MEMORIES ARE MADE OF THIS

MEMORIES ARE MADE OF THIS

June Francis

This first world edition published 2013
in Great Britain and in the USA by
SEVERN HOUSE PUBLISHERS LTD of
19 Cedar Road, Sutton, Surrey, England, SM2 5DA.

British Library Cataloguing in Publication Data

Francis, June, 1941-
  Memories are made of this.
  1. Missing persons–Fiction. 2. World War, 1939-1945–
  England–Liverpool–Fiction. 3. Domestic fiction.
  I. Title
  823.9'14-dc23

ISBN-13: 978-0-7278-8250-9 (cased)

All Severn House titles are printed on acid-free paper.

Severn House Publishers support the Forest Stewardship Council [FSC], the
leading international forest certification organisation. All our titles that are printed
on Greenpeace-approved FSC-certified paper carry the FSC logo.

MIX
Paper from
responsible sources
FSC® C018575

Typeset by Palimpsest Book Production Ltd.,
Falkirk, Stirlingshire, Scotland.
Printed and bound in Great Britain by
MPG Books Ltd., Bodmin, Cornwall.

Acknowledgements

I would like to thank Kath Williams who was a police officer in Liverpool during the 1950s for her willingness to help me with my research, as well as Kate McNichol, the Force Records Manager of Merseyside Police, for assisting my son Iain to research background information. It was much appreciated. I'd also like to thank Elsie from swimming for the information she provided me with about her job in the Cunard Building. I would add that my characters and plot are purely the product of my imagination and any factual mistakes in police procedure are mine.

Prologue

Liverpool: May 1941

'I never forget a face and I recognized your sort straightaway!' Ethel Ramsbottom ran a finger over the dust on the sideboard. 'Look at this! You're not only a whore but a slut. I told George he was making a mistake marrying you. You're far too young for him,' she said stridently.

Grace Walker's slender body shook and in a voice stiff with outrage, she said, 'This time you've gone too far, you're not running one of your prison landings now, you old bitch! In case you haven't noticed there's a bloody war on and a bomb dropped only yards from here last night. Everywhere's a mess. I've had enough to do today without worrying about a bit of dust. George has been far too tolerant of you, just because you're the last remaining link with his mother. Well, I've had enough! Since his first wife died you've made his kids' lives a misery. I'll tell you once and for all you're not going to do the same to our daughter. You can sling your hook! When I get back, I want you out of this house for good.'

Ethel's chest swelled with indignation. 'How dare you speak to me in such a tone! You don't really care about our George or his kids. It's all pretence with you. All dollied up to go out! You've got a fancy man, haven't you?'

Grace's green eyes glinted. She was so incandescent with rage, she could not speak. She had to get out before she did something she would regret. Carefully picking up the shopping bag with the small cake inside, she went out into the lobby. Taking her coat from a hook on the wall with trembling fingers, she shrugged it on and took several deep breaths before opening the parlour door and poking her head inside. Her seventeen-year-old stepson, Sam, was standing over by the bay window, hands in the pockets of his grey flannels, gazing out.

She cleared her throat. 'Sam, will you keep your ears open

in case Jeanette wakes up? The raid last night unsettled her. I have to go out.'

'OK,' he replied.

She thought his voice sounded strained and hesitated, wondering if she should tell him that Carol had called on them a couple of days ago and the old bitch had sent her packing. They'd had a row about that, too. But when he did not turn round and she caught sight of the time, she said, 'Thanks!' and closed the door behind her.

As she left the house, her mind buzzed with conflicting thoughts, but uppermost was her determination that her four-year-old daughter would have a happy life without the restrictions and constant questioning that had plagued her own growing years. She would have that old besom out if she was still there when she returned.

Three hours later Grace was standing on the step of a house in Toxteth taking her farewell of an elderly friend when the air raid siren sounded. 'Not again,' said the old lady huddled in the doorway. 'Well, let them come. They won't get me,' she said in a high pitched voice.

Grace frowned. 'You should go to the shelter, May.' Her fingers shook as she fastened a paisley headscarf over her light brown hair.

'Don't yous be worrying about me, queen. The Lord takes care of His own. It's good of yous to remember me birthday and I really enjoyed the cake.'

'It was a pleasure.' Grace's pretty features softened, and then she glanced up at the darkening sky, apprehension tightening her stomach. She imagined that she could already hear the drone of enemy aircraft in the distance. 'I'd better make a move. I'm going to have to walk home.'

'Yous have some distance to go, queen, and the bombs will be falling before you get there. Stay here! Yous'll be safe with me under the table. Proper oak that table is, belonged to me da! It's the same wood that built Nelson's navy.'

For several moments Grace dithered, wanting to get home to her daughter but scared of being caught out in the open. She remembered hearing tales of people running for cover and being targeted by the enemy. Perhaps she would be safe with May. Sam would take care of Jeanette, and George would not miss her. Being a policeman and the kind of man he was, he would be out all night because of the air raid. She chewed on her lip, thinking it was that old bitch Ethel's fault that had decided her not to leave her husband for the safety of the country-side. She had not been prepared to leave him and Sam prey to the old woman's poisonous tongue and strict regime. She thought of her ten-year-old stepdaughter, Hester, evacuated to a Lancashire village at the beginning of the war; at least she was well out of it. She grimaced. Too late now for second thoughts. She had to make the best of it. She took hold of May's arm and hustled her back inside the house.

'Time for another cuppa, queen,' said May, shuffling into the kitchen.

'I'll put the kettle on,' said Grace, assuming a cheerfulness that she did not feel.

'And I'll put some cushions under the table,' said May, obviously delighted that the younger woman had decided to stay with her.

An hour later Grace was under the table with her back against one of the legs, cushioned by a pillow. She was trying to match her soprano voice to May's slightly off-key rendering of 'The Lord's My Shepherd' in an attempt to drown out the sound of exploding bombs and gunfire. She thought, *I should have told Sam where I was going*, but it was too late now. She could only hope they would all come safely through this night. She had such a future planned for her daughter! Grace was still thinking of Jeanette when the bomb hit.

One

'It's raining again,' said Jeanette Walker, dragging a headscarf from the pocket of her maroon-check swagger coat.

'It's supposed to be bloody summer,' grumbled her workmate, Peggy, gazing at the glistening pavement outside the Odeon cinema. 'It's getting dark already. I hope the weather improves before me, our Lil and Mam and Dad go to Butlin's next week.'

'I wish I still had a mother instead of blinking Aunt Ethel! Your brothers not going?'

'No, they think they're too old.'

'I wish I could get away but I can't see it happening.' Jeanette flicked back her ponytail, and covered her light brown hair with the headscarf and knotted it at her throat. She would be lucky if she could manage a trip to New Brighton, what with her elderly aunt taking nearly every penny she earned. Her expression darkened at the thought of the old witch who had ruled the roost in the Walker household since Jeanette's mother had disappeared during the blitz. She sighed as she reached into a pocket and took out a paper bag. 'I'm hungry and I bet if there is any tea saved for me, it'll be burnt to a crisp.' She took out a pear drop and handed the bag containing the last remaining sweet to Peggy.

'Didn't you tell her you were going to the pictures straight from work?' Peggy popped the sweet into her mouth and shoved the paper bag in her pocket.

'Yes of course! I told her when Dad was there or else she'd have made some excuse to prevent me from going. As it was she had a right face on her and it'll be the same when I get home. Unfortunately Dad's on duty this evening.' Jeanette felt a chill go down her spine at the thought of having to face her father's only aunt, and crunched on the pear drop. She hoped her half-sister, Hester, would still be up when she got home, so she wouldn't have to confront the old woman alone.

'So what did you think of the film?' asked Peggy, turning up the collar of her coat and stepping onto the wet pavement.

'*The Weak and the Wicked*,' muttered Jeanette, following her out. 'At least it ended happily with our heroine saved by the love of a good man. Aunt Ethel doesn't agree with open prisons, though. She was once a prison wardress and is forever boasting about the efficiency with which her landings were run. Six of the best with the birch and solitary confinement on bread and water, that's what she'd prescribe.'

'She wouldn't be alone in that for some crimes, but surely not for fraud,' said Peggy, coming to a halt at the kerb and glancing right and left. 'Will she ask you about the film?'

'Depends on her mood. If she leaves it until tomorrow and the rest of the family are in, there'll be a helluva discussion about sentencing and corporal and capital punishment.' Jeanette stepped backwards as a car came too close to the kerb, sending a spray of water their way.

Peggy shouted a rude word at the driver before saying, 'Well, what do you expect with three coppers and an ex-prison wardress in the house?'

Jeanette sighed. 'Dad'll walk out after a few minutes and go into the parlour with the *Echo*. He hates raised voices at home, says that he hears enough dissension in his job.'

'If you don't mind my saying so, I'd hate to be part of your family,' said Peggy, crossing the road. 'At least you won't be joining the force, you're too short.'

'I wish I wasn't,' said Jeanette, hurrying in her wake. 'According to my brother, Sam, I take after my mother. He says she was petite, although I vaguely remember her appearing tall to me.'

'Glynis Johns is petite,' said Peggy, reaching the other side of the road. 'Maybe you should think about becoming an actress!' She smiled at her friend.

'She's got another film coming out this year,' said Jeanette, wiping her damp face on her sleeve.

'I know. It's in colour and she's a mermaid.' Peggy giggled.

'Fancy being half a woman and half a fish. It makes you wonder how they do *it*!'

'Hush, you!' hissed Jeanette, glancing about her. 'Someone might hear.'

Peggy rolled her eyes. 'Who cares! You are a prude.'

'No, I'm not,' said Jeanette indignantly. 'Anyway, you'd worry about being overheard if you had the old witch prowling around, trying to find out what you're up to.'

'Well, she's not here, is she? Shall we go and see the mermaid film when it comes out?'

Jeanette nodded. 'Although if the old witch gets to know it's called *Mad About Men*, I can guarantee she'll do her best to prevent me from going. She's a real killjoy! When I was growing up she was forever warning me what punishment would befall me if I didn't toe the line.' She linked her arm through Peggy's. 'Cor, I'm hungry!'

They began to walk in the direction of the T J Hughes department store. 'Do you know what—' began Peggy.

Jeanette interrupted her. 'I can smell chips!'

Peggy breathed in deeply. 'So can I. It'll be the chippy just round the corner in Norton Street, near Gianelli's ice cream parlour.'

Jeanette wrinkled her dainty nose. 'It's torture! I'm starving!'

'What d'you say to us getting some then?' suggested Peggy.

Jeanette hesitated. 'I don't know if I have enough money. Besides, unlike you, I've a bus to catch and I'm late already with us staying in to watch the second feature again.'

'If you're already late, what difference is another ten minutes or so going to make? The chippy's not far.'

'And what if there's a queue?'

'But there mightn't be,' said Peggy sensibly, avoiding a shower of water pouring from a broken drainpipe. She tugged on Jeanette's arm. 'Come on, I'll mug you.'

'I can't be taking money from you!' said Jeanette, sounding scandalized.

'Don't be daft. What are friends for?'

Jeanette's stomach rumbled. 'All right, thanks. I do have some money but I need it for my fare for today *and* tomorrow.'

'But we're not in work tomorrow,' said Peggy.

Jeanette smiled. 'I need to go into town, anyway. Don't be asking why right now. If things go the way I plan, then I'll tell you on Monday.'

Peggy shrugged. 'Be secretive then! I'm more interested in chips right now.'

Arm in arm, the two girls made their way to the chippy. Annoyingly, there was a queue, but they tagged on to the end, hoping they would not have long to wait. Jeanette heard one woman in front of them say, 'It's just like when everything was on bleedin' rationing the way we still have to queue up.'

Jeanette thought that was the kind of remark her great-aunt would make. But as the minutes ticked by, she began to understand how the older woman felt and to worry about getting into trouble at home. She was about to say to Peggy that perhaps she should go when a young man wearing oilskins joined them. Rainwater dripped onto the floor in a circle about him and he looked miserable. Jeanette smiled at him sympathetically.

He returned her smile and she thought how it altered his whole appearance. He was not bad looking at all, with greyish blue eyes fringed with black lashes. A lock of damp black hair curled on his forehead, and he had sideburns, as well as a faint tan. What with his wearing a sou'wester, she was reminded of the seaman on a tin of Skippers' sardines. Of course, this bloke was much younger, but with Liverpool being such a busy port, he could easily be a sailor. All different races landed up in the city and she was curious to know where he came from.

'Not a night to be out at sea,' she said.

He agreed, adding, 'Although I've known worse.'

Jeanette detected a familiar accent. He was British but not a Liverpudlian. Before she could ask where he was from she felt a tug on her sleeve. She glanced at Peggy. 'What?'

'See that bloke getting served,' hissed Peggy. 'He's Greg Riley who I told you about. The one I dated.'

Jeanette would rather her friend had not interrupted her, but she stared at the three lads at the front of the queue. Even from the back one could tell they were Teddy Boys with their DA haircuts, which was short for duck's arse and similar in style to that favoured by the film star Tony Curtis. They wore drape jackets and drainpipe trousers.

Peggy said nervously, 'I could do without him seeing me right now.'

Vaguely interested in why that should be so, Jeanette asked, 'Have you had an argument?'

'It's not so much what I've done but my brother—' began Peggy, only to stop as Greg turned away from the counter with the two other Teds. She ducked behind Jeanette, but she might as well have not bothered because she had been spotted.

'Hey yous, Peggy McGrath, I've a bone to pick with you!' shouted Greg, his swollen and bruised face twisted with anger.

A red-faced Peggy straightened up slowly. 'Well, I don't want to talk to you, Greg Riley, if you're going to take that tone,' she said tartly, slipping her arm through Jeanette's. 'Let's get out of here, Jeanette!'

'What about our chips?' she said, forgetting that she too had thought of leaving in a hurry earlier.

Peggy pulled on her arm. 'We can live without chips.'

'But I'm hungry,' protested Jeanette. 'Besides, we've been in this queue for ages and it seems daft to leave after waiting all this time.'

Greg seized hold of Peggy's sleeve. 'You have some explaining to do, girl, and yer not getting away from me that easy. What did you tell your Marty about me? I didn't get a chance to get a word in edgeways with him!'

'Ouch, you're hurting me,' said Peggy, flushing and attempting to tug her sleeve out of his grasp.

'You leave her alone,' said Jeanette, wondering if his black eye and bruises had been inflicted by Peggy's brother. The next moment, not only was Peggy catapulted against Greg, but because she and Jeanette were linking arms, Jeanette was dragged along with her. 'Let her go! You've no right to treat her so roughly.'

Greg squinted at Jeanette. 'This is none of your business, doll, so keep out of it or you'll be sorry,' he snapped.

Jeanette did not live in a household of three members of Liverpool's police force for nothing. 'Are you threatening me?' she said icily. 'Because if you are I tell you now my dad and brother are policemen, and my sister is on the force, too.'

His face hardened. 'So what? I can't see any sign of them here, so shut your mouth!'

'Don't you speak to me like that,' said Jeanette, glaring at him.

'I'll speak to you anyway I like,' said Greg. 'You're not from around here, are you, doll?'

'So what if I'm not,' said Jeanette, tilting her chin. 'You can't go round bullying me just because of that!'

Greg's lips tightened and then he called over his shoulder, 'Hey, Billy, grab hold of this one who doesn't know when to keep her bloody trap shut. I don't want her interfering with what's between me and Peggy.'

Jeanette felt her shoulder seized in a vice-like grip and gasped in pain. 'Let me go!' she said through gritted teeth, her green eyes flashing as she stared up at the other youth.

'Yous heard her, Billy,' said one of the women in the queue. 'Leave the girl alone! You Teddy Boys are nothing but trouble. You'll end up in hell if you don't change your ways.'

'Mind yer own business, yer old cow,' said Billy, swivelling his head briefly before giving his attention to Jeanette again.

She would have been a liar if she had said that she was not scared at that point. He was a big fella with shoulders as wide as a giant coat hanger beneath his drape jacket with velvet lapels. She felt not only powerless to prevent Peggy from being dragged outside by Greg, but unable to defend herself against this monster.

Then to her surprise came a voice from a different quarter. 'Let her go!'

She had temporarily forgotten about the young man in the sou'wester, and obviously Billy and Greg had not given him a single thought. Billy looked round to see who had spoken and Jeanette made the best of the opportunity presented to her to grind her high heel into his ankle. He swore and tightened his grip on her shoulder, causing her to scream.

'Didn't you hear me, you bloody bully?' said the young man, squaring up to him.

Jeanette could only stare at him in admiration, for he was not a big fella. In fact she could not help comparing him to the biblical David who had confronted the giant Goliath.

A smirk crossed Billy's face. 'Wait yer turn, mate! I'll deal with you after I've finished with her.'

Jeanette's gaze flew from Billy's face to that of the young man and she saw his eyes turn the colour of flint. *Oh dear! He must think he can beat this gorilla!* Her thudding heart began to beat even faster.

'If you know what's good for you, boyo, then you'll stop behaving like a louse and let the young lady go,' her David said softly.

Jeanette was not prepared for what happened next. Billy shoved her to one side and from his pocket he dragged a bicycle chain. She gasped in horror as he swung it and instinctively ducked as it whizzed through the air. She had no idea where it landed. Two women screamed and one threatened to send for the police. Then the two males grappled with each other. Jeanette could hear the breath whistling in their chests and the scrabbling of their feet on the floor. She had not expected them to fight over her and was at a loss how to stop them.

Then the other youth who had been in company with Greg and Billy launched himself onto her rescuer's back. She attempted to claw him off. He lost his balance and toppled backwards, knocking her off her feet, so that she landed on the floor with him on top of her. She could hardly breathe. As she struggled to push him away, she noticed the bicycle chain on the floor within arm's reach. But before she could seize hold of it, the youth on top of her grabbed it and threw it, shouting, 'Here, Billy!'

Billy managed to catch the chain, but it whipped around in his hand and caught her rescuer on the side of his face. He let out an agonized yell as it tore into his flesh.

'Oh my God!' gasped Jeanette, and pushed with all her might to rid herself of the youth who still had her pinned to the ground. He toppled sideways and she got to her feet. She hurried over to her rescuer, terribly aware of the blood seeping from his torn skin. She caught a whiff of oil as, with hands that shook, she removed the chain from about his head.

He was ashen beneath his tan and stumbled backwards against the counter, stretching out his arms and resting them on the ledge beneath the metal top. Blood dripped from his chin onto his yellow oilskins and he was gasping in pain. She was aware of the rain beating against the window and of her own rapid breathing. Then she felt a waft of cold, damp air on her neck as the door opened and someone entered the shop.

A deep male voice asked, 'What's going on here?'

The tension broke and the woman behind the counter, who was twisting her hands nervously, said, 'Father Callaghan, you've got to help us. I don't want to be losing me job by getting this place a bad name. I was just about to call the police, but if you can sort it out I'd really appreciate it.'

'Calm down, Mary,' ordered the priest, his eyes scanning the faces of those present and coming to rest on the bleeding face of the man resting against the counter. 'What happened here?'

'None of your business, Father,' sneered Billy. 'Why don't you just turn round and go out again?'

'And why can't you stay out of trouble, you young fool!' Father Callaghan shot out a hand and thrust it in Billy's face, sending him sprawling against his mate. 'If you must fight, come to the church hall. You can do a few rounds in the ring.' He turned to the young man in the sou'wester. 'What happened to your face?'

'Thanks for your concern, Padre, but I'm not of your flock,' gasped the young man.

'Anyone in trouble is my concern, lad! That looks nasty and I think the police should be informed. Mary!' he bellowed. 'Get on the phone!'

She scurried off to do what the priest said.

Immediately Jeanette wanted out of there. If this got back to her father and great-aunt there would be hell to pay, but she had to say her piece. 'He didn't make the first move,' she said hastily. 'It was those two,' she nodded in Billy and his mate's direction. 'This man here only got involved because he came to my aid. You ask anyone here.'

'It happened so fast, I couldn't see properly what was going on,' said one man.

'Yous'll need to speak to Gregory Riley, Father,' said an elderly woman, dragging her black shawl tightly around her humped shoulders. 'You knows him, and it was Billy who dragged the bicycle chain from his pocket. He needs a few rounds with yer champion in the boxing ring at the boys' club. Do him more good than being sent to any ol' Borstal.'

'Thanks for your advice, Josie,' said the priest, grabbing hold of the youth as he attempted to sneak out of the door. 'But it's too late for that now.'

'I must go,' rasped the young man, straightening up from the counter, 'I've a boat to catch.'

'I have to go, too,' said Jeanette hastily.

Father Callaghan blocked their way. 'Not so fast, the two of you!'

'Padre,' said the young man wearily, 'I really do need to be somewhere else. I can't afford to miss the boat.'

'And I have to get home,' said Jeanette. 'I'll be skinned alive if I'm late.'

Father Callaghan hesitated. 'You don't want to press charges for what happened to you, son? That's going to leave a scar.' He reached out and touched the young man's face. He winced and shook off the priest's hand.

'I'll see a doctor, don't you worry. Thanks for the concern. Now, please, let me past.'

Father Callaghan hesitated and then moved aside. 'Go! But if you're ever in Liverpool again and need help, you only have to ask here and they'll tell you where to find me.'

The young man gave a twisted smile and brushed past him.

Jeanette hurried after him. 'You really will get that wound seen to, won't you?' she asked.

He gazed down at her as they stood in the rain. 'I'm a big boy now, luv. I can look after myself.'

'I'm not saying you can't,' she said hastily. 'But men think they're invincible. Thanks for coming to my rescue. I'm Jeanette Walker, by the way.'

To her surprise, he lowered his head and pressed his lips against hers. The moment seemed frozen in time, until after several seconds he lifted his mouth. 'Bye, Jeanette Walker. Maybe I'll see you again some day.' He touched her damp cheek with a finger and was gone.

Jeanette watched him cross the road. A bus pulled up on the other side and he vanished from sight. Where did he have to be that he could not delay long enough to have that wound attended to? And what was he thinking of, kissing her?

She felt a hand on her shoulder. 'Come inside, Miss,' said Father Callaghan. 'He's made it obvious that he doesn't want any interference from either of us and I want to speak to you.'

Jeanette said, 'He didn't even tell me his name.' She sighed and pushed a strand of sodden hair inside her scarf. 'I'd best be going.'

'Hang on a little longer. You could be needed as a witness if you want justice to be done here,' said Father Callaghan, guiding her through the doorway. 'The police have been called and should be here soon.'

She pulled away from him. 'I have to go. My great-aunt will go mad if this gets back to her. She'll blame me for what happened. There's enough witnesses here to testify that Billy is guilty of GBH. If it's his first offence he'll probably get off with a warning and a fine. Whichever, I'd rather not have to go to court.'

'That lad needs a taste of the birch,' said one of the women behind the counter who had been listening to their conversation. 'It's all this rock'n'roll, it does their heads in. Jungle music, my fella calls it. I'll testify against him. Now what about your chips, girl?' she asked, changing the subject.

Jeanette rested her arms on the counter. 'Make it fast and be sure and put plenty of salt and vinegar on them if you don't mind, please. I'm starving.'

The woman glanced at the priest and he gave a ghost of a smile. She shovelled the chips onto paper and then sprinkled them liberally with salt and vinegar before wrapping them in newspaper. Jeanette handed over the fare she'd been saving for tomorrow and stared at Father Callaghan. 'You're not going to try and persuade me to stay, are you, Padre? You can't want me to get in to trouble with my family – and I'm a free citizen of this country.'

'Go on, off with you!' he said abruptly, jerking a thumb in the direction of the door.

She smiled at him. 'Goodnight!'

To her relief the rain had eased and she wasted no time making a hole in the steaming newspaper-wrapped parcel and digging out several chips. She ate as she strode to the bus stop, wondering where Peggy and Greg had gone. She hoped her friend was all right, but it looked as if she was going to have to wait until Monday to find out.

Her thoughts turned to the young man wearing the sou'wester. He had a bit of a cheek kissing her without a by-your-leave. Why had he done it? The kiss had made her feel weak at the knees. It would have been better if she had found the touch of his lips on hers distasteful instead of being set all atremble. She would probably never see him again.

She finished the chips and spotted a bus approaching, so she scrunched up the newspaper and stuck it in the bin attached to the bus stop. There was still no sign of a policeman responding to the call from the chippy, and for that she was glad. All she had to do now was gather her wits and courage and stand up to the old cow when she arrived home. Fingers crossed, Hester would be there to provide her with some support.

Two

As Jeanette jogged up her street, she spotted the squat figure of her great-aunt silhouetted in the light of the street lamp outside her father's house. For Ethel to have left the warmth of the fireside on that rain-soaked evening meant that her mood was probably meaner than usual, and Jeanette slowed down, needing to get her breath back before facing the old woman. As a kid, Jeanette had prayed and prayed that she would inherit the genes that made her half-brother, Sam, as tall as their six-footer father, and her half-sister, Hester, a good five foot seven inches, but fate had decreed that she inherit her mother's genes.

Jeanette was glad she was no longer a kid because the odds were that Ethel would not clout her across the head. A couple of years ago she would have done, depending on whether the old woman had given any thought to whether the neighbours, hearing the tap-tap of Jeanette's heels on the pavement, were peering through the bedroom curtains.

'Hello, Aunt Ethel,' she said, resisting the temptation to say, *What big teeth you have!*

Ethel made a noise in her throat and waited until her great-niece had walked up the step before poking her in the back with two sharp fingers that had enough force behind them to send Jeanette stumbling forwards so that she almost cracked her head on the front door.

'What time is this to be coming in?' hissed the old woman, reaching over Jeanette and pushing the door wider. She thrust a hand in the girl's back and sent her flying up the lobby.

Jeanette managed to grab a coat hanging on the wall, preventing herself from sprawling on the bottom stair. 'I told you and Dad that I was going to the flicks straight from work,' she cried.

'I don't believe you've only been to the cinema,' said Ethel, her thin lips twisting. 'Tell me the truth about where you've been.'

Jeanette forced herself upright, determined not to show her apprehension. 'I was hungry so I went with my workmate to the chippy afterwards. I'm sorry I'm late,' she apologized, although doing so almost choked her.

Ethel prodded her hard in the chest. 'You're not sorry at all, but you will be by the time I've finished with you. You've been with a lad, haven't you?'

Jeanette bit back an *Ouch* and wished her father was here to see how his precious elderly relative behaved when he was not on the scene. 'I have not!' she gasped, wishing she had the guts to poke her back.

'Don't lie!' Ethel thrust her face into Jeanette's and sniffed. 'You've been drinking! You're this late because the pubs have only just let out.'

'No, I haven't! Where would I get the money from? You take nearly all of it.'

Ethel gave her great-niece another poke in the chest. 'Don't give me cheek!' Jeanette rubbed her chest. 'You're weak and you're wicked, just like your mother. She was no bloody good for my nephew. A right flibbertigibbet! A spendthrift! Lazy! If she ran a duster over the furniture once a week that was as much as she did to keep the house tidy. It was a blessing when she disappeared – no doubt with a fella. She showed little love for you and the rest of this household, leaving the way she did.'

Jeanette exploded. 'Shut up about my mother! If she left the way you go on about, then she would have left a note. Why can't you accept that, despite her body never being found, she was killed in the blitz? She was most likely blown to pieces.' Her voice broke on a sob and she thrust a hand against Ethel's bosom. 'I don't want you speaking in that nasty way about my mother ever again! You wouldn't dare do it if Dad was here. He loved her despite all your accusations.'

Ethel's face turned puce and she grabbed Jeanette's arm. 'You keep George out of this! He married her for convenience! I won't believe he ever told you that he loved her.'

'He did!' lied Jeanette.

'Then he was kidding you, just to make you feel better about her. It's upstairs for you, my girl, and you won't get out of that bedroom for a week!'

Jeanette ignored the threat. There was no way the rest of the family would allow her great-aunt to lock her in her bedroom for that long. 'Let me go!' She tried to prise the old woman's fingers from her arm. 'I need a drink of water and to go to the lavatory.'

Ethel ignored her words and, despite all Jeanette's attempts to free herself, she could not loosen the old woman's grip and was forced up the stairs. Another shove in the back meant she almost fell into her bedroom. The door slammed behind her and a key turned in the lock.

'You'll have to let me out in the morning!' shouted Jeanette, thumping the bedroom door. 'I've work to go to.'

'Don't think you can fool me, girl,' called Ethel through the wood. 'It's your Saturday morning off and you'll spend it scrubbing floors.'

Jeanette dropped onto the bed, punched the pillow and swore. It was only possible for a woman like her great-aunt to be tolerated by her father because she was bloody crafty. George Walker had never lifted a finger in anger to any of his children and hated violence, so Ethel behaved herself when he was around and was saccharine sweet towards them. Not that it prevented her from saying things about their behaviour, but she said it in a way that made it sound like it was because she worried and cared about them. Sam had said on more than one occasion that he did not understand how his father could not see through her. Jeanette had even heard Sam wonder aloud how their father had managed to last so long in the police force with the belief that there was good in everyone.

Sam, on the other hand, believed firmly that some people were completely evil and that most people were capable of cruelty if circumstances conspired against them. Jeanette agreed with the latter, but never in a thousand Sundays would she have said it to her father about his mother's sister. Ethel had brought him up almost single-handed after his father had been killed in a terrible accident down at the docks where he was a fire bobby. His mother had been so traumatized that her nerves had been shattered and she had never recovered from the shock of it and had died when George was only ten years old.

Jeanette began to undress, inspecting her arms and chest for bruises. She presumed Hester was fast asleep, oblivious to her sufferings. She always went to bed early when she was on a seven-to-three shift in the morning. Jeanette only hoped that her half-sister was not cowering beneath the bedclothes, loathing herself because she was too cowardly to come out and see what all the commotion was about. Jeanette found it really odd that Hester did not think twice about confronting a criminal, but shrank from squaring up to Ethel. After all, she had been trained to defend herself and had even attempted to teach the much younger Jeanette some ju-jitsu.

As Jeanette dragged her nightdress over her aching head, she found herself resenting not being able to clean her teeth and having to use the chamber pot under her bed. If only she could discover some way of getting her great-aunt to alter her bullying ways, but she reckoned it would take a miracle. Ethel, like that Billy in the chippy, was too quick to use violence. It appeared it was embedded in her after years of being a prison wardress.

Jeanette wondered what had happened in the chippy after

she had left. Had the police turned up and put out a search for her and the missing victim of Billy's attack? She hoped nobody remembered having heard her name spoken by Peggy. Her father would be so disappointed in her if it came to his ears that she had been involved in a fight.

During Jeanette's growing years, he had suffered from a misguided belief that because Ethel was a woman, she knew best how to handle both his daughters and had left disciplining them to her. A big mistake! She believed that sparing the rod spoilt the child. Jeanette knew her only option to escape her great-aunt's domination was to leave home. But with her current financial situation being what it was that was definitely out of the question.

That night Jeanette slept fitfully. Her dreams were filled with jumbled thoughts of her mother made up to the eyeballs, dressed in high heels, low-cut blouse and a short skirt, singing as she pranced along Lime Street. The next moment the scene changed and she was smothered beneath a pile of rubble after a bomb had exploded. The noise of it in her imagination startled her into wakefulness, and when she finally fell asleep again, she dreamed of the young man who had come to her rescue, bleeding and in pain, on a rusting old steamboat with a drunken captain jabbing a hypodermic needle in him. Only in the peculiar fashion of dreams, the drunken captain turned into her great-aunt, who locked her into a cabin, saying she was weak and wicked for lusting after sailors.

Jeanette woke in the morning to find herself struggling with the bedcovers and became aware of footsteps on the landing outside. Recognizing them as Hester's, she tumbled out of bed and hurried over to the door. 'Hester, you have to let me out of here,' she croaked. 'I'm as thirsty as hell.'

The footsteps paused and retreated to her door. 'There's no key in the keyhole,' whispered Hester. 'Why has she locked you in this time?'

'I was late getting home and she accused me of going with fellas and being drunk,' answered Jeanette.

'The same old story,' said Hester.

'Yes! She said I'm weak and wicked just like my mother.' Jeanette's voice quivered.

'Ignore that! I don't remember Grace being weak or wicked. She was young and full of fun and the complete opposite to ol' misery guts. I will say, though, that you must have been really late in, because I didn't hear you and I lay awake for a while, thinking.'

Jeanette was glad that her half-sister had not lain there in a funk, listening to Ethel bullying her. 'I hate being lied to and treated like a child. I'm nearly eighteen for goodness' sake!'

'You've got years to go before she'll consider you're beyond her control. Look at the way the old cow treats me and I'm twenty-four.'

'That's because you let her! You should stand up to her,' whispered Jeanette. 'You've a responsible job in the police force and you haven't even got a regular boyfriend because she puts her spoke in whenever you let slip that you've been on a date. I don't know why you don't leave home! I could move out and live with you then.'

'It's not that easy, and Dad wouldn't like it unless I was getting married. Anyhow, what good does standing up to her do you?' hissed Hester. 'Did she attempt to clout you one?'

'No, she did her poking and pushing trick and you know how that hurts.' Jeanette inspected her chest. 'Damn, I really have got bruises!'

'I'm sorry.' Hester sighed. 'What did you want me to do, did you say?'

'Get me out of here. I told you I'm thirsty as hell and I would have been starving as well if I hadn't gone into a chippy after the film.'

'But you went straight from work, so you shouldn't have been that late,' said Hester.

'OK, I'll tell you the truth. We stayed to watch the second feature again and then a fight broke out in the chippy,' babbled Jeanette. 'There was this young man who came to my rescue. He was a dish. If you'd have seen him, you'd have thought so too.'

For a moment there was a breathless silence on the other side of the door, then Hester groaned. 'I knew there must have been more to it than your being late because you'd simply been to the pictures. You and your liking for fellas! I've a good mind to leave you in there. When are you going to learn not to flirt with lads? You'll end up getting yourself into trouble.'

'No, I won't! I know what's what,' said Jeanette indignantly. 'You've been listening to the old witch too much. I've never even been out on a proper date with a lad yet.'

'Humph! If you say so,' muttered Hester.

Jeanette bit back a swear word and got down on her haunches and peered through the gap under the door. She could see Hester's highly polished flat black shoes. 'I won't be seeing him again.'

'Why not?'

Jeanette sensed Hester's interest. 'He had to leave to catch a ship and I have no idea where he lives or what his name is. His face was in a right mess and he was in pain. I was really worried about him. I still am, to be honest.'

'Well, never mind him right now,' said Hester. 'I'm going to have to go.'

Jeanette gasped. 'Wait! If you don't want to admit to letting me out, just slide the key under the door once you get it.'

'What d'you mean, once I get it? If you think I'm going to creep into her bedroom, you've had it,' said Hester. 'If she caught me, there'd be hell to pay.'

'Don't be such a coward.'

'I'm not a coward,' replied Hester, exasperated. 'I'm just sensible. She's going to have to let you out when Dad or Sam make an appearance. You shouldn't have got caught up in a fight and stayed out late. You know what can happen to a girl of your age and with your looks roaming the streets after the pubs let out.'

'I wasn't in any danger. Anyway, the point is that this is my free Saturday morning and I've something terribly important to do. I have to be somewhere dead early, so you must let me out of here,' pleaded Jeanette.

'I won't let you out until you tell me what this terribly important thing is.'

Jeanette hesitated. 'The truth is that I'm going after a part-time job in a milk bar.'

'Good for you! I suppose I can guess why you haven't told her.'

'She'd have the money off me in no time. It's cash in hand so it's all mine.'

'That's illegal!'

'Oh, shut up, Hester,' hissed Jeanette. 'I'm talking about just a few bob for brushing up and clearing tables.'

Hester nibbled on her lip. 'I don't think I should encourage you to break the law.'

Jeanette swore beneath her breath. 'If that's the way you feel, and you want Dad getting all upset when he discovers the old witch has locked me in again, then go off to work and forget about me. You know how he worries about me.'

'I know he'd go off his nut if you ended up in the clink.'

Jeanette felt like banging her head against the door. 'Why should that happen to me? My mother was never in prison – was she?'

'It's just the way Aunt Ethel talked about your mother. I know I shouldn't have listened, but I did wonder when I was a kid if she had ever been in serious trouble. You know how soft-hearted Dad is and he's a great believer in giving people second chances. It's not as if we knew Grace before he brought her home. She was a lot younger than him, too. After my mother died I think he thought we needed a replacement.'

'But would he want someone who had broken the law? Unless she'd been wrongly accused,' said Jeanette brightly. 'The film I saw yesterday evening was about a girl who was unjustly condemned to prison. It was called *The Weak and the Wicked*.'

'The old witch wants to go and see it,' murmured Hester. 'Suggested that I go with her this evening.'

'It's worth seeing, but not with her,' whispered Jeanette. 'Now get the key and let me out of here before I die of thirst.'

'Don't exaggerate,' said Hester. 'But I'll have a go at getting the bloody key.'

A relieved Jeanette scrambled to her feet. She stood a moment, listening to Hester's retreating footsteps and imagining Ethel hitting the roof on discovering she had disappeared from her bedroom. If only she could get her hands on the post office savings book her father had put money in for her over the years, but the old woman looked after it.

The next moment she heard a noise outside on the landing

and a key appeared her side of the door. 'You can let yourself out, so I don't have to lie about having done it,' came Hester's voice, 'and you have to put the key back before you go out. Anyway, where is this milk bar you mentioned?'

'Leece Street. And thanks,' said Jeanette, relishing as little as Hester the idea of creeping into Ethel's bedroom to replace the key. 'Could you lend me a tanner as well?'

She heard Hester mutter under her breath and then two thrupenny bits were pushed under the door. 'Thanks, Hester,' she whispered.

Jeanette dressed and waited another few minutes before opening the door. She walked softly along the landing to Ethel's bedroom at the far end. She tried the knob cautiously, her hand pressed against the panel of the door as she felt it yield. Then she slipped inside like a shadow, glad that the curtains were dark ones so that it was almost pitch black in the room. She could hear Ethel snoring and wasted no time replacing the key. Then she paused in the middle of the room. It would have been a perfect opportunity to look for her savings book if it had not been so dark. She knew that Ethel had a tin box in which she kept such items.

Suddenly there came a break in the old woman's breathing and, like a bullet from a gun, Jeanette was out of there. She collected her outdoor clothes and handbag from her bedroom, made her way to the bathroom and locked herself in. Twenty minutes later she was in the kitchen, making herself a couple of jam butties and a cup of tea. She devoured her breakfast with pleasure and left the house, not knowing whether her father or Sam had come in during the night. They had been very quiet if they had done so. She was going to be early at the milk bar, but that was better than risk facing her great-aunt, and having to scrub floors, by hanging around the house. At least she'd have time to think up an answer when the old witch asked how she had managed to get out of her bedroom, so that Hester would not get into trouble.

As Hester rode up Dale Street on her bicycle she was wondering about the young man whom Jeanette had called a dish. What kind of dish was he? Tasty or poisonous? Her half-sister was far too young to make a proper judgement when it came to the opposite sex. She turned into the yard belonging to Liverpool police divisional headquarters, thinking: fair-haired, dark or ginger? Jeanette had not said and neither had she voiced whether he was British or not.

She mused on the little information Jeanette had told her about being involved in a fight and thought about Grace. If Jeanette's mother had ever appeared in court and gone to prison, then she and George had done an excellent job of keeping it from his children. Hester and Sam had welcomed her with open arms after six months of Ethel's depressingly strict regime. Both of them had seen the interior of the coal cellar more times than either of them cared to remember. It had been a terrifying place of dark, solitary confinement. Thank God all that had ended when George had married Grace. Grace had been as eager for affection as they had. She would play games with them indoors and out, and was always willing to take them and other children from the street to Princes Park nearby.

Although Hester had missed her own mother, Marjorie Walker had been sickly for a long time. She had willingly surrendered the care of her children to Ethel when she came to stay, not even bothering to argue with her over bedtimes and the buying of their clothes. Grace, on the other hand, had been an excellent seamstress and had consulted Hester on design and fabrics when it came to her having a new frock for Easter, Whit and Christmas – and she had defended Hester's taste against the criticism of her great-aunt.

When war came and Hester had been evacuated, she had left Liverpool with mixed feelings. Yet those months in Whalley in the Lancashire countryside had been some of the happiest of her life due to the affection she had received from the childless couple who had taken her in.

A sigh escaped her. It was thirteen years since she had seen the Joneses and at first she had missed them terribly. Yet she guessed life back in Liverpool would have been acceptable if Grace had been there to welcome her home. What had happened to her? Ethel might go on about her walking out on them and having a fancy man, but Hester found that difficult to believe. Grace must be dead. Which meant that Hester had had to cope with life as it was and make do with memories of happier times.

It was a while since she had dated a bloke. The last had been a sailor whose hands wandered far too much. She had put a stop to that pretty damn quick before he received the impression that she was an easy touch and not just desperate for affection. But it was not only due to dating the wrong blokes or her great-aunt making a fuss about her going out with men that caused Hester not to bother much with the opposite sex. It was the job. Working shifts and being called on unexpectedly often meant the hours she was available were unsociable. She enjoyed her work, but she would have enjoyed sharing a meal with an attractive man who had a sense of humour, good manners and a brain in his head.

She placed her bicycle in a stand and chained it up; one couldn't be too careful, even here in police headquarters. After checking the seams of her black stockings were straight and smoothing down her navy-blue skirt, she entered the building. The WPCs' rooms were situated on the top floor, and on entering their domain she discovered a couple of her colleagues were already there, reading the chief constable's orders and the crime reports.

She exchanged greetings and sat down next to her friend, Wendy. They had started their careers in the force together at the Bruche training camp outside Warrington, living in Nissen huts that had once belonged to the RAF. Hester had enjoyed her time there. She remembered the feeling of having a load lifted from her shoulders because she was away from Ethel's domination. Again she found herself thinking of her time as an evacuee in the village near Clitheroe, and of Myra Jones who had shown her such affection.

At first Hester had kept in touch with Myra after her return to Liverpool, but then the older woman's letters had stopped and Hester could only believe that she had decided the relationship was not worth keeping up. She had been miserable at first about that, but her brother had told her to get over it.

Hester smiled at the thought of Sam, who was seven years her senior. She loved him dearly, despite his having a biting tongue on him sometimes. When they were children, he'd had the courage to defy the old woman. Ethel had taken the cane to him time after time, but he had never whimpered or complained to their father. 'One day,' he had said to Hester, whilst lying on his front on his bed, 'I'll get back at her.'

Thank God the days when the old witch had punished him so cruelly were long gone. Sam's spurt of growth in adolescence had changed everything, and she remembered him snapping the cane in half and flicking both halves under the old witch's nose. Both of them would still like to see her punished, but they had yet to determine how that could come about. She was an old woman and their father's only link to a shared past with his mother, and she played both these cards for all they were worth.

Sam had joined the police force as soon as he could, and three years ago he had encouraged Hester to do the same. She would always be grateful to him. She had loved every minute of those early days of her training and had studied law and police procedure. She and the other women had been drilled by an ex-guardsman, and instructed in self-defence and ju-jitsu by an ex-Army PE Instructor. There had been so much to learn and lots of exams to take, but she had enjoyed the challenge. Gosh, those men had been tough, but they had not had her quaking in her shoes as much as her great-aunt did. Odd that she still had that effect on her despite all that Hester had learnt and knew of self-defence.

She and Wendy had stayed close since then, but not for much longer. The other girl was engaged and would be getting married later in the year and leaving the police force. Hester almost envied her for having found the right man, but not for having to give up her job to become a housewife and mother.

'Anything to report?' asked Hester of her friend.

Wendy glanced up. 'An incident at a chippy in Norton Street in which a bicycle chain was used as a weapon.'

Hester froze and then asked casually, 'Anyone hurt?'

'Some bloke who didn't hang around long enough to make a statement, and neither did a girl who was involved.'

'Did they get her name?'

'They have a lead and are hoping to speak to someone this morning.'

Hester's heart sank. 'Did they arrest whoever used the chain?'

'Local lad who claimed it was an accident. He's been in trouble before for pilfering. Anyway, our man spoke to the local priest, so we should find out more later. The chief constable is determined to put a stop to these Teddy Boys using bicycle chains and knuckle dusters. He wants the man and the girl found. Anyway, you can read the rest for yourself,' said Wendy, pushing a sheet of paper across to her friend.

Hester's fingers quivered as she took the paper, but she didn't read it immediately. Instead she thought about what Jeanette had said. She was going to have to report that the girl involved was her sister and dreaded doing so. It would create trouble at home with a capital T. She began to read the report, but then Wendy nudged her as several more women constables and a female sergeant entered the room and she had to pause.

'Anything going on down at the Pierhead that requires our presence?' asked one of the other WPCs.

'You should know by now that any trouble down at the waterfront is the province of the men,' said Wendy.

'That's the docks. It could be that the men will need a woman to help control the queues for the Isle of Man boats,' said the same WPC. 'There's bound to be women and children amongst 'em and there's those that believe we're better at dealing with 'em.'

A discussion ensued.

Wendy glanced at Hester and rolled her eyes. 'You going anywhere this evening?' she whispered.

'Supposed to be going to see that prison film with Aunt Ethel,' said Hester, pulling a face. 'I suppose you and Charley have plans?'

Wendy sighed. 'I'd love to go dancing, but we've still got a fair amount to do to the flat before the wedding. You are coming, aren't you?'

'I've put in a request to change my shift for that day, so fingers crossed I'll be there,' said Hester, smiling.

'Your Sam said that he's going to try and come to the evening do.'

'Great,' said Hester brightly. 'At least if no one else asks me to dance, I can dance with my own brother.'

'He's a marvellous dancer, your Sam!' A smile played around Wendy's lips. 'I know plenty of girls who would be happy to get whizzed around the dance floor by him.'

Hester said wryly, 'He always did say that doing a course in ballroom dancing would prove useful one day.'

'Are you ready for inspection?' interrupted the sergeant. 'Walker, we've had a request for a WPC from the CID. It would be appreciated if you volunteered since you have already done part of your plain-clothes training.'

'Yes, Sergeant,' said Hester, straightening up and squaring her shoulders. 'When do I have to go?'

'You'll be needed later this afternoon and for this evening, so you can go home now and report to the CID superintendent at two o'clock. You'll be given all the information you need then.'

'Can't you give me a hint what it's about, so I'll know what to wear?'

The sergeant shook her head. 'You know as much as I do.'

Hester knew Ethel was not going to be pleased about this change of plan, but at least it meant she could put off saying anything about Jeanette's involvement in the incident at the chippy. Besides, it could be helpful if she spoke to Jeanette a bit more about what had happened before she reported it. If she changed into the plain clothes she kept in her locker, she could visit that milk bar in Leece Street that Jeanette had mentioned. She would leave her bicycle here, preferring to walk than to weave through the traffic on her bike. It was the other side of town, not far from the cathedral, but it should not take her that long to get there.

Three

There was a spring in Jeanette's step as she walked past Lime Street station and the Punch and Judy cafe. She was glad to have escaped the house and be in town, despite having no money to spend. Hopefully she would be better off by the end of the day.

She dawdled past the Futurist and Scala cinemas, gazing at the publicity shots of forthcoming films and the main feature that evening. Then she crossed a side street to the Adelphi, considering it almost miraculous that the hotel should have survived the blitz undamaged when Lewis's department store just across the way had been completely gutted; it had since been rebuilt.

Thinking of the blitz reminded her of her mother and she wished that she knew for certain what had happened to her. With three members of the police force in the family, one would think they could get at the truth. She also wished she knew whether the young man who had sprung to her defence the previous night had seen a doctor. No doubt he would need stitches in that wound and she winced at the thought.

She carried on up Renshaw Street and stopped to gaze at the toys in the baby shop window, wondering if she would ever have children herself. How old had her mother been when she gave birth to her? Ethel always harped on about Grace being too young for George. How young was young in the old woman's eyes? Jeanette sauntered past the Methodist Central Hall and car showrooms, imagining life without Ethel and her spirits lifted. No more nagging, no more being locked in her bedroom. Suddenly, she remembered why she had been so desperate to be set free that morning and lengthened her stride, impatient now to reach the milk bar. She paused to gaze at Quiggins' window display of locks, where one of Peggy's brothers worked. If the shop had been open, she would have gone inside and asked if her friend had arrived home safely.

It was only a short distance from Quiggins to Leece Street where the milk bar was situated. The door was open and a man was carrying a crate of milk bottles inside. Jeanette took a deep breath before entering. A woman with blonde hair, showing dark at the roots, was leaning on the counter. She was dressed in a pale pink nylon overall, and a lighted cigarette appeared to be stuck to her scarlet-painted lower lip. Jeanette had judged her age to be about forty when she had spoken to her the other day.

Eyeing Jeanette up and down and drawing on her cigarette before blowing out a perfect smoke ring, she said, 'I didn't expect you to show up so early.'

'I want the job so I made sure I was in plenty of time, Mrs Cross.' Something different about the place suddenly caught Jeanette's eye and her face lit up. 'A jukebox! When did that come?'

'Yesterday.' Mrs Cross smiled. 'Interested in all the latest hits, are you?'

Jeanette nodded. 'Although I like all kinds of music.'

'Well, we'll be having just the most popular hits. Monster, isn't it? Let's hope it brings the youngsters in.'

'I'm sure it will,' said Jeanette, thinking there were few homes in Liverpool that had the means to play all the latest hit records from America. She unfastened her coat. 'Would you like me to start right away, and do you have an overall for me?'

'Sure you can start now! It'll give me a chance to see if you're worth the money I'll be paying you.'

Jeanette knew she was only getting paid buttons, but hopefully she would be allowed to wait on tables and if so she'd surely be left some tips. Although, as it was teenagers her employer was hoping to attract, she couldn't see herself making much that way.

As she worked, Jeanette's eyes kept straying to the jukebox. Presumably the youngsters Mrs Cross mentioned would be students from the university, as well as the Liverpool Institute and School of Art, when they reopened after the summer holidays. Her employer probably pictured them coming in here for a milk shake and a sandwich or sticky currant bun on their way down into the city centre, lingering once they set eyes on the jukebox. Although, surely there must be plenty of other young people needing a place to chat and listen to music. She wished Peggy was here to see the musical monster.

She frowned, wondering what had happened between Peggy and Greg that had caused her brother to beat him up. A sigh escaped her as she thought again of the young man who had come to her rescue. If she had known what was going to happen, she'd have been out of the chippy like a shot as soon as Peggy suggested leaving. Yet if she had left, he would never have kissed her. Wouldn't it be marvellous if one day he walked into the milk bar and swept her off her feet? She smiled to herself, hoping that it would not be long before some customers came in.

Jeanette did not have long to wait and for a while the place became so busy that Mrs Cross told her she could wait-on. She found herself quite enjoying the work. It was so different from her weekday occupation in a shipping warehouse office, and there was the added bonus of being able to listen to the music on the jukebox.

She'd had a closer look at the machine and seen that it played 45s, which meant because the records were smaller than the old 78s there were plenty of titles to choose from. She found it a struggle not to give in to the urge to jig around to Bill Haley & his Comets singing 'Shake, Rattle and Roll' as she carried dirty glasses and crockery to the kitchen. She grinned, imagining Ethel's horror if she were to listen to such music at home. The old witch dominated what programmes the family listened to on the wireless, so Jeanette scarcely ever got the chance to tune in to what she wanted.

Jeanette was taking a well-earned break when the door opened and Hester entered the milk bar, startling her so she dropped the last bit of bun in her tea, which annoyed her no end. Swiftly she rescued it before sliding from the stool behind the counter and facing her half-sister. 'What are you doing here?' she whispered.

'I'm glad to see you, too,' said Hester, glancing about her. 'Where's your boss?'

'In the back. Why?'

Hester leaned closer to Jeanette and said in a low voice, 'I've come to tell you that quite a fuss is being made of that fight in the chippy. A search is being made for you and that young man you mentioned.'

'Damn!' The colour ebbed from Jeanette's cheeks. 'Does Dad know?'

'I've no idea.' Hester pushed back a hank of dark hair and sighed. 'Your name wasn't mentioned but they have a lead that could connect to you. The chief constable is determined to put a stop to fights involving Teddy Boys and bicycle chains.'

Jeanette clung to Hester's arm. 'Please, don't tell your sergeant that I'm the girl they're looking for!' she pleaded.

'I don't know what to do,' said Hester unhappily. 'I should

have already reported that you were involved, but I wanted to talk to you first. It would be best if you came forward and told them what happened.'

Jeanette gulped. 'If I go and talk to the police, Aunt Ethel is bound to hear of it and I'll never live it down. She'll go on about me being like my mother!'

'I know, although if you were to tell Dad first, he might just keep quiet about it.'

'Fat chance of that,' said Jeanette gloomily. 'He'll want her to keep a better eye on me so I don't get into more trouble. I won't be allowed out evenings.'

Mrs Cross came in from the back and looked their way. 'That your boss?' asked Hester in a low voice.

'Yes.'

'Then I'd better order something.'

'Cup of coffee and a scone?' suggested Jeanette.

'Yes, that'll be fine.'

Hester perched on a stool and pulled off her gloves and shoved them in her pocket, watching her sister busy herself behind the counter. 'So how's it going so far?' she asked.

'All right,' said Jeanette, placing a coffee in front of Hester before picking up a buttered scone with a pair of tongs and putting it on a plate. 'So why aren't you wearing your uniform – although I have to admit I'm glad you're not.'

'I'm to report to CID later.'

Jeanette's green eyes showed interest. 'Doing what?'

'Could be that it's a raid and women and children are involved, so they want a woman on hand. Or undercover work, where I have to pretend to be a girlfriend of one of the men,' said Hester casually.

'I wish I had your job,' said Jeanette wistfully. 'Aren't you excited at the thought of doing something that years ago a woman wouldn't have been allowed to do?'

Hester looked thoughtful. 'It had to happen, but it was two world wars that helped bring it about – and we still haven't got equal wages with the men.'

Jeanette nodded, although she knew little about it.

At that moment the door opened and a couple of girls entered. 'You'd best pay me for that coffee and scone now,' whispered Jeanette. 'Mrs Cross is looking this way. She'll be expecting me to see to those two, I bet.'

'OK.' Hester took out her purse and glanced at the price list on the wall behind the counter. She placed the money on the table and slipped tuppence across to Jeanette. 'There's your tip. I'll go as soon as I've finished.'

Jeanette grinned. 'Thanks. Good luck for this evening.'

'I think it's you who are going to need the luck when you get home,' said Hester. 'It wouldn't surprise me if our Sam is involved with this CID business, so I'll be OK. You'll have to face Dad. Don't forget to tell him about your involvement in that fight in the chippy and he'll probably go with you to the bridewell for moral support.'

Jeanette pulled a face and glanced at her employer. 'I'm going to have to go. Mrs Cross will be on my back if I linger here any longer.'

'OK, but you are listening to me, aren't you? I don't want to have to report you to my sergeant. It's best coming from you.'

Jeanette nodded and left Hester to finish her coffee.

Jeanette was ready to collapse by the time she arrived home. And – oh joy! – she had the house to herself. Her feet and back had never ached so much. Only briefly had she given a thought to going into Quiggins as she passed the shop and speaking to Peggy's brother, only to decide she was too tired to cope with any hassle about what had happened Friday evening. She concealed her minuscule wages and the tips she had received in a safe place in her bedroom and was just considering having a bath when she heard the sound of a key in the front door. Her heart began to race. Most likely it would be Ethel and she still had not worked out exactly what she was going to say to her. Then the door opened and Sam entered the lobby.

Her half-brother was a good-looking bloke with a thatch of thick flaxen hair and chiselled features, just like the film star Douglas Fairbanks Jnr. He was also protective towards her, on the whole. She remembered him telling her that he was the last person to speak to her mother before she had left the house that fateful day in May 1941, when she had asked him to keep an eye on Jeanette.

'Am I glad it's you,' she said. 'Would you like me to make you a cup of tea?'

'You can if you want to get on the right side of me,' said Sam, hanging up his mackintosh.

She slanted him an uncertain look before hurrying into the kitchen. 'D'you want me to make you a cheese butty as well? I don't know what Aunt Ethel is planning for tea. She's out.'

'A couple of cheese butties will be fine. I'm working this evening, so I'll get something more substantial at the canteen later.' Sam sat at the kitchen table and drummed his fingers on the table top, gazing at her from narrowed brown eyes. 'I'm glad I found you here. Where were you earlier?'

'Working.' She filled the kettle and put it on the stove.

'Don't lie. Dad was in a right state this morning when I got up, and the old witch was blowing her top because you'd vanished. She swore that it was your Saturday morning off and, just to make sure, Dad phoned your workplace.'

Jeanette was horrified. 'Oh no!'

'He'd been informed that you were involved in an incident in the chippy in Norton Street last evening.'

'Oh bloody hell!' The tea caddy slipped from her fingers, but she managed to prevent it landing on the floor and placed it on the table. 'I was going to tell him when I saw him, but I haven't had a chance to do so yet.'

'So you don't deny being there,' said Sam, scowling.

'What would be the point if you already know? Who was it who gave my name to the police?'

'It was a friend of yours, Peggy McGrath.'

'Peggy!' Jeanette was stunned. 'Is she all right? Only she was dragged away by the fellow she'd been going out with. He said that he had a bone to pick with her. I suspect her brother beat him up because of something she had said about Greg.'

Sam rolled his eyes. 'Some old dear had suggested that he and Peggy McGrath might be able to help the police with their enquiries.'

'Blast and double blast,' muttered Jeanette. 'I bet she hates me now because a policeman turned up on her doorstep! I should have minded my own business, instead of thinking I had to stick up for her because she was my friend.'

'At least she won't have to go to court because she didn't witness the fight. But you might,' warned Sam.

Jeanette groaned. 'Does the old witch know about this?'

He raised his eyebrows. 'What do you think?'

Jeanette stared at him gloomily. 'Where are she and Dad now?'

'She mentioned having shopping to do, whilst he went off to see if he could find you.'

'Couldn't he have just waited until I came home?'

'Perhaps he thought you mightn't come home? You're forgetting you went out without saying where you were going and you must have known you were in trouble.'

'I sneaked out because the old witch locked me in my bedroom. Hester let me out because I'd found myself an extra job, working part time in a milk bar. I didn't want Aunt Ethel knowing because she'd take all my earnings.'

Sam's lips set in a grim line. 'I bet she didn't mention locking you in your room to Dad.'

Jeanette sighed heavily. 'I suppose I'd better go down to the bridewell and make a statement. Will you be here when I get back?'

'Probably not. Do you want me to come with you? I can do without the tea and butties if you're desperate for my company,' said Sam, his stern features suddenly relaxing into a smile.

Her eyes brightened. 'Oh, I do love you! I know I shouldn't expect any favours because three members of my family are in the police force, but I admit with you there I'm hoping they'll be lenient with me. I'd best get my coat.'

'Don't expect me to defend your actions,' he warned, switching off the gas under the kettle. 'You should have come straight home after the pictures, knowing Aunt Ethel would be watching out for you.'

'I didn't expect there to be a fight at the chippy.'

'All right. Now get a move on.'

She got a move on.

As they walked to the bus stop, Jeanette asked if he knew

whether the priest had been questioned yet. 'That I don't know,' replied Sam. 'Tell me exactly what happened.'

She told him most of it. Sam looked disturbed. 'Nasty. And like you, I hope the priest's words got through to the injured man and he went to the hospital.'

'I'd like to know what happened to him.' Jeanette sighed.

He fixed her with a stare. 'Don't go getting ideas about him, just because he came to your rescue. There's plenty of blokes who would have done the same where someone looking like you was involved.'

'There's nothing special about me,' protested Jeanette.

'You're petite and your figure's not bad at all. You've got a cute nose and unusual green eyes and there's an air of inno-cence about you. You stir up the protective instinct in men.'

Jeanette was so taken aback that she could not think of anything to say immediately. They walked on in silence for a while. Then she blurted out, 'I'm not an innocent, though! I know there's a lot of nastiness in the world and people can't always be trusted. I don't normally need a bloke to fight my corner.'

'Maybe not. I would hope you'd use your common sense and stay out of trouble. In the normal way of things, I'm here if you're desperate. You could have got the woman behind the counter to phone directly through to me.'

'But you mightn't have been available. I mean, you're going to be out this evening.' Jeanette glanced at him. 'I don't suppose you can tell me what it's about?'

He smiled slightly. 'Why d'you need to know?'

'I don't. I'm just interested.'

'All I can tell you is that I was down at the docks this morning.'

'On a job? Thefts from warehouses or ships?'

'We've been working in cahoots with the Customs on a case.'

'You mean smuggling?' Her eyes sparkled.

'I'm saying no more.' Sam changed the subject. 'You need to prepare what you're going to say to Dad when you see him. Aunt Ethel was going on at him about you running wild, saying you're completely out of control. You have to prove to him that you're not. Make sure there's no getting involved in incidents such as last evening again. And if you're a witness to such an event, no running away! You do the telephoning.'

Jeanette flushed. 'There won't be a next time,' she said in a low voice. 'Aunt Ethel will see to that. I'll be on bread and water and locked away.'

'Don't be melodramatic. She's no fool and knows she wouldn't get away with it these days.'

Jeanette stared at him and said seriously, 'You can say that, but she still hurt me and locked me in my bedroom last night. You can't always be there and neither can Dad. I have to find a way of dealing with her myself.'

Sam frowned. 'You know, there was a helluva row going on between her and your mother that evening she disappeared.'

'You've never mentioned that before.'

'That's because it was a terrible day for me and I don't like talking about it.' Before she could ask, he added, 'And I still don't!'

She dug her hands deep in her pockets. 'OK! I won't nose into your affairs. The day will come when the old witch pops her clogs and until then I'll put up with her. Unless—'

'Unless what?'

Jeanette's green eyes glinted. 'Unless she goes completely crackers. Then I'll have to retaliate in a way she'd never expect.'

'She's not worth swinging for, our kid.'

'I know that,' said Jeanette.

For a while they were both silent, and then she said, 'You don't think the old witch followed my mother and did something nasty to her?'

'You mean murdered her?'

Jeanette nodded. 'She could have removed all identification and hid the body. I hate to think of it and I suppose I'm talking nonsense in the light of what she says about my mother having upped and left because she had another man. I get the impression she still thinks she's alive.'

'Yes, and it's a mystery to me why she says it,' said Sam tersely. 'Your mother wouldn't have upped and left you.'

'So where was she going that evening? You're the detective!' burst out Jeanette. 'Can't you solve this mystery?'

'I wish I could find out the truth for you, but right now I have other things that need my attention.'

'Sorry,' said Jeanette, biting her lip. 'That was unfair of me.'

His face softened. 'No, I can understand your frustration, but digging up the past takes time, our kid.' He placed a hand on her shoulder. 'Here's our stop. Have you worked out exactly what you're going to say?'

'I'm going to tell the truth, the whole truth and nothing but the truth,' she said, taking a deep breath.

Jeanette had expected to feel much better when she emerged from the bridewell, and she did. Of course, having Sam with her had made a difference and, as it turned out, Billy had confessed to being in possession of a dangerous weapon and admitted to unintentional grievous bodily harm. It could be that he and his mate would be treated less severely than they might have been in the circumstances when they appeared before the magistrate at the juvenile court on Monday.

Four

As Jeanette closed the back door, she could hear Ethel talking, and then came the low rumble of her father's voice. She filled the kettle, expecting them to come rushing into the kitchen at any moment. She could feel her heart thudding in her chest and told herself that it was stupid to be so nervous. With her father present, Ethel was not going to hurt her.

She knew as soon as they realized there was someone else in the house. They went quiet, and despite their attempts to open the sitting room door without making a noise, she heard a hinge squeaking. Then came the sound of her father's size elevens and Ethel shuffling along in her slippers. Jeanette did not wait for her father to fling open the kitchen door, but did so herself and pinned on a smile.

'Cup of tea?' she asked.

'Don't you cup-of-tea me, my girl,' said Ethel, wagging a finger. 'Where've you been? We've been worried about you.'

'At the bridewell in town giving a statement. Our Sam went with me as I was a bit nervous about going on my own.' Jeanette poured milk into cups. 'I wanted to do my duty, but I was apprehensive. Who's to say that one of the youths involved in the fight won't come after me. What do you say, Dad?'

George felt a catch at his heart as he stared at his younger daughter – so like her mother when he had first seen her. He would never forget the fear and defiance in Grace's green eyes. She had reminded him of a stray cat he had once found in an overgrown garden. The animal had given birth to kittens and was prepared to defend them with her life. In Grace's case, the only life she had been defending was her own against a drunken ex-soldier from the Great War. She'd had a penknife and her hand was clenched so tightly on the shaft that George had a job persuading her to hand it over to him. He remembered she had been wearing a worn floral frock of red and green that was much too small for her, so all the more revealing of the feminine form beneath. He was newly widowed with two young children and she was a waif living on the streets, so she told him. Two months later he had asked her to be his wife.

'Cat got your tongue, George?' said Ethel. 'You're not going to believe all that, are you? It wouldn't take her all day to go to the bridewell and give a statement. You do realize that she lied to me last night!' Her voice sounded like a rusty nail being pulled out of a plank.

'That's not true!' Jeanette avoided looking at her great-aunt and concentrated all her attention on her father. 'I didn't tell any fibs, Dad. I just didn't tell Aunt Ethel the entire truth. I thought she might have nightmares, thinking how close I'd come to being killed. If you'd seen that bicycle chain flying through the air, Dad, you'd have been terrified for me.'

Aware that the kettle was boiling, Jeanette paused to give herself time to think; she switched off the gas and warmed the teapot, knowing that from the way he was looking at her and ignoring Ethel, her father was hooked. He really enjoyed a good story, consuming crime novels and westerns from the library at the rate of two a week. 'If I hadn't have ducked,' she continued, 'it would have been me who was hit in the face.' She shivered. 'Scarred for life! All my looks gone. If you could only have seen that young man, Dad, you'd have pitied him.'

'That still doesn't explain where you've been all day,' said Ethel, snatching the teapot from her and swirling the water around before emptying it in the sink.

'I returned to the scene of the crime, although I didn't go inside,' lied Jeanette. 'I also contemplated visiting the priest.'

'The priest!' exclaimed Ethel. 'Since when has this household ever had anything to do with priests?'

'Never! I know that, but needs must when the devil drives. Isn't that what people say when it's an emergency?' said Jeanette.

'Humph!' exclaimed Ethel. 'Do we believe that, George?' She stared across at her nephew who was pulling out a chair.

He sat down and his gaze rested on his daughter's face. 'Aunt Ethel thinks you might have known this young man already and the fight broke out over you, Jeannie, love.'

Jeanette's eyes widened. 'That's not true! You ask my friend Peggy.'

'My sources say she wasn't there for the fight,' said George.

'No, but we went into the chippy together, glad to get out of the rain. The young man came in shortly after. He was wearing oilskins and I thought he looked like a sailor and said it must be terrible being at sea in such weather. Then we were interrupted by Greg dragging Peggy out. There wouldn't have been a fight if it weren't for him,' said Jeanette.

'She denied having anything to do with him,' said George.

'I don't believe it!' said Jeanette, taken aback.

George said heavily, 'Actually, she admitted lying later when told there were those who swore they'd seen him there. She's not exactly what you'd call a reliable witness.'

Jeanette's eyes darkened. 'I'm going to have it out with her on Monday! What does she think she's playing at, telling such lies?'

'Never mind what she thinks,' said Ethel, pouring boiling water into the teapot. 'You shouldn't have been in that chippy. You knew I'd have your supper waiting for you.'

'Burnt to a crisp,' said Jeanette beneath her breath.

'What did you say?' snapped Ethel, rearing her head like a cobra ready to strike.

Jeanette met her great-aunt's eyes squarely. 'If you remember, Aunt Ethel, when I came in you didn't offer me any supper but hustled me upstairs. You didn't even give me the chance to go to the lavatory or clean my teeth.'

George placed a hand on his daughter's wrist. 'She's explained that, Jeannie, love. She'd been worried sick about you with it being so late and decided it was necessary to teach you a lesson.'

'That's true,' said Ethel, nodding several times. 'I've been thinking, as a treat, not as a punishment, you understand, Jeanette, you can accompany me to the pictures to see *The Weak and the Wicked* this evening.'

'But you know I saw that yesterday,' protested Jeanette, her heart sinking at the thought of sitting through the film with the old woman.

'Then you can see it again,' said Ethel softly. 'Anyway, to make up for your having no supper last night, you can help me make supper this evening.' She went over to the vegetable rack and returned with a full colander and placed it in front of Jeanette. 'Peel them!' She sat at the table and, staring at her great-niece, added, 'And you've yet to tell us what you said to this priest.'

Jeanette wished the old witch would remove herself. She could not resist criticizing the way Jeanette did things. According to her, Jeanette always removed too much of the white flesh from potatoes.

George intervened. 'Well, Jeannie, did the priest have anything more to say about the young man who got hurt?'

Jeanette inwardly counted to ten. 'I only thought about going.'

'I see. So you don't know the name of this young man?'

Jeanette shook her head. 'I barely got the chance to thank him, and I doubt I'll ever meet him again unless he gets in touch with the priest.'

'Well, I hope he does. I'd like to shake his hand for coming to your rescue,' said George.

'I don't know why,' said Ethel. 'When sailors come ashore they're looking to get into mischief. Wine, women and song, that's what they want. No doubt he was trying to get round our Jeannie and have his wicked way with her. No doubt she was flattered by his attention.'

George frowned. 'That's a bit prejudiced, Aunt Ethel. If you haven't got something good to say about people, don't say it is what I say!' He rose from the table and left the kitchen.

'Now see what you've done,' said Ethel wrathfully, glaring at Jeanette.

'It's not my fault if Dad wanted to get away from you. And he's right – you shouldn't tar all sailors with the same brush. It isn't nice.'

Ethel cuffed her across the head. 'Don't you be giving me cheek! And while I remember, how did you get out of your bedroom? I swear I locked you in.'

'Well, you could have been imagining you did,' said Jeanette, rubbing her head.

Ethel's eyes narrowed into slits. 'Are you suggesting I'm going senile? Well, let me tell you, girl, that I never forget a face.'

What had never forgetting faces to do with her escaping her bedroom? It was interesting, though, Ethel talking of going senile. Jeanette determined to watch for any sign of it and decided she must mention it to Hester and Sam, too.

As she peeled the vegetables, her thoughts were now of them. It was possible that they were working together, doing their part to catch those men whom the Customs had their eye on for smuggling in goodness knows what!

Hester glanced at her brother as he banged the knocker for a second time. After several minutes, the door opened in what could only be described as a furtive manner. Sam thrust his foot into the opening and produced a sheet of paper from an inside pocket. 'I have a warrant to search this house.'

'There's nothing here! You've come to the wrong address.' The owner of the voice was invisible to Hester, but she detected a trace of fear amid the bluster.

'We'll see about that,' said Sam calmly. 'Step aside, please, if you don't want to be hurt.'

A head peeped round the door and Hester found herself being inspected, along with the three uniformed male officers. 'You're making a mistake!' shouted the man.

Sam pushed him aside and told a constable to watch him.

Entering the house, he ordered another policeman to check the front room whilst the other searched upstairs. Sam told Hester to follow him and headed for the rear of the building.

This was not the first time she had been on a raid, but even so, Hester's heart was beating rapidly. She was close on her brother's heels as he flung open a door. 'So what's going on here?' he said quietly.

Standing at his shoulder, Hester was aware of a sweet pungent odour that was quite pleasant. She stared at the Chinese couple who were lying on blankets on the floor. Between them was a spirit lamp, and the man was in the act of taking a pipe from his mouth. Near to hand were two open packets, one of which had been used.

'Search the room, Constable Walker,' ordered Sam.

Hester did so whilst her brother spoke to the couple who appeared to be in a daze. On the mantelpiece she found two needles and a file, and on a ledge behind the window shutter were two opium pipes. She searched the wardrobe and discovered inside a coat pocket some raw opium and a tin containing five packets of prepared opium. She could hear one of the men saying in fractured English that he smoked opium to relieve the bad pain in his stomach. She might have felt sorry for him if her brother had not already told her that he had previous convictions for possession of drugs in London. He had also been convicted of gaming offences, so it wasn't as if he was unaware that he was breaking the law. She found another spirit lamp under the bed and that seemed to finalize everything.

After the arrests were made she accompanied the female prisoner, whilst two of the male officers dealt with the men. They travelled in a Black Maria to the bridewell in Cheapside, while Sam and the other officer went down to the docks. It was not long before her brother returned and she was told the white man who rented the room in the house was a ship's steward, and the Chinaman was a ship's cook and brother-in-law of the woman. She was pleased that everything had been accomplished without any violence.

'You can go off home now, Hester,' said Sam, stifling a yawn. 'I've some paperwork to do here.'

'It's a pity you can't come with me,' she murmured. 'You work too hard.'

He put down his mug and stared at her. 'I enjoy my job. You're not worrying about facing Aunt Ethel on your own just because you let Jeanette out of her bedroom, are you?'

She flushed and fiddled with her whistle. 'I know I'm stupid. I'm glad you were able to be of some influence, so Jeanette won't have to appear in court.'

'It had already been arranged that the evidence of the two women who saw everything would suffice,' he said, toying with a pencil. 'I do think she has too much to say for herself sometimes, though. One day it could get her into real trouble.'

'I agree. But I'd hate to see her put down so badly that she'd be scared to open her mouth.'

Sam agreed, leaning back in the chair. 'I'm fond of the kid. But you know what she said to me today?'

'What?'

'She wondered if the old witch had followed Grace and murdered her!'

Hester's eyes flared wide. 'What do you think?'

'Aunt Ethel did go out for a while. If I hadn't been so wrapped up in myself I might have asked not only her where she was going, but Grace as well. Jeanette reckons that with three members of the police force in the house, we should have a go at finding out what happened that evening.'

Hester pulled a face. 'As if we didn't have enough to do.'

'But you can understand why she said it,' muttered Sam. 'Three coppers in the house and we have no proof that Grace is dead or if she went off with another man. Surely Dad should have been able to find some trace of her?'

'Perhaps he never searched thoroughly enough because he believes there could be some truth in what Aunt Ethel said about Grace having someone else. It could be that she was seeing someone but had no intention of leaving Dad and Jeanette for him. Maybe she was with him when a bomb fell and destroyed wherever they were and that was the end of them,' said Hester.

'From what I remember she appeared to be very fond of Dad. I don't recall them ever arguing.'

'They might have done when we weren't there. So what are we going to do?' asked Hester.

Sam yawned and rubbed his face with his hands. 'I didn't say we had to do anything. I was just telling you what Jeanette said.'

'Yes, but you don't generally say something unless you feel something needs to be done about it,' persisted Hester.

'OK! I don't like it that Jeanette might believe we've failed her. I do have trouble accepting that our stepmother would have walked out on us, never mind her own daughter and Dad,' said Sam. 'Yet how well did we really know her? I know nothing of her background. She never mentioned family and we didn't ask. We were just glad to have a younger woman in the house who was on our side.'

'I'd like her to be alive,' said Hester softly. 'Perhaps she got caught up in the bombing and was so badly injured that she lost her memory? The only difficulty with that idea is that she would have had her identity card with her.'

Sam's eyes glinted. 'She kept it in her handbag and I'm sure she didn't have that with her that evening. I watched her from the window. She was carrying a shopping bag flat on her hand as if she was making certain whatever was inside would not spill or break.'

'She must have been going to visit someone.'

'But who? She never had visitors as far as I know,' said Sam.

'So what if she did have a friend and is walking around today, not remembering any of us, and has taken on a new identity?' suggested Hester.

Sam laughed. 'You're not thinking, our kid! If she had a friend from the time before she knew us, then the friend would know who she is.'

Hester smiled faintly. 'Could be that after losing her memory she took up with another man and married him and has another family. The old witch might have seen them together but has no intention of ever telling us the truth or informing Grace who she is and where we live now. Don't forget we were living in a different house back then.'

Sam reached for his mug. 'It's a lot to think about.'

'Then let's just mull it over. I'll see you later. Don't work too hard.'

'And don't you let the old witch get you down.'

Hester waved and left the office. Sam had given her a lot to think about but she had no intention of mentioning what they had discussed with Jeanette. And she was not going to be scared of her great-aunt either. So what if Ethel had worked out it could only have been Hester who had enabled Jeanette to escape? She should show some guts and tell Ethel what she thought of her.

As it was, when Hester returned home, it was to find that her father was the only one there. Immediately she relaxed, although she felt sorry for Jeanette when she heard that she had gone to the pictures with their great-aunt.

While Hester ate her meal, she told her father about the raid. He showed interest, and she might have gone on to put to him Sam's idea of what might have happened to Grace if he had not switched on the wireless to listen to *In Town Tonight*. She went upstairs and had a quick bath before going to bed with a Mills & Boon romance from the library. She fell asleep after reading only five pages to dream that she was marooned on a tropical island with a mystery man.

She was roused the following morning by the sound of church bells and her half-sister bringing her breakfast in bed. 'I believe you and Sam made several arrests,' said Jeanette.

Hester sat up and yawned. 'Who told you?'

'Dad. He's proud of you. Whereas I just remind him of the wife the old witch says he should never have married. You should have heard her go on at me on the way to the Odeon. I asked her point blank what she had against my mother and you know what she said?'

'What?'

'She was on the streets when Dad found her and she led him on!' Jeanette's voice shook. 'I told her I didn't believe her. I just can't see Dad marrying a prostitute, can you?'

Hester was shocked. 'No. He's fastidious is Dad. He wouldn't have a woman who'd sold her body, however sorry he might feel for some of those on the streets. You should have told him what she said about your mother and he'd have put you straight.'

Jeanette gave a grim little smile. 'I just couldn't bring

myself to say the word *prostitute* to him. It would appear as if I needed to ask him because I was unsure about the truth of the matter.'

'But you'd have let him know that his aunt was telling you lies.'

Jeanette toyed with her fingers. 'She'd talk her way out of it. She also went on about my mother being very young when he married her.'

'She seemed old enough to me,' said Hester. 'There were times when she got down to our level and then there were others when she was expecting you and just sat in a chair, knitting little garments with an altogether different expression, and I'd think: *You look older today, Gracie.* It was as if she realized having a child brought responsibility.'

Jeanette smiled. 'I can see how that could be. The old witch pulled the film to pieces, as well, you know. All the way home, she was going on about the prison governor and the wardens being soft on criminals and how it hadn't been like that in her day.'

'Typical of her.'

Jeanette nodded and gazed out of the window. 'It looks like rain again.'

'A blinking nuisance, the weather.' Hester sipped her tea. 'I know it's difficult to ignore what Aunt Ethel says, but I can tell you that Dad used to smile more often when your mother was part of this household.'

'D'you think he loved her?'

'To be frank, I don't know. He introduced her to us as *your new mam,* so I presumed that he'd married her to look after me and Sam. I have a vague memory that our dear great-aunt wasn't at all pleased and I prayed that she would leave. She didn't always live with us. I think I remember my mother saying that Ethel had a job where she lived in once upon a time.'

'Perhaps she was in service when she wasn't a prison wardress?' said Jeanette.

'Maybe,' said Hester, glancing about her. 'What happened to my Mills & Boon?'

'It's here on the floor,' said Jeanette, bending to pick it up.

She placed the book on the bed. 'Peggy reads them. Love's young dream she isn't,' she added, scowling.

Hester cocked an eye at her. 'They're relaxing reads. I suppose Dad was in need of a woman's affection after my mother died, and that could have been another reason why he married your mother.'

'Well, they must have slept together for me to have been born,' said Jeanette cheerfully. 'I wish I knew more about sex. What we were taught in biology class about reproduction makes it sound not worth bothering about.'

'That's what grown-ups want you to believe, so you won't get into trouble. The disgrace and the pain isn't worth it from what I've seen.' Hester changed the subject. 'Did Aunt Ethel say anything about you escaping from your locked bedroom?'

'I didn't mention your name if that's what you want to know,' said Jeanette, smiling. 'I gave her the impression she was getting forgetful and hadn't locked me in. She mentioned going senile and I took advantage of it.'

Hester's expression froze. 'I must try that myself. After all, she is getting on.'

'How old is she exactly?'

'She must be kicking seventy at least.' Hester yawned. 'What are you doing today?'

Jeanette grimaced. 'I'm confined to the house because of what happened on Friday. If it wasn't Sunday, she would have me scrubbing floors. Instead, I'll be preparing the vegetables and washing dishes. By the way, Sam knows about my part-time job but neither Ethel nor Dad does.'

'OK, but I don't know how long you think you'll get away with it,' warned Hester.

'I wish I could—' Jeanette stopped abruptly.

Hester smiled. 'What do you wish?'

'I wish I could get my hands on my savings book,' said Jeanette in a frustrated voice. 'If I had the money I'd be off like a shot. Not because I'm not fond of you, Sam and Dad, of course. All through the film the old witch kept elbowing me as if I needed to be reminded constantly what happened to girls that went astray. I wonder what she was like at my age?'

'Or mine,' murmured Hester.

'You should find yourself a fella, get married and leave home,' said Jeanette.

'Talking about fellas,' said Hester, reaching for her cup of tea, 'what about the one who was hit in the face?'

'What about him?' Jeanette said with a sigh. 'He'll probably be scarred for life and it's all my fault. I should have minded my own business,' she added, not for the first time. 'I think he's a sailor. I wonder if it's possible for me to discover the name of his ship?'

'How?'

'I'll have to think about that.'

'The trouble with sailors is that they can have a girl in every port,' said Hester. 'He could also be a lousy letter writer, and a girl has to have something to cling on to for a relationship to work.'

Jeanette nodded, hoping her sister was wrong on both counts. Summer would soon be over and with only Christmas on the horizon, it would be great to have a boyfriend, even one who wasn't around all the time; someone to exchange letters with, and to talk about to Peggy, assuming they were still on speaking terms.

Five

Jeanette was attempting to concentrate on typing a sheaf of bills of lading for various consuls throughout the world the following morning, but her mind kept wandering. She would be glad when she had finished the task. The paper was very thin and inclined to slip sideways between the rollers, and so did the carbon paper if she wasn't careful. She had come in early and checked Friday's arrivals, but the two ships that might possibly have had her rescuer amongst their crew had left on the early tide on Saturday.

She sighed and glanced out of the window, which had a view of the Liverpool Dock office. If she turned her head she could just about see the River Mersey. It looked like the weather was clearing and so she made up her mind to eat her sandwiches down at the Pierhead instead of in the windowless room where there was a kettle to make tea or coffee.

So far there had been no sign of Peggy, but then she was a staff member of a subsidiary branch of the warehousing company that employed them both, so that was not surprising.

'I've a bone to pick with you!'

Jeanette started at the sound of Peggy's voice and thought, *Talk of the devil!* Aware that the other shorthand typist was looking their way, she whispered, 'D'you mind keeping your voice down? I don't want everyone knowing my business.' She carried on typing.

Peggy placed a hand over the typewriter keys. 'Ashamed are you for causing a fight and getting me and Greg into further trouble? My dad almost had a fit when a policeman came knocking at our door!'

'Will you stop that?' hissed Jeanette, shoving Peggy's hand off the keys. 'You've made me make a mistake and I'll have to type this out again.'

'You should have stopped and given me all your attention,' snapped Peggy.

Jeanette glared at her as she removed paper, carbon and copies from the typewriter. 'Say what you have to say and go. I don't want to get behind with my work.'

Peggy sniffed. 'It's all right for you, but I'm in real trouble with my dad. He didn't half belt me one and then went round to Greg's house to tell him not to go near me. As if I wanted to see him again after what he called me on Friday night. Anyway, his dad threw a punch at my dad. Fortunately he missed because he was drunk.'

'So what was your quarrel with Greg all about? Why did your brother hit him?'

Peggy flushed. 'I'd rather not discuss it.'

Jeanette was disappointed. 'It must have been really bad if your brother beat him up.'

'Well, I'm not telling you,' muttered Peggy.

Jeanette thought about the love bites she had seen on her friend's neck. 'Please yourself. I'm sorry about what happened, but it's not my fault that your boyfriend and his mates got violent. It's a miracle I didn't get hit in the face instead of that poor sailor. As it is he could be scarred for life!'

'None of that was my fault! If you hadn't flirted with him, then most likely he wouldn't have interfered. Anyway, how d'you know he's a sailor?'

'He looked like a sailor! And I wasn't flirting with him,' said Jeanette, annoyance bubbling up inside her again. She reinserted paper and carbon in the typewriter. 'Anyway, that Billy deserves whatever he gets,' she muttered.

Peggy said moodily, 'You would say that because your father's respectable. Billy's dad is a drunkard and is in and out of work.'

'He didn't look like his family was hard up. That drape jacket he was wearing appeared brand new!'

'You think it was knocked off?' said Peggy, fiddling with a pencil on Jeanette's desk. 'I know he's been in trouble before for petty theft.'

'There you are then,' retorted Jeanette. 'It probably came off the back of a lorry.'

'You could be more sympathetic for them whose life is harder than yours.' Peggy dropped the pencil.

'I can't understand you – he's a violent troublemaker!'

'I know! Anyway, his mother has asked Father Callaghan to put a good word in for him. He has a boxing club for the lads and does good work.'

'Well, he failed with that Billy, didn't he?' said Jeanette in a hard voice, hurt by Peggy's suggestion that she didn't care about the underprivileged.

'You don't know how difficult life is for some lads in our neighbourhood,' protested Peggy, folding her arms across her ample bosom in the tight white blouse that was gaping at the front. 'I believed I could save Greg from the same kind of fate. Now it's all over! It was good whilst it lasted, but now I'll never speak to him again,' she said in a tight little voice.

Jeanette muttered, 'Well, you're not the only one who got into trouble. Aunt Ethel poked me in the chest and locked me in my bedroom. I can't see me having a night out anytime soon. At least you've got your holiday to look forward to.'

'With my mam and dad both having a face on them. Great!' cried Peggy, and flounced off.

Jeanette hit the typewriter keys hard, thinking most likely their friendship was at an end. Well, that was unfortunate, but she was not going to lose any sleep over it, although it could be awkward when Peggy came into the office. Perhaps it was time to look for another job. She felt fed up. After she had finished at commercial college she had seen this job as a stopgap until she decided what she really wanted to do with her life. If only she was five inches taller she would have been able to join the police force when she was twenty. It was discrimination against small women. She had once considered nursing as a career, but after a visit to a hospital she had decided that she wasn't cut out for a job that demanded a strong back, stomach and the patience and caring nature of a saint. Good training, she supposed, for marriage and kids.

As she typed, Jeanette imagined what it would be like staying at home and looking after children. Because it was not that long since she had been a kid herself, she thought it shouldn't be that difficult to take care of her own brood. Her thoughts turned to Hester who had helped rear her. No doubt that experience would stand her in good stead if she became a mother.

Jeanette rather liked the idea of being an aunt. Having the fun of playing with children without tying herself down for life too soon. But she would like a real boyfriend, one with whom she could go dancing and to the flicks, enjoy a day out at New Brighton or Formby beach in the summer. *But not if your boyfriend was a sailor who was away for weeks on end.*

'My David who fought Goliath,' she murmured.

'What was that you said?' asked Elsie, the other typist.

Jeanette smiled wryly. 'I was talking to myself.'

'We all do that at times.'

'Have you ever been out with a sailor?'

'Not for long. They come and go and it can feel like you're wasting half your life waiting for them to come home.'

'Maybe that kind of life suits some women. You wouldn't have to be too fond of them, though.'

'Hmm. And there's many a sailor just looking for a bit of fun when his ship docks.'

Jeanette remembered Ethel's words about sailors and sighed. It would be heartbreaking being parted if you loved each other, she thought. Well, it didn't look like she was likely to trace her sailor's whereabouts any time soon. She should start being sensible and put him out of her mind.

Despite having come to that decision, when Jeanette descended from her third-floor office and left the Cunard Building, her rescuer was still very much on her mind. She hoped he was not in too much pain and his wound would heal quickly. She did feel responsible for what had happened to him, because she had lied when she had said that she had not been flirting with him. Jeanette enjoyed flirting. It was fun if not taken too seriously, but Peggy had spoilt what could have been an enjoyable interlude.

Jeanette determined to banish the blues as she walked down to the river. The surface of the water dazzled her eyes and she held up a hand to shield them from the sun. Today she could so easily imagine the Mersey was the Mediterranean or the Caribbean. She had often dreamt of travelling to faraway places as she watched the ships coming and going. At the moment dreams were all she had.

The next few weeks passed slowly. The weather was a complete washout, but at least on the last day of the month there was a parade of veteran cars through Liverpool which excited Sam, who had it in mind to buy a car of his own and said so at the breakfast table.

'Perhaps you could take me on a trip then?' whispered Jeanette in his ear on her way out to work.

'How about abroad?' he responded, getting up from the table.

Her eyes widened. 'Are you serious? I'd have to get a passport.'

'What's this about a passport?' asked Ethel, glancing at the pair of them.

'Nothing! It was just a joke,' said Sam.

'What's there to joke about a passport? You thinking of leaving the country?' Ethel's eyes were suspicious.

Sam nudged Jeanette to get a move on. She hurried out of

the kitchen and he followed her, closing the door behind them. 'That'll have her wondering for the rest of the day,' he said, grinning.

'So it was a joke about going abroad?' said Jeanette, putting on her coat.

He shrugged on his mackintosh. 'I couldn't afford to buy a car and go abroad as well.' He reached for his trilby. 'You ready? Let's get out in case she comes asking any more questions.'

'She won't let it drop, you know. She won't believe it was a joke.' Jeanette fastened a scarf over her head as she followed him to the front door.

'Then I'll have to give her something else to think about,' said Sam. 'Such as why she insists your mother had a fancy man. Where's her proof?'

'I wish you luck in getting a straight answer from her.'

He opened the door and ushered Jeanette out. 'I wonder if it would be worth visiting the hospitals in the vicinity and asking to see their files for the week of the May blitz. Hester and I were wondering about the possibility that Grace received a head injury and lost her memory.'

There was a thoughtful expression in Jeanette's eyes. 'Now why haven't I ever thought of that? Dad must have reported her missing, and maybe there was a photograph of her in the *Echo*.'

Sam frowned. 'I can't remember seeing one.'

'Perhaps you should mention it to Aunt Ethel and watch for her reaction,' said Jeanette. 'She might even say something helpful.'

'And in the meantime she'll tell Dad about us discussing passports and he'll want to know if we're thinking of going abroad.' Sam chuckled.

As Jeanette caught the bus to work, she thought of Peggy who had been on holiday at Butlin's in Pwllheli. She knew that she was back in Liverpool but she had yet to talk to her. She missed her company and wished they could make up their quarrel. She decided to try sending friendly vibes Peggy's way.

A few days later Jeanette was cutting out the shipping list from the *Echo* when a voice said, 'So, anything of real interest in there today?'

She started, recognizing the voice, and glanced over her shoulder with a smile on her face. 'Hi, Peggy, I had hoped I might have seen you before now. Did you have a good holiday?'

'I wasn't sure you'd want to see me, so I kept putting off coming up here,' said Peggy, looking relieved.

'Of course I want to see you! So what was your holiday like?'

'Despite the weather, it could have been worse,' replied Peggy, perching on the edge of Jeanette's desk. 'There was plenty of indoor entertainment and I met this fella at one of the dances. You should have seen him bop. He had me up on the floor most nights, in between the ballroom dancing that is. Mam and Dad had fun, too.'

Jeanette did not like to ask: *What about Greg? Did you miss him? You never did tell me what he said to you that Friday night after he hustled you out of the chippy.* 'I'm glad you enjoyed yourself. I've missed you to be honest.'

'Nothing like getting away from everyday life to put things into perspective,' said Peggy. 'There was a couple of times when I wished you could have been there.'

'Only a couple of times,' teased Jeanette. 'No doubt it was before you met this bloke.'

Peggy grinned. 'How d'you fancy going to the Grafton on Saturday night?'

'I'd love to, only—'

Peggy's face fell. 'Your Aunt Ethel's still not preventing you from going out, is she?'

'I sometimes think it's her whole aim in life,' said Jeanette. 'But I haven't had anyone to go out with if the truth is known. Dad hasn't said that I can't go out. I'll mention it to him, so, fingers crossed, I'll meet you outside the Grafton at half seven.'

'It's a date then,' said Peggy happily. 'We just don't know who we might meet, and in a way that's more fun than going steady, don't you think?'

'I've never gone steady so I wouldn't know,' said Jeanette.

'A whole three weeks Greg and I were meeting secretly because he's a Proddy like you. I suppose it was that which made it so thrilling,' said Peggy, thoughtfully.

'But it's all over now?'

'Hell, yes! I don't want to be going out with someone who called me a tart and whose mate is in Borstal. See you at lunchtime? Perhaps we can walk down to the Pierhead and have our sarnies there,' suggested Peggy.

Jeanette agreed, thinking it was a dry day and who was to say that today she wouldn't spot her seaman. If not, maybe she should visit Father Callaghan and see if he'd been in touch with him. She did not have the address of his presbytery, but no doubt Peggy would be able to tell her where she could find him.

Jeanette had never set foot in a Catholic church before and soon realized that the interior was pretty much as she had imagined, with statues, candles and confessionals, and a faint sweet smell that she guessed was incense.

There were a couple of women arranging flowers and she recognized the priest at the front of the church as Father Callaghan. He was talking to another man and, not wanting to interrupt them, she perched gingerly on the end of a pew and waited for them to finish their conversation. She could not help but overhear some of what was being said because the man was talking at the top of his voice.

He was obviously annoyed with the priest and his language was choice. She decided he was drunk and it was not long before she realized that the priest was not prepared to put up with such behaviour. He seized the man by the back of his collar and escorted him from the church. She was about to follow them outside when Father Callaghan suddenly reappeared and collided with her. He steadied her with a large workmanlike hand.

'Sorry,' said Jeanette, her colour rising with embarrassment. 'I was in a rush to catch up with you. I didn't expect you to get rid of him so quickly.'

He fixed her with a penetrating stare. 'If I'm not mistaken, you're the young lady involved in the fight in the chippy some weeks ago. That was Billy's father.'

'Oh! You have a good memory for a face, Father Callaghan,' she said, impressed.

'A necessary part of my calling,' he said. 'My parishioners

don't like it if I can't put a name to a face. You're Jeanette Walker.'

'You *are* good! I suppose Peggy McGrath told you that.'

He smiled faintly. 'What can I do for you, Miss Walker?'

'I hope you can help me find him,' she said. 'I think you'll know who I mean.'

For a moment he simply stared at her, and then said, 'Shall we sit down? I've been on my feet all day.' He did not wait for her to answer but led the way to the nearest pew.

'Well, Miss Walker,' he said once they were both seated, 'I can tell you the young man has been in touch with me.'

Jeanette could scarcely control her excitement. 'Is he OK?'

'Yes, he did see a doctor and his wound is healing.'

She beamed at him. 'Oh, I'm so glad!'

'Me, too,' said Father Callaghan. 'I was concerned about him.'

'I dreamt about him being on a ship and being cruelly treated by a drunken captain,' she burst out.

Father Callaghan raised his eyebrows. 'You have a lot of imagination, Miss Walker.'

'It's a gift, so I've been told,' said Jeanette, her cheeks pink. 'Did he mention me?'

'I didn't speak to him. He wrote to me, care of the chippy, and they passed his letter on.'

'Oh, I thought he might have come to see you,' said Jeanette, disappointed. 'May I ask if he gave you his name?'

'Certainly. It's David Jones.'

Her face lit up. 'Did he tell you the name of his ship?'

'He didn't mention a ship. The postmark on the envelope was the Wirral, so it could be that he was just catching the last ferry that Saturday evening. When I received his letter I intended speaking to Peggy McGrath about it so she could pass a message on to you, but I'm sorry to say I forgot.'

'You're going to say he wanted my address?' said Jeanette, smiling.

He shook his greying head. 'He just asked me to let you know his wound was healing.'

She could not conceal her disappointment. 'Is that all?'

'I'm afraid so.' He paused. 'You might wish to know the reason why he was in such a hurry that evening.'

She nodded.

'He'd had a message that his father was on the critical list and he had to get to the hospital.'

She frowned. 'Now that I didn't expect. Poor David! Did he reach his father in time?'

'Yes, but he died shortly after he arrived at the hospital.'

'Tough,' murmured Jeanette.

'From what I saw of him and what I can gather from his letter, that young man is well able to cope with it all,' said Father Callaghan.

'Do you have an address where I can get in touch with him?'

Father Callaghan shook his head. 'He didn't put an address on the letter. He's helping his mother to move house, and when she's settled he'll be in touch again.'

'When he does get in touch, will you let me know?' she asked politely.

'I'll speak to Peggy McGrath and she can pass the message on to you.'

'OK. Although, if it was urgent and a Saturday, I work part time at a milk bar in Leece Street.'

He surprised Jeanette by saying, 'I know a young woman called Betty Booth who works part time in a coffee bar in that vicinity. She's a student at the School of Art. Perhaps you've come across her?'

'No, I know no one of that name,' said Jeanette. 'Is she one of your parishioners?'

'No. Now if that's everything,' said Father Callaghan, sounding weary as he rose to his feet, 'I'll see you out.'

'There's really no need,' said Jeanette hastily. 'I've taken up enough of your time. *Tarrah!*'

She left the church, thinking that at least she knew her rescuer's name. It was disappointing not knowing his address but hopefully it would not be long before he got in touch. At least she had some news to tell Hester and Sam.

But when Jeanette arrived home she walked straight into a row between Sam and her great-aunt. It wasn't often that her half-brother lost his temper, but sparks seemed to fly from him and he towered over Ethel in a way that surely must have frightened even her.

'What's going on?' asked Jeanette.

'You keep out of this, girl,' said Ethel, an ugly expression on her wrinkled face. 'You have too much to say for yourself as it is.'

'I've hardly opened my mouth,' protested Jeanette.

'Well, keep it shut,' said Ethel.

'Don't speak to her like that,' snapped Sam. 'You think you own this place. Dad's allowed you too much say in this house for too long.'

'I'll speak to her anyway I like,' said Ethel, squaring up to him and waving her fists in the air. 'You think yourself somebody, just because you made sergeant before your father did.'

'I worked bloody hard to get where I am,' said Sam, grabbing the fist that had nearly hit him on the nose.

Jeanette decided it was probably wisest for her to make herself scarce and headed for the kitchen, where she found a white-faced Hester sitting at the kitchen table, pushing her food around the plate.

'Where's Dad?' asked Jeanette.

'He's on duty. I'll be glad when he retires and he's around more often,' said Hester in a tight voice. 'Then I doubt she'll be able to conceal the kind of person she really is from him any more.'

'What's the row about?'

'Sam came home and found her sitting by the fire, reading letters that he recognized as belonging to him. She'd been in his bedroom, which you know he always locks. She swore that it wasn't locked and that she'd just been waiting for the opportunity to get in there and give it a good clean. He called her a liar and said that he never forgets to lock his bedroom because he doesn't trust her. It turns out that the letters are the ones Carol wrote to him and Aunt Ethel has already burnt some of them.'

'Carol! Who's Carol?' asked Jeanette, bewildered.

Hester sighed. 'Of course, you were too young at the time to know Sam had a secret girlfriend.'

Jeanette hastened to remove her supper from the oven and sat at the table opposite Hester. 'Tell me more!'

Hester leaned forward. 'Sam kept quiet about her for ages

because he knew how the old witch would react if she got to hear that he was seeing a girl.'

'What happened to her?' asked Jeanette, reaching for her knife and fork.

'She was killed in the blitz when she was only seventeen.'

'Oh no! How sad.'

'I didn't know she was dead until a few weeks after I arrived back in Liverpool. Sam was heartbroken and wouldn't talk about it.'

'So how did you get to know about it?'

'A mate of Carol's called Dorothy Wilson told me what had happened. We went to the same school but not at the same time. She was older than me. Still, she'd speak to me if she saw me in the street, with her knowing our Sam. I haven't seen her for ages. She loved the theatre and was always hanging around the Playhouse or the Royal Court. I think she eventually went on the stage and travels around the country.'

'So that's why our Sam doesn't bother with women,' murmured Jeanette. 'He's still in love with Carol. Poor Sam!'

'Those letters and his memories are all he has left of her.' Hester's eyes were bright and shiny.

'Don't be getting yourself upset,' said Jeanette, reaching out a hand to her.

Hester wiped her eyes. 'I know it's stupid because it's thirteen years since it happened and I never knew her that well. Even so—'

'It's not stupid! You love our Sam and that's why you're sad. The old witch doesn't care whom she hurts. He's in a right temper with her so perhaps this time he'll seriously think of leaving home.'

Hester dug a fork into a sausage. 'If he does we'll miss him, won't we?'

At that moment they heard the front door slam. They both started to their feet and hurried from the kitchen. They were too late to see who left the house, but as they reached the front door, Sam appeared in the parlour doorway, sucking his wrist.

'What happened?' asked Jeanette.

'She bit me! She's stormed out, said something about none

of us deserving her and that we'll miss her when she's gone,' he replied.

'I'd miss her like a hole in the head,' said Jeanette, her eyes glinting.

'She'll be back,' said Hester gloomily. 'She hasn't had time to pack any clothes.'

'She's not going to leave,' growled Sam, reaching for a cigarette.

Hester and Jeanette sighed in unison. 'If only wishes could come true,' said Hester. 'Anyway, are you OK, Sam? Do you need some antiseptic on that bite?'

'Probably. I managed to keep my hands off her throat, but it was a struggle and I think she knew it,' he said grimly. 'Not that she apologized for her actions, and she must have known the letters she burnt meant a lot to me after the fuss I made. This time she's gone too far!'

Six

'So what are you going to do?' asked Jeanette.

'I'm thinking about it. Right now I want something to eat,' said Sam, heading for the kitchen.

Hester followed him but Jeanette went upstairs, hoping Ethel had not locked her bedroom and she could search for her savings book and snaffle her own bedroom key. She was out of luck and so returned to the kitchen.

She was just in time to hear Hester say, 'I just wish she didn't put me in such a quake. It goes back to when I was a kid. One look from her used to fill me with dread and have me quivering in my wellies!' She glanced across at Jeanette as she sat down. 'I've just remembered. I'm on nights this week. If she comes back, you'll be all on your own.'

'Yes, I'm out, too,' said Sam.

'When's Dad due home?' asked Jeanette.

'I don't know,' said Hester.

Jeanette sighed.

'You can always put a chair under the door handle on the inside,' said Sam.

'We shouldn't need to take such measures,' said Jeanette angrily.

'No, we shouldn't,' said Sam, grim-faced. 'Dad should be tougher with her. I'm really fed up of her.'

Hester said, 'You can't change people.'

'I don't agree,' said Jeanette, picking up her plate of food and putting it back in the oven to heat up. 'So what are you going to do, Sam? Leave home?'

He hesitated. 'I thought of it but she'll think she's won if I do that.'

It was not until he finished his meal and lit another cigarette that he spoke again, his voice harsh. 'I might have thought twice about eating my supper if she'd cooked it after our row.'

'You really think she'd poison you?' Jeanette was astounded.

'A lot of murders take place in families,' said Sam.

'But aren't they generally crimes of passion?' said Jeanette.

'I think she's always hated me with a passion,' said Sam, his eyes hard as he gazed at his sisters through the cigarette smoke.

'She hates me, too,' said Jeanette, frowning.

'And me,' said Hester. 'It makes you wonder why she stays around.'

'Where else would she go?' said Sam. 'In all the years she's lived with us, I've never heard mention of any friends.'

'That's because she's a nasty bit of work. I suppose it's her having been a prison wardress that makes her the way she is,' said Hester.

'They can't all be like that,' said Jeanette. 'Maybe she was always a bit of a bully? For reasons we don't know she could have hated her sister because she was pretty and then envied her having a husband and child.'

'Talking of violent old women, you'll never guess what happened today,' said Hester, getting the biscuit tin from a cupboard. 'A friend of mine arrested a seventy-two-year-old widow for slashing clothes in Marks and Sparks with a pair of scissors.'

Sam said, 'Did she give a reason why she did it?'

'Not that I know.'

'I reckon they'll put it down to nerves and senility,' said Sam. 'She could have lost her husband in the Great War and possibly sons in World War Two.'

'Maybe Aunt Ethel did have a fella and he was killed at the front, and that made her resentful of those who still had husbands and explains why she finds it difficult to love people,' mused Jeanette.

Sam rolled his eyes.

'I think she might love Dad,' said Hester.

Jeanette stood up. 'I'm not so sure about that. I'm going to listen to the wireless and forget about her. *Ray's a Laugh* is on soon.'

'I think I'll listen with you before I go out,' said Hester. 'I could do with cheering up. You all right on your own, Sam?'

'Of course I am,' he said shortly.

Sam drank his tea and then took Carol's remaining letters upstairs. There had been a time, just after Carol was killed, when he could not bear reading them. He sat on his bed and unfolded one of them, noticing that the ink was fading in places. It was bad enough that his great-aunt had destroyed several, without the knowledge that one day soon he might not be able to read those he still possessed. Why had she had to go and burn them? It mattered, even though he knew the contents off by heart.

He sighed, thinking if only Carol had stuck to their original plan, which was for him to visit her at her aunt's smallholding near Ormskirk, she would still be alive. According to her aunt she had been missing Liverpool and had planned to surprise him. What so upset him was that he had never got to see her when she did arrive in Liverpool. She had been killed before he discovered about her plan to visit. He gazed down at Carol's neat copperplate handwriting and thought he must find another hiding place for the letters.

He lay on his bed, staring up at the ceiling, wondering, despite what he had said to his sisters, whether it was time for him to move on and find himself not only a place of his own – not easy with the housing situation being what it was – but a wife as well. He had begun to yearn for the comfort that only a woman could provide. He had been having dreams about Dorothy Wilson, who had been Carol's best friend, that just wouldn't go away. He had briefly caught sight of a woman coming out of the stage door at the Playhouse a short while ago and had been convinced it was Dorothy. If he had not been in a rush, he just might have checked her out there and then. Maybe it was guilt that had prevented him from visiting the theatre later to see if it really was her.

He closed his eyes and the memory of the younger Dorothy's face impressed itself against his eyelids. He imagined burying himself in her soft feminine body and could almost smell the sweet fragrance of Pond's face cream and 'Evening in Paris' scent. She had been slightly older than Carol. His heart began to race. She was smiling eagerly at him and her lips were swollen from his kisses. Her hair was the colour of ripening wheat, a lighter shade than his own, but hers had a silky texture to it that his lacked. He remembered how it had brushed against his bare chest. They should never have done what they did, but both of them had been hurting, so they had spent that May evening of Carol's funeral in Dorothy's parents' bed, whilst her mother was at the munitions factory and her father in the army on the south coast.

He remembered how Dorothy had encouraged him to let himself go, despite his attempts to hold back. At least from the noises she had made he knew that she had got pleasure from the act. Maybe that was why afterwards they had avoided meeting again? Eventually, he heard that she was carving out an acting career for herself and was on tour with a theatrical company. He had worried briefly that she might have got pregnant, but obviously she had been OK or she would have been in touch.

A wry smile twisted his mouth, remembering how she had talked about one day seeing her name up in lights. At least she hadn't given up on her dream. He would like to see her again but had no idea where she was right now. Maybe he should visit her widowed mother? That was if she was still alive. He had not been able to face her after having spent a couple of hours in her bed with Dorothy and so had avoided the street where she lived for years.

'Are you all right, Sam?'

Hester's voice startled him and he banged his head on the headboard as he sat up. 'Damn!' he groaned, rubbing the sore spot. 'Did you have to shout so loud?'

'Were you asleep?'

'Almost,' he lied, yawning loudly. 'What do you want?'

'To talk to you about something our Jeanette's just told me.'

'Is it important?'

'I think so, but if you'd rather I left you alone . . .'

There was a note in her voice that caused him to roll off the bed and open the door. 'No, it's OK. Come in.'

Hester entered the room and rested her hands on the foot of the bed. 'Jeanette went to see that priest!'

'What priest?'

'The priest who was at the chippy!'

Sam stared at her. 'I suppose she's hoping she can make contact with that bloke who was hit in the face?'

'Too right she is,' said Hester.

'So what did he have to say?'

'Apparently the bloke was in a rush that evening to see his father who was seriously ill in hospital.'

'Do we have his name?'

'David Jones.'

Sam's eyebrows shot up. 'Now there's a name that's two a penny. So when is she planning on seeing him?'

'She's not because he didn't put an address on his letter to the priest. Apparently his father died and he's helping his mother move house.' Hester smiled. 'Interesting, though, that his name is David Jones. The couple I stayed with when I was evacuated were called Jones. If you remember I wrote to Myra for a while but then she stopped writing. I've always regretted losing touch with her. She had a nephew called David. He called a couple of times at the house, so it's possible it's the same person.'

'So what are you planning on doing? Writing to Myra Jones to see if, by the strangest coincidence, her nephew is Jeanette's David Jones?'

Hester's face fell. 'You think it's a daft idea?'

'I didn't say that.'

She gnawed on her lip. 'I don't want to be a nuisance.'

'Why should you think you'd be a nuisance?'

'Aunt Ethel said that was why Myra stopped writing – because she couldn't be bothered with me. Do you think—?'

'Do I think the old cow was jealous of your relationship with her? It wouldn't surprise me if she destroyed Myra's letters to stop you writing to her,' said Sam.

For a moment Hester was too choked to speak, and then she managed to say, 'I've no proof.'

'What's that matter? Write to the woman and see what she has to say.'

Hester took a deep breath and there was a militant light in her eyes. 'I will!'

'Good on you, girl,' said Sam, smiling.

'I won't mention it to Jeanette unless I hear back. She told me she's going to the Grafton on Saturday with that friend of hers, Peggy McGrath.'

'The one that was really the cause of all the trouble in the chippy?' said Sam, shaking his head.

'Should we try and put a stop to her going?'

Sam hesitated. 'No. She's rebellious enough as it is, and we don't want her to think we're siding with Aunt Ethel against her. She's told you what she's planning on doing, so let's be happy with that and hope she's got enough common sense to stay out of trouble this time.'

'Jeannie, is this yours?' Mrs Cross held up the oiled cloth bag containing a frock and sensible low-heeled shoes.

Jeanette looked up from wiping a table top. 'Yes, Mrs Cross. I hope you don't mind my leaving it in the back, only I'm going dancing this evening at the Grafton and I didn't want to go home first.'

A young man over by the jukebox glanced her way and for a moment she thought he was going to speak, but then he looked away and put a coin in the slot and the next moment the strains of 'Three Coins in the Fountain' sung by Frank Sinatra came flooding out. Earlier she had thought the young man looked vaguely familiar.

'I love this, don't you?' said a girl seated at a table near the window. She and the young man had entered the milk bar about a quarter of an hour ago and ordered milk shakes and sticky buns. Jeanette had heard him call her Irene.

'I've seen the film,' said Mrs Cross. 'You should go and see it, Jeanette. It's almost as good as a holiday, and much cheaper. You can imagine yourself in Rome. Louis Jourdan who plays a prince is so handsome, you wouldn't believe it.'

'He's a bit of a playboy in it, though,' said Irene. 'I preferred Rossano Brazzi myself. I've never seen him in anything else before but he's a real dish.'

'I'd like to go to Italy,' said Jeanette. 'My brother's saving up for a car and he was talking about going abroad.'

'I've an older friend at the art school who's hoping to go to Italy to study next year,' said Irene.

'Lucky her!' said Jeanette. But before she could continue the conversation another girl entered.

She was pretty with pale ginger hair, a slender figure, and was wearing a swagger jacket and a straight skirt in dark green gaberdine. Accompanying her were two young men who were good looking and so alike that they had to be twins. One of them had a limp. 'So you and Jimmy made it then,' said the girl, walking over to the table where Irene sat.

'We're here, aren't we, Maggie?' said Irene in a tone of voice that told Jeanette that the other girl was not one of her favourite people. '*Ciao*, you two! I haven't seen you for a while,' she nodded to the twins. 'How's tricks?'

Jeanette stood over by the counter whilst the three newcomers sat at the table with Irene. She waited a few moments whilst they scrutinized the menu, interested in how they knew each other. Jimmy was still standing next to the jukebox, looking at the list of records. One of the twins beckoned Jeanette and she went over to the table and took their order as 'Three Coins in the Fountain' came to an end. Maggie did not seem able to make up her mind. As Jeanette stood waiting, she heard the click of a record dropping and the seductive tones of Alma Cogan singing 'I Can't Tell a Waltz from a Tango' almost had her dancing back to the counter.

'They're all so fattening!' complained Maggie, tossing the menu aside.

'Stop worrying about your figure, Maggie,' said Irene. 'You know you never put a pound on.'

'That's because I watch what I eat and care what I look like, unlike my dear cousin.'

Irene frowned. 'Why bring Betty into this? She's not fat!'

'You would say that because you're not exactly slim either,' said Maggie bluntly.

'Don't you two start,' said one of the twins. 'It's only puppy fat with Irene, and you are too skinny, Maggie.'

She pouted. 'I have the perfect figure for a model, and when I leave school that's what I'm going to train to be. Betty's trouble is that she gobbles down what's nearest to hand because she can't be bothered cooking a proper meal when she's painting.'

'You could cook her a proper meal,' said Jimmy, pulling up a chair and sitting next to her.

Maggie shrugged. 'She won't eat what I eat.'

'You can't blame her for that,' murmured Irene. 'And our Jimmy has obviously never tasted your cooking. You can't cook for toffee, so that's why you make do with rabbit food and tinned soup.'

Jeanette cleared her throat. 'Is that it, then?' she asked.

'No, I do want something to eat,' said Maggie hastily. 'I'll have a lemon tea and a buttered teacake. But don't go putting too much butter on the teacake, waitress. Put it on and then scrape it off.'

'Yes, Miss,' said Jeanette in a colourless voice, thinking she would have a job scraping off melting butter. The twin with the limp caught her eye and winked. She smiled involuntarily before turning away.

She wasted no time in dealing with their order and carried it over to the table just in time to hear Irene ask, 'Why aren't you working today, Pete?'

The twin who had winked now frowned. 'I've been in the office this morning. There's talk of a possible dockers' strike. Have you heard anything, Jimmy?'

He nodded. 'I hope to God it's not true. They'll finish Liverpool if they're not bloody careful. As it is, although the ferries will still be running, a strike will prove a bloody nuisance if the dockers go ahead with it.'

Such talk filled Jeanette with dismay. If the dockers carried on taking such action, she worried that there would soon be no ships coming to Liverpool. Some companies had already transferred to Southampton.

'Well, if there's a strike it's not going to affect me,' said the other twin, 'although it will our Pete with him working in a shipping office.'

Jeanette was tempted to tell them it would affect her too, but kept her mouth shut, wondering which shipping office Pete worked in as she placed the bill on the table. As she walked away she heard Jimmy say, 'So who's going the Grafton tonight? Did Betty say she'd come?'

Jeanette shot a look at him and wondered if she would see him there.

Seven

'Can you see any sign of that Jimmy you served in the milk bar?' asked Peggy, glancing about the ballroom.

Jeanette did not answer, having spotted a vacant table not far from the edge of the dance floor. She claimed one of the chairs and took a sip of her lemonade and gazed about her. Already there were plenty of people dancing to the music of a live band playing a quickstep. She was aware of a simmering excitement, despite being unable to spot Jimmy amongst those who had taken to the floor or who were sitting out this dance, having a drink and taking in the scene before them.

Then suddenly she spotted him dancing with a girl. 'There's Jimmy, with that redhead!' she cried.

'Where, where?' asked Peggy.

Jeanette did not answer, wondering if the redhead could be the Betty mentioned earlier that day. She knew the moment Jimmy spotted her because his eyes widened and then he bent his head and whispered in the girl's ear. She looked in Jeanette's direction and smiled. But it was not until the number ended that the couple made their way towards where Jeanette and Peggy were sitting.

'Hi!' said Jimmy, smiling. 'It's Jeanette, isn't it? I wondered if I'd see you here.'

'I felt the same about you,' she said, returning his smile.

Suddenly one of the twins appeared at his shoulder. 'Well, if it isn't the waitress from the milk bar,' he drawled.

'I saw her first,' said Jimmy, his smile vanishing.

Jeanette caught the redhead's eye and expected her to look annoyed, but she just stood there with a wry smile on her freckled face. 'Shut up, you two,' she murmured. 'If I were you, Jeanette, I'd have nothing to do with either of them. They're both terrible flirts.' She held out a hand. 'I'm Betty Booth. It's nice to meet you.'

'It's nice to meet you, too,' said Jeanette, shaking her hand. 'Are you the Betty studying art?'

'Don't get her started on art,' said the twin, taking out a packet of Players. 'She'll be having you visiting the Walker to see her father's painting next.'

'Your father has a painting hanging in the Walker Art Gallery!' Jeanette was really impressed.

Betty flushed. 'Yes, but no credit to me.'

'I'd like to see it.'

'Now you've done it,' groaned the twin.

Betty turned on him. 'If you don't want to listen, then go and dance with our Maggie.'

He ignored her and stared at Peggy. 'So who's this?'

'My name's Peggy,' she said, smiling. 'Me and Jeanette work in the Cunard Building.'

'You don't say,' he murmured, putting away his cigarettes. 'D'you want to dance?'

'I wouldn't say no,' replied Peggy.

Without another word, the twin grabbed her arm and walked her onto the dance floor.

'Well, that's got rid of him,' said Jimmy, offering Betty the vacant chair.

She sat down opposite Jeanette. 'There was a time when Norm didn't have much to say for himself, because he was in his twin's shadow, but after Pete's accident Norm found himself having to make his own decisions and go places on his own.'

'Pete is the twin with the limp?'

Betty nodded. 'He doesn't do dancing.'

Jimmy rested both hands on the back of Betty's chair. 'I used to have a twin. He got run over during the war when we were only little. My dad got killed down at the docks during the blitz not long before, so it was a terrible time for my mother.'

'That's so sad,' said Jeanette. 'My mother went missing during the blitz. Her body was never found.'

'I lost my dad at Dunkirk,' said Betty. 'Not that I remember him.' She frowned. 'It was much worse when Mam was hit by a car and died a few years ago.'

Jeanette grimaced. 'I can imagine.'

'Fortunately I have cousins, as well as a half-sister I never met until a couple of years ago,' said Betty.

'How come?' asked Jeanette, experiencing a fellow feeling with both Betty and Jimmy.

'Emma was brought up in Whalley, near Clitheroe, by her maternal grandparents,' replied Betty. 'She didn't know I existed until she found a letter from my mother when she was clearing out after her grandfather's death. She's since married my cousin Jared and so I see more of her now.'

Jeanette was fascinated by the story. 'I presume your father married twice?'

'That's right.'

'How does it feel meeting someone like that after being parted for years?'

'Oh, we took to each other straightaway,' said Betty.

The three of them were silent a moment and then Jeanette said, 'So Norm's twin, Pete. You mentioned an accident, is that how he was crippled?' Betty and Jimmy exchanged looks that caused her to add hastily, 'You don't have to tell me if you feel it's something I shouldn't know.'

'No, that's OK,' said Jimmy. 'The twins also lost their dad during the war.'

'We should form a club,' murmured Betty.

'Well, we have, sort of,' said Jimmy, squeezing her shoulder.

'We all support each other. Even Maggie's part of it, although she didn't lose her parents until after the war.'

'Let's not talk about our Maggie,' said Betty. 'Stick to talking about Pete.'

'OK!' exclaimed Jimmy. 'He used to be a real daredevil. He and Norm were always up to mischief, but Pete was the leader. But they had a bossy older brother to keep his eye on them.'

'I suppose they rebelled?' said Jeanette.

'Aye, I won't tell you how it came about but Pete fell from an upstairs windowsill.'

Jeanette gasped. 'It's a wonder he wasn't killed!'

'It's a wonder the pair of them weren't arrested!' said Betty. 'Fortunately their brother is a policeman.'

Jeanette was about to remark about the coincidence because of her family, when Jimmy said, 'Here comes your friend with Norm and she's limping!'

Jeanette's head turned and she spotted the couple making their way around the edge of the dance floor. Peggy's face was drained of colour and she was being half-carried, half-dragged along by Norm. Jeanette stood up and hurried towards them. 'What happened? Are you OK?'

'No, I'm not bloody OK,' said Peggy tearfully. 'I think I might have broken my foot. Some bloody fool tripped and fell against me and crushed it with his damn great big number twelve shoes. I'm going to have to go home.'

'Shall I phone for a taxi?' asked Jimmy, looking concerned.

'I'll come with you so Peggy can have her chair back and sit down,' said Betty. The pair hurried away.

Jeanette helped her friend to sit down. 'It's a blinking shame,' she said, carefully inspecting Peggy's swelling ankle and foot.

'Yeah! Just when we were getting into the groove,' said Norm.

'Well, forgive me for getting in the way of that idiot's foot,' said Peggy pettishly. 'I'm sorry to spoil your fun.'

His mouth tightened. 'I didn't say it was your fault.'

'Sorry,' mumbled Peggy, tears in her eyes. 'I'm in pain and I feel so frustrated. I'm sorry for you, too, Jeanette. I didn't want to spoil your evening.'

'It can't be helped,' said Jeanette. 'There'll be other dances.'

'Would you like me to go in the taxi with you, Peggy?' asked Norm.

'Best not,' she said hastily. 'Jeanette will come with me.'

He hesitated. 'If that's what you want.'

She nodded. 'You don't have to hang around, Norm.'

'Well, if you don't need me, I'd better check that Maggie's OK. I noticed that she had a bit of a face on her when we danced past. She's really too young to be here, but you wouldn't think so the way she dresses and slaps on the make-up.'

'Don't let me keep you,' said Peggy.

He nodded, then walked away.

'Well, that's him gone,' said Peggy, her face tight with pain.

'Didn't you like him?'

'Oh, I liked him all right, but he'll be going off to a shipping yard in Glasgow next year as part of his apprenticeship to be a marine engineer. I wouldn't be seeing much of him then, would I?'

Before Jeanette could comment, Jimmy and Betty returned and told them that the manager had phoned for a taxi and it would be here shortly. Between the three of them, they had no trouble getting Peggy up from the chair and out into the foyer. Jeanette went and collected their coats from the cloakroom and she arrived at the front entrance just as the taxi drew up. There was a flurry of goodbyes as Betty and Jimmy waved them off.

As Peggy and Jeanette flopped down in the back of the taxi, they both let out a sigh of relief. 'Well, this evening didn't turn out in the least like I hoped it would,' mourned Peggy. 'I'm just worrying now what my mam and dad are going to say. It could mean that I'll have to stay off work and Mam's not going to like that.'

Jeanette thought it highly likely that Peggy would have to rest her foot. She imagined it could be days before she was able to walk without difficulty. She only hoped that Peggy's parents would not direct their annoyance at her. From some of what her friend had said, it was clear they still partly blamed Jeanette for a policeman landing on their doorstep after the trouble in the chippy.

★　　★　　★

Peggy's foot was not broken, but it was badly bruised and swollen which meant she did have to take time off from work. Jeanette popped in to see her a couple of times during the week. They had discussed that evening at the Grafton, and on Sunday afternoon when she visited the question on Peggy's lips was whether Norm or Jimmy had called in at the milk bar on the Saturday.

'No, as it happens,' said Jeanette. 'I can only think that they're occupied elsewhere.'

'So Norm doesn't have my address.' Peggy sighed.

'Obviously not.' Jeanette wondered why Peggy should think she would have given it to him when Peggy had made it clear that she thought going out with him was a waste of time. Besides, she was determined not to get involved in Peggy's love life again. Her friend's father had wanted to know everything that had happened the night of the Grafton incident. She had backed up what Peggy had told him, but he had looked at her as if he doubted her word. She had also been aware of Peggy's brother Marty's eyes on her. Maybe he didn't believe her either.

'Perhaps I'll see one of them next week,' said Jeanette.

'Your great-aunt hasn't discovered you're working part time at the milk bar yet?' asked Peggy.

'Surprisingly, no. I can only believe she really is getting senile.'

'Well, I'm hoping to be back at work on Monday,' said Peggy. 'I'm real fed up being stuck at home.'

The following morning, no sooner had Jeanette walked into the office than Elsie, the other typist, greeted her with the words, 'Have you seen this?'

'Seen what?' asked Jeanette, removing her headscarf and fluffing out her light brown hair.

'The dockers are on strike – which means if they're all out, there'll be no ships getting loaded or unloaded today!'

A dismayed Jeanette remembered Norm and Jimmy mentioning a strike. 'That could mean we might be laid off and have money docked from our wages!' she cried.

'I know, although I've still got some work to do,' said Elsie. 'Bills to type and a couple of letters from yesterday.'

Jeanette pulled a face. 'I haven't! I just hope to God that there'll be some ships arriving in the Mersey today despite the strike. Perhaps some will get unloaded. Are today's expected arrivals listed on the board?'

Elsie nodded. 'But it's reckoned that there are already forty-four ships idle on both sides of the river. If any ships do dock today, they could be here for some time. Fruit could rot in the holds. I'm not sure what will happen with the frozen meat from Australia and New Zealand.'

'Surely they'll just keep the freezers going, and where the fruit's concerned it shouldn't be too bad because it's not as if it's high summer. I wonder if the boss will decide to send us home early?'

'I wonder. Do you have something you can be doing at home?' asked Elsie.

Jeanette removed the cover from her typewriter. 'I guarantee that, if I were home, my great-aunt would find me something to do that I don't want to do. It's not that I'm averse to a bit of housework or cooking, but I'd rather be earning my living.'

At that moment the door to the manager's office opened and both girls turned to give him their attention.

There was not much for them to do that day after all, but they weren't sent home. At twelve fifteen Jeanette found Peggy making tea in the room where they ate their lunch. They discussed the strike and Jeanette mused aloud as to whether it would affect Pete as he also worked in a shipping office. 'I wish I had thought to ask which company he worked for,' she murmured.

'Is he the spitting image of Norm?' asked Peggy, her expression brightening.

Jeanette nodded.

Peggy asked no more questions, but sat looking thoughtful.

At the end of the afternoon the manager told Jeanette and Elsie to come in the following morning as not all the dockers were on strike, adding the proviso, weather permitting. A blanket of fog had descended over the course of the afternoon, so that by going home time, the Pierhead was invisible and the mournful sound of a ship's foghorn could be heard from the Mersey.

As Jeanette and Peggy left the building there was hardly a tram or bus to be seen, so they decided to start walking home. As they made their way up Water Street, Jeanette could hear footsteps behind them.

'D'you hear that?' she whispered, quickening her pace.

'Hear what?' Peggy's voice was muffled through the scarf covering her mouth and nose.

'It sounds like someone dragging their foot.'

In the silence that followed they heard a quickening footstep followed by that dragging sound again.

'It reminds me of a Sherlock Holmes film,' said Peggy.

'Maybe someone has fallen and hurt their foot just like you did,' suggested Jeanette.

They both turned and a moment later a limping figure materialized out of the fog. He lowered the football scarf swathed about his neck and mouth and said, 'It is Jeanette, isn't it?'

She nodded.

'He does look the spitting image of Norm,' said Peggy, a hint of wonder in her voice.

Pete stared at her. 'I'm his twin. You must be Peggy, and I take it your foot's OK now from the speed the pair of you were walking?'

'It still gives me some gyp now and again,' said Peggy. 'I take it your Norm mentioned me?' She sounded gratified.

'That's right. He asked me to try and look out for you.'

'You chose a good night,' said Jeanette, deciding to get a word in, and remembering the way he had winked at her in the milk bar.

He grinned. 'Luck of the draw.'

'So where do you work?'

'King's Dock.'

Peggy looked from one to the other. 'Can we get a move on?'

'Sure! Sorry to keep you,' said Pete, an edge to his voice.

Peggy said hastily, 'It's just that it's freezing standing here and it's my first day back at work. I'm wishing I was indoors by a lovely roaring fire. Don't you?'

'Sure.'

'Me too,' said Jeanette. 'Shall we get going?'

'I must admit I'm hoping there's some buses or trams running,' said Pete, limping between the pair of them. 'I don't fancy walking all the way to Bootle in this damn fog. Where d'you live, Jeanette?'

'Not your way. Besides, I thought I'd drop in on my brother and sister at police headquarters. I just might be able to get a lift in a shiny black police car. Sam is a detective sergeant,' she said with a hint of pride.

'Now there's a coincidence,' said Pete. 'My older brother's in the Bootle division.'

'You mean your brother is a policeman?' said Peggy, sounding dismayed.

'Yeah, and you don't have to sound like that,' said Pete grimly. 'I don't like it either. Since our Dougie joined, me and our Norm have been expected to toe the line and not make a wrong move. If he hadn't wanted us to be saints, I wouldn't be a cripple now.'

'I have my dad always going on at me, wanting to know what I'm up to,' said Peggy. 'It's not just policemen who are like that.'

'I have the same worry,' said Jeanette. 'Except it's my great-aunt I have breathing down my neck. My dad's lovely and our Hester and Sam aren't bad, but Aunt Ethel is an old witch. She was a prison wardress!'

'Bloody hell!' exclaimed Pete. 'Doesn't it drive you crazy? I'd be leaving home.'

'That's what I want to do but I can't afford it just yet,' said Jeanette.

The three of them walked on in silence until they came to a bus stop. There Peggy halted. 'My foot's hurting and maybe if we wait here for five minutes, a bus might come along.'

'That's a good idea,' said Jeanette. 'You're both going the same way. I'll say *tarrah* now. If you can pass on a message to Betty and Jimmy, Pete, tell them I did enjoy their company.' She hurried away, calling over her shoulder, 'See you in the morning, Peggy!'

She arrived outside police headquarters to the rear of the fire station in no time at all, although she had no intention of

going inside. It had just been an excuse in case Pete offered
to see her home after asking where she lived. She hadn't wanted
to put him to any trouble. She carried on walking, wondering
what he and Peggy would talk about on their way home.

By morning the fog had evaporated and after listening to the
news on the wireless, Jeanette was ready to leave the house
when the post arrived. She picked it up before Ethel had a
chance to get her hands on it and rifled through the envelopes
and found one for Hester. She had not long left and had gone
on foot. It was possible that Jeanette might catch her up if
she hurried herself.

She reached the main road and spotted Hester a few yards
ahead of her. Despite being out of breath, Jeanette shouted
her name. At first Hester appeared not to have heard her,
and then she turned her head. At the same time, Jeanette
heard the sound of a bus and she ran for all she was worth.
Fit to collapse with running so hard, Jeanette was heaved
aboard by her half-sister. There were no seats available so
they had to strap hang.

When Jeanette got her breath back she handed the envelope
to Hester. 'This just came for you.'

Hester's face lit up. 'It's from Myra Jones. I recognize her
handwriting.'

'You mean the woman you stayed with when you were
evacuated?'

'Yes!' said Hester. 'Oh, I'm glad she's still alive. Neither of
them were young and I was worried in case they'd died. Myra
had a nephew, David Jones.'

'You're kidding! Is that why you wrote to her?' asked Jeanette.

'Partly. But I was very fond of her and I really liked the
area where I stayed.'

'I can't see how it can be the same person as my David
Jones,' murmured Jeanette. 'Wrong direction.'

'He didn't live in Whalley. Anyway, I've been thinking about
the past and wondered if they'd be able to help me find someone
as well,' she added casually.

'Who?' asked Jeanette, taking a couple of coins out of her
pocket ready to pay her fare.

Hester did not answer but murmured, 'Memory is a strange thing.'

Jeanette slanted her a startled look. 'What d'you mean?'

Hester folded the envelope and placed it in her pocket. 'I met a lad whilst I was staying with Myra. I never did get his name or give him mine, but I think he must have been an evacuee too because he mentioned living in the city. He made me laugh.'

'Was he lodging in the same house?' asked Jeanette.

'No. I met him when I tripped over some wire across a hole in a hedge and landed in a patch of mud. He'd done the same thing a few minutes earlier and he helped me up. The wire had cut into my shin and he said I needed to put some iodine on it.' She paused and added in a surprised voice. 'I've never told anyone else that before.'

'Well, now you have, tell me more about him.'

'OK! I said that I would put iodine on the cut and then I straightened up. We looked at each other and burst out laughing because we were covered in mud.' Hester's face was soft with remembrance.

'So what happened next?' asked Jeanette, nudging her to continue.

Hester sighed. 'The farmer came along, cuffed him over the head and hauled him away.'

'So did you meet again?'

'Oh yes, but only briefly.' A small smile played about her mouth. 'I was ten when I'd left Liverpool almost two years earlier, and I was just sprouting a bust and starting to find boys not so much of a nuisance. There was this . . . this feeling there between us. I felt excited and scared at the same time in his company. Anyway, he suddenly grabbed me and kissed me.'

'Was he a good kisser?' Jeanette was remembering how David Jones had kissed her so unexpectedly.

Hester's smile deepened. 'It didn't last long enough for me to tell, even if I'd had any experience to judge it by. It was my very first kiss, so I've never forgotten it. Anyway, that was the last time I saw him because Aunt Ethel came and took me back to Liverpool shortly after.'

'And you never heard from him again. What a shame!'

'I know the city was in the north, so maybe he came from Bolton or Blackburn.'

'And you thought Mrs Jones might have been able to help you trace him?'

Hester shrugged.

Jeanette was fascinated by this glimpse into her half-sister's past. 'The farm could still be there, you know. You really should go and see if you can find him.'

'Don't be daft! He'll have forgotten about me.'

'You haven't forgotten about him.'

'No, but men and women are different. Besides, I mightn't be able to find the farm. I remember blackberrying and gathering hazelnuts along the hedgerows nearby, but there are plenty of lanes like that around Whalley.'

'Whalley? I've heard that name somewhere else recently.' Jeanette frowned in thought but could not remember, adding, 'You shouldn't give up, you know.'

Hester looked amused. 'It's not a matter of giving up. I never got started searching for him.'

'But he could have been the one fated for you,' whispered Jeanette, suddenly aware that people were listening to their conversation.

'I don't believe that there is one man in the world destined for one person,' said Hester.

'But you read Mills & Boon,' protested Jeanette. 'Isn't that what they're all about?'

Hester did not answer.

The conductor came for their fares and after they had paid they were silent, wrapped up in their own thoughts as the vehicle made its way into town.

Suddenly there was a loud bang, startling them so much that the sisters clung to each other. Through the window they saw a car hurtling across the road and onto the pavement where it shuddered to a stop.

Eight

Their bus came to a halt and, without a second thought, Hester forced her way past the people standing in her way. Determined not to be left behind and wanting to be of help too, Jeanette followed her, guessing that, as a policewoman, Hester saw it as her job to see if she could be of assistance. They soon realized that another bus had skidded to a halt near Erskine Street and was blocking the way. A couple of men, one wearing a soldier's uniform, were already making their way towards the car.

Jeanette clutched Hester's arm as she caught sight of an unconscious woman hanging out of the passenger side. Her legs were pinned by the door so that she could not move.

The two men managed to open the door wider and lift the woman out. Hester hurried round to the other side and opened the door. The driver's face was grazed and he looked blank when she spoke to him. She eased him out of the driving seat, talking to him in a calm manner.

Jeanette's insides were quivering as she went to the rear door. With the help of two passers-by, she assisted the two female passengers from the vehicle onto the pavement. She was aware of a bus driver hovering a few feet away. 'It . . . it was my bus that caught the side of the car. It . . . it seemed to come out of nowhere,' he stammered.

'It happens,' she found herself saying to comfort him. 'What's important is to help the injured.'

'None of my passengers are hurt so . . . so we could take these two women over to my bus where they can sit inside until an ambulance arrives. It's bloody freezing and it will be warmer in there than out here for them.'

Jeanette agreed that his idea was a good one. Between them, they helped the women onto the bus. Then she returned to see how Hester was getting on with the more seriously injured. Straightaway she realized that the woman was in a far worse condition than the male driver. The two men who had lifted her out had laid her on the ground. Blood was trickling from her mouth and she was still unconscious.

Hester spoke to the two men and the soldier nodded and looked serious. The other man surprised her by saying with a smile, 'I'm in the police force. It's handy that you are, too.'

'Now there's a coincidence,' said Jeanette, winking at Hester.

Hester gave her a reproving look and told her to get out of the way. Jeanette did as she was told, watching as the woman was carried onto the bus. She noticed her hat on the ground and, picking it up, hurried after Hester. Handing the hat to her, she asked, 'What should I do next?'

'You're not needed now,' said Hester absently, gazing down at the woman. 'You might as well get on the bus that was taking us into town and go to work. I'll have to wait for the ambulance to arrive and get statements from a couple of people who saw what happened.'

Jeanette was full of admiration for Hester, but baffled as well. How could she be so calm and controlled in such circumstances and yet get into a tizzy when having to confront their great-aunt? 'I'll see you this evening. I hope that woman will be all right.'

'So do I,' muttered Hester, and roused herself to watch Jeanette climb aboard the bus that was revving up. As it drove off, Hester turned and went to speak to the soldier to whom she'd given little attention. He seemed now to be in a tearing hurry. He described what he had seen succinctly, and gave her a name and address before hurrying off, saying he was late for an appointment. Only then did she turn to the policeman and found herself thinking, *Now wouldn't it be lovely if he was the one for me* . . . He had a swarthy, handsome face and the darkest eyes she had ever seen.

He held out his hand and smiled. 'Perhaps we should introduce ourselves. I'm PC Cedric Dobson. I'm with the Bootle division.'

'PC Hester Walker. I'm stationed here at Liverpool headquarters and I've been seconded to the CID these last few months,' she said, shaking hands. She forgot that there was work to be done and could only stand there, returning his smile like a fool, clinging to his hand until he reminded her that they had best get on with the job. *The job!* Probably that's all this was to him. She recalled how only a short while ago she had been telling Jeanette about the Lancashire lad. Now here she was, feeling slightly starry-eyed over this policeman: it was time to pull herself together.

It was only after she and Cedric had left the hospital and telephoned both their headquarters to explain the situation that he asked Hester if she would like a bite of lunch. 'That's if you're not in a rush to go anywhere?' he said, stroking his cheek with the side of his left index finger.

'No. I'd like that, but I need to report in by quarter past two at the latest,' she replied.

He looked put out. 'Then we've only just over an hour.'

She flushed. 'Sorry about that but you know how it is. Orders are orders. Maybe we should forget lunch and just have a coffee and a cake?'

He agreed and they went to the Kardomah cafe in Church Street. Despite it being a busy time of the day, they managed to get a table without any difficulty. He ordered and, while they waited, asked her what had made her decide to join the police force.

'My father's a policeman and so is my brother. It seemed a natural course to take.'

He could not conceal his surprise. 'What did your mother have to say?'

'My mother's dead.'

'So who does the housework, shopping, cooking?' he asked, leaning back in his chair and looking her straight in the eye. 'Or is there enough money for you to hire a housekeeper?'

'We're not wealthy,' said Hester, not having expected such a conversation. 'My father's aunt lives with us.'

'So she's taken over your mother's role.'

'I wouldn't say that! She hasn't a maternal bone in her body, but for years she's tried to rule the roost and keep us girls in particular in our place. For a short time I had a stepmother who was lovely.'

'I presume your stepmother was never a policewoman?'

'What's that supposed to mean?' Hester toyed with her fingers. 'You don't approve of women in the force, do you?'

He leaned towards her and covered her hands with his. 'I didn't say that. You did a good job back there. I just like a woman to fulfil the role that God intended.'

Hester withdrew her hands from beneath his. 'I don't believe God ordained that every woman should be a wife and mother, if that's what you're getting at. There are plenty of working women in the Bible. Lydia in the New Testament, for instance. She was a seller of purple, an expensive dye.'

He tapped his fingers on the table. 'There's no need for you to get on the defensive. My taste doesn't run solely to the "little woman" who takes care of the house and her husband, brings his slippers, cooks his meals and looks after his children. I like strong, independent women, as well. So, do you enjoy chasing criminals?'

She found him baffling. 'I don't often do any actual chasing.'

'Typing reports?'

'Some of the time.'

'Perhaps you joined the force because you thought you could influence women who broke the law?'

His words surprised her. 'If that was so it wasn't consciously. It was my brother's suggestion that I join.'

Cedric smiled. 'You'll have had training in self-defence?'

'Of course.' His questions continued to surprise her.

'So what rank do your father and brother hold?'

She felt as if she was being cross-examined and slightly resented it. 'My brother's a detective sergeant and only received his stripes in spring. My dad is also a sergeant and plans to retire next year.'

'So is it your aim to become a sergeant, too? Because, if so, you'd better get your skates on. I should imagine someone with your looks won't remain single for much longer.'

Hester flushed. 'You flatter me. I'm not that special that I have men fighting over me.'

'So you don't have a boyfriend?'

'I'm a career girl. I enjoy my job and, yes, I would like promotion. I know it can happen sooner than with you men because a lot of WPCs do leave to get married after only a few years in the job.'

His dark eyes held hers. 'Don't you want to marry and have children?'

The colour in her cheeks deepened. 'There's more to life than marriage. I don't see anything odd about a woman wanting a career. It's what Mrs Pankhurst and other women of her ilk fought for. Women having the vote and equal rights and pay with the men.'

'You misunderstand me,' said Cedric, covering her hand with his again. 'I agree that marriage isn't for everyone.'

'I'm not saying that I'll never marry. I'm just not in any hurry.' She attempted to free her hand but his fingers curled round hers firmly.

'Why don't you come out with me on Thursday evening? We could go dancing. No strings attached.' He released her hand.

She hesitated. 'Let me think about it.'

He frowned. 'What's there to think about? Is it that you don't trust me?'

The question surprised her. 'Trust has nothing to do with it. It's just that I never know when I might be needed with my being seconded to the CID. It's not easy having a social life.'

'We could still arrange to meet, and if you don't turn up then I know the job's got in the way.'

She hesitated and then nodded. 'OK, and if you don't turn up I suppose I can assume the same?'

'Yes,' said Cedric, and arranged a time and a place to meet.

Only after they parted did Hester realize she had no idea where he lived. She had deliberately withheld her address because she did not want him trying to get in touch with her at home. She found him physically attractive but was unsure whether she liked him or not. What he thought about a woman's role was not so different than a lot of men, though. Not for one moment did she really believe he approved of strong women. Still, she was looking forward to going dancing. She just hoped Jeanette would not mention him to anyone at home.

Only when she arrived at headquarters did she remember the letter from Myra. Despite being in a hurry, she slit open the envelope and read what she had to say. Sadly Myra's husband had died, but she was delighted to hear from Hester. She herself was keeping in good health, except for a touch of rheumatism. Her nephew David Jones was working in a factory in Blackburn, and he and his wife came to visit her, bringing their little girl, once a fortnight. She visited them occasionally and once a year she went on holiday with them. She asked Hester to keep in touch.

Hester decided that she must try and visit her, but knew that it wouldn't be easy finding the time. One thing was for sure: it was highly unlikely Myra's nephew was Jeanette's David Jones.

Jeanette was late getting into work that morning, but as the boss had not arrived either, she only had to explain to Elsie what had delayed her. After that they discussed the strike. There were hundreds more dockers out, and not just on Merseyside but in London, Manchester and Southampton. The dispute had something to do with overtime, and the TUC were condemning the strike, saying 'it was bringing the union movement into disrepute'.

'So what do we do, Elsie?' asked Jeanette, not bothering to remove her coat.

The other typist shrugged. 'Perhaps we'll be sent home when the boss comes in.'

'Unpaid leave. I don't fancy that,' muttered Jeanette gloomily.

As it turned out they were not sent home that morning but were set the task of writing letters to some of their customers. That afternoon they left early and were told to come in at eleven o'clock the next day as hopefully, by then, the strike might have been settled. On the way home Jeanette read the notices on all the newspaper stands blazoning the news that the Queen's scheduled tour of Liverpool had been altered, so as not to include a visit to the docks. It looked like the police were going to have their hands full dealing with all that was happening in Liverpool at the moment.

★　　★　　★

'I've a bone to pick with you, girl,' said Ethel, seizing hold of her great-niece's shoulder as soon as Jeanette entered the house.

'Ouch, that hurts,' said Jeanette, attempting to shrug off Ethel's hand, thinking the old woman had fingernails like talons. 'Let me go, I must have a word with Dad.'

'Not so fast,' said Ethel, seizing the back of Jeanette's cardigan as she struggled to get free. 'I want answers, girl.'

'What about?' asked Jeanette warily.

'I've kept quiet so far because our George said you're nearly eighteen and you work all week and so you're entitled to do what you want with your free time Saturday afternoons, but I want to know what you do then because you're never in, so where are you going and who with?'

Jeanette had, of course, been wondering when the old witch would raise this matter and was still reluctant to give her an honest answer, so she decided to answer her with a question. 'You don't think I've a boyfriend, do you?'

Ethel hesitated before saying, 'I might think that if I saw you dollying yourself up in front of the mirror.'

'But you haven't, have you?' said Jeanette promptly.

'No, I have to admit I haven't,' replied Ethel grudgingly.

'Well, there you are, Aunt Ethel, nothing for you to worry about. I'm not going to get myself in to trouble if I haven't got a boyfriend, am I?'

Ethel glared at her and her grip on Jeanette's cardigan tightened. 'No, but you still haven't answered my question, girl!'

Jeanette sighed. 'If you must know, I meet some friends in town and listen to music.'

Ethel thrust her face into Jeanette's. 'Where? You don't have money to spend.'

Jeanette jerked back her head. 'People have houses where they play music. I go to one of those,' she lied.

'That's not a good enough answer. Where?'

Jeanette was beginning to get really annoyed. 'How well do you know Liverpool? I mean . . . I was wondering the other day where you were born? You don't speak like a Liverpudlian.'

Ethel sniffed. 'I should hope not. Terrible accent. I was born in Manchester, if you must know.'

Jeanette was taken aback. 'Was Dad born there as well?'

'None of your business.'

'Of course it is! He's my father. What brought you to Liverpool?' she asked.

'That's none of your business either,' snapped Ethel, giving her a push in the direction of the kitchen.

Despite her curiosity, Jeanette wasted no time hurrying into the kitchen. There she found George, sitting at the table, eating his supper.

'You OK, Dad?' she asked, putting an arm about his shoulders, thinking he looked tired.

'Don't like this weather. I see our Sam and Hester are both still out. What about you, Jeannie? How badly is the dockers' strike affecting you?'

She had been about to mention the crash that morning, but changed her mind and sat down opposite him. 'I must admit the strike is a pain. I just hope to God it finishes soon. Were there many strikes when you were young, Dad?'

He put down his knife and fork. 'There was the police strike in 1919.'

The police strike she already knew about. 'Any strikes earlier than that?' she asked.

He looked thoughtful. 'Could be that you're thinking of the transport strikes of 1911. I was only a kid then, but I remember the riots and the fighting between the strikers and the police here in Liverpool. It started with the seamen and then the railwaymen and dockers. The army was brought in and there was a naval ship in the river because the government was convinced anarchy would break out if they didn't put on a show of strength. A couple of civilians were killed and hundreds of people injured during the sectarian fighting that followed. Several bobbies ended up in hospital.' He picked up his fork and stuck it in a morsel of stewing steak. 'That was bad. It's not that I blamed the workers. Wages were low and the conditions some of the poor lived in were terrible. The women in particular suffered, often going hungry themselves to feed their children. It was a good thing that their better off sisters decided to do something about it.'

'You mean the suffragettes?'

'Yes. Most were upper or middle class, with time on their

hands, who wanted the vote for themselves. Although not all were concerned about their poorer sisters.' He chewed thoughtfully.

'Do you think our Hester would have joined the suffragettes if she'd been around then?'

George swallowed. 'She'd have been a suffragist. They didn't believe in using violence and were keener to help the poor. Mind you, the police in Liverpool have always tried to help poor families. Even then they had a special charity to provide clothing and shoes for the destitute.' He hesitated. 'I remember your mum telling me she'd been a charity case.'

'Did she?' Jeanette was shocked. 'I know hardly anything about her, Dad. When did she tell you that? How did you meet her?'

'During the thirties. Life was hard and Sam and Hester's mother had just died after a painful illness. She was a good woman but frail. Grace, on the other hand, was tough. She had to be after spending time with foster parents that really didn't love her and then running away and living rough. I found her defending herself against a drunk, so I decided to take her under my wing. She fought me all the way because the last thing she wanted was to be treated like a charity case.'

'Did you love her?'

George turned brick red. 'You young people today with your talk of love. I blame the cinema. What is love? She needed a settled home, regular meals, someone to care for her and to care for – and that's why I asked her to marry me. I can't tell you how upset I was when she went missing. I did my best to try and find her but the Luftwaffe weren't leaving us alone that week in May and I had a job to do. Afterwards, it just seemed as if she'd disappeared off the face of the earth.'

'Aunt Ethel seems to think—'

'I know what she thinks,' interrupted George, 'and I wouldn't blame your mother if she'd upped and left because of the interfering old besom,' he muttered. 'I'd just like to know for certain what happened to her.'

'Me too,' said Jeanette, reaching across the table and placing her smaller hand on top of his large one. 'She was only young when she had to fend for herself, and then to have me, well . . .'

He said gruffly, 'I've sometimes wondered if she had a
nervous breakdown and couldn't face coming home with Ethel
there. I did visit several hospitals, but there were those that
were hit by incendiaries and were on fire and you can have
no idea how chaotic everything was. Records were destroyed
and—'

'I wish that we could see her again,' said Jeanette wistfully.

'Me too, but wishing doesn't get you anywhere. We just
have to get on with life and hope for the best.'

She was touched and surprised by all that he had told her.
Slowly she removed her hand. 'Hester and I were on the bus
this morning and we saw an accident so we got off and helped.
Our Hester was marvellous the way she handled things. Oddly
enough, there was another policeman there who gave her a
hand. They seemed to work well together.'

'Hester's a good girl,' he said, flushed with pride. 'Never
been any trouble to me.'

'Unlike me, hey,' said Jeanette, kissing his cheek.

'Now don't you be saying that,' he said, patting her shoulder.

'I'll leave you to get on with your supper, Dad.'

Without another word she went upstairs to think over what
he had said and all that had happened that day.

Nine

'So who's this policeman who was at the accident scene the
other day?' asked Sam.

Hester felt the colour suffuse her cheeks. 'Why are you
asking?'

'Because you haven't mentioned it. Jeanette told Dad that
there was a policeman who gave you a hand. She admires you,
thought you handled it brilliantly.'

'She's easily impressed.' Despite her words, Hester was pleased
by the compliment.

'I wouldn't say that,' said Sam. 'She gives credit where it's
due. So . . . good looking, was he?'

'He's all right,' she said casually.

'Name?'

Hester frowned. 'Why d'you need to know his name?'

'Because I'm nosey and I reckon from the way you're blushing, he's asked you out on a date,' said Sam.

She hesitated.

'I could look up the report,' he murmured, reaching for a file he needed to read.

'He's with Bootle division and his name is Cedric Dobson. Happy now?' she said, and flounced out.

Sam guessed she did have a date with him. But why couldn't she have given his name immediately? Sam decided to check him out. He wondered what Jeanette had thought of him and decided it might be worth having a chat with her next time he saw her.

Jeanette was feeling restless that day and suggested to Peggy that they walk down to the Mersey at lunchtime and eat their sandwiches there.

'You're crazy. The strike isn't settled yet and you could get caught up in a scuffle or anything. You do realize there are three hundred ships lying idle in the Mersey?'

'Yes, I read the *Echo* too, and it says that over forty-three thousand men are involved,' said Jeanette. 'If things look like getting nasty, I'll come straight back. I need to stretch my legs and get some fresh air.'

'OK, but you can go on your own,' said Peggy. 'My foot's still giving me gyp and I'd rather rest it up.'

'That's understandable,' said Jeanette warmly. 'It's surprising how long these things can take to heal.'

'You never asked me how I got on with the twin after you left,' said Peggy.

'Sorry, I forgot! How did you get on?'

'All right. I only wish he could move a bit faster. I can't see us going dancing. We're a pair of crocks.' Peggy pulled a face.

'What about the flicks?'

'It's a thought. I can see I'll have to put myself in his way,' said Peggy, smiling slightly.

★   ★   ★

Later, as Jeanette walked down to the Mersey, she felt depressed. She feared that Liverpool would go down the drain if these strikes continued. Some ships with perishable cargoes had already decided to unload at ports where there was no industrial action, and it worried Jeanette that their owners might choose never to dock in Liverpool again. She sighed as she forced her way through knots of men and women gathered at the Pierhead and managed to make her way down to the landing stage. At least the ferries were still sailing and there were plenty of police about to deal with matters if the situation was to get out of hand.

She watched the Seacombe boat approach the landing stage. The tide was in and water surged and foamed in a frothy mix of cream and khaki, as ropes, thick as saplings, were thrown. She watched a young ferryman dressed in navy-blue sweater, trousers and peaked cap, help tie up the ship. Suddenly she realized it was Jimmy and called out to him.

He glanced around. She waved and he stared and then lifted a hand in acknowledgement. As the gangplank was lowered, she stepped out of the way to allow passengers to stream past her. As the rush thinned to a trickle, she walked over to him. 'Fancy meeting you here,' she said. 'I didn't realize you worked on the ferry boats. Do you only ever work on the Seacombe one?'

'No. Do Birkenhead sometimes. Are you coming aboard?' he asked, pushing back his cap and grinning at her.

She smiled. 'I wasn't planning on doing so. I just came down for a walk and some fresh air.' She paused. 'I wonder . . .'

He cocked an eyebrow. 'Wonder what?'

'If you've seen a bloke with a nasty cut on his face on your travels backwards and forwards across the Mersey lately?'

'Can't say I have. Who is this bloke?'

'Oh, someone I met briefly. We got caught up in a fight in a chippy and he was hit in the face with a bicycle chain.'

Jimmy gave a low whistle. 'Nasty. When did this happen?'

'August. Hopefully it would be healed by now, so you'd be looking for a bloke with a scar. I just want to know if he's all right.'

'I'll keep my eyes open for him. Does he have a name?'

'Yes, according to Father Callaghan it's David Jones.'

'Father Callaghan?'

She nodded. 'D'you know him?'

'Know him? He's the brother of Mrs Gianelli, who used to run the nursery Mam took me and our Irene to during the war. Although she was a Mrs Lachlan then and a widow, the same as Mam.'

'Oh, was he living in Liverpool then?'

'Yeah. I believe he used to help dig people out during the bombing and give the last rites to the dying.'

Jeanette was fascinated, but before she could ask a further question there was a sudden whistle.

Jimmy's head turned in the direction of the ferryboat. 'I'm going to have to go. See you around.'

There came another whistle and Jeanette was left staring after him, a chill wind blowing in her face, thinking of her mother.

'Hey, Jeannie, come here!'

Jeanette paused on her way upstairs a few days later and looked down at her half-brother. 'Is it important? I was just going to get changed.'

'Just a few words,' said Sam.

She retraced her steps. 'What's it about?'

'The policeman at the accident where our Hester helped out – what was your opinion of him?'

The question took Jeanette by surprise. 'Why?'

'Answer my question,' ordered Sam.

She sighed heavily. 'You're not half bossy sometimes. I'm not a member of your squad, you know. He was good looking in a Tyrone Power kind of way, but I didn't really take that much notice of him.'

'Do you think our Hester fancied him?'

Jeanette's brow knit in thought. 'Maybe. She had talked on the bus about a lad she'd met when she was evacuated. He gave her her very first kiss. I'm thinking she wants someone to go out with.'

Sam looked thoughtful. 'Thanks, kid. You can go now.'

'Ta very much,' she said flippantly, and ran upstairs, wondering where Hester was this evening. Perhaps she had a date with that policeman.

'So you came,' said Cedric, taking Hester's hand and drawing it through his arm.

Hester felt a tremor go through her. 'You came too,' she said lightly.

His dark eyes searched her face. 'I hope you're glad I did.'

'Well, I'd have felt a right ninny standing here waiting if you hadn't.' She could feel her cheeks getting hot because he was staring at her intently. 'Shall we go in?'

'That's what we're here for,' he said, pushing open the glass-panelled door that led into the foyer of the Locarno. 'I hope you can dance.'

'It's a bit late to be asking me that when you arranged to meet me outside a dance hall,' said Hester drily.

'Just testing,' he said, his smile revealing Maclean-white teeth.

He proved to be a decent dancer. Showy, but she could forgive him that because not once did he tread on her toes, although there were several occasions when he held her too close for comfort. He also didn't bother making small talk whilst they danced, although when they sat out he commented on other people's dancing and also asked if she had worked on any exciting cases lately.

'If I want excitement I read *Real Crime* magazines or Edgar Lustgarten books,' she said lightly, not wanting to talk about work.

She had obviously caught his interest because his handsome face creased into a smile. 'You're a fan?'

She could not help returning his smile. 'Yes, you?'

He nodded, and for the next quarter of an hour, instead of taking to the dance floor, they discussed crime writers. By the time the evening ended, Hester could honestly say that she had enjoyed the date and they arranged to meet again. She told him not to bother seeing her home, and as they were going in opposite directions, parted outside the dance hall.

When she arrived home she found Jeanette making cocoa in the kitchen.

'Make us a cup too, please,' said Hester.

Jeanette did so, and when she placed it in front of her, asked, 'Do you know how that woman is who was injured in the crash the other week?'

'As far as I know, she's OK,' said Hester, reaching for the cocoa cup. 'By the way, I had our Sam asking me about Cedric.'

'Is Cedric the policeman?'

'Yes.'

'He asked me what I thought of him.' Jeanette took a sip of cocoa.

Hester frowned. 'I don't know why he has to be so interested in him.'

'He's your brother!' said Jeanette, as if that was answer enough. 'So, are you dating Cedric?'

'What if I am?' said Hester casually.

'I'm glad you've got a boyfriend. I hope it lasts.' Jeanette grinned at her, stood up and left the kitchen.

Hester stared after her, frowning. What had she meant by that − *I hope it lasts*? Perhaps she was thinking of Aunt Ethel putting her oar in or Sam checking Cedric out − maybe see if he had a couple of wives tucked away somewhere, she thought, exasperated. Why did her family have to poke their nose into her affairs?

By Friday there was not much change in the strike situation in Liverpool, but in London there was a move back to work by the dockers. Jeanette was glad when Saturday arrived, as she was hoping she might see Jimmy at the milk bar. As it was she only saw Norm and Maggie. Even so, both were chatty, and when Betty came into the conversation Jeanette remembered it was Maggie's artistic cousin who had mentioned her half-sister having lived in Whalley.

'That's right,' said Maggie. 'She was an Emma Booth, but she's now a Gregory because she married my brother, Jared. They live in Formby, but she still has a cottage in Whalley and in summer she usually opens up the front room and back garden and serves teas and light meals and sells local crafts. She's reluctant to get rid of the cottage as not only her grandparents lived there but her great-grandparents, too.'

'Emma must have been living there when my half-sister

Hester was evacuated to Whalley. I wonder if they knew each other?' mused Jeanette, thinking she must try and remember to ask Hester who was going out that evening. No doubt she was seeing Cedric but had kept mum about where they were going. Could be that her question about Emma would have to wait until tomorrow.

Hester felt a thrill go right through her as she glanced at Cedric's handsome profile. Was she falling in love with him? Just the touch of his sleeve against hers distracted her attention from the stage when she wanted to concentrate on the players. She had noticed a name in the programme that she recognized, so was trying to spot the actress.

Cedric whispered, 'Are you enjoying the play?'

She said in an undertone, 'Of course I am.'

'Shush!' came a voice behind them.

They fell silent and she was aware of his fumbling for her hand. Her heart skipped a beat. Now she really was finding it difficult to concentrate on the play. Then suddenly she thought she recognized a trace of a Scouse accent in the voice of the actress who had just come on stage and stared intently at her. Beneath the stage make-up she could not recognize Dorothy Wilson, but Hester determined to go backstage when the play finished and see if it was her.

Unfortunately, Cedric was not in favour of the idea when she broached it during the interval, while they were having a drink. 'I don't have the time to hang around stage doors, Hester.'

She was disappointed. 'But you don't understand! She was a great friend of the girl my brother was in love with who died during the blitz. I haven't seen her for ages.'

He shrugged. 'I'm not preventing you from speaking to her, but it does mean you'll have to see yourself home. I have to be in at a certain time, otherwise my mother worries about me. She's getting old, and you know what old people are like.'

'Only too well,' said Hester, thinking of Ethel. 'I'm perfectly capable of seeing myself home, just like I did last time.'

He reached out and squeezed her hand. 'You do understand I'd much prefer to spend the time with you?'

She nodded.

His dark eyes held hers and he raised her hand to his lips. 'How about meeting outside Owen Owen on Thursday at seven o'clock. We could go and see the new Robert Taylor film. It's set in Egypt and the sight of a bit of sun will cheer us up.'

'Sounds good. I'll look forward to it.' She hesitated. 'What about next Saturday? Will you be free?'

'I don't know yet, Hester. I'll let you know on Thursday.'

'Couldn't you ring me at headquarters before then?'

He hesitated. 'I'd rather leave it until Thursday. I'm taking Mother to the hospital earlier in the day and until I know what the doctor says, I can't make a decision.'

She said no more, thinking it was enough for now, knowing she would see him in a few days' time. Should she tell Sam that he lived with his mother? Thinking of her brother brought her mind back to Dorothy Wilson and her decision to go backstage later.

Ten

Hester and Jeanette did not get the opportunity to talk to each other over the weekend, as by the time Hester arrived home Jeanette was in bed, and the following morning she had an urgent call to report to the CID. So it was not until Monday evening that the pair of them had the house to themselves.

'*Why do girls leave home?* Have you seen this?' Jeanette glanced up from the evening's *Echo* and stared at Hester. 'You being a policewoman, I thought you might be interested. Some of them don't just leave home, they go missing.'

'Yes,' said Hester, looking at her through blurry eyes as she stirred sugar into her cocoa. Her head was throbbing and she felt as if she had a cold coming on. *Damn!* 'Apparently they're seeking happiness. I hope they find it,' she added, putting her feet up on the pouffe and sipping her cocoa. 'I didn't tell you, did I, that I went to the theatre on Saturday – and who did I see?'

'Who?'

'Dorothy Wilson, Sam and Carol's friend, up on the stage.'

'Fancy that! I didn't tell you, either, that I remembered where I'd heard Whalley mentioned before,' said Jeanette. 'It was to do with some customers who come into the milk bar. They know someone who grew up there. She used to be an Emma Booth but now she's married to Maggie's brother.'

'Emma Booth!' Hester sat up straight. 'I remember her. I attended the same school whilst I was there. She lived with her grandparents. Well, well, it's a small world.'

Jeanette smiled. 'Isn't it just. Did you get to speak to Dorothy Wilson?'

'Yes, I decided that I couldn't let the opportunity slip by. She remembered me and asked after Sam. Her mother died last year and she's all alone in the world. I meant to mention seeing her to him, but it slipped my mind.'

'You should tell him.'

'I will,' said Hester, putting down her cup hastily and reaching for her handkerchief. She sneezed into it.

'You're not getting a cold, are you?' asked Jeanette, pushing her chair further back. 'If you are, I don't want it.'

'I don't want you to get it,' said Hester in a muffled voice. 'By the way, when are you going to see that new Glynis Johns' film?'

'Don't know, why?'

'Because Dorothy is in it. She only has a tiny role but it made her rethink what she'd really like to do.'

'Tell me what she looks like and I'll watch out for her. There was a review of it in the *Echo* last week and an interview with Glynis Johns, but it won't be showing until the week before Christmas.' Jeanette yawned.

Hester stuffed her handkerchief up her sleeve. 'I wonder where Aunt Ethel has gone?'

'I don't know and I don't care, just as long as she's out of the way.' Jeanette turned a page of the *Echo* and a few moments later asked, 'What do you think of bigamy?'

'What on earth makes you ask that?'

'Because of what it says here. Apparently the reason why some people go missing is because they've committed bigamy. They find someone else and because they don't want to cope with going through a divorce, they change their name, pretend the first marriage never took place and marry someone else.' She lifted her head and stared across at Hester. 'It happened quite a bit during the Great War and afterwards. Now it's not so easy to just change your name and get a job when you move somewhere else because of National Insurance numbers. Unless you get a job cash in hand like my part-time one.'

'Why are you so interested in this subject?' asked Hester, stifling a sneeze.

Jeanette sighed. 'Dad and my mother didn't marry for love, you know. What if she did fall in love with someone else and couldn't bear to live without him and—'

'You don't really believe that, do you?' asked Hester, lowering her handkerchief.

'I don't want to, but it would mean she was still alive somewhere.'

'She loved you too much to go off with another man,' said Hester firmly. 'Unless it can be proved, I'm not going to believe it. Now, if she had lost her memory and remarried, that would be different.'

'Dad told me he visited several hospitals in search of her but everything was in such a mess – records destroyed, and so on,' said Jeanette softly.

'Let's change the subject.'

'OK. Tell me something more about Dorothy Wilson?'

Hester leaned back in her chair and closed her eyes. 'She's been involved in all kinds of plays, and not only in the theatre. She's been on the wireless and even on the television. She's interested in what goes on behind the camera as well. She told me she'd enjoy filming a documentary in Liverpool.'

'What kind of documentary?'

'I'm not sure.'

'I don't know why she doesn't make a thriller. One of those black and white gritty films with sailors, a tart with a heart, fog and a juicy murder,' said Jeanette with relish.

'Murders aren't fun in real life.' Hester reached for her

handkerchief and sneezed again. 'Damn!' she exclaimed in a muffled voice. 'I really have got a cold coming on and it's bloody inconvenient.'

'Would you like me to make you a hot-water bottle?' said Jeanette, putting down the newspaper. 'You're probably best going to bed early.'

Hester thanked her and within the hour she was tucked up in bed, praying that she would feel better in the morning.

Feeling worse if anything the following day, Hester struggled into work, rather than being home at Ethel's mercy. She dosed herself with Aspro and bought a bottle of lemon, honey and glycerine to ease her sore throat, determined to be fit for her date with Cedric.

She had told her friend Wendy about him, and she had suggested that Hester pass on an invitation to the evening do of her wedding. 'I can't wait to see him,' she had added, her eyes twinkling.

Hester had yet to mention it to Cedric and knew that she was leaving it a bit late to extend the invitation because it was for the coming Saturday. She crossed her fingers and hoped for the best. Unfortunately by Wednesday her cold was no better and she began to doubt that she would be fit enough to attend the wedding if she didn't take a couple of days off. On Thursday morning she was still feeling rough and knew that she would have to cancel her date. As Cedric had told her he was taking his mother to the hospital that day, she knew it was no use phoning through to his station. So she decided to ask Jeanette to do her a favour.

'Anything within reason,' she said.

'I want you to meet Cedric for me this evening on your way home from work and give him a message.'

'OK. Where and what time?'

Hester told her, adding, 'Explain to him that I've been ill but hope to be better by Saturday. Wendy's invited him to her evening do. Ask after his mother and see if he can come. It's at the Co-op hall in Edge Lane. I'll meet him outside at seven thirty.'

'OK,' said Jeanette, making for the door.

Hester called after her. 'You do remember what he looks like?'

'No doubt I'll recognize him when I see him,' said Jeanette, and was about to close the bedroom door when she remembered something. 'By the way, did you tell Sam about seeing Dorothy Wilson at the theatre?'

Hester sagged against the pillows. 'No, I'll tell him when I see him.'

'Okey doke! I'll see you this evening.'

Jeanette groaned as she came out of the Cunard Building that evening to swirling fog. She wished Peggy was with her, but she had not turned in to work that morning. Jeanette drew up her scarf over her mouth. Hopefully it would not take her more than a quarter of an hour to reach Clayton Square.

As she began to walk she found herself thinking of a Sherlock Holmes film called *The Pearl of Death*, which had a villain called the Creeper. She almost jumped out of her skin when a man loomed up out of the fog. He hurried past her. Sighing with relief, she just hoped that Cedric would be at the appointed place when she got there.

To her annoyance there was no one who looked the least like the man she vaguely remembered waiting in Clayton Square. She was hungry and cold and decided to hang around outside Reece's for a quarter of an hour, and if he didn't come in that time she would go home. After ten minutes there was still no sign of him and her feet were in danger of turning into blocks of ice. She walked to Kendall's and gazed at a colourful display of raincoats and umbrellas, and was on her way back when a man stepped out in front of her.

Jeanette started, gazing up at the tall figure in a dog-tooth checked overcoat and a trilby pulled low over his forehead. The bottom half of his face was concealed by a scarf. 'Are you Cedric?'

He pushed back his hat and drew down his scarf. 'That's right. You wouldn't be Hester's sister, would you?'

'Yes. Hester can't come. She's a rotten cold but is hoping to be better by Saturday.'

'That's a shame. I was looking forward to spending time with her this evening. There was a film I wanted to see. I don't suppose you'd like to come in her stead?'

The question took her aback. 'I couldn't! I've no money and besides, she'll be waiting to hear what you had to say. I was also to tell you that it's her friend Wendy's wedding on Saturday and you're invited to the evening do.'

He frowned. 'It's a bit short notice. Is Wendy her friend who's also a policewoman?'

'That's right. No doubt there'll be several members of the force there. My brother's going. You know he's a detective sergeant?'

'Yes,' he said shortly. 'I doubt I'll be able to make it. My mother wants me to take her to see an old friend. You'll give Hester my best wishes and tell her that I hope she is up and bouncing about soon. I'll be in touch.'

'I'll tell her,' said Jeanette, thinking her sister was going to be very disappointed. Suddenly she remembered something else she was to ask him. 'Oh, she mentioned your mother. She wanted to know how she was after her trip to the hospital.'

For a moment he stared at her blankly and then said hastily, 'She's not as bad as we feared, but she's got to have treatment.'

'I'll tell her. *Tarrah!*' She hurried away in the direction of the bus stop, not really knowing what to make of him. He might be tall, dark and good looking, but fancy asking her to go to the pictures with him? Perhaps she had better not mention that bit to Hester. She did not want her thinking that any female would do to keep him company. It was a pity he hadn't thought of sending Hester his love. *My best wishes* sounded a bit formal. It would also have been kind of him to offer to escort her home, so that he could see how Hester was for himself.

As soon as Jeanette saw Hester's expectant face, she wanted to hit Cedric. He could have come home with her, but she bet a pound to a penny that he had gone to see that film he mentioned.

'Well, was he there?' she asked eagerly.

'You feeling better?' said Jeanette, sitting across the table to her.

'Yes! But was he there?' whispered Hester, glancing towards the door.

'Yes, he was there.' Jeanette glanced at the door. 'Is Aunt Ethel in?'

'No, she's out, but one never knows when she's going to suddenly appear like the wicked witch in a pantomime.' She smiled at Jeanette. 'Anyway, what did he have to say? Was he disappointed I didn't turn up?'

'Of course he was disappointed. He'd been planning on taking you to the pictures.'

Hester sighed. 'We were going to see *Valley of the Kings* with Robert Taylor.'

A voice from behind Jeanette said, 'I remember when our Jeanette had a crush on Robert Taylor.'

She swivelled round. 'Where did you spring from, Sam?'

'Came in the back way.' He took his dinner from the oven.

'It's ages since I fancied Robert Taylor,' said Jeanette.

'It was last year,' said Sam. 'There's another dinner in here. Is it yours, Jeanette?'

She nodded, getting up and going over to the oven. 'This looks good.'

'I cooked it so you're safe,' said Hester.

'You must be feeling better if you made supper,' said Jeanette.

'Never mind that now,' said Hester. 'I want to know what Cedric said about Wendy's wedding. Can he go?'

'Cedric! I still think it's an unusual name for a policeman,' said Sam.

Hester flushed. 'It's just uncommon. Whereas Sam is really common.'

'Thanks very much,' said Sam, grinning. 'It's the same as David Jones. Really popular.'

'I wish you'd shut up about names,' said Jeanette severely. 'I want to say what I have to say.' She paused. 'Sorry, Hester. He can't go. He has to take his mother to see an old friend. His mother, by the way, turned out to be not as bad as they thought when he took her to the hospital, but she's got to have treatment. He said he'd be in touch.'

'His mother?' Sam slowly reached for the pepper.

'Yes, he has a mother,' said Hester, pulling a face at him. 'Not a couple of wives hidden away.'

Sam raised his eyebrows. 'Why should I think he's a bigamist? Anyway, when are we going to meet him?'

'It's early days for you needing to meet him. Although you

could have met him at the wedding,' said Hester. 'By the way, I meant to tell you that when I went to the Playhouse with Cedric the other evening, Dorothy Wilson was in the play.'

'I know she was,' said Sam casually, sprinkling pepper over his food. 'It's the second time she's appeared in a play in Liverpool in the last year.'

His sisters stared at him. 'Did you go and see her?' asked Hester.

'Yep. And she's hoping to come to Wendy's evening do with me.'

'Wow! You're a quick worker,' said Jeanette.

Sam grinned. 'I always did like Dorothy. Pity about Cedric.'

Hester frowned. 'Now what do you mean by that?'

He raised his eyebrows. 'Pity he has to let you down.'

'It can't be helped.'

'No, of course not,' murmured Sam, forking more food into his mouth. 'He seems to do a lot for his mother.'

Hester stared at him. 'I find it rather touching that he's so solicitous about his elderly mother. I'd hope you'd be the same if our mother hadn't died.' She got up and walked out of the kitchen.

Jeanette stared at Sam. 'Why did you go on about Cedric and his mother?'

Sam was quiet.

'You don't think he's good enough for our Hester, do you?'

'No.'

'But why? You've never met him – or have you? I have and I think he's odd. He asked me to go to the pictures with him in Hester's place.'

Sam lifted his head. 'Did he now!'

She nodded. 'I haven't told her.'

'Perhaps you should have. It would have really had her questioning what kind of man he is.'

Jeanette frowned in thought. 'I've just remembered something. I know these twins who come into the milk bar. I'm sure their brother's in the Bootle division. D'you want me to ask if he knows Cedric and what he thinks about him?'

'No! I have my own methods of gathering information. Don't you worry about it. I'll sort Cedric.'

'OK, I was only trying to help.'

They were silent as they finished their meal. Then as she gathered their plates and cutlery, she said, 'I'm glad you're going out with Dorothy Wilson.'

He smiled. 'I'm glad you're glad.'

'Does it mean you're over Carol? I still feel something for Davy Jones, although I scarcely know him. Strange, isn't it?'

'Not if it's gratitude for his coming to your rescue,' said Sam, reaching for a cigarette. 'I don't suppose you'll stop mooning over this Jones bloke until you see him again and realize you've built up a picture of him that proves false.'

'Thanks for spoiling my fantasy!' said Jeanette drily. 'I think I'll leave you to drink your tea alone, while I have a bath and daydream of Robert Taylor,' she added mischievously. 'I wonder where the old witch has gone? She's been going out a lot in the evenings lately. Perhaps she's found herself a fancy man.'

'That'll be the day,' drawled Sam.

Jeanette grinned, trying to imagine Ethel made up to the eyeballs, billing and cooing on the back row of the pictures with a mustachioed elderly gentleman.

Later, as she turned on the bath taps and reached for Hester's jar of lavender-scented bath salts, she wondered if David Jones really would turn out to be a disappointment if she did meet him again. Somehow she didn't think so.

She drowsed up to her neck in the warm, scented water. It was the sound of footsteps on the stairs that roused her and instantly she was on full alert. They stopped outside the door and she was glad that she had locked it. She watched the doorknob turn before being rattled.

'Who's in there?' demanded Ethel. 'I'm armed if you're a burglar.'

Jeanette stifled a laugh. 'What burglar locks himself in the bathroom, Aunt Ethel? I'm having a bath and won't be long.'

'You damn well better hadn't be long, whoever you are.'

'It's me, Jeanette,' she called, wondering if the old woman really was going senile.

'Well, you can get out of there! Using up all the hot water is selfish,' grumbled Ethel. 'You girls don't know you're born! If it weren't for George, I'd make you take cold showers as I

did my other girls. I'm going downstairs to make myself a cup
of cocoa and if you're not out by the time I get back, you'll
have a taste of the birch.'

The birch! Jeanette wondered if her great-aunt had been
drinking. She waited until she heard her go downstairs before
getting out of the bath. Once dressed, she unlocked the door
and ran along the landing to Hester's bedroom. She knocked
on the door. 'Can I come in? The old witch threatened me
with cold showers and the birch.'

The door opened and Hester grabbed Jeanette by the front
of her nightdress and dragged her inside. 'I wonder where she's
been this evening,' said Hester.

'We should try asking her.'

Hester shook her head. 'Let's not bother. I've enough on
my mind right now without worrying about her.'

'Cedric,' said Jeanette, then wished she had not mentioned
him because her half-sister looked so fed up. She had been
going to tell her about his asking her to go to the pictures
with him but changed her mind.

'I'd planned on buying a new dress. A real fancy one.'

'Well, what's stopping you from still doing that? You are still
going to go to the wedding, aren't you?'

Hester hesitated, then nodded. 'Of course! Wendy would
be upset if I wasn't there. We've been friends since we joined
the force.'

'Well, you forget about Cedric for now and buy a new dress
that will knock the socks off all the men there,' said Jeanette,
relishing the thought of Hester finding another bloke to take
her out.

Eleven

'I'm in a dancing mood. A gay romantic mood,' sang Sam as
he fastened his tie.

Hester met her brother's eyes in the mirror above the fireplace
and rolled a bit more Max Factor pan stick over the redness

about her nose. 'I must admit I'm looking forward to this evening more than I was the other day.'

'You be careful your skirt doesn't catch fire,' warned Ethel, glowering at Hester who was wearing a turquoise taffeta dress with a sweetheart neckline and full skirt, under which she wore a pale blue, starched nylon underskirt.

'Leave her alone,' said George, rustling the newspaper. 'She's not daft. The fireguard's in place.'

Ethel said, 'You can't be too careful. I remember a young girl's nightdress catching fire years ago and she burnt to death.'

'Go on, Aunt Ethel, cheer us up,' muttered Hester, outlining her lips with a coral lipstick.

'Where's Jeanette?' asked Ethel, glancing about her. 'I wanted her to do something for me. I have something to show her.'

'Don't tell me you've forgotten already that she's gone to the pictures with her friend Peggy?' said George, wishing he was in his son's shoes and looking forward to spending the evening dancing with a young woman in his arms. Instead, he was going to have to keep his aunt company because, according to Hester and Jeanette, Ethel could be going senile. He hoped not. Lately he had begun to look forward to retiring from the police force and putting in a bit of detective work trying to find out what had happened to Grace. But if his aunt was starting to lose her marbles, that meant he was going to have to be around to keep his eye on her.

Ethel sniffed. 'I can't be expected to remember everything at my age. I hope she gets home at a decent hour or there'll be trouble. Where's she been this afternoon, that's what I'd like to know?'

Sam and Hester exchanged looks. 'How old are you, Aunt Ethel?' asked the latter, placing her lipstick in a black patent leather handbag along with a clean handkerchief and her purse.

'The same age as my hair and younger than my teeth and that's all I'm saying,' answered Ethel, sitting down and switching on the wireless. 'I wish you'd hurry up and go out, so me and our George can have a bit of peace. I'm getting a headache with all this chatter.'

'We're going,' said Sam, shrugging on his overcoat and

heading for the door, where he paused. 'Pity you couldn't have come too, Dad. You could do with having a bit of fun.'

'I'm OK, son. You go and enjoy yourself,' said George, his face softening as, with an ache in his heart, he gazed at his only son, of whom he was so proud. If only Sam could find someone who could make him happy for the rest of his life.

'Bye, Dad. See you later.' Hester kissed the top of his head before tying a headscarf carefully over her newly set hair and grabbing her coat.

'No one ever bloody kisses me,' grumbled Ethel.

That's because you don't deserve it! thought Hester as she followed her brother out of the house. As they walked up the street to the main road, she said, 'I thought Dad looked a bit down.'

'Well, he would, wouldn't he? Stuck in with the old witch while we're out enjoying ourselves,' said Sam.

Hester glanced at him. 'I'm glad you're convinced we're going to have a good time.'

Sam hesitated. 'I'm going to tell you something that you're not going to like, but hopefully it'll make you determined to enjoy yourself.'

She stopped in her tracks. 'It's about Cedric, isn't it?'

'Yeah. I've made a few enquiries about him, and one of the men remembers him from when he first started with the force in Liverpool. He didn't trust him, especially around women. Cedric's beat was the area around Canning Street and you know what that's known for. Another bloke mentioned Cedric not being married but living with his mother. He remembers him taking time off to attend her funeral.'

Hester was shocked and baffled. 'Why lie to me about her?'

'Exactly. Why does he feel he needs an alibi for the other Thursday?'

'You mean the day he supposedly took his mother to the hospital?'

'You're not the only one he lied to. I spoke to his sergeant and Cedric gave him the same reason for asking for the day off. It's not the first time he's used his mother as an excuse since he's been there.'

'Oh!' Hester began walking very fast. 'It doesn't say he's

been up to mischief. And he could have lied about his mother's funeral years ago.'

'Accept, Hester, that she's dead,' said Sam. 'His sergeant is keeping an eye on him because he has a feeling Cedric is up to something and he wants to find out what it is. I don't have the time to investigate him any further. After all, he's Bootle's responsibility now. I suggest you have nothing more to do with him.'

Hester was silent, thinking about what her brother had told her. She felt angry and sick at heart and knew she was going to have to decide herself how to deal with Cedric.

They took the bus to Tunnel Road and walked the rest of the way to Lodge Lane. Hester had been at the wedding ceremony earlier but had returned home to have a rest and change for the evening do. The sound of a band, the buzz of conversation and bursts of laughter could be heard coming from upstairs in the Co-op hall as they paused on the pavement below. A man stood watch in the doorway, smoking a cigarette. Hester recognized him as a member of her division. For a few moments he and Sam discussed the football match at Goodison Park earlier that day, before Hester and Sam climbed the stairs to the function room above.

Almost immediately they were spotted. Wendy, still wearing her white satin and lace wedding gown, hurried over to them. 'Dorothy's here, Sam,' she blurted out. 'I told her I didn't think you'd keep her waiting. She's been signing autographs. Quite a few people recognized her from that telly programme she was in not so long ago – and, of course, some had seen her at the Playhouse.'

His gaze swept the hall for Dorothy.

'Let's both go and say hello to her,' said Hester.

'No, no,' said Wendy hastily, seizing her friend's arm. 'I've someone else I want you to meet.'

'If it's a bloke—' began Hester.

'Of course it's a bloke,' said Wendy, her eyes sparkling. 'And I've been told he's a great dancer. One thing is for certain, he won't trample on your feet in size thirteens like some men I could mention.'

'I'll see you later,' said Sam, and walked away.

Hester thought, *What the hell!* She had come here to dance.
She allowed herself to be hustled to the other side of the hall
where several people were grouped around two tables that were
almost covered in glasses, some empty, some half full.

'Who is this bloke?' she asked in a low voice.

'He's a mate of Charley's cousin and came home from
Germany only two days ago. He popped in to see the cousin's
family in Blackburn and they twisted his arm to drive them
here.'

'Is he in the army?'

'Yes, but he'll be getting demobbed soon. He's not half bad
looking and I've been told that he'll be putting money into
a garage when he finishes. Apparently he served his time as a
mechanic and built his own car out of old spare parts before
doing his national service later than usual.'

'OK, you don't have to sell him to me,' murmured Hester,
her eyes running swiftly over the men in the group they were
approaching. 'Which one is he?'

'The one laughing with the reddish brown hair and the
dimple in his chin.'

Hester spotted him and thought he must have been at
the wedding that afternoon because he seemed familiar. There
was something infectious about his laugh, and she wondered
what the joke was because he was not the only one who
looked amused. 'At least he's cheerful,' she said.

Wendy agreed. 'I like happy faces around me. Come on, let
me introduce you.'

Hester allowed herself to be led forward and shook hands all
round. One or two said they remembered seeing her earlier at
the church. Wendy managed to persuade them to shift around
to make room for Hester between the soldier, introduced to
her as Ally, and Marion, one of Charley's cousins.

'So you're in the police force as well,' Marion said, once
Hester was settled.

'That's right,' murmured Hester. 'What do you do?'

'I'm married. My husband's stationed in Germany and I'm
hoping to go and join him soon.'

Hester glanced at Ally. 'Are you and he both in the same
unit?'

He shook his head. 'I'm in the Lancashire Fusiliers, and so was my father. He fought in the trenches during the Great War but was lucky enough to survive because he was sent home just before the big push.' All signs of laughter had vanished from his eyes. 'They wanted him to train men for the front, which he had mixed feelings about. Still, it saved his life and he died only recently.'

'Let's talk about something more cheerful,' said Marion. 'This is a wedding after all.'

He nodded and turned again to Hester. 'Do you dance?'

'I'm no expert, but if asked I do my best,' she said lightly.

'They're playing a quickstep. Would you dance with me?' He stood up and she realized they were much of a height, which made a change from very tall policemen.

She rose to her feet and her skirts swirled round her calves. 'I hope I don't let you down. Wendy told me you're a good dancer.'

He smiled ruefully. 'I suppose Charley's sister told her that and she had it from my sister.'

She returned his smile. 'I've no idea. Why, isn't it true?'

'What a question to ask me,' he said, taking her hand and leading her on to the dance floor. She could feel his palm rough against hers and remembered what Wendy had said about his working as a mechanic.

They began to dance and did not speak for a minute or two. Then he said, 'Tell me, how was it I missed you at the reception?'

'Probably you had more important people to talk to,' said Hester.

'I wouldn't say that.' He stared at her intently. 'Although I must have noticed you because you seem familiar.'

Her eyes met his. 'I thought the same about you. What's Ally short for?'

'Alexander.' He grimaced. 'A bit of a mouthful. It was my sister who first called me Ally when we were kids because she couldn't get her tongue round it and it stuck.'

'Wendy said you drove Charley's family here from Blackburn. Are you staying with your sister whilst you're on leave?'

He nodded. 'She's determined to see me settled and thinks dancing is one way of capturing a woman's heart.'

Hester smiled. 'I have a sister who's the same, but I enjoy my job too much to give it up for marriage just yet.'

'Ah, a career girl! I've met a few of them in the army and sooner or later they change their minds about staying single.'

'I've met other men who think like that,' she said, an edge to her voice. 'And I suppose I have to agree with you that lots of women do change their mind when they meet the right man. But I bet it's the same with men, or are you planning on remaining a bachelor, despite what your sister says?'

'No, I want to get married,' he said firmly, drawing her closer.

She was surprised by the frisson of excitement that pulsed through her as their bodies brushed with the movement of the dance. Why should he make her feel like this? It was not as if he was as handsome as Cedric, but she felt much more at ease with Ally. There seemed to be an instant rapport that had been missing with her fellow policeman, and talking to him was so easy.

'So what do you do in the police force?' asked Ally after they had circled the dance floor once again.

'I'm attached to the CID. I occasionally go on raids,' she said slightly breathlessly, for he was an energetic dancer.

'So you're a detective?'

'I wouldn't say that exactly. It's my brother who's the detective.' She glanced about her but could not see Sam amongst the swirling couples. 'He's here somewhere. He's a good dancer, too.'

'He must have been told the same as me, that it was the way to attract the girls,' said Ally, twirling her around.

'If he was then it wasn't me who said it,' gasped Hester. 'Don't you think it's possible he just might enjoy dancing?'

'An excuse to hold a pretty girl in his arms? It's one way to get close up and have an almost private conversation. My mother was a great Fred Astaire and Ginger Rogers fan. She used to take me and my sister to see all their movies.'

'Sam and I enjoyed their films too. *Top Hat*, *Swing Time*, *Flying down to Rio*!' Hester named a few of the famous couple's hits.

'I wish they'd show them again. The films today seem much more serious,' said Ally.

'No, you're wrong,' said Hester firmly. 'There are still some good musicals and comedies out there.'

'Name one.'

'*Calamity Jane* came out last year and that was good. I haven't seen *Seven Brides for Seven Brothers* yet, but Howard Keel is in it and he can really belt out a song.'

'All right, I'll give you *Calamity Jane* because I've heard Doris Day's "Secret Love" played plenty of times, even in Germany, but I don't think she was much into dancing.'

'No, but—' Hester got no further because the music came to an end.

Some couples began to leave the dance floor, but her partner made no move to do so. He stood there, holding her and swaying slightly as if the music was still playing. 'I wouldn't mind seeing the Howard Keel movie you mentioned,' he said.

'It might be showing somewhere in Liverpool,' she responded, 'although I presume you'll be returning to your sister's farm this evening?'

'Not until Monday. The family would like to make the most of the opportunity to do some Christmas shopping while they're here and I don't blame them. If you're free tomorrow we could go to the pictures.'

'But I don't know if the film *is* showing anywhere,' said Hester, flustered by the unexpected invitation, 'and besides—'

'Besides what?' His eyes held hers and she could not look away. 'You hardly know me,' he added softly.

'Yes, but I wasn't going to say that.'

'What were you going to say?' asked Ally.

How could she say that she enjoyed dancing with him even more than she liked dancing with Cedric? He was bound to ask who Cedric was, and he was the last person she wanted to discuss right now. No doubt Ally would soon be returning to his unit; she would enjoy getting to know him better before he left.

'That there are other films,' she said at last.

The band launched into another number.

Ally smiled and raised his eyebrows. 'How d'you feel about the polka?' He did not wait for her answer, but caught her close to him and then they were dancing in wild abandon. It was such fun she wanted to laugh and laugh. The other couples on the floor passed by in a blur and it was only when the music ended and he brought her to a swinging halt, that she saw her brother a few feet away with his arm around Dorothy Wilson's waist.

He winked at Hester and she gave him a smiling nod.

'Hello, Hester,' said Dorothy, who looked as flushed and sweaty as Hester felt, but who Hester considered much prettier. 'That was a fast dance.'

Hester gasped. 'I've never danced like that in all my life.'

'Perhaps we should put in a request for the next one to be a waltz,' said Ally, his hazel eyes amused as he gazed down into her face.

'Good idea,' said Sam. 'I'm Hester's brother, by the way.'

Ally nodded in his direction. 'Pleased to meet you. I'm Ally Green, a mate of Charley's cousin. I've just asked your sister if she would like to go to the pictures with me tomorrow. You don't have any objections, do you?'

Sam said, 'She's over twenty-one and doesn't need my permission.'

'I should think not,' said Dorothy, tapping the side of his face gently. 'If I'd waited for permission to leave home to become an actress, I wouldn't be where I am today.'

'Sam encouraged me to join the police force,' said Hester swiftly, 'so I have a lot to thank him for. And Dad supported me, too.'

'No need to leap to my defence, our kid,' said Sam, taking Dorothy's hand and kissing it. 'I believe you're in the army, mate?'

'Be getting demobbed at the end of the year,' said Ally.

The band suddenly struck up and Sam said, 'Good for you. By the way, I think we're getting what we asked for. Unless I'm mistaken they're playing the "Tennessee Waltz".'

Ally turned to Hester. 'Shall we?'

She nodded, thinking that she could happily dance all night with him.

All too soon the evening came to an end and Ally asked if he could see her home. As it had gone midnight and there were no buses running, she was about to say that it was a bit of a walk when Sam approached.

'I've ordered a taxi, Hester. It'll be here in ten minutes. We'll drop Dorothy off at her hotel and then go home.'

Hester turned to Ally and said regretfully, 'I'm sorry, but it will save you the walk.'

He shrugged. 'You've nothing to be sorry for. Hopefully I'll see you tomorrow.'

She nodded. 'What time?'

He suggested that they meet under the clock in Lime Street station at four thirty and she agreed. For a moment longer they stood there, looking at each other, then he said, 'Goodnight!' and walked away.

'Goodnight!' she echoed, and then let out a sigh.

Sam looked down at her. 'I think Ally is definitely a better bet than Cedric.'

'I wouldn't argue. I'll go and get my coat and meet you and Dorothy out front. I must thank Wendy and Charley and their parents for a great evening first.'

As she made her way to the cloakroom, she was already going over in her mind what she might say to Cedric if he should get in touch and ask whether she had enjoyed herself at her friend's wedding.

Twelve

'So how was the wedding do?' asked Jeanette, turning from the sink as Hester entered the kitchen the following morning.

'Good,' said Hester, stifling a yawn as she sat down at the table. 'Do you know where last night's *Echo* is?'

'Last time I saw it Aunt Ethel was reading it,' said Jeanette. 'She might have placed it down the side of her chair. Why, what d'you want it for?'

'I want to see what's on at the cinema. Is there any tea in the pot?'

'I'd make fresh if I were you,' said Jeanette, placing a bowl on the draining board. 'So what made it so good?'

'I danced nearly every dance.' Hester stood up and did a twirl. 'I'll go and see if the *Echo* is where you say it is.'

As she went out of the room, humming a dance tune, Jeanette smiled to herself, glad that her half-sister appeared to have had a good time. *Eat your heart out, Cedric!* she thought.

A few minutes later Hester re-entered the kitchen and sat down at the table with the newspaper. She unfolded it and pulled a face before turning to the front page.

'What's the face for?' asked Jeanette, emptying the teapot.

'It was open at the Deaths section. I suppose at Ethel's age you can get into the habit of checking if there's anyone you know who's died.'

'Cheerful!' Jeanette's eyes gleamed. 'Perhaps I should ask her?'

'No, leave well alone!' said Hester, glancing over at her. 'What was the film like you went to see last night?'

She shrugged. 'It was OK.'

'Only OK.' Hester smiled. 'I don't suppose there was any dancing and singing in it?'

'No. Anyway, it finished last night. If you're after a bit of music, then *Rose Marie* with Howard Keel is on at the Forum.'

'I suppose that'll do us,' said Hester, her face brightening.

Jeanette darted her a glance. 'Us?'

Hester tapped her nose. 'Never you mind.' She turned the pages of the *Echo* back to the Deaths section and was about to fold it in half when she noticed a name had been circled and began to read.

Jeanette placed Hester's cup and saucer on the table within reach. 'What's that you're reading?'

'A piece about someone called Lavinia Crawshaw,' said Hester, without looking up. 'Her age is given as seventy-four and apparently she was active in the suffragette movement in her younger days. In 1910 she was imprisoned in Walton gaol for fourteen days' hard labour.' She paused. 'I wonder if she was one of Aunt Ethel's charges? Anyway, there's to be a service at St Agnes Church in Toxteth Park on Friday at four o'clock. It says here that she was the only daughter of William Crawshaw who was once a leading cotton merchant of Liverpool. Maybe Aunt Ethel is planning on going.'

'I bet the father had some money,' said Jeanette.

'And position, no doubt.' Hester reached for her cup.

Jeanette was puzzled. 'I wonder if Aunt Ethel ever considered joining the suffragettes?'

'Not if she was for law and order.'

'Is there any mention of Lavinia being married or having relatives?'

'It says *Miss* Lavinia Crawshaw.' Hester sipped her tea. 'Hmm. Another little mystery for you to solve if your interest is more than idle curiosity.'

'I bet you ten bob that her having been locked up in Walton gaol will have been reported in the Liverpool *Echo* at the time.'

'Central Library will have old newspapers in their archives,' said Hester, looking thoughtful, 'although the police would have arrested her and no doubt there'd be stuff in the police archives, too.'

'So you could look it up if you wanted to,' said Jeanette.

'If I wanted, but I'm not that interested.'

'I am because of the suffragettes, although I'm more inter-ested in finding out what happened to my mother,' said Jeanette. She was halfway through the doorway when she remembered something. 'So who were you dancing with all evening?'

'A soldier,' said Hester.

'A soldier!' Jeanette supposed that made a change from a policeman. 'What about our Sam? Did he meet him?'

Hester smiled. 'Of course. He was dancing with Dorothy Wilson. They seemed to be hitting it off OK, so maybe he'll be seeing more of her. That's if she's not touring the country with a theatrical company or making films. Don't mention any of this to the old witch or she'll be poking her nose in, wanting to know the ins and outs of our business.'

'My lips are sealed,' said Jeanette, closing the door behind her.

Jeanette collided with Ethel as she turned to go upstairs.

'Why are your lips sealed?' asked the old woman, fixing her with her dark, beady eyes.

'That would be telling, Aunt Ethel,' said Jeanette. 'Now can I get past? I'm going to church.'

Ethel's jaw dropped. 'Church! I hope you aren't visiting that priest again.'

Jeanette smiled. 'You don't have to make it sound as if I'm committing a deadly sin. I'm going with my friend, Peggy, because I need to ask him a question. See you later.'

She managed to squeeze past the old woman, remove her coat from the hook and scuttle down the lobby. Even as Ethel called her back, Jeanette was putting on her coat. She dragged a scarf from a pocket and checked she had enough money for her fare and collection before opening the door and hurrying outside. She had arranged to meet Peggy outside St Joseph's Church and did not want to be late.

There was no hymn singing of the sort Jeanette really liked, such as 'Jerusalem' or 'I Vow to Thee, My Country'. The service was in Latin, so she could understand very little of it. Peggy hissed a sort of translation to her. At least the sermon was in English and wasn't highfalutin' but down to earth. Jeanette decided that was Father Callaghan to a T. As she made for the church door afterwards, she wondered if he would recognize her or whether she'd have to introduce herself all over again.

She need not have worried. He recognized her straightaway and thought he knew why she had attended the service before she even had a chance to speak.

'No, I haven't heard from him, Jeanette Walker.'

'I wasn't going to ask you that. It's about my mother.'

He looked surprised. 'Your mother?'

'She disappeared during the blitz but her body was never found,' said Jeanette. 'She just went out one evening and didn't return. I was told that you helped with digging people out of bombed houses.'

'Sadly, it is a fact that some were never dug out and identified,' said the priest, a shadow in his eyes. 'It was a terrible time for all of us here on Merseyside. My own mother was killed in Bootle during the blitz. Fortunately, my sister Lottie, who was with her at the time, survived, and my other sister, Nellie, was in the Lake District teaching nursery-aged children when it happened. She returned home almost immediately to take care of our grandfather and youngest sister.'

Jeanette said hastily, 'I'm sorry, Father, I didn't mean to revive sad memories for you.'

He nodded absently. 'I assume you have no idea where your mother was going that evening?'

'No. I was tucked up in bed. My half-brother, Sam, was keeping his eye on me and she didn't tell him where she was going. My father was on duty. Later he did try and find her, visited several hospitals, but without any luck. We'd accept she was dead, only my great-aunt says nasty things about her and is of the opinion she's still alive.'

'Does she have any proof of this?'

'She's never produced any, and those who knew my mother believe that she would never have walked out and left me. We've considered memory loss but . . .' She shrugged.

Father Callaghan was silent for what seemed a long time. Then he said, 'I'll tell you what, Jeanette. If you have a photograph of your mother you can let me have, I know a number of men who were involved in rescuing people during the blitz in different parts of Liverpool. It's a long shot, but someone just might remember if they dug her out and she survived with memory loss.'

Jeanette's face lit up. 'Thank you!'

'Don't build up your hopes,' he warned. 'It might lead nowhere.'

'It's worth a try, though. I'll see you get a photograph. Oh, and by the way, we were living in a different house to the one we're in now. It was not far from Princes Park on the edge of Toxteth.'

'I see. I'll take that into consideration when I mention it to the men.'

Jeanette thanked him again and left the church with Peggy. 'What do you make of that then?' she asked.

Peggy squeezed her arm. 'I think it'll be good if he can find someone and you discover for certain what happened to your mother. So what are we going to do now? Shall we walk into town and do some window shopping?'

Jeanette nodded. Window shopping wasn't as good as real shopping, but she could dream of what she would buy if she had money to spend.

Thirteen

'When I'm calling you-oo-oo!' sang Ally as he and Hester came out of the cinema on Lime Street.

'Hush,' she hissed, forcing back a giggle. 'We don't need the "Indian Love Call" here in Liverpool.'

'Perhaps not,' he said, slipping an arm around her shoulders. 'It wasn't a bad film if you like Howard Keel dressed up as a Mountie, but I'd have liked some dancing.'

'Me too,' said Hester, conscious of that strong arm holding her against him, 'but it wasn't that kind of film.'

'No, much more serious than *Top Hat*.' He gazed down at her. 'So what do we do now? Shall we go for a drink or do I see you home?'

'You don't have to take me home when your hotel is here in the city centre,' she said hastily.

'But I want to take you home,' he said firmly. 'What if something were to happen to you on the way and I was not there? A gentleman always sees a lady home.'

'I'm no lady, I'm a policewoman,' said Hester, amused, 'and I can take care of myself.'

He shook his head. 'I'm coming with you. I'm not expecting to be invited in to meet the family if that's what's worrying you.'

'After just one date that didn't occur to me,' said Hester. But now he had mentioned it, she was struck by the thought that her great-aunt might peep through the curtains and see her with a man. She didn't want to be put through the third degree once inside the house.

'If it's that you just don't want to inconvenience me, forget it!' said Ally. 'I'm going to have to return to my sister's farm near Blackburn tomorrow, so I don't mind going out of my way if it means spending more time with you now.'

The thought of his wanting to spend more time with her made her feel warm inside. Was that how he felt? She could hardly believe that this attraction between them had developed so quickly. It seemed odd to think that they had only met for the first time yesterday. Although there had been a couple of times in the cinema when she had caught a glimpse of his profile and been convinced that she had seen him before. It was a possibility, because if his father and uncle had lived in Liverpool and Ally had done so too, then they might have passed in the street or even seen each other coming out of a cinema.

'See me to our street then,' she said, smiling, 'but not to my front door. I don't want the neighbours gossiping.'

He gazed down at her quizzically. 'You care about what they say that much?'

'I don't like being the centre of attention. I like my privacy.'

'So do I, but in the army it's something you get little of,' said Ally wryly.

'But you'll be leaving the army soon.'

'Aye, but I've yet to make up my mind where I'd like to settle. Could be I might decide to emigrate,' he said.

She felt a stab of dismay but tried not to show it. He was obviously trying to gauge her reaction to his words. Emigrate! It was something that she had never given any thought to and she did not want to do so now.

Even so, she felt compelled to ask, 'Why d'you want to emigrate? Where would you go?' She was aware of a sharpness in her voice and wished she could have controlled it.

'Maybe to Canada or New Zealand. I don't like too much heat, so Australia is out of the reckoning for me.'

'Well, that's the where,' she said, attempting to lighten her voice, 'but you haven't told me the why.'

'They're two countries I'd like to visit to see if I can build myself a good life out there,' he said slowly, removing his arm from about her shoulders. 'Haven't you ever wanted to move away from Liverpool?'

Instantly the feeling of closeness vanished. Obviously what he was talking about was extremely important to him and he wanted to distance himself from her because, with their bodies touching, he had been only too aware of her reaction to his words. But why did he have to bring such a topic up so soon?

They scarcely knew each other and it was serious stuff. And now he was waiting for an answer and she felt cross with him for disturbing the harmony that had existed between them.

'You haven't, have you?' he said, gazing at her intently.

'Twice I've lived away from Liverpool and was happy,' she said slowly. 'Once up in Lancashire, as it happens, and then when I did my police training Warrington way.'

His expression altered. 'So you're not against the idea of uprooting yourself?'

'No, but the reason would have to be a good one. I'm very fond of my father, Sam and Jeanette. My great-aunt I can easily live without,' she replied. 'Now can we change the subject? There's a lot we don't know about each other. We don't even know when next we'll be able to meet.'

He surprised her by kissing the side of her face. 'I know the most important thing and that's that I want to get to know you better. I think I could fall in love with you.'

Her head was in a whirl. 'It's too soon.'

'Why? People fall in love at first sight.'

She remembered how she had felt when she had met Cedric. It seemed to her now that the attraction she had experienced then had simply been physical. There was no way she had felt as good as she did being in Ally's company. He made her think and feel on a different level and, most of all, he made her laugh.

'Let's cross the road,' she said rapidly. 'We can catch a bus in front of St George's Hall.'

He took her hand and they headed for the bus stop. He lightened the mood by making a joke about something that had happened to him in Berlin and linking it to a black and white film of Ginger and Fred. Once seated on the bus, she did not know what to expect from him conversation-wise. He asked about her job and she found herself talking about the accident involving the bus and car.

He stopped her in mid-sentence. 'I don't believe it! We have met before. I was on compassionate leave and I helped get the injured woman out of the car. I wasn't really taking notice of what you looked like and besides, that bloke who said he was a bobby obviously wanted to take command.'

'Cedric? He's a bobby from Bootle,' said Hester, unable to take her eyes from Ally's face. 'You were the soldier! I've been thinking since yesterday that I'd seen you before. But I wrote your name down. Why didn't I recognize it?'

'Why should you remember it? No doubt it just didn't occur to you that I could have been that soldier.' He hesitated. 'This Cedric?'

She stiffened. 'What about him?'

'Good-looking bloke.'

Her heart had begun to thud. 'Yes, I went out with him a few times but . . .' She hesitated, not wanting to open up to him quite so soon or for him to think she was just someone who dated loads of men.

Ally's expression had altered. 'You look so serious. I've been making a fool of myself, haven't I?'

'No! I've enjoyed your company. I'd like to see you again,' said Hester earnestly.

His hazel eyes narrowed. 'But what about Cedric? He's a bobby. You must have plenty in common with him.'

She heaved a sigh. 'I can see why you might think that . . . and it's true that we're both interested in the psychology of crime.'

Ally gave a low whistle. 'The real funny stuff.'

She would have preferred to tell him the truth about that funny stuff, as he called it, but felt unable to discuss with him what Sam had told her about Cedric, so she decided to try and make a joke of things. 'Yes, but he doesn't like musicals! Fred and Ginger definitely aren't to his taste. I've told you how much I like them.'

'OK, we have stuff in common, too. So what next?'

'What do you mean?'

He did not answer immediately, but gazed out of the window. She so wished he would look her in the eye. Then he turned, and reaching for her hand, squeezed it. 'Right, you've put your cards on the table and have said you would like to see me again. I think I know where I stand. Perhaps we could take in a film again when I'm back in England.'

Her heart lifted. 'You mean after you're demobbed?'

'It could be before then.'

'Right,' she said, smiling.

By the time the bus arrived at Hester's stop, they were discussing forthcoming films and Hester expressed a wish to see *Mad About Men*.

As they got off the bus, Ally said, 'Hopefully we'll be able to see it together.'

'I'd like that,' said Hester, relieved beyond measure that they were to meet again.

Ally took out a scrap of paper and pencil. 'Your address?'

Hester halted beneath a lamp post and gave it to him. She watched him write it down and pocket the paper and pencil before beginning to walk past St John's Church on the corner of Richmond Terrace. He fell into step beside her as they turned into it. Neither of them spoke and he made no attempt to put his arm around her. She had mixed feelings about that, because she liked the security it gave to her, but she did not want the neighbours talking if they happened to be looking out of their windows.

She came to a halt a couple of doors from home and looked at him, unsure what to say to bring the evening to an end. Would he be expecting a goodnight kiss? Hesitantly, she held out a hand.

Immediately Ally took it and shook it. 'Are we being watched?' he said in a low voice.

The words brought a smile to her face. 'Oh, what the heck!' she exclaimed, leaning towards him and kissing him. It was a mere brushing of lips before she drew away. 'Goodnight, Ally.'

He moved purposefully towards her, kissing her in a way that left her breathless. 'Goodnight, Hester. Till the next time!' The words wafted to her on the breeze as he walked away.

She could hear the laughter in his voice and then he was gone. She had an urge to run after him, but instead she took a deep breath, walked the few yards to the house and opened the front door with the key she had received on her twenty-first birthday.

Fourteen

'I spoke to Father Callaghan the other day,' said Jeanette.

Hester and Sam gazed across the landing to where their half-sister stood in the bathroom doorway.

'Why?' asked Sam.

Jeanette tapped her toothbrush against her palm. 'We discussed my mother.'

'Your mam!' exclaimed Hester, closing her bedroom door behind her.

'He was here during the blitz and knew a number of the men involved in digging people out. He suggested I give him a photo of my mother and he'll show it around and see if anyone recognizes her.'

Sam frowned in thought. 'He could be lucky, but I wouldn't build your hopes up too much, Jeanette.'

'That's what he said and I'm not!' she said earnestly. 'But what with the way Aunt Ethel goes on about Mam, I thought it was worth a try.'

'I'm sure it is,' said Hester in a comforting tone. 'Anyway, there's a good photo of your mam in Dad's bedroom. You could ask to borrow it.'

'That's what I thought I'd do, although he might not approve of my involving a Roman Catholic priest.'

'I wouldn't have said Dad was prejudiced against Catholics,' said Hester, surprised. 'Anyway, he'd miss it if you didn't ask and it's a better picture than the one in the sideboard drawer downstairs.'

'Thanks!' She switched her attention from Hester to her brother. 'I'm not daft, you know, Sam. I do realize it's a long shot that anyone would remember her from a photograph after all this time.'

'OK.' He sighed.

She gave him a penetrating stare. 'Are things OK with you? How's Dorothy?'

'She's in Birmingham in some play. Different from the usual thing, she says.' He pulled a face and reached for a cigarette. 'Less middle class, more working class and down to earth.'

'When will you see her again?'

He shrugged. 'She's hoping to be back here next week. The play's experimental apparently, so it's only on for a few days.'

'Well, give her my best. Perhaps I'll get to meet her one day,' said Jeanette.

He nodded and lit his cigarette, his eyes narrowing against the smoke.

Jeanette and Hester exchanged looks and left him alone.

Shortly after, Jeanette asked her father about the photograph of Grace, but despite what Hester had said, she didn't tell him the real reason she wanted to borrow it, just that she wanted to show it to her friend Peggy. Later, as Jeanette gazed at her mother's likeness, she could not help wondering what might happen if Father Callaghan was able to connect her with someone who could provide them with a definite answer to what happened that night in May over thirteen years ago. What if her mother was alive and different from what everyone but Aunt Ethel believed her to be?

She decided not to wait until the weekend before getting the photograph to Father Callaghan, and instead placed it in an envelope with a short note and handed it to Peggy, asking if she could put it through his letterbox on her way home from work.

'OK, if that's what you want me to do,' said Peggy. 'What about Saturday evening? Are you doing anything? I wondered if you'd seen the twins at all?'

'No,' said Jeanette. 'I take it you haven't?'

Peggy shook her head. 'I thought I might have caught sight of Pete down by the King's Dock, but I haven't.'

'I'll tell you what,' said Jeanette. 'If they drop into the milk bar this Saturday, I'll drop a hint that we wouldn't mind going to the pictures with them.'

'OK,' said Peggy. 'But how will you let me know?'

'I'll drop in at Quiggins and tell your brother.'

Peggy grabbed her arm and said, 'Wait!'

Jeanette looked at her enquiringly. 'Something wrong with that idea?'

'He'll want to know everything. Where I met them and where we're going,' groaned Peggy.

'No different from my dad or Sam then. I won't mention the twins, so there's nothing for you to worry about,' said Jeanette in a comforting voice.

In the meantime, perhaps she should call in at Central Library and see if she could discover more about Lavinia Crawshaw and the suffragettes. Considering they had done so much for the cause of women's rights, she didn't remember learning anything about them at school.

So on Friday evening, Jeanette set out to walk to Central Library. During the blitz, the library and the museum had been badly damaged by firebombs and closed for quite a while, but after renovation they were now open.

After filling in a form and providing evidence of her name and address, she was given a library ticket and the newspapers of January 1910 were made available for her perusal. She did not have to read far before coming upon a report of a suffragette called Jane Wharton being arrested for throwing stones at an MP's car in Liverpool. She was sentenced to fourteen days' hard labour in Walton gaol.

Jeanette read on until she came to another mention of Jane Wharton, who was actually a Lady Constance Lytton in disguise. She looked frail in the newspaper, which was not surprising since she had been force-fed eight times and suffered a heart attack. Jeanette marvelled at the courage of the woman and continued her research. At last she found a mention of Lavinia Crawshaw. Not only had she spent time in Walton gaol, but also in Manchester for suffragette activities. Wanting to discover more about both women, she asked whether there were any books about them she could borrow.

'Well, Lady Constance Lytton did write a book called *Prisons and Prisoners*,' said the librarian.

'Do you have a copy?'

'Yes. It's not read much these days, but I'll find it for you.'

Within ten minutes, Jeanette had left the library with a thin book in her handbag. She began to read it on her way home and found it gripping. Lady Constance had spent time in Holloway and had planned to carve the words 'Votes for

Women' on her body to prove how seriously she regarded their cause. Jeanette grimaced at the thought and then discovered that her ladyship had been prevented from self-harming by the authorities. But more importantly, her ladyship had become very sympathetic towards women prisoners who were poor and ill-favoured in appearance, so she had disguised herself as Jane Wharton, a seamstress, even going as far as cutting off her hair to make herself look less attractive to draw attention to their plight.

Jeanette had to stop reading as she had reached her destination, but she could not wait to find out what Lady Constance had to say about her time in Liverpool and whether Lavinia was mentioned in the book. To her relief the house was empty, so she made a cup of tea and a jam butty and went upstairs. She stretched out on her bed and ate the jam butty, making sure she wiped her fingers before reaching for the book.

She was almost at the end when she heard the front door opening. Marking her place, she went onto the landing and peered over the banister. Ethel was sitting at the bottom of the stairs dressed in black, whilst George was standing over her, speaking in an urgent low tone.

'Dad, is everything all right?' she called down.

He broke off from what he was saying and called up, 'Nothing for you to worry about, Jeannie.'

'Don't believe him,' said Ethel, getting to her feet.

Jeanette hurried downstairs. 'Have you been to a funeral?'

'None of your business. Out of my way, girl. I want to go up and get changed,' said the old woman.

Jeanette squeezed past her and only now noticed in dismay that her father had a bandage about his head. 'What happened to you, Dad?'

'A confrontation with some troublemakers demonstrating against the city councillors,' he replied, removing his greatcoat.

'Did they knock your helmet off? It was the kind of thing the suffragettes did. I'll make you a cup of tea.'

'Thanks, luv,' said George, looking drawn.

'What's this about the suffragettes?' asked Ethel, thrusting her face close to Jeanette's and seizing her wrist. 'What's your interest?'

Jeanette wrenched herself free. 'Let go, Aunt Ethel!' She slipped her hand through George's arm. 'You come and sit down and have a rest.'

George allowed himself to be ushered into the kitchen. He was feeling a bit faint if the truth were known. He sank into a chair and closed his eyes. 'I'm getting too old for this game,' he muttered.

Jeanette gazed at him anxiously. 'Did you go to the hospital, Dad?'

'Naw, I much preferred coming home.'

'But what if you've cracked your skull? It could be serious.'

He opened his eyes. 'If I have fractured it, there's nothing they can do. It'll have to mend itself. Anyway, I've a day off tomorrow, so I'll have a rest.'

Jeanette knew it was no use arguing with him. Maybe Sam would be able to talk sense into him and make him go to the hospital. She put the kettle on before turning to him. '*Has* Aunt Ethel been to a funeral?'

'Aye, some woman she knew years ago,' he said shortly.

'Lavinia Crawshaw?'

He blinked at her. 'How d'you know that?'

'She'd circled the name in the Deaths section in the *Echo*. Lavinia was a suffragette and spent time in Walton gaol.'

'Stupid woman,' he growled. 'They wanted to go to gaol; wanted to be martyrs to the cause.'

'Being force-fed wasn't nice, Dad. I don't think I could have put up with it,' said Jeanette, reaching for a couple of mugs.

'I should hope you'd have more blinking sense,' said George fiercely. 'She should have had more thought for those dependent on her.'

'Who was dependent on her?' asked Jeanette, surprised. 'Her father was a cotton merchant and rich, so hardly a dependant.'

'She had a baby!' he burst out.

Jeanette stared at him. 'But she wasn't married.'

'You don't have to be married to have a child, girl,' he said, exasperated.

She thought he had never sounded so cross with her. 'I know that. But how do you know she had a child?'

'Because Aunt Ethel told me so, not half an hour ago.' He

took a deep breath. 'I shouldn't be talking about this to you. You're only a child yourself.'

'No, I'm not,' she retorted, her eyes flashing with annoyance. 'I'll be eighteen in December.'

'That's as maybe, but you've been protected.' He looped his hands together and stared at her. 'It's the eyes . . .' he muttered.

She wondered if the blow to his head had knocked him silly. 'What d'you mean, it's the eyes?'

'Your mother had the loveliest green eyes, just like yourself, and according to Aunt Ethel, so did this Lavinia Crawshaw.'

Jeanette sat down abruptly. 'What are you saying, Dad?'

'It's not me, it's Ethel! She says there was a baby girl born in the prison hospital. Apparently, this Lavinia Crawshaw told her that she couldn't keep the little mite and to take it away. Her father would have disinherited her if he'd known about it − as if the poor man didn't have enough to worry about with her involved in the suffragette movement.' George paused a moment, holding his head and wincing before continuing, 'Worse was, she also believed in this free love business, but she kept that from him too, according to Aunt Ethel. He was a High Anglican and that would have been a step too far for him.'

Jeanette could not help but be fascinated by the story. 'Was the baby born in Walton gaol?'

'No, Manchester. Ethel was a prison wardress there at the time Lavinia Crawshaw went into labour.'

Jeanette moistened her lips. 'Do you believe her, Dad? I find it incredible that she tells you all this out of the blue.'

'It was seeing Lavinia Crawshaw's death in the *Echo*. It brought it all back to her. Now she's got it into her head that Grace is Lavinia's daughter, and I know why − she's convinced there's money in it!'

A flabbergasted Jeanette stared at him in silence, and several seconds ticked by before she said, 'Surely she's mistaken. She'd need more proof than me having green eyes to convince a lawyer that I'm Lavinia's granddaughter. The birth was kept secret, wasn't it? We'd have to produce a birth certificate with Lavinia's and Mam's name on it and there isn't one, is there?'

'Not that I know of.' He rubbed the back of his neck and

muttered, 'Aunt Ethel has a bee in her bonnet over this, and if there's money I'd like you to have it.'

'Heck, Dad, I can't believe that she's almost got you convinced!'

The kettle began to whistle and Jeanette made tea and toast. Her hands were trembling and she was thinking that it was like something out of a book or a film. It just couldn't be true! If her mother had been the baby in question, surely she would have grown to look a bit like Lavinia, and Ethel would have noticed a similarity between them when Grace had married George.

Another thought occurred to her as she sat opposite her father. 'You say Aunt Ethel took the baby away as soon as it was born because she was told to do so by Lavinia Crawshaw. I hate to say this, Dad, but I think I know a different side to her than you, as do Sam and Hester.' She took a deep breath. 'I'd be more inclined to believe that she'd have dumped the baby and let it die.'

George's lips tightened and he reached for his mug and gulped half the tea down. 'I'm not as blind as you seem to think,' he said grimly. 'I know she has strict rules that she feels she must abide by. She used to be forever saying that Mam spoilt me by letting me get away with this, that and the other, and she made up for it by making sure you lot toed the line. But Aunt Ethel wouldn't stoop to murdering an innocent baby. Lavinia Crawshaw was not the first woman to give birth in the prison hospital, you know. Apparently a number of mothers did so, and some kept their children because they had husbands, whilst some unmarried ones were allowed to keep their babies with them for a short time and then they were taken away for adoption. Lavinia Crawshaw had money, so apparently she told Aunt Ethel to hire a wet nurse for the child and see she was looked after. Ethel knew an organization that housed unmarried mothers and their babies until the children were weaned, so she got in touch with them.' George reached for a slice of toast and crunched into it.

'You mean Barnardo's?'

'No, it was a Church of England home. Once the baby was weaned, the mother was free to leave and the child was placed in the Home for Waifs and Strays up the coast in Formby.'

Jeanette's fingernails dug into the palms of her hands. 'That's not so far away. We could go there and find out what happened to her.'

'It's not that simple, Jeannie. Those in charge at the home aren't going to give away the identity of the couple that took the child in. Grace told me that she ran away because she was unhappy with them – but was she telling me the truth?' George finished his tea and toast before leaning back in the chair and closing his eyes.

Jeanette wanted to ask him more questions, but he looked so tired and she was worried about that knock on his head. She should never have badgered him about this business with Lavinia Crawshaw. 'You rest, Dad. This can wait,' she murmured.

George opened his eyes. 'No, let's get it over with. Next question.'

Jeanette hesitated. 'Was Mam legally adopted? I remember reading somewhere that families often just took a child in and cared for it when a mother died or could not cope with an extra mouth to feed. There was no law protecting such children for years. What if she was Lavinia's daughter and because Lavinia had money she was able to have a say in who looked after her child? What if Mam knew who her mother was and was deeply hurt because she had given her away.'

'No, she told me that she believed herself to be the couple's natural child. The trouble came when she went for a job. Some companies insist on seeing a birth certificate for proof of age. How would you feel if you discovered the people you believed to be your parents weren't related to you? Whichever way you look at it, Jeannie, legally adopted or not, Grace was angry, hurt and rebellious.'

Jeanette gnawed on her lip. 'So she went off the rails and ended up living rough. In that case we have no way of finding out if she was Lavinia Crawshaw's baby or not.'

'No,' said George, his head drooping.

Jeanette said no more, but could not help considering how different her future would be if it could be proved that she was Lavinia Crawshaw's granddaughter.

'Even after all this time, I miss your mother,' said George. 'Having you around has helped me get over her loss, but sooner or later you'll meet a nice young man and get married and I'll be stuck here with Aunt Ethel. I had thought about trying to solve the mystery once I retire, but . . .' His voice trailed off.

Jeanette debated whether she should tell him the truth about why she had wanted the photo of her mother, but decided he might find the thought too disturbing right now. Instead she said, 'Aunt Ethel is not going to be here forever, Dad. Anyway, if I can't find Mr Right, I won't be getting married.' She brushed crumbs from her chin.

'What about the one who was hit with the bicycle chain, have you given up all hope of seeing him again?'

She shrugged and, getting to her feet, said, 'Not completely. Is there anything else I can do for you, Dad?'

'No, Jeannie. I'll just sit here for a while and rest.'

'OK. I'll leave you in peace. I've a library book I want to finish.'

To Jeanette's annoyance, when she reached her bedroom she found Ethel sitting on her bed reading *Prisons and Prisoners*. 'What are you doing, Aunt Ethel? I hope you haven't lost my place.'

Ethel looked up at her with an odd expression on her wrinkled face. 'Lady Constance says we were kind to her. Must have gone wrong there.' She dropped the book on the bed. 'If you were looking for a mention of your maternal grandmother, then don't bother. I do believe Lavinia Crawshaw must have asked for her name to be kept out of it. She caught religion, no doubt because she wanted forgiveness for her sins after her father died of a stroke when she was imprisoned for a fourth time.'

Jeanette sat down on the other side of the bed to the old woman. 'How is it you're talking so freely about this to me now?'

Ethel smiled grimly. 'You mentioned suffragettes, so I reckoned you already knew something. Did your mother ever say anything to you about her being adopted?'

'Of course not! I was only a little girl when she vanished,

if you remember. You're not going to be able to prove anything, so there's no way you're going to make money out of me.' Jeanette picked up her library book and flicked over the pages until she reached where she had marked her place.

Ethel fixed her great-niece with a baleful glare. 'You always have to think the worst of me. It's you I want the money for.'

'Thousands might believe you, Aunt Ethel, but I don't. You've never liked me and now because of the death of a woman I've never heard of until recently, you're saying you want to help me claim an inheritance. Well, I'm not going to play ball, even if you come up with a way of proving the whole thing. And, as my mother is missing, I don't see how you can do that.'

'She left a note.'

For a moment Jeanette thought she had not heard right. 'What did you say?'

Ethel chomped on her lower lip. 'Grace left a note.'

Jeanette felt a surge of anger. 'I don't believe you. You'd have never kept it secret from Dad and me.'

'Why not? I could have just wanted to keep you guessing.'

'You called her a whore and said that she had run off with a man! A note would have proved you were right. I think you're going doolally in your old age and making this up.'

Ethel flushed. 'Believe what you like, but it's true. I destroyed the note. I didn't want George hurt.'

'That remark doesn't hold water. If you didn't want him hurt you'd have never spoken of your suspicions that she'd run off with someone else.'

'Your mother's alive. I just feel it in my bones. She left a note and I destroyed it.'

'Rubbish!'

Ethel smirked and folded her arms across her chest. 'You're starting to have your doubts, aren't you?'

'No,' said Jeanette fiercely. 'You've never given me reason to trust you to tell the truth about my mother.'

Ethel poked Jeanette in the chest. 'I've helped rear you, haven't I? You haven't turned out too bad, although you have far too much to say for yourself. George is too soft with you.'

Jeanette drew back. 'Don't poke me! One day I'll retaliate and forget you're an old woman and you'll be sorry!'

Ethel's expression turned ugly. 'Who d'you think you are to threaten me? Your mother was just the same.'

'I heard you used to row. Was that why she walked out – because she couldn't put up with you any more?'

Ethel did not answer immediately, but she was obviously struggling with her emotions from the way she was biting her lips and clenching her hands. 'She threatened me, told me to get out!'

Jeanette's eyes narrowed. 'So what did you do? Follow her and bash her over the head then hide her body where nobody would think of looking for it?'

Ethel flinched. 'You think you're so clever! Well, let me tell you this, girl. She didn't care a bugger about you.'

'You'd like me to believe that, but I don't because Hester and Sam don't.'

'You'll never know the truth unless you find her, so why don't you get looking for her?'

'Just to please you, you old witch! You can get lost,' said Jeanette, her green eyes glinting with anger as she walked out of the room.

Ethel shambled after her and, as Jeanette reached the top of the stairs, seized her by the hair. 'Don't you call me an old witch! You come back here,' she snarled.

'Will you let go of my hair!' cried Jeanette, fearing that if she struggled too much, they'd topple down the stairs.

There was the sound of heavy footsteps below and the next moment George shouted, 'What the hell d'you think you're doing, Ethel? You just let her go!' He started up the stairs.

Jeanette felt Ethel's grip tighten. The pain was excruciating and, reaching up, she attempted to prise her great-aunt's fingers from her hair. They swayed backwards and forwards and for a moment Jeanette thought they were both going to fall down the stairs, but then she became aware of her father acting as a bulwark a couple of steps below. He reached over her and seconds later the pain lessened in her scalp and she was free.

'Thanks, Dad,' she gasped.

George eased her past him and told her to go downstairs

and put some coal on the fire. She hurried to the foot of the stairs and then turned and looked up to see what was happening.

'Don't you ever do that again to her!' roared George, gripping Ethel's arm. 'It's not in the rule book and you could have both been killed, you stupid old cow!'

'But . . . but she gave me cheek,' protested Ethel, shrinking back from him.

'I bet you provoked her! Why can't you accept that you can't always have your own way in this house. Any more of this behaviour and you're out.'

'You wouldn't,' said Ethel, blinking rapidly. 'I'm . . . I'm an old woman and where would I go?'

'The old people's home on Belmont Road,' said George.

Ethel drew in her breath with a hiss and Jeanette waited for the explosion of words. She was as shocked and surprised as her great-aunt by her father's threat and yet, at the same time, she was elated. 'This family have never appreciated all I've done for it,' shrieked Ethel.

'That works two ways,' snapped George. 'It's time you showed some gratitude for what you have here. Now why don't you go and rest on your bed? It hasn't done you any good attending that funeral.'

She sniffed. 'Perhaps I will go and rest, but it's cold up there.' She glanced down the stairs and saw Jeanette standing there. 'Jeannie, you fill me a hot-water bottle. I think I've caught a chill standing at your grandmother's graveside.'

Jeannie bit back a swear word. 'You don't give up, do you? I'll fill you a hotty because I want you to stay up there. But you can blinking forget about my being Lavinia Crawshaw's granddaughter because you're never going to be able to prove it!' She hurried into the kitchen and put on the kettle. She couldn't wait to tell Hester about all that had happened since she had arrived home that evening. She would be as thrilled as she was that the worm had turned at last and their dad had told the old witch just where to get off. Could be that bang on the head had affected him. She only hoped that he wouldn't have any more damaging side effects.

Fifteen

As Hester pedalled along Breck Road and turned at the church on the corner, she was thinking back to Sunday evening when Ally had seen her home. She wondered when she would hear from him again and wished that Wendy had not had to finish work after she married. She would have to arrange with her to meet up in a fortnight or so in order to catch up on each other's news. No doubt Wendy would have something to say about Ally, but she was bound to mention Cedric and ask whether Hester had seen him since the wedding.

She hadn't done so, but whilst she was out earlier that day, he had left a telephone message for her, suggesting that they meet on Tuesday outside the Forum cinema at seven thirty. Her first instinct had been to return his call straightaway and tell him that she couldn't make it due to work commitments, but she had been unable to use the telephone. Even if it had not slipped her mind later she would not have had time to try again. Besides, she was more interested in a poster on the notice board advertising a weekend conference on the 'Psychology of the Murderer'. Apparently there were still a few places available and one of the speakers was her favourite crime writer; the venue was also in the Clitheroe area, not far from where she had been evacuated, and what clinched it for her was the opportunity to arrange to visit Myra whilst she was up there.

The front lamp on her bicycle lit up the gate post and she slowed to a halt. As she wheeled the bicycle up the path, she caught sight of someone silhouetted in the parlour window. From the shape of the outline she guessed it was Jeanette. A few moments later her supposition was proved right as her half-sister opened the front door.

'You're home at last,' whispered Jeanette. 'I've been waiting ages for you to come in.'

Hester's sharp ears caught the note of suppressed excitement in her voice. 'What's up?' she asked, accepting Jeanette's help to lift her bicycle over the step and into the lobby.

'First, Dad was hit on the head during a demonstration but he didn't go to the hospital. There's no need for you to worry,' she added hastily, hearing the sound of Hester's breath catching in her throat. 'He's OK. Better than OK, actually, because he threatened Aunt Ethel with banishment to the old people's home in Belmont Road if she didn't behave herself. He's gone to bed and is sleeping.'

A weary Hester said, 'Well, that's good to hear, but does he mean it? What did she do?'

'She only nearly killed me.'

Hester's gloved hands slipped on the handlebars. 'What did she do?' she repeated, aghast.

Jeanette grabbed the bicycle and leaned it against the wall. 'Come into the kitchen and I'll tell you.'

'You're OK, obviously,' said Hester, accepting a helping hand to shrug out of her greatcoat. She tossed her hat on the hook above and headed for the kitchen. 'I take it there's no supper?'

'I thought you'd have eaten in the canteen. D'you know what time it is?'

Hester yawned and sat down. 'It seems ages ago since then and I've cycled home and worked up an appetite.'

'Then I'll boil you an egg,' said Jeanette, taking one from the bowl on the windowsill. 'The old witch nearly scalped me bald, as well as pushing me down the stairs. Fortunately Dad came thundering to the rescue.'

Hester expressed her horror and said, 'She's losing her marbles. I've been called in on a few domestics, and what you've told me is as bad as any between a married couple.'

'Thank God I'm not married to her,' said Jeanette, grinning. 'But I've more to tell you.'

Over supper, Jeanette told Hester what she had found out about Lavinia Crawshaw as well as everything else that had happened that evening. Hester stared at her with growing incredulity. 'She has definitely flipped her lid if you ask me.'

Oddly, Jeanette felt a vague disappointment. 'You don't think there could be any truth in it?'

Hester spluttered as she took a mouthful of cocoa and had

to pause to mop up the mess before saying, 'You can't believe her! I mean . . . wait a mo, what is it precisely you're asking? About your mother leaving a note or whether she's the illegitimate daughter of Lavinia Crawshaw?'

Jeanette said slightly dreamily, 'There's something to be said for being the granddaughter of one of the suffragettes. She must have had guts to be prepared to go to prison for her beliefs.'

'I wouldn't deny it, but she must also have been one of those suffragettes who resorted to violence to be put in prison four times. Anyway, setting that aside, the conclusion you have already reached is that a pair of green eyes doesn't constitute proof.'

Jeanette blinked and sighed. 'OK. So the note . . . do you believe Mam left one?'

'No.' Hester sipped her cocoa. 'Now let's forget all this and just hope Dad will have no further ill effects from that clout on the head. It's time you were in bed. Are you working in the morning?'

Jeanette nodded and rose to her feet. 'Any news of Cedric?'

Hester stood up. 'He telephoned the station and left a message.'

'Did he want you to meet him?'

'On Tuesday outside the Forum,' said Hester. 'I was going to telephone and say I couldn't make it.'

'Oh! Has this anything to do with the soldier you met at the wedding?'

'You could say he has something to do with it, although he's gone back to his unit and I'm not sure when I'll see him. We had planned to meet again.'

'So what are you going to do? Just not turn up at the meeting place? I'm sure Cedric will get the message.'

'That would be bad manners,' murmured Hester. 'Maybe I'll meet him this one last time and tell him it's over.'

'He'll want to know why,' said Jeanette. 'Are you going to tell him the truth?'

Hester shrugged. 'I'll play it by ear.'

Jeanette hoped that all would go well with the new bloke, and then put Hester's affairs out of her mind, thinking instead whether she should do anything more to discover what had happened to her mother. Should she put a notice in the *Echo*? Maybe it would be best to wait. Having made that decision she went to bed.

'Those sticky buns look nice,' said a familiar voice.

Jeanette turned back to the counter and stared at Maggie. 'Hello! You on your own?'

'What does it look like?' said Maggie, shrugging slender shoulders clad in a woollen check coat with a fur collar.

Jeanette looked behind the other girl to the jukebox and was pleased to see Irene with a black-haired youth. 'I see Irene's here. Who's the lad she's with?'

'Tonio Gianelli. They've known each other since they were in nursery together. His stepmother organized one in her house during the war and for a while after.'

'I've heard of his stepmother! She's the sister of a priest I know.'

'Father Callaghan!' Maggie nodded her head sagely. 'Tonio was actually born in Italy but his father's half-English. Tonio has a gorgeous voice and plays the guitar. His stepmother plays the piano and his father sings. They're a real musical family and attend the opera at Verona when they go over to Italy. She has a much younger half-brother living there. My cousin Betty will be visiting them when she studies art next year.'

'How lovely! No twins meeting you here today?'

'They're both busy.' Maggie rested her elbows on the counter.

'So what can I get you?' asked Jeanette, knowing that Peggy was going to be disappointed.

'I'll have three buns, two coffees and one tea,' said Maggie.

'You're not watching your weight today then?' asked Jeanette.

Maggie froze. 'What does that mean?'

'Nothing.'

'So you're not saying I've put on weight?'

'No! You've got a good figure. You have nothing to worry about. Go and sit down and I'll bring your order over.'

Maggie did not budge, but watched Jeanette as she executed the order. 'You've met our Betty, haven't you?'

Jeanette nodded.

'How did you find her?'

'OK!' Jeanette's face lit up. 'I've found out something that you could pass on to her if you would.'

'What's that?'

'My half-sister, Hester Walker, remembers her half-sister, Emma, from when she was evacuated to Whalley during the war.'

Maggie stared at her. 'You're kidding!'

'No. Hester attended the same school as her whilst she was living with a couple called Jones. I think the woman was called Myra.'

'I'll tell her.' Maggie turned away and went over to a table by the window. Jeanette watched a moment, aware with half her mind of the jukebox playing Rosemary Clooney singing 'This Ole House' as Irene and Tonio joined Maggie.

Immediately Maggie began to talk to Tonio whilst Irene gazed out of the window with a moody expression on her face. When Jeanette went over with their order, she asked after Jimmy.

A fleeting smile crossed Irene's face. 'He's OK, just been making me feel a bit of a heel. Mam wants us all to go to her brother's house for Christmas this year, but Betty has asked me to a party at her flat on Christmas night. Mam hasn't been well lately and he thinks I should do what she wants and go with them. I'm really torn. He knows that Betty will probably be in Italy next Christmas, so this one is special.' She sighed. 'I suppose it'll all sort itself out.'

'Can't you do both?'

'No, if we visit my uncle's it'll mean driving there and staying overnight. Anyway, what are you doing for Christmas?' she asked brightly.

'Nothing special that I know of,' replied Jeanette. 'Like millions of other women I'll be helping get dinner on the table.' She placed the bill on a saucer on the Formica table top and walked away, wishing her life was a bit more exciting.

She was glad when the afternoon came to an end and wasted no time in pocketing her wages, putting on her outdoor clothes and leaving the milk bar. There was a sharp wind blowing as she turned the corner into Renshaw Street and hurried down to Quiggins, hoping she would find Peggy's brother, Marty, in the shop.

She pushed open the door and immediately recognized him, despite his having his back to her. He was of stocky build and had a shock of blond hair that was styled in the fashionable Tony Curtis cut. She cleared her throat and he turned to face her.

'Can I—' He paused and stared hard at her from pale blue eyes. 'I've seen you before. Aren't you our Peggy's mate from work who got her into trouble?'

'I didn't get her into trouble,' retorted Jeanette indignantly, remembering catching sight of him the evening Peggy had damaged her foot at the Grafton. 'It was that mate of the bloke she was going out with that caused the trouble. Anyway, that's water under the bridge now.'

'Let's hope so. What can I do for you?'

'I want you to give Peggy a message.'

He rested an elbow on the counter, placed his chin in his hand and smiled. 'What kind of message, kid?'

'I want her to meet me outside Reece's at seven o'clock this evening.'

His expression sharpened. 'Why? Where are you going?'

She sighed. 'It's really none of your business.'

'Are you meeting fellas and going to the dance there?'

'No!'

His eyes narrowed. 'I don't know if I believe you.'

'I'm telling you the truth. We'll probably just go to the pictures. I'm not saying I wouldn't prefer going out dancing with a couple of fellas,' she mused, 'but there you are, Robert Taylor and Tony Curtis can't make it tonight.'

He smiled unexpectedly as he straightened up. 'I can see why you were at the centre of a fight. You have spunk. Are you doing anything next Friday night?'

'What!' Jeanette could not believe her ears. 'Are you asking me out?'

'What's wrong with that? Think you're too good for me?'

'No, but I'm a Proddy, you know.'

'So? I'm not planning on marrying you. My ma would have a fit if I brought a Protestant girl home.'

'Good.' She hesitated. 'I'd rather not go out with you, thank you.'

'Then I won't pass on your message to our Peggy.'

She gasped. 'But that's blackmail.'

'Not really. It's just an exchange of favours. I've a couple of tickets for the Stadium to see the wrestling, but me and my girlfriend have had a row and now she's sent me a message saying she's going with someone else.'

Jeanette's eyebrows shot up. 'You take your girl to the wrestling?'

'Why not? She loves it.'

'But surely it's all men shouting and swearing at two blokes knocking the hell out of each other?'

He grinned. 'It's true there is some of that, but quite a few women attend. They really enjoy it and call the wrestlers names I wouldn't repeat in front of me ma. Still, you can always close your ears.'

'I didn't say I was going.'

'No, but give it a try. It'll be a new experience for you,' he said coaxingly. 'Besides, I'd like Bernie to see me with a pretty girl on me arm.'

Jeanette could not help but be flattered and amused. 'Do you really think I'm pretty enough to make her jealous?'

'I wouldn't say it if it weren't true, but you're in no danger of me making a pass at you. I told you, Ma wouldn't like it.'

Jeanette chuckled. 'Is that a promise?'

'Cross my heart and hope to die.' He sketched a cross on his chest.

'Who's wrestling?'

He looked taken aback. 'You wouldn't know if I told you and I don't want to put you off.'

'Dirty Jack Pye?' she asked.

His blond eyebrows shot up. 'I'm impressed, kid.'

'I saw his name in the *Echo*.'

'Rightio. I'll meet you outside Exchange Station at six o'clock on Friday.'

She tapped her fingers on the counter. 'That means I'll have to come straight from work. I'm going to be hungry.'

'So will I. I'll take you for a bite to eat so you won't starve to death.' He held her gaze. 'Now don't go mentioning it to our Peggy. She's got a big mouth and I don't want her telling Bernie it's a set-up to make her jealous. She likes Bernie.'

'OK.' Jeanette would probably have mentioned it to Peggy if he hadn't asked her not to. 'I'll see you then.'

He came from behind the counter, opened the door for her with a flourish and bowed her out. She could not help smiling as she hurried along Renshaw Street. It did not bother her in the least that she was only being taken out in order to make another girl jealous. It would be an experience going to the wrestling, and at least Marty had a sense of humour.

A few hours later Jeanette arrived outside Reece's in Clayton Square to find Peggy already waiting for her. 'So no twins,' she said.

'So your Marty gave you my message,' said Jeanette.

'Of course, otherwise I wouldn't be here,' said Peggy. 'But I've got a message for you.'

'Who from?' asked Jeanette, slipping her arm through her friend's.

'Father Callaghan.'

Jeanette's stomach began to churn. 'Is it about my mother?'

'No, it's about that bloke you fancied from the chippy who got hit with the bicycle chain,' said Peggy in a rush.

'Oh!' Jeanette's heart lifted.

'Is that all you can say – oh!' said Peggy, pulling a face. 'Apparently his mother and her sister are going to share an apartment here in Liverpool and should have moved in by Christmas.'

Jeanette waited for her to say something more and continued to wait with growing impatience. 'Is that it?' she asked.

'Sorry, my mind drifted,' she said mischievously. 'You were right about David Jones being a seaman.'

Jeanette's face lit up. 'I thought I was. Did Father Callaghan tell you the name of his ship and when it'll dock next?'

'No, but he said it docks in Liverpool regularly.'

'That could mean a week, a month or every three months or more,' murmured Jeanette.

'At least you know he'll be back,' said Peggy, and changed the subject. 'So where are we going? The flicks?'

Jeanette nodded. But for the rest of the evening she had difficulty concentrating on anything other than the thought of David Jones coming to Liverpool. She wished he had written her a note, but maybe he hadn't had time. She would just have to be patient and wait until she heard from the priest again.

When she arrived home, she walked in on Sam and Hester having a low-voiced conversation in the kitchen. They stopped as soon as they realized she was there.

'Cocoa, you two?' she asked. Without waiting for their answer, she set about making a jug of cocoa. 'You can carry on talking. Interesting conversation, was it?'

'Don't be nosey,' said Sam.

'Is it about Dorothy? When's she coming for dinner?'

Sam scowled. 'She's away a lot.'

'I thought you said she was going to be back in Liverpool this week.'

'She's been and gone and spent half the time talking to women and about this film she wants to make. I feel as if she's no time for me. She's obsessed.'

'Poor Sam,' said Jeanette sympathetically. 'We can all get obsessed at times. Some might think I've been obsessed by David Jones and finding out what happened to my mam.'

'I wouldn't say you were that obsessed,' said Hester. 'Anyway, I've just been telling Sam about the old witch trying to kill you. He reckons we should put her in the cellar for a week on bread and water.'

'Don't forget the birch,' said Sam, visibly relaxing. 'At least ten whacks should finish her off.'

'If only,' said Jeanette. 'But that wasn't what you were talking about earlier, I reckon. Well, you don't have to tell me.' She stared at them hopefully but they were not to be drawn, so as soon as she had made the cocoa and a hot-water bottle, she went up to bed.

Sam and Hester exchanged glances. 'We should have said that we were going to book the old witch into a cosy cell and throw away the key,' said Hester, her hands cupped around her mug.

'It could be arranged,' said Sam, his eyes glinting. 'We could tell dear old Aunt Ethel that it was for the film Dorothy has in mind to produce and direct.'

Hester looked surprised. 'You are joking? How often is a woman given the opportunity to take charge like that?'

He shrugged. 'I tell her that, but she gets all tight-lipped and says she's got to give it a go. Let's get back to what we were talking about before Jeanette walked in. You've got to cancel your date with Cedric.'

'It's too late! I'll meet him and explain that I can't see him again.' Hester scowled. 'Fancy him asking our Jeanette to go to the pictures with him. She should have told me at the time.'

'She thought you'd be hurt. It was bloody odd of him, though, wasn't it?'

Hester agreed, thinking she couldn't wait to dump him.

Tuesday evening was cold and damp and Hester was feeling far more nervous than she liked to admit as she stood waiting for Cedric to arrive. When she eventually caught sight of him, her heart began to thud but she pinned on a smile as he approached and said, 'Hello, long time no see!'

He returned her smile. 'It does seem a long time, doesn't it? You look as if you're bursting with health now, though.'

'I'm as fit as a fiddle,' said Hester. 'You?'

'I'm as you see me,' he said, spreading his arms. 'A gift to a woman!'

She thought, *he really is extremely handsome, but he sure as hell knows it.*

He dropped his arms and took hold of her hand. 'How was the wedding? I was sorry I couldn't make it.'

She allowed her hand to lie limp within his grasp. 'Yes, it was a shame you couldn't be there. It was really enjoyable and the bride looked lovely.'

'Perhaps another time,' he said smoothly. 'But weekends aren't good for me. Mother's still ailing. Shall we go inside?'

Liar! thought Hester. She was about to make some excuse as to why she couldn't go into the cinema with him, but he was pulling her up the steps and before she knew it she was inside the foyer. She was reluctant to make a fuss, surrounded as they were by a bustling crowd. Finishing with him was going to have to wait.

Once inside the auditorium and settled in their seats, she

felt as tense as a coiled spring. When the lights dimmed and the title of the supporting film came up, his arm went about her shoulders and he nuzzled her neck. She stiffened, wanting to shrink from his embrace. She could not help comparing her feelings towards him now with how she felt about Ally.

'What's wrong with you?' he whispered in her ear.

'I want to watch the film. I thought you would, too. It's an Edgar Lustgarten real-life murder case.'

His hands, which had begun to wander, stilled, and to her relief he drew away from her. For the rest of the film he kept his distance, although she was aware that several times he glanced her way. She did her utmost to keep her eyes firmly fixed on the screen.

It was during the interlude when he returned with ice creams for both of them that he mentioned the conference. 'I don't know if you've seen the poster about the "Psychology of the Murderer", but I thought you might like to go with me.'

Hester's heart began to thud in that uncomfortable fashion again and she thought swiftly. 'I have, but my brother says that there's something big coming up and I'll be needed.'

Cedric frowned. 'That's a shame. I thought it would be the perfect opportunity for us to get to know each other better.'

'Work has to come first.'

'Sure,' he said in clipped tones, 'although I would have thought it right up your street.'

'It is, although I'm surprised at you considering going away for the weekend — what with your mother to worry about,' she said, interested to see what answer he would come up with.

'For something special like this conference, I would have arranged for a neighbour to look after her.'

'What a shame you couldn't have made a similar arrangement and come to my friend's wedding,' said Hester sweetly. 'That was special to me and could have made a lot of difference to how I feel now.'

He stared at her. 'Are you criticizing me?'

'I wouldn't dare,' she murmured.

'What d'you mean by that?' he asked sharply.

She spooned up the last of her ice cream. 'Some men can't take criticism.'

'I know what this is about. You're bloody annoyed with me because I didn't want to go to your friend's farting little wedding,' he said, an ugly expression on his face as he noisily spooned out the melting remains in the cardboard tub.

His crude remark angered her further and she found herself ignoring the people glancing in their direction. 'It was a lovely wedding and if you want to know, I met someone there with much better manners than you.' She stood up. 'Goodnight, Cedric. I don't think we'll be meeting again.' She picked up her coat from the back of her seat and, smiling down at the woman in the next seat, asked her to excuse her. Without a word, the woman made room for her to ease past.

'Hey, you can't leave just like that!' hissed Cedric, grabbing Hester's arm, his fingers biting into her skin through the fabric of her sleeve. 'You've got some explaining to do.'

She wrenched herself free. 'Oh, can't I? Enjoy the film.' With her coat bunched under her arm, she squeezed past people until she reached the aisle.

As she made for the exit, the lights began to dim. She glanced back to where she had been sitting and saw Cedric staring after her. He mouthed something but she could not read his lips. No doubt it was something rude. Once in the foyer, she donned her coat, conscious of a pulse beating in her ears. She had finished with him, thank God! Sam and Jeanette would have been proud of her.

Sixteen

Jeanette was trying to imagine Liverpool having clean air as she stood outside the Exchange railway station, muffled up to the eyeballs because it was freezing cold. The weather had been terrible that week, but the smog in London had been so bad that more people than usual had died. All the headlines in the newspapers were about the Government passing a Clean Air Act. But at least Liverpool was fog free.

Seeing a bobby walking along the pavement towards her

immediately reminded her of her father and what he might say if he were to discover that she was planning on attending a wrestling match. He wouldn't like it one little bit. As for Aunt Ethel, she would act as if her great-niece had committed all of the seven deadly sins. She prayed Marty would not be much longer. The bobby passed her by. If only Marty would hurry up and come!

'Been waiting long?'

Jeanette almost jumped out of her skin and turned hastily to see her date standing a couple of feet behind her wearing a trilby and overcoat. 'You frightened the life out of me.'

'I spoke to you twice but you didn't appear to hear me the first time,' he said, hunching his shoulders. 'You were in another world.'

'I was thinking.' She sighed heavily. 'It's blinking cold standing here. The wind from the Mersey comes tearing up, cold enough to freeze your socks off.'

'Stop moaning! We'll soon get you warm. A nice steamy, smoky pub that sells Scouse pies and mushy peas and a decent pint is what you need,' said Marty, taking her arm.

'I'm under age,' said Jeanette, alarmed.

'That's OK. I won't force you to drink alcohol. It's not as if I want to have my wicked way with you.'

She gasped. 'Don't joke! I've persuaded myself that you can be trusted.'

He laughed. 'You think I'd mess around with my sister's best friend! Stop worrying, luv. I've my eye on another and you're going to help me get her back.'

'This is daft,' said Jeanette as they walked in the direction of Old Hall Street. 'I don't know why I came. I could have got away with not coming.'

He stopped and stared at her. 'We had an agreement and you coming was part of the bargain. What's there to complain about? You're not going to have to spend a penny. Grub and entertainment free, so relax and enjoy yourself, kid.'

She realized he was right and smiled. 'OK! I have to be home by eleven, though.'

'We'll leave before all the bouts are over if necessary.' He pushed back his trilby. 'Now, food. I'm starving!'

She was hungry, too, so did not dither when he led her into a pub. But she clung to his arm when she realized she was the focus of more pairs of men's eyes than she cared for. 'Don't be worrying,' he said. 'No one's going to jump on you while I'm here. Now grab a table and sit down while I see to the grub.' He removed her hand from his arm and left her alone.

She chose a table over by a window with a view of the entrance and once seated took a folded magazine from her bag and pretended to read it.

'I got you a small lemonade,' said Marty, placing a glass in front of her.

'Thanks.' She glanced at him over the magazine and reached for the glass of lemonade. 'So tell me about this Bernie you're going out with.'

'She's a cracker, but has a temper. I have a temper, too, but have better control of it, thanks to me dad. She's the youngest of ten and spoilt rotten. But I'll tame her once we're married.'

'Tame her? Haven't you ever heard that women are equal to men? We fought for the vote!'

He gave a cheeky grin. 'Just teasing. All you need to do is behave as if I'm the best thing since sliced bread,' said Marty, taking a mouthful of ale.

'I don't like sliced bread. I like the crusty kind from the bakery that you can cut nice and thick.'

'OK, I'm a crusty slice of bakery bread and you want to take a bite out of me,' said Marty.

Jeanette giggled. 'I'm that hungry I would take a bite out of you if you were a loaf.'

Marty grinned. 'Well, the food won't be long coming, so control yourself, girl.'

He was right. Within minutes their meal arrived and soon they were tucking into a plate of Scouse pie and mushy peas. She thought food had never tasted so good and it was soon gone.

'I enjoyed that,' she said, wiping her fingers with her handkerchief. 'Do we go now?'

'In a minute. I'd like time to smoke a ciggie and then we'll be on our way.'

Once inside the Stadium, the noise was so tremendous she decided it would be a waste of time trying to make conversation, so she just sat there, watching what Marty was doing and waiting for the action to begin.

'There she is,' he said suddenly in her ear.

Oh hell! thought Jeanette, feeling her stomach turn over. She hoped that she wasn't going to throw up. 'Where?' she croaked.

'Don't look, don't look,' he said. 'Bloody hell, what's she doing with him?'

'Who's she with?' asked Jeanette, looking around wildly.

While she was trying to see whom Mary was referring to, unexpectedly she spotted Billy, whom she had believed was in Borstal, sitting between a couple of blokes. 'What's he doing here?' she gasped.

'Who?' asked Marty.

'That Billy who started the fight in the chip shop and hit David Jones in the face with a bicycle chain.'

'Oh him! His dad was drunk and fell in a dock. They pulled him out dead. His mam immediately put on a grieving act and said she needed her son home. They let him out for the funeral and to help her with the arrangements, but if he dirties his nose, he'll be for prison, I bet.'

She cast a surreptitious look at Billy and for a moment she thought he saw her and she immediately ducked her head. The last thing she wanted was for him to notice her. She wished fervently that she'd had more sense than to agree to come here with Peggy's brother.

'What are you doing?' shouted Marty. 'Keep your head up and look at me like I was that crust you're hungering for. She's spotted us!'

Jeanette felt her hair being pulled and her head was jerked upright. 'That hurts!' she cried.

There was a sudden roar that drowned out his words but she read his lips. 'Smile, honey bunch,' he commanded.

She smiled.

After that she almost relaxed. The crowd's attention, including Marty's, was centred on the boxing ring, which was not a ring at all but a square, which made Jeanette wonder why it was so misnamed. But she soon forgot such things and even Billy's presence was pushed to the back of her mind as the wrestlers did what they did best, whilst the crowd roared, groaned and whistled, and the women nearest the ring catcalled, insulted and advised the competitors what to do to each other as they slammed bodies onto the canvas or got their opponent into dangerous-looking headlocks. Jeanette had never felt so exhilarated, whilst at the same time she was on pins and wanting to get out of there.

'Enjoying yourself?' asked Marty during a lull in the proceedings.

'I'm exhausted,' said Jeanette. 'And thirsty – and what's that smell?'

'I presume you don't just mean the stench of sweat and beer but the overpowering odour of liniment and embrocation, my girl,' said Marty, grinning. 'I wonder where Bernie's gone? He's still there but I can't see her.'

Jeanette did not care where his girl had gone. She'd had enough and wanted to leave. Her watch said that it was getting on for ten. 'Listen, Marty. I think it's time I went.'

'It'll be finishing soon. Just hang on a bit longer, kid,' he coaxed. 'I'll see you onto a bus.'

Jeanette heaved a sigh. 'OK.'

'And who is this?' demanded a silky feminine voice, seemingly out of nowhere.

'Bernie, what are you doing here?' asked Marty, looking as if butter wouldn't melt in his mouth as he gazed up at her.

Jeanette looked the girl over and thought there was no accounting for taste: dyed red hair, eyelashes thick with mascara and lipstick so red it could have been blood. As for what Bernie was wearing beneath a rabbit skin coat – her Aunt Ethel would have ripped it off her back. The woman's breasts were hanging half out of a midnight-blue satin blouse.

'You knew I'd be here. I told you so,' snapped Bernie. 'Who is this . . . this person?' She leaned across him towards Jeanette and glared into her face.

On closer inspection, Jeanette realized Bernie was younger than she had first thought. 'I don't think I'm any of your business,' she said, tilting her chin.

'Oh no?' cried Bernie, and lashed out at her.

A shocked Jeanette felt the air rush over her skin as the other girl's fingernails narrowly missed their target.

Marty put an arm around Bernie's waist and yanked her backwards. 'Are you bloody daft?'

'Let me go! Let me get at her!' shrieked Bernie.

Jeanette pushed herself up out of her seat and said, 'I'm going, Marty.'

She did not wait for him to argue with her but excused herself along the row in the opposite direction to Bernie until she reached the aisle. Then, clasping her handbag to her chest, she ran for the exit. She had just passed the end of the building outside when a figure suddenly loomed up in front of her and she almost died of fright.

'So where do you think you're going, doll?' Billy grabbed hold of her shoulder and his grip was so painful she screamed. 'Shut up,' he bellowed, wrapping his arm about her throat.

She panicked and kicked backwards and caught him on the shins with the heel of her shoe. He swore and his grip tightened about her throat. She could feel herself losing consciousness. Then a voice that seemed to come from a far distance, said, 'What's going on here?'

She felt Billy's grip slacken and although her head was swimming, she managed to jerk herself free and stagger away from him. Without bothering to see who had spoken, somehow she found the strength to keep on moving. As soon as she turned the corner into Dale Street, she took to her heels. Even so, she kept glancing over her shoulder every time she heard footsteps behind her. At last she arrived at the bus stop and stood, shivering, praying her bus would come soon. When a hand suddenly seized her by the shoulder, she cried out.

'Did I give you a fright?' asked Sam, gazing down at her.

She collapsed against him. 'Am I glad to see you. Take me home, please!' she cried, bursting into tears.

Seventeen

Jeanette sat at the kitchen table, warming her hands on a mug of cocoa and trying to avoid her father's eyes. 'Sam said you were frightened but wouldn't tell him why you were in such a state, where you'd been or why you were on your own, stinking of cigarette smoke and beer,' said George.

'I haven't been smoking or drinking,' said Jeanette, rearing her head.

'So you told him, but you've been somewhere that goes on. When Aunt Ethel told me you hadn't come home from work, I presumed you'd gone to the pictures with your friend, Peggy, but that can't be right because there aren't any cinemas near Dale Street.'

'I didn't tell her that I was seeing Peggy,' said Jeanette. 'I'm going out with her tomorrow night to a dance.'

'No you're not, my girl,' said George firmly. 'You're not going anywhere until I know where you were tonight. And while we're having this little talk, I'd like to know where you go every Saturday during the day when you're not in the office or at home.'

'I work part time in a milk bar.' Jeanette gulped a mouthful of cocoa. 'Aunt Ethel takes almost all of my normal wages and I'd have scarcely anything to spend if I didn't have this extra little job.'

George took a deep breath. 'Right, I'll check that out and if you're lying to me—'

'I'm not lying!' she cried. 'Ask Hester, she's known right from the beginning because Aunt Ethel locked me in my bedroom the night before and I had to ask Hester to let me out, otherwise I wouldn't have made it in time.'

George swore beneath his breath. 'Right, now tell me what you were doing this evening.'

Jeanette hesitated. 'I was returning a favour.'

George visibly relaxed. 'Now we're getting somewhere. What kind of favour?'

'I'd asked someone to pass a message on for me and in return I said that I'd help them out. They said it would be an experience for me,' she said in a rush.

He paled. 'What kind of experience?'

Jeanette bit down on her lower lip, knowing she had said too much.

'Come on, explain, girl!' he rasped. 'What kind of experience? Do you know how many young people end up in trouble because they want to experience stuff that is bad for them?'

Her green eyes flashed. 'Don't give me that, Dad! I'm not stupid. I haven't done anything bad. I just went somewhere that I knew you wouldn't approve of and I wish I hadn't gone, but there it is, I went.' She took another mouthful of cocoa. 'Now can I go to bed? I'm shattered.'

'No you bloody well can't go to bed! I'll have you here all night until you tell me where you've been,' shouted George, slapping a large hand on the table.

She jumped and the cocoa went down the wrong way and she burst into a spasm of coughing. He swore again and got up and went round the table and banged her on the back.

'What's going on?' Hester placed a hand on her father's shoulder.

Neither had heard the front door open and Hester come in.

George removed her hand and told her to sit down. 'Why didn't you tell me that Jeannie had a part-time Saturday job?' he asked.

Hester said, 'Now calm down, Dad. It's nothing for you to get worked up about. You don't want to knock her through to next week – which you would have if you'd kept banging her on the back. It's not like you to be violent. You don't realize your own strength.'

Jeanette gulped. 'He hasn't hurt me,' she said hoarsely. 'The cocoa went down the wrong way. I'll come clean. I went to the Stadium to see the wrestling and this girl attacked me. I also saw that youth, Billy, who started the fight in the chippy, and I had such a fright. He followed me outside and had a go at me. I thought I was going to die! If it hadn't been for someone coming along, I think he might have killed me. Instead, I managed to get away and ran for my life.'

For several moments George stood silent and still, and then he reached for a chair and sat down heavily. It was Hester who asked, 'What's he doing out of Borstal?'

'Apparently his father got drunk, fell in a dock and drowned. They let Billy out for the funeral.'

Hester and her father exchanged looks. 'We'll have to get someone onto this straightaway, Dad,' she said.

He nodded. 'But let's get this cleared up first.'

'OK,' said Hester.

Both looked questioningly at Jeanette. 'I went with Marty,' she said.

'Marty. Who's Marty?' demanded George, throwing his arms in the air.

'Peggy's brother. He's OK – and she knows nothing about this. Bernie, the girl who attacked me, is his girlfriend and he was trying to make her jealous by taking me somewhere he knew she would be.' Jeanette looked at her father hopefully. Surely that explained everything and he would allow her to carry on with her part-time job and go to the dance tomorrow evening.

'He took you to the Stadium to make her jealous?' George looked as if he could not credit it. 'And she attacked you?'

'She didn't hurt me. I pulled away and got out of there fast. Up until then Marty was going to see me to the bus stop, but I didn't wait,' said Jeanette. 'I wish I had,' she added with a shiver.

Hester put an arm around her. 'I wouldn't ask any more questions, Dad. I can't see our Jeanette ever going there again.'

'It was smelly and really noisy and crowded – and just horrible,' added Jeanette as an afterthought. 'Now can I go to bed?'

'Yes, but you're not going out over the weekend. You're staying put and you can scrub the floors for Aunt Ethel,' said George in a voice that brooked no argument.

'But . . . but what about my Saturday job?' cried Jeanette, starting to her feet.

'I presume they have a telephone? You can give them a ring and tell them you won't be in,' he said.

Tears started in Jeanette's eyes and she shrugged off Hester's arm and marched out of the kitchen and upstairs. She slammed the bedroom door and then threw herself on the bed and wept.

Downstairs in the kitchen, Hester managed to restrain her father from going upstairs after Jeanette when the bedroom door slammed. 'Leave her be, Dad. She's had a terrible fright. You heard what she said – she thought she was going to die. This Billy is the one who used the bicycle chain.'

'I know that,' growled George. 'Now, is one of us going to see to his being brought in?'

She nodded. 'I'll make the call.' As she made for the door, she stopped and turned. 'Where's our Sam?'

'He had to go out again.'

She looked thoughtful but did not say anything and left her father alone. He sank down onto a chair and put his head into his hands, glad that Hester was there and a woman of such good sense.

'Our Jeanette had a lucky escape,' said Hester.

It was the following morning and she was at police head-quarters talking to Sam. He gazed at her pale face and rubbed his unshaven jaw wearily. 'Do we tell her about the stabbing or not?'

'I think we're going to have to. Her friend Peggy's brother was at the Stadium and most likely he'll be aware of what happened,' she said, slumping in the chair on the other side of his desk.

'Until the doorman comes around from the anaesthetic, we've no proof that it was Billy who did it,' said Sam.

'Surely the fact that he didn't come home last night and is still missing says something,' said Hester.

Sam nodded, knowing a watch was being kept not only on Billy's mother's house, but on that of his former mates. 'I wish I knew where the hell he was because I feel our Jeanette won't be safe until he's found.'

'He'd be a fool to go after her,' said Hester.

'I agree. But he's already shown that he lacks any self-restraint and common sense.' Sam leaned back in his chair and closed his eyes. 'Bloody hell, I'm tired.'

'You need your bed,' said Hester, getting up. 'I'm off home. I need some shut-eye myself.'

Sam opened his eyes. 'Hang on a mo! You never told me how you got on with Cedric on Tuesday.'

'I finished with him. I told him there was someone else.'

'I bet that didn't please him.'

Hester smiled. 'No, I don't think it did. Anyway, it's over.'

'Good.'

She took a deep breath. 'I feel so much better. I was thinking of dropping in on Wendy later. I'm off duty until early tomorrow morning. She just might have something to say about Ally.'

Sam grinned. 'Give her my regards.'

She nodded. 'D'you want me to tell our Jeanette about the stabbing?'

'If you would. You'll do it so much better than me. But I'll phone through to Dad at the bridewell and let him know.'

'See you later,' said Hester.

Sam nodded and reached for the telephone as she left the room.

Jeanette wiped her sweaty forehead with a damp arm, seemingly unaware of the soapy water dripping from the scrubbing brush onto her apron as she looked up at Hester. 'You don't think the man is going to die, do you?' she asked, a tremor in her voice. 'I'll feel it'll be all my fault if he does.'

'Don't be daft!' said Hester, resting her feet on the crossbars under the kitchen table as she returned Jeanette's regard. 'The person responsible is the one who stabbed him. Anyway, the man's still alive.'

'I hope he stays that way.' The scrubbing brush slipped from Jeanette's fingers and dropped into the bucket of water, splashing her front. 'I wish—'

'Wishing does no good,' said Hester briskly. 'What's happened has happened and now I'm going out and leaving you to get on with washing this floor.'

Jeanette pulled a face and fished out the scrubbing brush. 'At least Mrs Cross accepted that I couldn't go in with an upset stomach. Can't be passing on germs to the customers.'

'Too right you can't,' said Hester, getting up and carefully stepping over the wet patches of tiles onto a sheet of newspaper and another until she reached the door. 'See you later and no skiving off!' She heard her half-sister sigh as she closed the door and headed off to catch the bus to Charley and Wendy's flat.

'I'd been wondering when you'd come,' said Wendy, grabbing Hester's sleeve and pulling her inside. 'How long can you stay?' She beamed at her friend. 'Oh, I do miss you and work!'

'And we miss you,' said Hester, following her upstairs to the flat over the shop below. 'I can stay long enough to have a cup of tea and a chat. Is Charley in?'

'No, he's gone to watch Liverpool play away,' replied Wendy. 'Why, did you want to speak to him as well?'

'No, I just don't want to be interrupted,' said Hester.

'Is it police business? Because I tell you now he'd go mad if it was and he was here. He said I've got to forget all about criminals now I'm married and just concentrate on looking after him. I love the bones of him, but I'm not going to have him telling me what to do when he's not here.'

'I'm glad to hear it,' said Hester. 'Just let me get my coat off.'

'I'll put the kettle on,' said Wendy.

A quarter of an hour later the pair of them were sitting on the sofa in front of the fire with cups of tea and a plate of biscuits to hand.

'I hear you went to the flicks with Ally,' said Wendy, smiling.

'Not from him, surely?' said Hester, startled.

'No, from one of Charley's cousins. Ally's gone back to Germany. I thought he might have been in touch with you.'

'Not so far,' said Hester, 'although we did talk about meeting up again when he comes home.' She sighed. 'I really like him.'

Wendy reached for a biscuit. 'I'm glad. What about Cedric?'

'I've finished with him. I told him I'd met someone else.'

Wendy smiled. 'I'm glad. Ally's a good egg, so Charley says.'

'Hmmm! But I'm not seeing him at all right now,' said Hester forlornly. 'Even when he comes back, I don't know what will happen between us. He's considering emigrating but

I like my own country. To go so far away from my family would take some doing.'

Wendy's smile vanished. 'You're not regretting giving Cedric up, are you?'

'No! He didn't like it, though,' said Hester. 'He's a liar and I can't abide liars. He's what Charley would call a rotten egg.'

Wendy stared at her. 'Are you going to tell me why you say that?'

Hester hesitated. 'Sam told me he's under investigation. I know he's lied to me, and not only to me. But worse than that was when I had that rotten cold, he asked our Jeanette to go to the pictures with him in my place!' Her voice rose with indignation. 'Now don't you think that's definitely unacceptable behaviour? Besides, any decent caring bloke would have taken a risk and come to see how I was.'

'I'm sure Ally would have,' said Wendy. 'What did Cedric lie to you about?'

'His mother. He makes her his excuse for not being places when all the time she's dead.'

Wendy's eyes widened. 'You're joking!'

'No, honestly. When I started going out with him, our Sam made enquiries about him. He used to be a member of the Liverpool force before he went to Bootle and some of the PCs remembered him. Apparently he used to live with his mother but she died and he took time out to attend her funeral.'

'That's really, really odd,' murmured Wendy. 'Who'd lie about their mother like that?'

Hester nodded. 'Sam reckons it's to give himself an alibi.'

'How does Sam work that out? If it was checked out, it would be known his mother is dead.'

'I know! It could be he thinks nobody would check whether he has a sick old mother. He could be using her to take suspicion away from what he's doing when he's supposed to be with her.'

'Did Sam find out anything else about him?'

'Apparently he has an eye for the girls, and his beat when he was in Liverpool was the Canning Street district.'

Wendy took a deep breath. 'Seamen's Club and prostitutes.

He could have been accepting backhanders to turn a blind eye or taking advantage of what's on offer.'

Hester nodded. 'The thought had crossed my mind, although I admit I didn't want to believe it. It bothers me that my judgement was way out when I agreed to go out with him. Anyway, the ball's in Bootle division's court now.'

They were both silent for several moments. Then Hester said, 'Before I forget, I must tell you that Ally's met Cedric. Remember that accident between the bus and the car? He was the soldier who was on the scene and helped out. How's that for a coincidence?'

Wendy's eyes sparkled. 'Well, his dad and uncle lived here in Liverpool, didn't they? You could have easily bumped into Ally anywhere in town.' She dunked a fig roll into her tea. 'It seems that you and he were fated to meet. How did he react when you told him you'd been out with Cedric?'

'I don't think he was pleased, but he behaved in a civilized manner. After all, it was our very first date and he was returning to Germany. Even so, I'm sure he didn't take to Cedric – and, thinking about it, his judgement was better than mine.'

'A bit of competition makes a bloke all the keener,' said Wendy. 'You'll see – Ally'll be in touch. He obviously likes you,' she added, offering the plate of fig rolls. 'And hopefully you won't hear from Cedric ever again.'

Hester bit into a fig roll, hoping Wendy was right and remembering how Ally had said that he could easily fall in love with her. 'Ally and I both like musicals and he has a sense of humour.'

'And Cedric doesn't?' asked Wendy with a smile.

Hester rolled her eyes.

'What about your Sam and Dorothy Wilson? Are they still in touch?'

'Yes, but if it's love between them it's not going smoothly,' said Hester. 'She's away so much.'

'The woman's a fool! A gorgeous bloke like your Sam and she's not spending every second she can with him,' cried Wendy.

Hester sighed. 'I understand why you're saying that, but I like her and I think she has a right to follow her star. Even so, he could do with getting married and having a home of his own and kids.'

Wendy agreed. 'Someone has to give in and do what the other one wants if a marriage is to work.' She did not wait for Hester to come back at her about that but said, 'What about your Jeanette?'

'Our Jeanette!' Hester groaned. 'I don't know where to start with our Jeanette.' And she proceeded to tell Wendy all about the Stadium episode and their great-aunt being convinced that Jeanette was the long-lost granddaughter of a wealthy suffragette who had recently died.

Wendy laughed about the latter, but just like Hester was concerned about the attack on Jeanette and the stabbing of the doorman. 'You have to find that Billy. He's trouble with a capital T. You haven't heard the end of him. You need to keep your eye on her.'

'Can't do that all the time,' said Hester, draining her teacup. 'So tell me, how's married life treating you when Charley's not telling you what to do?'

Wendy proceeded to advocate the marital state, obviously convinced that a husband was what Hester needed to be truly content. This despite the fact that Wendy was obviously not completely fulfilled being a stay-at-home wife. Hester sighed and thought of her brother and Dorothy. She found it hard to imagine Dorothy ever willingly giving up her career for the love of Sam, and wondered why it seemed so hard for men and women to achieve a successful compromise. Was it one she would be called upon to make herself one day?

Eighteen

It was not until Monday morning that Jeanette accepted that her punishment could have been a lot worse. She might have the beginnings of housemaid's knee and her hands looked little better than wrinkled monkey's paws despite her having rubbed lemon and glycerine into them, but she still had her

Saturday job. Her father had not insisted on her giving in her notice.

And she had been able to catch up on a few things over the weekend, such as writing a rough draft of the notice she planned to put in the *Echo* about her missing mother. She had also recovered somewhat from the shock of Billy almost throttling her. The news that the doorman had recovered consciousness and been able to give the police a description of his assailant had made her feel better; she had been so worried he might die.

Hester had come with her on the bus to work, and Jeanette suspected that her half-sister would do this as often as she could until Billy was caught. They spoke scarcely at all. Hester seemed to have a lot on her mind.

When Jeanette entered the office, humming the latest hit in the pop charts, the other typist was already putting up the ships' arrivals and departures on the board. She glanced over her shoulder at Jeanette. 'You sound cheerful.'

'The fog's lifted, that's why, and it looks like the sun's going to come out.'

'That wind's sharp, though,' said Elsie, 'and have you heard about the *Royal Iris* and the *Egremont* colliding at Seacombe in the fog?'

Jeanette thought of Jimmy. 'Was anyone hurt? I know someone who works on the ferries.'

'I don't think so. It says that the boats were only slightly damaged.'

'That's a relief. Even so . . .'

Elsie stared at her. 'Even so . . . what?'

'I might nip down to the landing stage in my lunch hour and see if I can find out anything more,' said Jeanette.

The door opened even as she spoke. 'Find out about what?' asked Peggy, standing in the doorway.

Jeanette told her.

'I'll go with you. I've something I want to discuss,' said Peggy. 'See you later.'

Jeanette guessed that Peggy knew about the incident at the Stadium and her possible involvement. The dockers having returned to work a while ago, Jeanette spent a very busy morning typing out bills and letters. By the time her lunch hour arrived, she was ready for a break. She met Peggy downstairs and they headed for the river.

Jeanette did not have long to wait before her friend said, 'It's all over the neighbourhood that Billy's wanted for stabbing the doorman at the Stadium.'

'Did your Marty tell you he took me there and I saw Billy?' said Jeanette, instinctively glancing behind her at the sheer mention of her attacker's name.

A serious-faced Peggy shook her head. 'It was Bernie who told me. She turned up at our house Saturday morning, wanting to know all about you. I was really annoyed with you for not telling me anything about it, so I put her straight where you were concerned.'

'What d'you mean by that?' asked Jeanette.

Peggy smiled. 'I told her she had nothing to fear as you fancied someone else. Afterwards I spoke to our Marty and he told me it was a put-up job to make Bernie jealous, so all's well that ends well. They've kissed and made up and I wouldn't be surprised if they got engaged at Christmas.'

'Well, good luck to them both,' said Jeanette, although she almost felt sorry for Marty because Bernie had real claws.

She and Peggy walked on in silence for a few minutes before Peggy said, 'So what happened after you scarpered?'

'Billy surprised me outside the Stadium and—' Jeanette broke off abruptly, reliving those moments.

Peggy stared at her. 'You've lost your colour! You don't have to tell me what happened if it's too upsetting.'

'He attacked me! Nearly choked the life out of me,' said Jeanette rapidly. 'I managed to kick him in the shins and . . . and the . . . the doorman – I reckon he saved my life. I . . . I didn't see what happened between them because I just beat it out of there. But was I in trouble when I got home!'

'You poor thing,' said Peggy, squeezing her arm. 'But you're OK now?'

'Beyond being terrified he might attack me again? Yes.'

'He's not going to touch you,' said Peggy comfortingly. 'He knows they'd get him for it. He'll keep his head down and try and get on a boat to his relatives in Ireland if he's got any sense. He might have done that already.'

Jeanette remained silent. She just wanted her life to get back to normal and Billy caught and punished.

They came to the landing stage where surprisingly there were plenty of people about despite the chill breeze. As it happened, a ferry boat had just come in and Jeanette was able to ask one of the crew about the collision. He knew Jimmy and was able to reassure her that he was all right.

They made their way to a bench under cover and sat down to eat their sandwiches and watch the ships coming and going on the river.

'Pity we couldn't see Jimmy,' said Jeanette. 'We could have asked him about the twins.'

'One of those twins wouldn't be me, would he?' said a voice behind them.

The girls' heads turned and they saw Pete standing there. 'Have you come to have the cobwebs blown away too?' asked Peggy, smiling up at him.

He rested both hands on the back of the bench and agreed that it was windy. Peggy said softly, 'Why don't you sit down?'

'No room,' he said.

Instantly Peggy moved her bag and Jeanette shifted over. He came round and sat between them. 'So how have things been with you two?'

'Jeanette was attacked on Friday by the bloke who used the bicycle chain in the chippy,' said Peggy.

Pete stared at Jeanette. 'Bloody hell!'

She felt herself begin to tremble inside. 'I know, it was really scary. Now if you don't mind, I don't want to talk about it, so I'm going for a walk.' She stood up and almost ran from them. She hoped neither would follow her. She still had her sandwich in her hand and ate it as she walked along the landing stage until she arrived at the place where the Isle of Man boats docked. There was one tied up and so she stood gazing up at it and noted it was named *Mona's Isle*.

'Hey there!' shouted a voice.

Startled, Jeanette tilted her head even further back and saw a sailor leaning over the side of the ship on what must have been the top deck. She could not make out his features because the sun was shining in her face. 'Were you talking to me?' she called, shading her eyes with a hand.

'I am that. Could you wait there until I come down?'

'Could you give me a good reason why I should?' Even as Jeanette spoke, she realized that she was wasting her time because the sailor had vanished. For a few moments she stood there indecisively and then turned and looked at the clock on the Liver building. Really, she shouldn't be wasting her time standing here.

She began to walk slowly back the way she had come, only to pause when she heard someone shouting her name. She turned and saw a man running towards her. It was only when he was about a couple of feet away from her that she was able to see the scar on his cheek. Her heart began to thud.

'It's Jeanette, isn't it?' he asked, smiling. She was in such a state of shock that for a moment she could not speak. His smile faded. 'Don't you recognize me?'

'You . . . you look different.' Her voice was strained.

'Ugly, you mean,' he said.

'No, don't alter my words!' she said hoarsely. 'The last time I saw you, you were wearing a sou'wester, you were soaking wet and your face was bleeding and dark with streaks of oil.'

His eyes hardened. 'I haven't forgotten. That sou'wester didn't do anything for me. I looked like the old seafarer on the Skippers' sardine tin.'

'No, you're exaggerating,' she said swiftly. 'He's much older and has a big bushy beard and—' She stopped. 'You're joking, when really there was nothing to joke about then. Your poor face . . .' She reached up to touch it and then withdrew her hand slowly. 'Does it still hurt?'

'Don't be daft, lovey. It's months ago now.' His serious, grey blue eyes searched her countenance. 'I recognized you almost immediately. You stood there, just staring, and I thought, *It can't be her!* Unless she's come looking for me.'

'I didn't know you were on this ship,' blurted out Jeanette. 'But I did want to see you again. I asked the priest about you and he told me why you were in such a rush that night. More recently I discovered that your mother had moved to Liverpool to live with her sister and that you were a sailor, just as I thought. I had wanted him to give you my address and for you to write to me. I was worried about you, you see.'

He smiled ruefully. 'I'm sorry, lovey. I didn't speak to the priest because the ship was ready to sail. It was a quick turnaround. I asked a mate to deliver a message for me. When he got no answer at the priest's house, he told me he just scribbled off a note and pushed it through the letterbox. Later I got in touch with my mother and asked her if she could sort things out, but obviously she didn't. She's not been herself since Dad died and she gets forgetful.'

'I'm sorry about your father and your mother,' said Jeanette. 'I wish I could talk more now but I have to get back to work.'

'But we must meet again,' he said firmly, his eyes gleaming. 'I was planning on treating you to some fish and chips next time I saw you.'

'Tha-that would be nice,' said Jeanette, unable to tear her eyes away from his.

'I'd have liked to have done that now, but as you say you've got work and we'll be sailing soon. My name is David, by the way,' he said. 'David Bryn Jones.'

She smiled. 'I knew about the David and the Jones but not the Bryn. Father Callaghan told me your name.'

'Good.' He returned her smile. 'How about the weekend? I'll be back here then and will have a twenty-four-hour shore leave.'

She took a deep breath in an attempt to steady the nerves in her stomach. 'OK! Time and place?'

He thought a moment. 'The Titanic Memorial, Sunday afternoon at three o'clock.'

'OK.' Whatever might happen in the meantime, she determined to be there. She glanced up at the clock on the Liver building. 'I'll have to go.'

David reached out a hand to her and she placed her hand in his. 'See you then, Jeannie with the light brown hair and green eyes,' he said softly.

She smiled. 'See you, David Bryn Jones.'

He squeezed her hand before releasing it. She hurried away, feeling as if her heels had wings – a description that fitted perfectly the floating sensation she was experiencing. It was so different from the fear that had gripped her such a short while ago. She had found her David Jones and she did not know whether to tell Peggy that her search was over or keep it to herself.

'You're looking pleased with yourself,' said Peggy, as she approached.

'That's because I am pleased with myself,' said Jeanette. 'Thanks for waiting. Pete gone back to work, has he?'

'Yes. We'd better get a move on, too.' Peggy sighed.

Jeanette stared at her. 'You don't look happy. What's up?'

'Nothing.'

'Don't be daft! There's obviously something wrong. Is it Pete?'

'Yeah,' said Peggy. 'Although I do sympathize with him not being able to dance like his brother and do all the other activities he used to do, I can't let that guide me. Anyway, there can be no future for him and me together.'

Jeanette was startled by the remark. 'Does there have to be a future together for the two of you? I mean, I know you like him so what's stopping you going out together?'

Peggy sighed again. 'I find him really attractive, but he's a Proddy like you. I've decided that I can't afford to get involved. It could prove too painful . . .' She let the sentence tail off and slipped her hand through Jeanette's arm. 'Shall we go? On the way you can tell me what got you smiling.'

'I've found him,' said Jeanette, a wobble in her voice.

'Found who?' asked Peggy.

'Don't be thick!' cried Jeanette.

Peggy came to an abrupt halt. 'David Jones?'

'David Bryn Jones! And he recognized me from way up on the top deck of the Isle of Man boat.'

'Bloody hell!' exclaimed Peggy, brushing a strand of hair blown by the wind from her eyes. 'I suppose you'll be seeing him again?'

'Of course,' Jeanette said blithely. 'Sunday afternoon. We've a date then.'

'I suppose this means I'll be seeing less of you,' said Peggy gloomily.

'Don't be daft! He's a sailor, so his job isn't nine to five and home every night.' Jeanette thought that the weekend could not come quickly enough for her. She would not mention him to the family yet. She would hug the knowledge of their meeting to herself and tell them about him when she was good and ready.

'So what are you so happy about?' asked Ethel on Friday evening.

Jeanette stopped mid-note of the fourth line of 'Some Enchanted Evening' and took her hands out of the dishwater. 'It's the weekend. I know that makes no difference to you, Aunt Ethel, because you don't go out to work. Most days must feel the same to you – but for me the weekend is special.'

'Hah!' exclaimed Ethel, scowling. 'Where d'you think you'll be going when last Friday you blotted your copybook?'

Despite her great-aunt having been in bed when Jeanette had arrived home with Sam a week ago, she had been told some of what had taken place that evening. Jeanette decided she needed a good excuse to leave the house alone on Sunday. 'I thought I would go to church again,' she said casually. 'Confess my sins and ask for forgiveness and all that. You should try it sometime.'

Ethel made to cuff her across the head but she ducked. 'Don't you be giving me cheek, girl! You're not too old to have your bottom smacked.'

'I blooming am,' said Jeanette, flicking dishwater in Ethel's direction. 'I'm not one of your former prisoners, you know. And don't you forget what Dad said about putting you in a home. You need to make sure that you don't blot *your* copybook. I'll be eighteen in less than a month. If you didn't take most of my money, I could move out and get a bedsit.'

Uncertainty flickered across Ethel's wrinkled face. 'George wouldn't put me in a home and he wouldn't allow you to leave home at your age.'

'We'll see about that when the time comes,' said Jeanette, thinking that there was just one more full day before her date with David Bryn Jones, and tomorrow should go swiftly what with working at the milk bar. She had thought her father might forbid her to go, but so far he had said nothing about it. Perhaps he had decided that as Billy had no idea where she lived he was worrying unduly about her safety.

The following day Jeanette was waiting-on at the milk bar when a policeman and policewoman entered.

'Now what do they want?' muttered Mrs Cross, glancing across at the navy-blue uniformed figures.

'It's my dad and half-sister,' Jeanette whispered. 'I'm sorry, Mrs Cross. They must have a message for me.'

'Well, get them out of here as quickly as you can. They're not good for trade.'

George came over to the counter and nodded at the woman. 'Morning! Nothing for you to worry about, missus. We just popped in to see my daughter and whilst we're here we'll have two cups of tea and two toasted teacakes.'

'You heard your father, Jeanette,' said Mrs Cross, pinning on a smile. 'Let him have them on the house.'

'That's generous of you, missus,' said George. 'But I always pay my way.'

'Well, that's up to you, Sergeant. I'll leave you to it.' She hurried into the back.

'What are you both here for, Dad?' asked Jeanette, cutting teacakes in half.

He did not answer immediately because he was looking about him. 'Nice little caff,' he said.

She nodded. 'We don't get any trouble here.'

'I'm glad to hear that.' He patted her arm. 'I'll go and sit down by the window with Hester and you can bring the order over.'

'OK.' She watched him warily as he sat down next to Hester at one of the tables usually occupied by Maggie, Irene and their friends and she wondered if any of them would come in today.

Just as Jeanette was ready to carry the order over the door opened and Maggie entered with a man and woman. She came over to the counter whilst the couple made for one of the vacant tables by the window.

'Hi,' she said. 'Three cups of tea and three buttered scones, two with jam when you've got a moment.'

'OK. Any of the others dropping by today?'

Maggie rested her arms on the counter and smiled. 'I don't know. I haven't seen the twins since last Saturday and Irene wasn't sure what she was doing today. I've come to see you and brought along my brother and his wife Emma, the one your half-sister knows. She wants to speak to you.'

'Blinking heck!' Jeanette's face lit up. 'You're not going to believe this but Hester's here now with my dad. That's them over there. I'm just about to take them their order.'

'That policeman is your father?' exclaimed Maggie.

'Yes, what's wrong with that?' asked Jeanette sharply.

'Nothing!' cried Maggie. 'He's a fine figure of a man. You're lucky, having a dad. I lost mine to a wasting disease a few years back. Then I lost my mum last year.'

'I am sorry. You go on ahead and I'll follow you over.'

Jeanette picked up the tray, thinking to make some introductions as soon as she reached the table, but she had not counted on an excitable Maggie saying, 'You're not going to believe this, Emma, but you're sitting right next to Hester Walker!'

Both Emma and Hester swivelled round at the sound of their names and stared at each other. 'I don't believe it,' said Hester, a smile breaking over her face.

'Me neither,' said Emma, 'although I came here specifically to see if I could get in touch with you. Fancy you being a policewoman!'

'I believe you're married,' said Hester.

'That's right,' said Emma, beaming at her. 'This is my husband, Jared.' She touched his shoulder. 'And we're having a baby. It was confirmed yesterday.'

'I couldn't be more pleased for you,' said Hester.

'We're delighted.' Emma placed her hand over that of her husband.

'It does mean, though, that there's decisions to be made,' he said, squeezing her fingers gently.

Her smile faded. 'They'd be easier to make if Betty wasn't going to Italy next year. I really don't want to get rid of the cottage and cut my ties with Whalley, but I need someone I can rely on to help me out next summer by living there and running the tearoom.'

All this time Jeanette had been placing George and Hester's order on the table in front of them, whilst her father had sat in silence, a smile on his face, listening to the conversation. She thought it was time she said something.

'Hester, don't you think you should introduce Dad?'

Hester glanced up at her and instantly she introduced not only her father but also Jeanette to Emma and Jared. That done, Jeanette got on with the task of carrying out Maggie's order. Later, when she carried it over, Hester and Emma were talking earnestly about someone called Lila who apparently had married a policeman called Dougie Marshall who lived in Bootle. As she emptied the contents of the tray onto the table, she caught Maggie's eye who mouthed 'He's the twins' brother!', and she remembered what Betty had told her that evening at the Grafton. Thinking of the twins reminded her of Peggy and their conversation down at the landing stage, and of her own meeting with David Jones. She felt a surge of happiness. She could not wait to see him again.

Nineteen

By the time Jeanette reached the Titanic Memorial, the wind had got up and it was drizzling. She thought how when you lived by the sea, the weather was always changeable. She had put on her best frock and cardie and had hoped for sunshine, but had her mac and umbrella as well, so she felt a bit like Debbie Reynolds in *Singin' in the Rain*. She certainly had a glorious feeling inside her. To her relief, David was waiting for her, and as soon as he spotted her he came hurrying over. He looked as pleased to see her as she was to see him.

'I'm glad the weather didn't put you off,' he said, taking her hand.

Her green eyes sparkled. 'What weather?'

His smile deepened and he placed her hand in the crook of his arm. 'Let's not hang around here or you'll get soaked.'

'I feel like pinching myself. I can scarcely believe you're here at last.' She did not feel a bit shy of him, but was so excited that she was trembling all over. 'Wh . . . where shall we go? I wish it could be somewhere—'

'Different?'

'Somewhere the sun is shining. It would be great if we could take a liner and sail off to a beautiful beach with warm seas,' said Jeanette.

'You're a dreamer,' said David, a hint of laughter in his voice.

'We all need our dreams,' she said firmly. 'More often than not, I have to be practical.'

'There are some good beaches on the Isle of Man, but I can't promise you everlasting warm waters and dawn to dusk sunshine if you were ever to sail with us,' he warned.

'How long have you been working for the Isle of Man Steam Packet Company?'

'I only joined them recently. Before then I worked on the banana boats and sailed to the Canaries and to the Caribbean.'

'Now those places sound more like it.' She sighed happily, conscious of their bodies brushing as they walked. 'What on earth made you change companies?'

'My father's death and the need to resettle my mother somewhere more affordable.' He paused as they came to James Street. 'So where do we go?'

The wind blew Jeanette's skirt against her legs and was that strong she clung to his arm. 'If it weren't that we've a lot of catching up to do, I'd have suggested going to the flicks where it would be warm and comfortable,' she gasped.

'Another time. Shall we go for a drink?' he suggested.

'I don't drink,' she said frankly, remembering saying those very words to Marty. 'At least not until the twenty-first of December when I'll be eighteen. That's not to say we can't go into a pub if you feel like a pint. Are you hungry as well?'

'Do you know, during the war there were girls of fourteen who pretended they were over eighteen so they could go in pubs and mix with the Yanks.' He gazed down at her, a smile in his eyes. 'I'm glad there's no such pretence where you're concerned. I'm twenty-five. I presume you've had Sunday lunch?'

She nodded. 'Have you?'

'Yes. We'll have the fish and chips I promised another time. Let's find a cafe and have a pot of tea and cakes.'

'That sounds good.'

They walked up James Street without speaking, but kept glancing at each other and smiling. When they reached Castle Street, they turned right and hurried along the wet pavement until they came to a Kardomah. It was not until they were settled at a table in the warm, steamy atmosphere and had placed their order that he said, 'You first. Tell me all about yourself.'

'There's not much to tell,' she said hastily. 'I'd rather hear about you.'

He shook his head. 'Your life can't be that dull. Not after the way we met.'

'All right! You know my name is Jeanette Walker. I live with my father, George, my great-aunt Ethel, half-brother Sam, and half-sister Hester.'

'And your mother?'

Jeanette blew out her cheeks and then let out a breath. 'She walked out during the blitz and never came back. I've just put a notice in the *Echo* in the hope that I'll discover whether she's alive or dead. My great-aunt insists that she went off with a fancy man, leaving a note which she was so angry about that she destroyed.'

'You poor kid! It must drive you crazy at times, not knowing one way or the other.'

She nodded. 'My great-aunt is an old faggot! I don't believe her about the note. I'm just hoping that my piece in the *Echo* will trigger someone's memory – and as well as that I've Father Callaghan on the case.' She paused. 'What about your family?'

'No, you can't just leave your story like that. How does the Padre come into this?'

'He was here during the war and helped give the last rites to the dying. He knew a lot of those who helped dig people out.' She sighed.

'Tough,' said David, frowning. 'We'll change the subject.' He rested his arms on the table and leaned towards her. 'What do you do for a job?'

'I work in a shipping warehouse office in the Cunard

Building. It was just pure chance that I went down to the landing stage and you spotted me.'

'I would have found you sooner or later. You were often on my mind, but I had to sort Mam out first and I knew I had that contact with the Padre.'

'Honestly, I understand why us meeting again has taken so long,' she said, placing her hand on his.

He caught hold of her fingers. 'Thanks. After Dad died, we came to the decision that it would be best for Mam to leave the house on the Wirral, and you know the rest. She now lives with her sister on the outskirts of the city.'

Her eyes lit up. 'So . . . so does that mean your home is in Liverpool, too, now?'

'We-ell, I have somewhere to kip when the ship docks, and it means I can keep my eye on the two women. Mam was forty when she had me, so she's no spring chicken. There's times when they need a man's help.' He toyed with her fingers. 'It also means that you and I—' He broke off as the waitress arrived with their tea and cakes.

Both withdrew their hands and watched the waitress place their order on the table. As soon as she left, Jeanette picked up the teapot and filled their cups, hoping he would continue with what he was saying. When he did not pick up the thread of the conversation she was disappointed, thinking that perhaps he'd had second thoughts. She so wanted something to come from this date with him.

Suddenly she realized that there was something important that she had not told him. 'You won't have forgotten Billy who hit you in the face.'

'Of course not.' David's expression was grim as he spooned sugar into his tea.

'Well, his father fell into a dock and drowned. His mother said that she needed him, so they let him out of Borstal to attend the funeral.'

He stilled and then offered the plate of cakes to Jeanette. 'Pretty much like my mother needed me, one might say.' His voice was expressionless, but she sensed the anger in him.

'There's more,' she said, taking a chocolate éclair whilst she thought about what to tell him. The last thing she wanted to admit to was going to the Stadium with another man and seeing Billy there, but she could not see how she could get round it.

He stared at her. 'Go on.'

She bit into the chocolate éclair. 'These are lovely.'

He looked only faintly amused as he stretched forward and wiped cream from the tip of her nose. 'What's he done now? I guess he's done something wrong if you've brought him up.'

She ate the whole éclair and wiped her fingers on a napkin before saying, 'He attacked me and then he stabbed a man.'

David paled and shot out a hand and gripped her arm. 'When did this happen? Were you hurt?'

'It happened only the other week. I was shocked and frightened more than anything. I've a few bruises but I managed to get away when the doorman intervened. I didn't realize Billy had a knife. Fortunately the doorman survived. Now Billy's on the run and the police are looking for him. A friend did suggest that he might have caught the Irish boat and be hiding out there.'

'You don't think the police would have put a watch on the Irish ferry terminals here in Liverpool? Because if he was really crafty, he'd have made for Holyhead and taken the ferry to Ireland from there. Or travelled to Heysham up Lancashire and taken the ferry to Douglas and from there to Ireland.'

Jeanette's eyes widened. 'I never thought of that.'

'You wouldn't, and neither would I most likely if I didn't now work on the Isle of Man boats. We go back and forth to Ireland as well.'

'My dad and brother want to get their hands on him.'

He nodded. 'You're not short of protectors. I know I wouldn't mind having a go at him.'

'I did manage to kick him in the shins,' said Jeanette almost casually.

'Good for you.' He looked amused as he reached for the teapot. 'D'you want a top-up?'

She nodded and decided to change the subject. 'This will make you laugh. My great-aunt thinks my mother, who apparently was fostered or adopted and ran away from home, was the daughter of a lady suffragette who gave birth in prison.

She died not so long ago and according to my great-aunt she was rich. I'm supposed to prove I'm her illegitimate grand-daughter so as to claim my inheritance.'

As soon as David grinned, Jeanette knew that she had managed to steer him away from the subject of Billy. 'I can dream!' she cried. 'I want to leave home but have no money to speak of, and a luxury apartment would be great.'

'A house even better,' he said.

She agreed and reached for another cake, and so did David. Their hands touched and she felt a frisson of pleasure. 'Your choice first,' she said, blushing.

'Ladies first.'

She took a cream horn and he chose a cream cookie.

'What does your dad think of your leaving home?'

'I haven't mentioned it to him. He still thinks of me as his little girl and would like me to stay at home a while longer.'

'Doesn't see you getting married soon then?' asked David, his eyes intent on her face as he bit into the cream cookie and jam and cream squished out.

She did not get to answer his question but giggled. 'Oh, lor – you want to see your face!' She reached into a pocket and withdrew a hanky which she handed to him. 'You've cream and jam on your chin and nose!'

David took the hanky and to her surprise leaned forward and wiped her mouth. 'I'm not the only one making a mess.'

His touch caused her skin to tingle and she thought, *I must be in love with him, the effect he's having on me.* She murmured a word of thanks.

They both sat back and finished their cakes before resuming their conversation.

'So your sister and brother, are they courting?' asked David.

'A short while ago I would have said no, but things have changed since they went to Hester's best friend's wedding where she met a soldier called Ally. Sam's going out with a girl he knew years back. She's an actress.'

'What will your father do if they get married?' asked David.

'I think he'll be happy for them.' She hesitated. 'He knows about you – what with him being a policeman. I didn't tell him that I'd be seeing you today.'

'Why, doesn't he approve of me?'

'It . . . it's not that. I wanted to keep it to myself. Sort of our secret. I will tell him, though, if . . .' She paused.

'If we were to go steady,' he said quietly.

She blushed and nodded.

He smiled. 'How about the flicks next time?' he suggested. 'Unless you'd prefer to do something else.'

Immediately she imagined him whirling her around the dance floor of the Grafton or dancing cheek-to-cheek. 'Perhaps we could go dancing another time, although there is a film I want to see,' she said.

'The flicks it is then,' murmured David.

They left the Kardomah and walked in the direction of Dale Street. 'So what bus do we catch to your house?' he asked.

'Haven't you got to return to your ship?'

'Not today. Anyway, I'd see you home first,' he said in a voice that brooked no argument. 'I want to make certain you get there safely.'

'Thanks!' She appreciated the thought and wondered if he was always so assertive. Just as long as he didn't insist on seeing her to the front door. She needed to let the family know first that they had met up again.

'So what are you doing over the Christmas break?' he asked once they were seated on the bus.

'I generally spend it at home with the family, but that's not set in stone.' She gazed at the scar on his cheek and experienced a pang of regret. 'I might be seeing my friend Peggy on Boxing Day. She's feeling a bit down.'

'Peggy,' he said thoughtfully, wrapping the bus tickets round his finger. 'She's not the same friend from the chippy, is she?'

She stared at him. 'You've a good memory.'

'So what happened to her and the boyfriend?'

'They split up but she's over him. There's someone else she likes but he's not Catholic. I told her there's no reason why they can't just have fun together, but she's not having it. Her family wouldn't like it.'

His mouth twisted in a smile and he searched for her hand and held it tightly. 'I'm glad we don't have that problem. So when would you like to go to the flicks?'

They arranged a date and then Jeanette mentioned her birthday and Christmas, thinking it would be lovely to spend time with him. 'I suppose you'll be tied up over the festive season because you have to consider your mother though? After all, it'll be her first without your father.'

He nodded. 'I was thinking I need to do something to cheer her up.'

'I should imagine she would want a quiet Christmastide with her sister and you. The quicker it's over with the better. Too many memories of happy times with your father would prove painful.'

David rubbed the space above his nose with two fingers and sighed. 'I'm not so sure. Mam and Dad always spent the evening of Christmas Eve doing what they each wanted. He was a manager of a departmental store in Birkenhead and by the time he arrived home, he only wanted to collapse in an armchair by the fire and fall asleep. Mam would take one look at him, fill her shopping bag with goodies and go and visit my aunt and her family. When Uncle Jack was alive, he would bring her home in his little black Ford just after midnight. She'd be slightly tipsy and full of the Christmas spirit. Dad would be in bed by then but I would wait up for her. She would tell me all about the party and I'd wish I'd gone with her, but she never suggested it. Christmas Day was always a bit of an anti-climax. And when Uncle Jack died the whole Christmas thing was worse for her because the parties stopped. I'm just hoping she and my aunt living together will work.'

'You make me want to do something for her,' said Jeanette, squeezing his hand.

He shrugged. 'At least she knows about you.'

'Does she?'

'Of course she does. I told her and she knows I was meeting you today.'

Jeanette wondered how his mother had responded to the news. She could not imagine that she would welcome her with open arms, especially when David was her only child. But it was stupid for her to start worrying about that now. For the moment she and David had found each other again and she could not have been more happy.

She had explained to him why she didn't want him seeing her to her front door and he seemed to understand her reasons. Even so, she was aware of him standing beneath the lamp post a few doors away, watching her to her gate.

She saw the lobby light go on and glanced to where David had been, but he was no longer there. The door opened to reveal Sam. 'The old witch said that you'd gone to church,' he said.

She took a deep breath. 'I confess I told a lie.'

Sam frowned and moved out of the way so she could wipe her feet on the mat. 'Where have you been?'

She did not answer immediately, but took off her scarf and coat and hung them up before facing her half-brother. 'I've found him. We've just had a date, me and David Bryn Jones. He used to be on the banana boats but now works for the Isle of Man Steam Packet Company.' The words came out in a rush. 'We spotted each other down at the landing stage. His widowed mother recently moved to Liverpool and is living with her sister.'

Sam stared at her for a long moment. 'I take it you're hoping to see him again.'

She detected disapproval in his voice. 'Ye-e-es. You have something against that?'

'Did he see you home?'

'Almost.'

'Then bring him in next time,' said Sam sternly. 'You've got to look at this from Dad's point of view. David Jones was involved in a fight and didn't hang around to talk to the police.'

She was taken aback. 'But you know why. His father was dying and he had to get to the hospital to see him.'

'I accept he had a good reason, but bring him home so Dad or I can judge whether he's a reliable person for you to go out with.'

She felt a spurt of anger. 'You're saying that my judgement can't be trusted? I thought you were on my side.'

Sam scowled. 'I am on your bloody side, idiot!' he snapped. 'From what he's told you, he sounds on the level, but he could be lying to you. You're obviously starry eyed about him, so you could be seeing him through rose-tinted specs.'

She did not want to accept what her half-brother was saying and blurted out, 'You should give me more credit for having some common sense.' A thought suddenly occurred to her. 'Anyway, he's visited Father Callaghan and he seems to think he's OK.'

'A priest is supposed to see the best in people.'

'He's also aware that people are sinners,' retorted Jeanette.

'OK, I won't argue with you,' said Sam. 'When will you be seeing him again?'

'Wednesday. We're going to the pictures.'

'OK. You just bring him in when he sees you home. I won't say anything to Dad right now.'

'OK!' She had a strong urge to walk out of the house there and then but instead said, 'Where's our Hester?'

'Working extra hours. There's some conference on the "Psychology of the Murderer" she wants to attend. It's up near Whalley.'

Jeanette blinked at him. 'Sounds interesting.'

'A famous crime writer is going to talk and she really likes his stuff.'

'I see. No doubt there'll be other members of the police force there.'

'I have thought of that. I hope she has too. Policemen are only human, you know!'

She bit back a laugh. 'I live with three coppers, so I certainly know they're no saints.'

Sam flinched. 'You're as bad as Dorothy.'

'Why, what's she said?'

'Mind your own business,' he snapped.

Jeanette swore beneath her breath and ran upstairs. She told herself that she was not going to let what Sam had said about David ruin her new-found happiness. She liked it that her brother cared about her, especially in the light of what had happened with Billy. But maybe sometimes he was too protective. She flopped down on her bed and imagined David's reaction on Wednesday when she said that her father wanted to meet him. She groaned. It was positively Victorian! She would have liked to put off their meeting a little longer. She should have said nothing to Sam. What was up with him that he was so bad tempered? Could it be that he and Dorothy had broken up, having decided that their lives were incompatible?

Twenty

'Listen to that wind,' said Jeanette, walking into Hester's bedroom and perching on the edge of her bed.

'I'm glad I'm not on duty tonight,' said Hester.

'Or at sea.' Jeanette took several pipe cleaners from the pocket of her housecoat and placed them on the eiderdown. The weather reminded her of the evening she had met David in the chippy. 'Do you want to put these in for me? I'm going out straight from work tomorrow night and I want a bit of curl in my hair.'

'With David Jones, I know. Sit down here,' said Hester, indicating the stool in front of the dressing table.

Jeanette did as she was told and once settled said, 'I suppose our Sam told you. Have you heard from Ally?'

Hester smoothed her left eyebrow with a damp finger and didn't quite meet her sister's eyes in the dressing table mirror. 'No, I think Ally must be too busy to bother getting pen and paper out and dropping me a line.' There was a tremor in her voice. 'I've decided to put him out of my mind. I'm attending a conference this coming weekend and I'm making time to visit Myra Jones in Whalley. I might even see Emma up there. Her husband's in the building industry and he's planning on doing some renovations to the cottage. Anyway, why didn't you tell me straight off that you'd met up with David Jones again?'

'I didn't know how it would turn out. Anyway, I haven't seen much of you.'

Hester nodded. 'So, tell me all about it.'

'Our Sam will have told you some of it. David seemed as

made up to see me as I was to see him and we had a good chat and decided we wanted to see each other again.' Jeanette smiled. 'If possible I'd like to see him some time over Christmas but he has to consider his widowed mother. What'll you be doing? If Ally were to turn up, would you be seeing him?'

'Let's wait and see, shall we?' Hester picked up a pipe cleaner and a length of Jeanette's light brown hair. 'I believe we might be seeing David Jones tomorrow night?'

Jeanette nodded. 'Our Sam insisted on it. I'm going to mention it to Dad in the morning. I suppose as soon as the old witch learns of it, she'll have something to say.'

'What did you expect?' Hester wrapped a length of hair around the pipe cleaner and then bent both ends towards each other.

'Exactly that. So what's up with our Sam and Dorothy?'

'Oh, he's in a twist because she wants to interview me for that film she's planning next year. She's going to have to finance it herself and he thinks she's making a mistake.'

'I did wonder if they'd broken up,' said Jeanette. 'Why is she having to finance it herself?'

'Because she's a woman, of course! The bosses in the film industry are all men and think women should be in front of the camera, not behind it. The men like to be in charge, as we all know.'

Jeanette did not argue with her. Hester was right. Despite all that the suffragettes had achieved, it was still a man's world. 'So is it going to be a documentary or what?'

'Yes, it's about women of Liverpool.'

'Such as who?'

'Kitty Wilkinson, Eleanor Rathbone, Bessie Braddock, me!' Hester struck a pose.

Jeanette chuckled. 'Because you're a policewoman, I suppose.'

'Yes. Not that I can compare with those famous women. But I'm young, female and set on promotion in a male-dominated workplace, and although I work as hard as any man, I don't get paid the same.'

'Dorothy should include the suffragettes being force-fed in Walton gaol,' said Jeanette. 'I suppose Aunt Ethel could help, with her having been a prison wardress.'

'I'll mention it to Dorothy but can you see the old witch agreeing?'

'You never know. She might be bowled over at the idea of seeing herself up on the big screen.'

'I think it's for television,' said Hester. 'Anyway, let's forget it for now. It's not as if it's going to happen tomorrow. As soon as I've finished your hair, I'm going downstairs. There's a new series on called *Journey into Space*. I thought I'd give it a go.'

Jeanette showed interest and shortly after the pair of them went downstairs to discover the programme was already on and Ethel was asleep in a chair by the fire. Hester put a finger to her lips and sat down, but Jeanette wandered over to the window, lifted the curtain and peered out. 'You're not going to believe this,' she whispered. 'It's snowing!'

'You're kidding!' said Hester, and joined her at the window. 'I hope it doesn't stick or I mightn't be able to get to the conference.'

'I like the snow,' murmured Jeanette, her nose pressed against the pane. 'It hides all the dirt and makes everything look magical.'

'It's inconvenient,' said Hester, turning away from the window.

Jeanette remained where she was, gazing out at the falling snow whilst half listening to *Journey into Space*. She remembered when she was a kid and the snow had lain on the ground for what had seemed weeks. She had a sudden memory of sitting on a sledge with her mother. Somewhere there was a photograph of them. It used to be on the sideboard, but a couple of years ago it suddenly vanished. It was probably lying in one of the drawers, removed by Ethel no doubt. She thought of the photograph she had lent to Father Callaghan. Perhaps she should give him another visit soon to see if he had turned up any information about her mother. She had not heard anything in response to the notice she had put in the *Echo*.

Journey into Space came to an end on a cliffhanger and she heard Hester leave the room. Jeanette felt suddenly restless, thinking of David perhaps out at sea in this blizzard. She felt a need to stretch her legs, anything to get rid of the fidgets. Quietly, so as not to wake Ethel, she put on her outdoor clothes and left the house.

She found it exhilarating being blown along with the whirling snow towards Whitefield Road. She hoped the little sweet shop around the corner would still be open because she fancied some chocolate limes. The old woman who owned the shop stocked sweets of every different kind in tall glass jars with glass stoppers.

To her disappointment the shop was closed and so she turned back, only to collide with a bulky figure wearing a thick coat, trousers, a striped scarf and a woolly hat pulled right down so one could see little of the face.

'Sorry,' said Jeanette. 'I didn't see you there.'

'That's all right, dear, easily done,' said a muffled voice.

'We must be daft coming out on such a terrible evening,' said Jeanette, aware that she was being scrutinized by a pair of dark eyes.

'Do I know you?' asked the muffled voice.

'Well, I live around here. My name's Jeanette Walker. Goodnight!' said Jeanette, continuing on her way.

A faint, 'Goodnight, Jeanette,' drifted on the wind towards her.

Jeanette glanced back and saw that the figure was still standing outside the sweet shop. She lifted a hand and waved before turning the corner and hurrying home.

That night she slept fitfully due to the sound of the wind in the chimney and the noise as it rattled the sash window. When she did sleep, she dreamt of that mysterious figure in the snow and woke convinced it was a woman, despite the trousers and the muffled voice. Who was she?

By morning the snow had stopped but the wind was still strong and tearing the clouds apart to reveal a clear blue sky. By the time she arrived at work, Jeanette had every hope that when she left that evening David would be able to meet her outside the cinema on Lime Street. But one look at the arrivals and departures board was enough to make her change her mind. A number of ships were either not sailing, or had not been in touch, or were fortunate enough to have been able to take shelter in the nearest port. She felt on edge, worried that after finding David, she might be about to lose him.

Unable to relax, she decided to go down to the landing

stage in her lunch hour and see whether the *Mona's Isle* had docked. But she did not even get near the landing stage as the passengerway had been closed off because the Mersey ferries were not sailing that day. She wasted no time in retracing her steps and telephoning the Isle of Man Steam Packet Company. She was informed that the *Mona's Isle* had not left Douglas and would not depart until tomorrow. At least she could relax, knowing that David was safe in the Isle of Man.

As she left work that evening, she mentioned it to Peggy. 'I'm supposed to be taking him home. At least I didn't say anything to Dad this morning as he was still in bed after being on a late shift last night.'

'We could go to the flicks together if you want,' suggested Peggy.

'OK, but we'll go and see a different film because I have a feeling that David was quite keen on seeing the Alfred Hitchcock one,' said Jeanette.

That evening when she and Peggy were in the cinema, Jeanette was making her way back from the toilets to her seat when she caught sight of Cedric. He was not in uniform and appeared to be talking to a woman in the seat next to him. She could not see her clearly but the feather in her hat kept bobbing about as if she was nodding. Jeanette wanted to go and have a closer look at the pair, but that would mean disturbing people just as the lights were dimming, ready for the main feature. It seemed that he had got over Hester quick enough.

For a while, as she watched the film, Jeanette forgot about Cedric, but as soon as it ended she looked towards where she had seen him. Her vision was obstructed by other cinemagoers standing up and making their way towards the exits, so she followed the crowd outside but there was no sign of him.

Jeanette parted from Peggy in Lime Street because she saw her bus coming and made a run for it, so it was only half past nine by the time she arrived home. Hester was there and so was Ethel. They were sitting in what at first felt like a companionable silence, one sewing whilst the other was reading the newspaper.

'Cocoa anyone?' asked Jeanette, squeezing between the two armchairs and holding her hands out to the fire.

Hester looked up from the sock she was darning. 'So where is he?' she murmured. 'Cold feet?'

Jeanette shook her head. 'No. He's stuck in the Isle of Man, so I went to the flicks with Peggy instead.'

'Shame! Good film?' asked Hester.

'It was OK.' She hesitated. 'I saw Cedric there, not that I spoke to him. He was talking to a woman in the next seat to him.'

All that Hester felt was relief at such news. 'It didn't take him long to find someone else.'

Before either of them could comment further, Ethel interrupted them.

'Have you seen this in the *Echo*, Jeanette?' She slapped the open page with the back of her hand.

Distracted, Jeanette said, 'No, Aunt Ethel, I've only just got in. Is it something exciting?'

'You should know. It's got your name on it.' Ethel's eyes shone. 'You are making an effort to find Grace after all.'

Jeanette sat on the arm of the chair and looked at the piece in the newspaper. 'I wonder why they've put it in again.'

'I can tell you why,' said Hester. 'It's opposite an article about missing persons. With Christmas coming up it's an emotive subject.'

'I see what you mean,' said Jeanette slowly. 'It's when families get together and think of those far and near.'

'Well, Grace has never been in touch,' said Ethel, 'but maybe this time, so near Christmas, it will bring her out of the woodwork.' She folded the newspaper and shoved it down the side of the cushion.

Jeanette exchanged looks with Hester and rolled her eyes before asking again did anyone want cocoa. As she went into the kitchen, Sam and her father came in. They were discussing a couple of cases of arson and a spate of burglaries. Hester joined in their conversation and so Jeanette went to bed.

It was not until Friday that Jeanette heard from David. She arrived at work to find an envelope on her desk. There was no stamp on it but she had a feeling she knew who it was from and slit it open immediately. As she had suspected it was from David and he had popped it into the letterbox in the Cunard Building as soon as the *Mona's Isle* had docked. He explained what she already knew about the weather delaying the ferryboat sailing and asked if she could meet him that evening at the same time and place.

Smiling, she replaced the letter in its envelope and, getting up from her desk, went and gazed out of the window towards the river. The snow had melted and the wind had dropped and all was right with her world. She thought of Hester who had left before dawn that morning to catch the coach that would take her to the conference. It was a shame that she had left so early because a letter had come for her by first post. Jeanette had placed it in a drawer in Hester's bedroom out of harm's way, convinced it was the one she had been waiting for from Ally because it was postmarked Germany. She just hoped Hester enjoyed her weekend away. At least she would be delighted to find the letter on her return.

Twenty-One

Hester settled herself happily by the window and considered herself fortunate to have found an inside seat unoccupied. Most seats on the coach were now taken and it was due to leave in ten minutes. She reached for the book in her bag and had just flicked over the pages to where she had placed her bookmark when a familiar voice said, 'Well, well, well, look who's here!'

Her heart sank and she did not immediately look up. It had occurred to her that Cedric might attend the conference, but she had hoped he wouldn't.

'Aren't we speaking?' he continued. 'I've no hard feelings, Hester.'

Was that true? Slowly she lifted her head and looked up at him. He was smiling down at her as if she was the best thing he had seen in a long time. She found it hard to believe that he could be so forgiving of the embarrassment she had caused him in the cinema by walking out on him the way she did.

'I wasn't sure you'd be attending the conference,' she said, far more calmly than she felt.

'I thought you weren't going either. Work commitments, wasn't it?' His smile did not quite reach his eyes this time.

'I decided that you were right and the conference was an event I just had to attend, so I put in extra hours beforehand and stated my case to my inspector.'

'Now that's what I call sensible,' said Cedric, reaching up and placing his overnight bag in the luggage rack overhead. 'You don't mind if I have the seat next to you, do you? Most are taken.'

She had seen that question coming and sensed that it was a rhetorical one. Already he was lowering himself into the seat beside her and removing his trilby. She noticed a book in the pocket of his mackintosh. It looked like he had intended reading. Good. Without another word, she dropped her gaze to the open pages before her. Hopefully she was giving him the impression that she didn't care what he did and that her novel was far more interesting.

'I'm not squashing you, am I?'

She did not look up. 'As long as I can move my elbows to turn the pages.'

'Doesn't reading on a coach make you sick? A girl I once knew always felt nauseous if she tried to read while travelling.'

'No, not at all!' she said firmly. 'Truthfully, I get bored if I don't have a book with me when I travel. I don't get enough time for light reading with the job.'

'I don't suppose you'd like to talk.'

'You suppose right.'

There was the sound of the coach engine starting up and she breathed a sigh of relief, glad to be on the way. She had been looking forward to the journey, but now she felt that the sooner it was over the better.

Shortly after they left the coach station she felt Cedric's elbow dig into her arm and her stomach muscles clenched. One more dig like that and she would have something to say to him. Fortunately he shifted slightly away from her and a few moments later she heard the rustle of pages being turned over. She waited several minutes before glancing at the cover of his book.

It was a dog-eared copy of *No Orchids for Miss Blandish* and caused her to raise her eyebrows. She had found the book disturbing. It was about ruthless gangsters in America during Prohibition with no heart when it came to dealing with people. She hadn't finished it because some of the descriptions were so unpleasant and she hadn't read any more books by that author. She gave her attention to her own library book that was much more pleasant.

'So what do you think of the programme?' asked Cedric.

'I know exactly which talks and discussions I want to be in on,' said Hester absently, without looking up.

'I wish I did.'

She was surprised into glancing at him. Having read two of the main speaker's books, she was eager to hear what he had to say. She would have thought Cedric would have felt the same.

He smiled at her. 'That got your attention.'

She took a deep breath and counted silently to ten, then lowered her gaze to her book again.

'I see you're reading Helen MacInnes,' he said.

'Hmmm.'

'So what's she like?'

Hester decided she did not mind talking about books with him. 'This one's more of a love story, but I have read her wartime spy stories and there's a thriller element in this, too,' she said.

'I saw the film of *Above Suspicion* with Joan Crawford, but I've never read anything of hers,' said Cedric.

'She's good. Different from the author we'll be listening to this weekend, but well worth a read.'

'I'll get my skates on when I get home and borrow one of hers from the library. Mind you, I'm going to be busy when I get back. Won't have time for reading.'

She guessed he wanted her to ask what he would be doing. Maybe it would be useful to know. 'What will you be doing?'

He grinned. 'Have you heard about that new system for fingerprinting?'

She nodded. 'My brother mentioned it. The Nynhydrin treatment.'

'Smart girl!'

Irritated by his patronizing tone, Hester decided not to rise to it but continued, 'It can be used when prints can't be seen by normal photography or the naked eye.'

'Criminals beware!' he said, smirking. 'When you think it's sixty years since fingerprints were first used in bringing criminals to justice, yet there's still those who don't have the sense not to leave any.'

'I wonder what the next big thing will be?'

'I wonder.' He stifled a yawn. 'I hope there's a decent bar in this place.'

'It says in the leaflet that there is one,' said Hester, opening her book again.

They both fell silent. A short while later when she glanced his way, he appeared to be asleep. Relieved, she smiled to herself and was taken by surprise when he said, 'What are you thinking?'

She did not immediately answer, wondering how he would react if she told him the truth. Instead she said, 'It shouldn't take us much longer to get there.'

'How do you know? Have you been up this way before?'

'I was evacuated not far from where we're staying.'

'No! You never said anything.'

'Why should I? I'm planning on visiting the woman I stayed with.'

He frowned. 'When?'

'Sunday afternoon.'

'So you won't be coming back on the same coach?'

'No.' She fell silent, thinking of Myra and then of Emma and their conversation outside the milk bar when they were alone for a few moments. They had discussed their half-sisters and Hester had told Emma about Jeanette's narrow escape from Billy. Emma knew a little about him as a description of him had been reported to Dougie Marshall when he had responded to a cry for help in Bootle. A woman in one of the houses

Billy had burgled had surprised him in the act and his finger-prints were found using the new system they'd just discussed. He had knocked the woman out and made his escape. Billy had still not returned home, so the question was, where was he hiding?

She sighed.

'What's the sigh for?' asked Cedric.

'I was just thinking of that young man who stabbed the Stadium doorman. You must have heard about it.'

His eyes flickered over her face. 'Sure I did. He attacked your sister, didn't he?'

'Yes. I want him caught,' she said in a hard voice.

'I can understand that. Pretty girl, your sister,' said Cedric, closing his eyes.

She stared at him and then reached for her book, resisting the temptation to hit him with it. She would be glad when they reached their destination.

Hester slumped against the pillow and yawned. Her head was buzzing, despite having drunk only one glass of wine. She was glad that she had come, despite Cedric. She liked her bedroom and had a lovely view from her window over part of the garden and beyond that Lancashire farmland. The first talk had held her attention and the conversation afterwards had been stimulating. She had met people whose company she had so enjoyed that she was looking forward to talking to them again. A fair number had no connection to the police force. Thankfully, she had seen little of Cedric. Once the talk was over he had made for the bar and had still been there when she had passed by. He had waved to her to come over but she had shook her head. He had scowled and then ordered another drink, from what she could see.

She washed her face and cleaned her teeth in the washbasin in her room and then put on pyjamas and housecoat to go to the lavatory just up the passage. When she returned, the door was slightly ajar and that puzzled her because she could have sworn she had closed it. Once inside the room she was about to lock the door when an arm slid around her waist and a hand covered her mouth. She started with fright and if she had not been so shocked, her reactions would have been swifter. As it was she only had a few moments in which to catch a glimpse of Cedric's profile before he had her face down on the bed and was astride her.

'Cedric, what are you playing at?' she said angrily, lifting her head from the pillow.

'I'm just testing the author's theory that surprise is everything,' he said.

An icy chill crept down her spine and she attempted to throw him off. 'You've proved your point. Now get off me!' she gasped.

He pushed her head down and stretched out on top of her. 'Like hell I will. Even someone who's been trained in ju-jitsu like you will have trouble getting out of this position.'

Her fear intensified when she heard a jangling noise and out of the corner of her eye saw that the noise came from a pair of handcuffs. Again she tried to buck him off but he was too heavy.

'Th-this isn't f-funny,' she stammered. 'Will you please get off me!'

'No, I told you, I'm trying to prove a theory.' He held her wrists in a vice-like grip and raised himself slightly. She struggled but it was no use and he managed to fasten the handcuffs about one of her wrists and then to the bedpost.

Oh dear God, she thought, panicking as she struggled to rid herself of his weight. She could hardly breathe. 'I know what this is about,' she gasped.

'I should think you do. No one makes a show of me the way you did in the pictures. Who's the bloke you prefer to me?' he snarled. 'I bet he doesn't exist. It's just that you don't want a real man.'

She was tempted to tell him the truth but knew that would be a mistake in her position. She had to try and appease him. 'I'm sorry. You're right. Now please, let me go.'

'No, I'm enjoying myself,' he said against her cheek. The smell of alcohol was so strong that she almost passed out.

'You're drunk,' she panted.

'No, not drunk, just less inhibited than usual. Pity you're not much of a drinker. You'd relax more and enjoy this.'

Never in a million years! 'Please, Cedric, let me go and we'll forget this ever happened. What would your mother think if she was here today?'

'My mother? The old bitch is dead! Never left me in peace morning, noon or night, always on at me to do something or other.'

She felt him slide his hand down her pyjama bottoms and clasp her bare buttock and her fear began to spiral out of control. 'Please don't do that,' she squeaked.

'I like your pyjamas. I thought you might have been wearing a frilly nightie, but not you. You're a tease. Still, the bottoms will come off easy enough.'

She felt as if a whole block of ice slithered down her spine as he began to drag them down. 'D-Don't be a fool!'

'A fool! Is that what you call me? You've proved a big disappointment to me, Hester.'

'I'm sorry. Please let me go!'

'Say pretty please.' He bit her neck and she screamed. 'Naughty-naughty,' he said.

Then he stopped talking and she was helpless to prevent what happened next. Into her head came the words: *Don't provoke an assailant into taking that step too far. Keep calm.* But how could she remain calm when he was behaving like an animal on heat? She wanted to scream and go on screaming, but instead she felt as if she was suffocating in a wave of horror and pain. Then, as suddenly as the nightmare had begun, he removed himself. She could breathe again, but strangely she could not move her limbs. She could hear him gasping as he staggered about the room, then the door opened and closed.

She lay there, bruised, humiliated and utterly terrified that he'd return. Tears trickled down her cheeks, for not only had he raped her, but he had left her handcuffed to the bedpost.

Her teeth started to chatter. Nervous reaction, she told herself, gazing about and praying he had left the key behind. Then she saw it on the bedside table. She managed to pick it up and unlock the cuffs before collapsing on the bed.

Then it was as if a light came on in her head. She had to wash herself! She must have a bath. Had to get rid of all trace of him, otherwise she just might get pregnant.

She forced herself upright, not bothering with her pyjama bottoms, and donned her housecoat before grabbing a towel, soap and flannel. She prayed that she would not meet anyone on the way to the bathroom. She intended locking the door to her room this time, but dropped the key twice before she managed to get it into the lock and turn it on the outside. She hoped no one had heard her. How could she face her new friends feeling as she did right now?

The water ran lukewarm but she did not care what the temperature was because she only needed a few inches to sit in. She felt better once in the water and with the door firmly locked. As she sat there, a longing for her mother came over her. The feeling was so intense that she felt her heart would break. She stuffed the flannel in her mouth to stop herself from howling.

Finally, she managed to pull herself together and rubbed herself vigorously with the towel. At least he had admitted that his mother was dead – he had hated her by the sound of it. She forced herself to walk sedately back to her room and, once inside, locked the door and climbed into bed still wearing her housecoat. She was shivering and would have liked a hot-water bottle, but that was out of the question.

Yet she could not lie still, knowing it was here that he had defiled her. She slid out of bed, dragged off the quilt and coverlet and took a blanket and wrapped it round her. Going over to the window, she drew back the curtains and stared out. There was a full moon shining over peaceful fields. She sat down in a chair and for the rest of the night remained there, trying not to think about what had taken place in this room a short while ago.

She must have fallen asleep at some time because she woke to the sound of knocking on her door. Her heart jerked in her chest and the memory of last night came flooding back, drenching her in fear. The knocking came again and she managed to ask who was there.

A woman answered and she recognized the name as belonging to one of the group she had been talking to the evening before. For a moment she thought of saying that she was unwell and must go home, but she could not face going home yet. 'Give me a few minutes,' she called in a voice that sounded surprisingly normal. 'Perhaps you should go down and I'll join you there.'

'No, I'll wait for you,' said the woman.

Hester did not insist on her going. She felt stiff and sore as she got up from the chair, but managed to dress without too much difficulty. She brushed her teeth, ran a comb through her hair and applied lipstick. She gazed at her reflection in the dressing table mirror and forced a smile that was more like a grimace. Her father used to tell her to think happy thoughts when she was troubled. It took a real effort for her to smile naturally. She felt a completely different person from the one who had left Liverpool the day before.

Cedric. How was she going to face him? She couldn't do this . . .

'Will you be much longer?' called the woman outside.

From somewhere deep inside herself, Hester found the strength to reply, 'I'm ready now.' She picked up her handbag and unlocked the door.

The woman stared at her and then smiled. 'You look nice.'

'Thanks, so do you,' said Hester. 'Shall we go?'

When they arrived in the dining room, Hester blindly followed the woman to a table where two places had been kept for them. Only when she was seated did she look for Cedric.

Despite having no wish to ever set eyes on him again, she knew that she had to face him. Yet she could not see him. Perhaps he was sleeping off the daddy of all hangovers. God, she hoped so. She wanted him to suffer.

She felt light headed. What if he could not remember what he'd done to her last night? What if he denied it had ever happened? The thought enraged her. She had to force herself to eat, not wanting her lack of appetite to cause comments from the group she now seemed to be part of. Every few minutes her eyes darted towards the doorway in case Cedric should enter.

There was still no sign of him when the criminal psychologist, whom the writer consulted for research, began his talk. Hester had trouble concentrating on what he had to say. Every now and again an image of what had happened last evening would flash up in her mind. She tried to suppress it but was only partly successful.

Cedric was not in the dining room at lunchtime or at the discussion that afternoon either. Where was he? Was it possible that he was too ashamed to face her? Could he be in the bar? Her anger was such that she could not keep still. She wanted him on his knees, begging for her forgiveness. She had an overwhelming desire to put her foot on his head and squash it.

He was not in the bar.

Eventually, when the tension inside her was too much to bear, she went to reception and asked after him.

'He's left, Miss Walker,' said the receptionist.

Wordlessly, she stared at the woman and then turned on her heel and hurried away. There were questions she could have asked, but at that moment she could only think that she desperately needed some fresh air. She went upstairs for her outdoor clothes and to change her shoes. The handcuffs had gone. She felt a spurt of rage. Somehow he must have entered her bedroom and taken them whilst she was elsewhere. That meant he had not been so drunk that he had forgotten what he had done.

She needed to think about what action to take. She went outside and took deep breaths of frosty air as she circumnavigated the grounds. Part of her wanted to walk out of the place and not return. She could understand now why people disappeared. She wanted to slam a lid on the last evening and pretend it had not happened. Yet another part of her was so outraged by what Cedric had done to her that she wanted to scratch his eyes out at the very least. He deserved to be punished for the degrading way he had invaded her body. She felt sick thinking about it. Suddenly it occurred to her to wonder what he had thought she might do. She was a police officer after all, and he might believe that what she had to say would carry some weight if she should accuse him of rape. What an ugly word that was!

A shiver ran through her and she wrapped her arms about herself. What was she going to do? Of course if she did lay a charge against him for rape, he could counter that charge by saying she had been willing. It was her word against his and the police force was still very much a man's world. But surely they would take her seriously – especially as Cedric was being investigated? But there was no doubt about it, what had happened would upset her father once it was out in the open. She could picture George's broken-hearted expression only too easily, and as for Sam – what would he do? Beat Cedric to a pulp? And what if she were to get pregnant? The thought made her feel icy cold. She needed time to think, somewhere away from this place. Then she remembered her plan to visit Myra Jones. The shock of what had happened had driven it from her mind. She went inside, packed her bag, handed in her key and left.

Twenty-Two

'The holly and the ivy, when they are both full grown,' sang Jeanette, wiping a table top.

'It's not Christmas yet, you know,' said Mrs Cross, slamming the till drawer shut.

'It's only a week to go,' said Jeanette, straightening up and easing her back. 'And on Tuesday it's my eighteenth birthday.'

'My, you're getting old,' said Mrs Cross in a droll voice. 'I wish I was eighteen again.' She sighed. 'You make the most of being young, girl.'

'I aim to,' said Jeanette, glancing around the milk bar. 'I've finished here now. Is it OK if I go ten minutes early? I've got to get home, change, cook a meal, and my boyfriend is coming to pick me up.' Her heart seemed to lurch sideways, thinking that this evening would be the first time David would meet the family. Last night had been a no-no because her father and Sam had been working, so it had to be this evening. She prayed that all would go well.

'All right, but don't think I'll allow it every Saturday,' said

Mrs Cross. 'I'll see you in a fortnight on New Year's Day.' She sighed. 'Nineteen fifty-five! Where do all the years go?'

Jeanette made no comment, but threw the cloth in the washing basket and then rinsed and dried her hands before reaching for her coat. 'Thanks, Mrs Cross. I hope you have a good Christmas – and thanks for the bonus.' She wasted no time leaving the milk bar and walked swiftly in the direction of Renshaw Street.

She was passing Quiggins when a voice hailed her. She turned and saw Marty standing in the doorway, smoking a cigarette. 'You off home?' he said.

'Yes, I can't stop.' She made to walk on by but he grabbed her arm.

'Hang on a mo! Our Peggy was telling me that fella that got hit in the face is back and you're going out with him?'

'That's right,' said Jeanette. 'Have you heard anything on the grapevine about Billy?'

'No,' said Marty, dropping the butt of his cigarette and grinding it out with his heel. 'If I had the faintest idea where he was, I'd grass on him like a shot.'

A shiver went through her. 'Do you think he's lying low in Liverpool somewhere or that he's scuttled off to Ireland?'

'I can't say for certain, but I am keeping my eyes peeled and my ears to the ground,' said Marty. 'If I do discover anything, you'll soon know.'

Jeanette thanked him, reckoning that he would tell Peggy and she'd pass it on to her. She continued on her way, thinking about the meal she was to cook that evening before going out, and wondering how Hester was getting on at the conference.

Hester felt a strange calm come over her as she stepped off the train at Whalley station. The heaviness of her spirit caused by the horror of last night lifted, and as she handed over her ticket and walked through the barrier and down the main street she experienced a sense of homecoming. Why had she left it so long before returning? She should have put what Aunt Ethel said about Myra Jones to the test and visited Whalley on a summer's day, making a visit to the ruined abbey an excuse and called in on her. She took a deep breath. Well, she was here now and, pray God, she would soon be seeing her.

The house was not far from the Co-op. She still remembered Myra's divvy number that she used to repeat every time she went shopping there. She came to the house and noticed that there were still net curtains at the windows and the door was painted green. She sighed and banged the knocker but no one came. She wielded the knocker again but there were no footsteps hurrying to answer the door. Her mood of calm began to evaporate. Myra had to be in!

She thumped on the door with her fist and called her name but there was still no response and she slumped down and sat on the step. Suddenly she thought of Ally and wished he was here right now to comfort her. But he was in Germany and she doubted there could be a future for them. What with him wanting to emigrate, and besides . . . Suddenly words were tumbling into her head: he wouldn't want her now. She was spoilt, besmirched, used goods because of what had happened last night. A sob burst in her throat and she bent over and burst into tears.

'Hester?'

Her head jerked up and she saw Emma standing a few feet away. 'What is it, love? You can't be breaking your heart crying just because Myra's gone to visit her nephew. She'll be back tomorrow.'

Hester stared at her dumbly, the tears trickling down her cheeks. Emma covered the distance between them in no time and crouched beside her, putting an arm around her. 'There now, tell me what's wrong and we'll see if we can sort it out.' Her voice was so sympathetic that all that had happened last night and what was worrying Hester now came out in fits and bursts between sobs.

'Oh, poor Hester!' murmured Emma, rocking her as if she was a baby.

'What am I going to do?' asked Hester when she gained some measure of composure, relieved that there was no one else around. 'How can I tell Dad and Sam?' she whispered.

'You must! You can't let him get away with it. Let your menfolk deal with him.'

'They'll want to kill him. I don't want them getting into trouble,' said Hester, mopping her eyes with her handkerchief. 'Besides, I feel too ashamed . . . and anyway, I'm forever saying women are equal to men. I should deal with him. I got myself into this, I should get myself out of it.'

Emma looked at her in dismay. 'Hester, there are just some things that men are best left to deal with. What can you do?'

'I don't know yet. I need to think some more when I'm in less of a state.'

'But what if . . .' Emma paused.

Hester stared at her. 'If I'm already pregnant, you mean? I'll worry about that if and when I know for sure. One thing is for certain – I won't be able to stay in the police force if I am.' Her eyes filled with tears. 'Dad will be so upset.'

Emma was silent for several moments, and then she said, 'Well, you know where to come if you need a refuge. You can stay at my cottage. You're not the first person this has happened to.'

Hester blinked at her. 'You mean it happened to you?'

'No! It happened to Betty,' she said in a low voice.

'Your half-sister?'

'Aye, although she's not really my half-sister, but that's another story.'

'I don't understand. I thought—'

'So did I, but apparently her mother was already pregnant when she married my father. Her sister, who was Jared's mother, told him shortly before she died and he thought I should know the truth. But I couldn't bring myself to tell Betty.'

'What do you know about her real father?'

'He was an actor with a travelling company and apparently he died of blood poisoning and never knew Betty's mother was pregnant. They were in love.'

'How sad!'

'Aye.' Emma sighed. 'But it's the past and right now we have to think what to do about you.'

'I came to see Myra. She was like a mother to me and will expect me to visit her tomorrow afternoon.' Hester's tears spilled over again.

'You can still see her. You can stay with Jared and me tonight.'

Emma stood up and helped Hester to her feet. 'Now let's go and have a cup of tea. I've made some scones. We'll have them and then we'll make something hot for supper. Jared is busy planning a bathroom. He thinks it will be an asset whether we keep the cottage and rent it out or sell it.'

'Thank you. You're so kind,' said Hester, and freed a deep sigh of relief.

'I'm sure you'd do the same for me,' said Emma, leading the way.

Hester picked up her overnight bag and followed her, thinking over all that Emma had said and questioning whether she should take her advice about letting her menfolk deal with Cedric. She wondered what exactly had happened to Betty that was similar to her own situation. Presumably she had been raped, but had it resulted in a pregnancy, and if so had Betty had the baby adopted or had an illegal abortion? She supposed it was really none of her business, but it was possible that she might have to make such a choice. She felt sympathy and admiration for the girl without having even met her. To suffer such abuse left its mark. She thought of Ally and felt a different kind of ache about her heart and wished she could turn back the clock.

Twenty-Three

'What's this?' asked Ethel, poking the food on her plate with a fork.

'It's cottage pie,' said Jeanette.

Ethel tasted a mouthful. 'It's got baked beans in it! Hester wouldn't put baked beans in cottage pie.'

'Hester isn't here,' said Sam shortly. 'Besides, what's wrong with baked beans? It tastes fine to me.'

Her father glanced across at Jeanette. 'So what time is this David Bryn Jones coming?'

She glanced at the clock on the mantelpiece. 'He should be here any minute now.'

As if on cue, the door knocker rat-a-tat-tatted. She jumped to her feet and hurried out of the room, switching on the lobby light as she did so for it was pitch black outside. As she opened the door and smiled at David, she thought no doubt there would be some of the neighbours taking note of the stranger calling at their house.

David smiled down at her. 'You OK?'

'I'm great.' She thought of this time yesterday when they had met in town and he had kissed her, there outside the Forum cinema, not caring who might be watching them.

'Your dad and brother in this time?'

She nodded, thinking that he had taken the news that her father and brother wanted to meet him surprisingly well. 'Come in!'

He stepped over the threshold and closed the door behind him. His lips brushed hers and she felt a warm glow. She helped him off with his navy-blue reefer coat and hung it up. All was quiet and she guessed that the family had their ears pricked. She glanced at him and he winked.

Taking a deep breath, she opened the door and said in a voice that quivered slightly, 'Dad, Sam, Aunt Ethel, meet David Bryn Jones.'

George rose to his feet. 'We're just having our meal, lad. Perhaps you'd like to sit down and have a cup of tea with us?' He glanced at his daughter. 'Jeannie, fetch the lad a cup!'

David removed his cap to reveal curling black hair, and squared his shoulders. 'Thanks, Mr Walker. A cup of tea's always welcome and it's a chilly evening.'

'Perhaps he'd like to sit by the fire,' said Ethel, surprising her relatives. 'We can all move round.'

'Thanks, Miss Walker, but I'm used to the cold. You stay where you are,' said David.

'Please yourself,' she said, 'but the name's not Walker, it's Ramsbottom.'

'That's a good Lancashire name,' said David.

Jeanette flashed him a smile as she poured his tea.

'Aye, it is,' said Ethel, blinking at him. 'So how's that face of yours? You should stay out of fights.'

'I have every intention of doing so, Miss Ramsbottom,' he said politely.

'It's Missus, actually,' she said, glancing slyly at her family. 'I married a distant cousin.'

'You never did!' said George, staring at her. 'What kind of joke is this?'

Her mouth quivered. 'It's no joke. I've never seen the point of mentioning it before, but after talking to that young film woman, I changed my mind. My husband died within two days of us tying the knot.'

'You've talked to Sam's Dorothy?' said Jeanette.

Ethel said smugly, 'She came knocking at the door this morning while you were all out. My young man was like this one here, with dark curly hair and nice manners.'

'Good God, Aunt Ethel, I wish you hadn't chosen now to drop such a bombshell,' said George, rubbing the back of his neck. 'And what's this about our Sam and a film woman called Dorothy?'

'She's determined to make a film about women of Liverpool,' said Jeanette.

'Shall we set this aside?' said Sam sharply. 'Mr Jones has come here to meet Dad. Bearing in mind how you two first met, we're naturally concerned that he stays out of trouble. After all, sailors are famed for getting into fights when they come ashore.'

David gave him a straight look. 'I don't go looking for trouble, Mr Walker, but I could no sooner ignore Jeanette's cry for help that evening in the chippy, than I could a kitten thrown in a bucket of water to drown. I'm a third marine engineer, hoping to work my way up to first, and it pays me to keep my nose clean.'

'What if you were to meet the youth who did that to your face again?' asked Sam.

'That would depend on the circumstances. If Jeanette was present, I'd send her to ring for the police.'

'Good answer,' said Jeanette, handing David his cup of tea. 'We'll have to go soon if we're to make the start of the film.'

'Hang on,' said Sam. 'We need to know more about him before you go off with him.'

'Let it go, son,' said George quietly. 'There'll be other evenings. Best drink that tea quickly, lad,' he added, turning to David.

David wasted no time in downing the tea, guessing that the old aunt's bombshell had given him an easier ride than he might have had if she had kept quiet. For now he was accepted by George Walker as fit to go out with his daughter, although it was obvious that her half-brother did not feel the same way.

'Ready?' asked Jeanette.

David nodded, and with a swift tarrah they left the house.

'I can hardly believe we escaped so easily,' she said, as arm in arm they hurried up the street.

'You know why,' said David. 'Your old aunt saying what she did.'

'I can't believe she's telling the truth,' said Jeanette. 'What's the point of keeping the fact that you were once married a secret?'

'You heard her. She didn't think it was worth it because she was only married for two days.'

'It seems a daft reason to me. I wonder what Sam will do now? He must be mad as a hatter with Dorothy coming to the house and speaking to Aunt Ethel. They've fallen out over her wanting to produce and direct this film about Liverpool women. She's putting her own money into it and he thinks she's crazy. He's having trouble accepting that times are changing and women can make their own decisions and aren't going to be content to be tied to the kitchen sink.'

'You mean women won't be satisfied with marrying, staying at home and having babies any more?'

'Some won't,' said Jeanette firmly. 'But I rather like the idea of running my own home and having children and bringing them up.'

David leaned towards her and kissed her cheek. 'That's useful to know.'

Jeanette blushed and did not ask why. Somehow she felt certain that she would get to know sooner rather than later.

'I've something to tell you,' said David, as they headed for the main road. 'I've fixed it so we can spend a good part of the Christmas break together. I'm giving Mam and my aunt a two-night break in a hotel in Chester for their Christmas present. They're made up. They love Chester.'

Jeanette's face lit up. 'That's great!' She hugged his arm.

'Now your birthday—'

Her smile faded. 'You'll be working.'

'Depends on several factors, but I'll try and make it.'

'I understand, but I was hoping we could go and see *Mad About Men.*'

'Let's wait and see.' He smiled down at her. 'And in the meantime, we'll make the most of this evening.'

To their surprise, when they came out of the cinema and were walking to the bus stop they saw Father Callaghan in conversation with a tramp.

'I want to speak to the Padre,' said Jeanette. 'I need to ask him a question.'

'OK, but make it quick,' said David. 'I don't want to miss the last bus after seeing you home.'

Jeanette tapped the priest on the arm and he glanced around. 'Hello, Padre. I'm sorry for interrupting, but can I have a word.'

The priest excused himself and smiled at them both. 'I see you found your friend, Jeanette. How can I help you?'

'Have you had any luck in finding anything out about my mother?' asked Jeanette.

Father Callaghan hesitated.

'Please, even if it's bad news, I must know the truth,' she pleaded.

He nodded. 'All right. One of my contacts showed the photograph to a man he remembers being in the auxiliary fire brigade during the blitz. He's certain he recognized her. She was unconscious and filthy dirty when she was dug out of a bombed building. He spent some time waiting with her to be transported to Fazakerley hospital.'

'Fazakerley!'

'Yes. The Royal Southern hospital had been moved into its grounds in temporary accommodation because its building in Toxteth was being used for naval training, with it being close to the Mersey. So the wounded in Toxteth had to go to Fazakerley.'

'We used to live just a short bus ride from Toxteth,' said Jeanette, trying to control her inner trembling.

Father Callaghan smiled kindly. 'There you are then. Perhaps you'd like the photograph of your mother back? I've been carrying it around with me since it was returned to me.'

'Yes,' she said. 'I might have need of it myself.'

He fumbled in his jacket pocket and produced the envelope with the photograph inside. 'You're very like her,' he said.

'So my father says. Thank you, Padre.'

'Now if you'll excuse me,' said Father Callaghan.

Jeanette turned to David. 'I thought I was prepared for such news, but I wasn't. Look at my hands!'

She held them out to him and he saw that they were shaking. He took the photograph and pocketed it before taking one of her hands in his. 'Let's go.'

As they waited at the bus stop, he said, 'I suppose you'll be wanting to visit Fazakerley hospital as soon as you can?'

'I'm not sure. The records for the Southern might be back there now. I'll speak to Dad. It's possible it's one of the hospitals he checked out when he was trying to find her.'

'Makes sense.' He put his arm around her shoulders and looked down at her with concern. 'You OK now?'

'Sure. At least Mam was still alive when she was taken to hospital. Even if she died later, she might have come round and managed to speak to someone.'

'Maybe. But best not to play guessing games.'

She agreed.

They were both silent on the bus, busy with their own thoughts. When they arrived outside her front door, Jeanette asked was he going to come in?

'No, I have to get back. Hopefully I'll see you on your birthday. I'll get a message to you by the same method as before.' He lowered his head and kissed her. 'Goodnight.'

'Goodnight, David,' she whispered.

He nudged her lightly on the chin with his fist and then turned and walked away.

She was about to knock on the door but it opened and her father stood there. 'Come in, luv,' he said. 'Enjoy the film?'

She nodded and followed him inside, wondering how to

broach the subject of her mother. Maybe she should leave it until the morning? She did not want him to have a sleepless night. So she asked if Ethel had said anything more about the man she had supposedly married, and where and when the wedding had taken place.

'She's not saying, luv,' said George. 'Sam and I tried to get it out of her but she sat there looking smug until in the end our Sam upped and left the house. He still hasn't come back.'

'Maybe she'll tell us tomorrow,' said Jeanette.

'No, I don't think she will, luv,' said George with certainty. 'She kept saying, "Wait until the film comes out".'

Jeanette had another restless night, and she wished Hester was there so she could talk over all that was bothering her. She fell asleep just before dawn and so overslept. When she went downstairs about ten o'clock there was no one there, so she could only think Ethel had nipped to the newsagent's and Sam and her father were on duty. She poured cornflakes into a bowl before switching on the wireless. In front of her she placed her mother's photograph. What were the odds that someone would remember Grace if she had still been alive when she reached Fazakerley? It was not as if it was just down the road, but up from the docks and on the other side of Liverpool, not far from Aintree race course. She felt depressed, wishing someone would come in so she could talk to them about this. But not Ethel. She wanted Hester but was unsure exactly when she planned to arrive home, so decided she might as well get on with peeling the vegetables for dinner.

It was not until four o'clock that George came in. Jeanette and Ethel had eaten their Sunday dinner, having decided it was no use waiting for the two men. 'No Hester yet?' he asked. Having changed out of his uniform into tweed trousers, checked shirt and a Fair Isle pullover, he was now sitting at the table.

Jeanette shook her head. 'Sam's not in either.'

'He could be anywhere. I'm not worried about him,' said George, folding the Sunday newspaper and then propping it against the teapot. He picked up his knife and fork and read whilst he ate his meal.

Jeanette went upstairs to get her clothes out ready for work in the morning, thinking she would talk to her father later about her mother. But when Hester had not arrived by seven o'clock, George went to the front door and looked out.

'Any sign of her, Dad?' asked Jeanette from the top of the lobby. She hoped everything was all right with her sister.

'No. I think I'll walk up the street. You put the kettle on. She'll be ready for a cup of tea when she gets here,' said George.

'I'm not exactly sure when she said she'd be home,' said Jeanette. 'She was going to see Myra Jones. Still, I'd like to come with you for the walk.'

She told Ethel, who was in the parlour rooting through drawers in the sideboard, where they were going. She hardly seemed to hear her and Jeanette wondered what she was looking for but left her to it. She put on her coat and scarf and left the house, linking arms with her father as they walked up the street. 'I've something to tell you, Dad,' she said.

'What's that, Jeannie?' He gazed down at her from his great height.

She told him about giving the photograph to Father Callaghan and what he had said to her last evening. She watched his expression change to incredulity and waited for him to speak. 'You've done more than I would have given you credit for, girl. What's the next step, that's what I ask myself?'

'The hospital records, Dad?'

He shook his grizzled head. 'No, I'd like to speak to the man who identified her from the photograph if possible. There's always more a person knows than he actually realizes. Could be, though, that I'll have to leave it until after Christmas.'

'OK, Dad, you're the policeman,' said Jeanette.

They had reached Breck Road and now stood on the corner looking in the direction of the bus stop. After three buses had come and gone with no sign of Hester, George said, 'You go back, luv, before you catch cold. I'll stay a bit longer.'

'No, I'll wait with you, Dad,' said Jeanette, huddling into her coat.

They waited another quarter of an hour in silence and then it began to rain.

'Let's go home,' said George heavily. 'It's possible she might have come West Derby Road way, despite it being longer, and she's waiting for us at home right now.'

She wasn't.

But they had not been in the house long when Sam turned up. Immediately Jeanette grabbed hold of him. 'Our Hester hasn't arrived home yet. D'you know if she's on an early shift in the morning?'

Sam's cheerful expression was replaced by a frown. 'I can't remember. But there's no need to start panicking. If she's gone to visit Myra Jones and she's on a later shift, she might have been invited to stay the night and will come back in the morning.'

'That makes sense,' said Jeanette.

Sam exchanged looks with his father, who still seemed worried. 'I don't like it. I'm sure she said that she'd be home this evening,' said George.

'She's a grown woman, Dad,' said Jeanette.

'Yes, look at Dorothy. She goes all over the country and doesn't come to any harm,' said Sam.

Jeanette thought he looked quite cheerful when he said that and was tempted to ask if he and Dorothy had solved their differences.

'Perhaps you could phone the conference centre and see when she left, Sam?' said George.

'D'you remember the name of the place?' asked Sam.

Jeanette said, 'I remember her showing me a leaflet. Maybe she wrote it down somewhere and it's in her room.' Without wasting time, she hurried upstairs, spotted the leaflet on the floor and ran downstairs with it.

Sam took it from her and gave it a quick perusal. 'I'll go and ring them from the telephone box.' He added as an afterthought, 'It's time you got a telephone put in, Dad.'

Jeanette and George waited impatiently for Sam's return and she filled in the time by telling him about David's mother and aunt going to Chester for Christmas, and asked would it be all right if he had Christmas dinner with them? He nodded, but she guessed he was only half listening.

Sam arrived back just over half an hour later and his expression was grim.

'What's wrong?' asked George, turning pale.

'She left yesterday,' he said, shrugging off his damp overcoat. 'I'm hoping that she went to stay with Myra Jones a day early.

I did ask whether Hester had given a reason why she was leaving early. The receptionist said no, but she did add that Hester had asked about one of the other guests, Cedric Dobson, that morning. When she told her that he'd left earlier in the day, Hester appeared shocked.'

'That name seems familiar,' said George.

'He's trouble,' said Sam tersely, and proceeded to tell his father that Cedric was being investigated.

Listening intently to all that was said, Jeanette broke into the conversation. 'But if they left separately, I can't see how there's any need for us to be worrying about Hester. Maybe it was just the sight of him there that upset her and she decided that she preferred spending time with Myra. She'll either be home later this evening or tomorrow morning, you'll see.'

As if on cue, there came the sound of a key in the latch and the front door opening. 'Hello, anybody at home?' called a familiar voice.

'Hester!' Jeanette shot out of the room and flew up the lobby. She flung her arms around her half-sister. 'We've been worrying about you. Dad got into a tizzy about you because he thought you should have been home by now. Then we discovered you'd left early and that Cedric had been at the conference. Are you OK?'

A shocked Hester dropped her holdall. She had been prepared to put on a smiling face for her family but now she felt all hot and bothered. How did they know about Cedric? 'Jeanette, let me get through the door, I'm that tired, I don't know what to do with myself,' she said huskily.

Jeanette moved out of the way. 'Did you go and see Myra Jones?'

'Yes! She made me very welcome.'

Jeanette took a deep breath. 'What's happened? How was the conference? Did you enjoy the special speaker or did Cedric being there spoil it for you?'

All sensible thought deserted Hester and she just stood there, staring at her half-sister. Then George appeared in the doorway of the sitting room.

'What are you two talking about? If you're talking secrets, bring them out into the open,' he said. 'This Cedric—'

Hester's face crumpled and she burst into tears. Instantly, her father put his arms around her, rocking her and whispering soothing words. 'There, there, love, you're safe. You tell Daddy and he'll sort the bugger out.'

At any other time his use of a swear word would have shocked his children, but not now. Yet still Hester could not bring herself to tell him the whole truth. 'He assaulted me, Daddy! He was so angry with me for finishing with him and got so drunk that he completely lost it.' She lifted her head and saw Sam standing behind her father, his face tight with fury. This time she addressed her brother. 'He told me that his mother was dead! He called her a bitch! It was obvious that he hated her.'

Sam jerked his head sharply. 'Let me past! I'm going to get the bastard.'

George looked at Jeanette. 'You look after your sister. Call the doctor. I'm going with Sam.'

Jeanette took his place at Hester's side, put her arm around her waist and ushered her into the sitting room and over to the fire. She helped her off with her outdoor clothes and eased her into a comfy chair. 'You stay there and don't move. I'm going to fill a hot-water bottle and make you a nice cup of cocoa. Then you're for bed. After that I'll go out to the phone box and call the doctor.'

'No!' cried Hester in fright. 'I . . . I've already seen a doctor. I saw one when I stayed with Myra. I'll be OK. I'm just feeling bruised and battered and terribly shaken up. I wasn't going to tell any of you because I didn't want to upset you.' She kicked off her shoes and rested her head against the back of the chair. Sobs still shook her body. She didn't want to see a doctor. He'd want to give her a thorough check-up and would discover she had been raped. She could not cope with that right now. She just wanted to be left alone and for her menfolk to deal with Cedric.

'What's going on here? What was all the commotion about before?' Ethel's voice disturbed the peace. 'Where's George and Sam gone?'

Hester thought she was the last person she wanted to talk to and did not even bother opening her eyes. It was Jeanette who answered their great-aunt. 'Hester was assaulted and Dad and Sam have gone to get the sod who did it,' she said.

'What? When was this?' asked Ethel.

'While she was away,' replied Jeanette. 'Now you just be nice to her, Aunt Ethel, and don't be bothering her with questions.'

'It seems a rum do to me,' said Ethel. 'That's what happens with giving girls too much freedom.'

'Oh shut up!' muttered Hester. 'You don't know what you're talking about. Now leave me alone. I need to rest.'

'Don't you speak to me like that,' said Ethel.

'Aunt Ethel, you heard her, leave her alone,' said Jeanette firmly, and seizing the old woman by the waist, she found the strength to propel her out of the room. She closed the door on her and turned back to Hester. 'That woman!' was all she said, picking up the hot-water bottle and handing it to her half-sister. 'I'll just get your cocoa and then I've got some good news for you.'

Hester opened her eyes and stared at Jeanette's retreating back. What good news could this be?

A short while later Hester opened the drawer in her bedroom and removed the envelope that Jeanette had placed there. For a moment she stared down at the bold handwriting depicting her name and address on the envelope postmarked Germany, and then she slit the envelope open with a finger.

Hello, Hester,

Sorry I haven't been in touch sooner but life's been hectic with too much to do, but you've been in my mind constantly, with me wishing I was with you instead of here finishing things up. By the time you receive this letter I should be on my way back to England. I've my fingers crossed I'll be able to see you before Christmas. I'm hoping Wendy and Charley will be able to put me up in their flat for a couple of nights. Will be in touch when I get to Liverpool.

Love Ally.

She had thought she had finished with weeping for that evening, but now the tears trickled down her cheeks. She was damaged goods and she could not pretend differently. If she agreed to meet Ally, how could she smile into his face and behave as if everything was hunky-dory? What if she was already pregnant? The thought terrified her. At the moment she could not imagine herself ever being able to bring herself to tell him about what had happened. He knew that she had dated Cedric several times and it was possible he might, just might, believe that she had not finished with him after all. A deep sigh passed through her body and she sank onto the bed. At that moment she could not imagine herself ever being happy again.

It was gone midnight when Sam and George returned. Jeanette had not gone to bed but was curled up in a chair in front of the fire. As soon as she heard the key in the door, she stood up and hurried out into the lobby. 'Well?' she asked.

Neither answered her, but removed their coats and hung them up. She backed into the living room and went and put the kettle on before returning to the sitting room. They both stood in front of the fire, holding their hands out to the glowing embers.

'He's done a runner,' said Sam, without turning round.

'The bloody swine! He knew he'd gone too far,' muttered George. 'We'll get him, though. Sooner or later, he'll be found. It's not only us that want to speak to him. He's suspected of taking bribes, fraud and arson. We'll get the bugger.' He stared at Jeanette. 'Did you get the doctor?'

'No. Hester said that she'd seen a doctor while she was staying with Myra in Whalley. She told me that she just feels bruised and battered and that she hadn't been going to tell us about what had happened because she didn't want to upset us.'

'I'm glad she came to her senses and did tell us,' said George. 'He has to be caught and punished.'

Jeanette agreed, and having told them Hester was tucked up in bed, she went and made tea, hoping the police would catch Cedric soon, yet fully aware that so far they had failed to find Billy.

Twenty-Four

'Christmas is coming, the goose is getting fat. Please put a penny in the old man's hat,' sang Jeanette, applying glue to a paper chain.

'Do you always have to be singing?' grumbled Ethel. 'I don't know why you're putting up decorations. There's no children in this house to make it worth the bother.'

'Don't be a misery, Aunt Ethel. Christmas isn't just for children, you know,' said Jeanette, determined to put a bright face on things. The rest of her family seemed to be able to think of nothing else but getting Cedric behind bars. Not that she blamed them. Although Hester had said no more about what form his assault had taken at the conference, she looked tense and wan. It was obvious the swine had hurt her in a way that had deeply shocked her sister. She sighed, hoping that Hester would recover soon. At least Ally should be able to help her do so – if she allowed him to.

Her thoughts were interrupted by Ethel snapping, 'Have you done anything more about finding Grace?'

Jeanette reached for a strip of red paper and wielded the paste brush. 'I don't know if I should tell you what I've found out, seeing as how you're keeping quiet about supposedly having been married.'

'So you have found out something then,' said Ethel, smiling.

Jeanette hesitated and then gave in. 'We know that someone looking like Mam was dug out of a bombed building. She could have been taken to Fazakerley hospital because the Southern hospital was taken over by the Royal Navy at the beginning of the war.'

Ethel made a sound in her throat, but Jeanette did not get to hear what she was about to say because there was the sound of a key in the lock and a draught of freezing air puffed round her ankles. The door opened and her father appeared. The shoulders of his navy-blue overcoat were dusted with snow, which started to melt as he stood there. 'Before you start thinking we're going to have a white Christmas, it's only a sprinkling, but it's gone cold. It wouldn't surprise me if there's a frost in the morning.' He placed his helmet on the sideboard.

'Don't put your helmet there,' said Ethel, shuffling over and removing it.

Jeanette smiled at him, thinking he seemed to have aged in the last few days. 'Come over to the fire, Dad, and get a warm. You look done in.'

He removed his overcoat and placed it over the back of a chair. 'I've had news about that swine Cedric. Our Sam got in touch with me and he and Hester have been given permission to go and speak to Cedric's inspector in Bootle.'

'What did Sam tell you?' Jeanette hastened to put the paste brush away.

George stood in front of the fire, warming his hands. 'A couple of timber yards were set alight within a short distance of each other. One was completely destroyed and the other one would have been, too, if a passer-by hadn't seen the flames and alerted the fire bobbies. They rescued a youth but also found a dead body. It's been identified as Cedric's.'

'Bloody hell!' Jeanette was shocked and sank into a chair. 'I wonder how Hester's feeling right now?'

At that moment Sam and Hester were gazing down at the charred timbers that still smouldered beneath a starry sky. 'What a bloody fool!' she whispered. 'He could have had such a good, worthwhile life if he hadn't given in to temptation.'

'You're too forgiving,' said Sam. 'He was bloody wicked!'

'Oh, I haven't forgiven him for what he did to me,' said Hester, her expression hardening. 'Don't ever think that. I bet Billy's mother will never forgive him either.'

'He was calling Cedric everything evil under the sun,' said Sam grimly. 'He's been carted off to hospital; his hands and face are in a bad way. Anyway, that priest our Jeanette knows has been sent for to accompany his mother to Stanley hospital. It'll be prison for Billy when he recovers. He's still wanted for the attack on that doorman. Cedric would have known that because his photograph has been up in every station on Merseyside. Just like him, he deserves what he got. Others could have been killed in those fires and they weren't the only cases of arson, as we know.' Sam tilted back his trilby, gazed up at the sky and changed the subject, not wanting to upset his sister further by going on about it. 'I hope the weather stays dry. Dorothy was planning on doing some filming tomorrow.'

Hester was glad to talk of something else. She rubbed her eyes, which were watering due to the acrid smoke, and said, 'So you've seen her recently?'

'On Saturday. I've asked her to marry me.'

'Oh!' Hester could not have been more surprised. 'So you've made up your quarrel then?'

'Sort of. She said she'll think about it and if she says yes, there'll be certain conditions, including a year's engagement.' He said gloomily, 'At one time a woman would have been thrilled to have a proposal and couldn't wait to get married.'

Hester managed a laugh. 'Times they are a-changing, brother. Although I'm sure there are still plenty of women around who would jump at the opportunity to accept a proposal from you. But Dorothy obviously enjoys what she does and has no intention of you putting a stop to it. You've already tried by speaking against it when you should have encouraged her.'

'I wouldn't have been honest if I'd done that,' said Sam. 'I want children and a home of my own and someone to look after me and them.'

All men want to be put first, thought Hester, but she understood his dilemma. 'Did you think of mentioning the word "love" to her? Not that a man always means it when he says it,' she muttered. Was Ally any different? She hoped so, even if there was no future for them together.

Suddenly she heard the click of fingers in front of her face.

'You seem to have gone off in a trance,' said Sam. 'Of course I mentioned the word "love". I wouldn't have asked her to marry me if I didn't love her. I'd have found someone else who was more willing to fall in with my wishes.'

Hester shrugged. 'OK, I believe you.'

Sam squeezed her shoulder affectionately. 'Buck up, our kid! This time next year hopefully everything will have worked itself out.'

But she could not bring herself to smile. 'I think I'll go along to the hospital and have a word with the priest. Our Jeanette will be interested in what he has to say about Billy and his mother.'

Sam nodded and went off to talk to the inspector.

'Constable Walker?'

Hester rose from the chair outside the room where Billy was lying moaning in pain. His burns were swathed in ointment and gauze and he had just received an injection of morphine.

'Father Callaghan?'

'That's right! You're Jeanette's sister?'

'Yes, I'm Hester.' They shook hands.

'This is a bad do,' he said. 'I had hoped that Borstal might have taught him a lesson, but then he attacked Jeanette, who was lucky to get away relatively unharmed, unlike the doorman. Billy's fortunate that he did not die. Now this latest evil . . .'

'He's paying heavily for it,' said Hester.

'Yes, he'll have weeks of dreadful pain and then court and prison.' Father Callaghan sighed heavily.

'I feel sorry for his mother. If only she had informed us where he was hiding this wouldn't have happened.'

'He would never have forgiven her,' said Father Callaghan sadly. 'It's not easy being a mother.' He paused. 'Talking of mothers, if Jeanette would like to speak to a nurse who thinks she saw her mother the day she was dragged from the ruins, then it's possible she'll be at a Christmas concert we're giving at the church hall.'

'What?' Hester could scarcely believe it.

'A woman came to see me. Her brother was in the auxiliary fire service. She would say no more than that she would try to be at the concert if Jeanette wished to speak to her.'

'What day is the concert?' asked Hester, thinking this news should delight Jeanette.

Jeanette heard the front door open, yawned and turned over in bed. She stared at the alarm clock. It was seven in the morning and her eighteenth birthday. She could hear voices below and hoped that meant someone was going to bring her breakfast in bed. She still didn't know for sure if David would be able to meet her today. She waited for ten minutes and when there was still no sound of footsteps on the stairs, decided she had better get up if she was going to be in work on time.

The lino was cold beneath her feet and she dressed in haste and scuttled to the bathroom. Ten minutes later, she went downstairs and entered the kitchen where she found Hester and Sam eating bacon and eggs in silence.

'I'd have enjoyed a cooked breakfast,' said Jeanette, taking a packet of cornflakes from the kitchen cabinet.

'Well cook it yourself,' said Sam. 'We've been out most of the night.'

'Of course, I'm sorry,' murmured Jeanette. 'So Cedric's dead?'

Hester and Sam looked at each other. 'Yes, he's dead,' said the latter, and carried on eating.

'Did Dad tell you about Billy?' said Hester.

Jeanette's hand stilled. 'He told me a youth had been injured.'

'Billy's face and hands were badly burnt.'

Jeanette gasped.

Hester continued, 'I spoke to your priest at Stanley hospital. I was to tell you that a nurse who thinks she saw your mother in hospital could possibly be at a concert given in the church hall tomorrow night.'

Jeanette sank onto a chair. 'That's the last thing I expected you to say,' she croaked.

'I was surprised, too.' Hester carried her empty plate over to the sink and then without another word left the kitchen.

Jeanette looked at Sam. 'Is she OK?'

'Cedric's death was a shock but she'll get over it.' Sam spread butter on his toast. 'Interesting message from the priest for you.'

Jeanette nodded, thinking not only of her mother but of Billy burnt and in hospital. No need to keep looking over her shoulder now, worrying that he wasn't in Ireland and might discover where she lived. She put him out of her mind and thought instead of the news from Father Callaghan. Perhaps Peggy would be going to the concert and she could go with her.

Jeanette was still eating her breakfast when the post arrived. Only two birthday cards for her: she recognized Peggy's writing, and David's from the note he had sent to her. He had sent his love and said that he would be able to make the cinema that evening. She hugged the thought to her, wrote a note to Ethel and her father saying she would be out, and propped it up against the clock and left for work, slightly miffed that no one in her family had remembered she was eighteen that day.

'Happy birthday to you, happy birthday to you,' sang Peggy, entering the office with a small, neatly tied parcel. 'This is for you.' She handed it over to Jeanette. 'It's a—'

'Don't tell me,' interrupted Jeanette. 'It takes away the fun of opening it.'

'Sorry,' said Peggy, perching on her desk. 'I hope you like the colour.'

Jeanette rolled her eyes. 'Thanks.' She opened the parcel and took out a Max Factor lipstick and a bar of Fry's chocolate cream. She removed the lipstick from its box and saw that it was coral. 'Perfect. I'd have hated bright red.'

'My pleasure,' said Peggy, beaming at her. 'So what are you doing tonight? Meeting lover boy?'

'Yes. We're going to see Glynis Johns in the mermaid film.' Jeanette paused. 'I was going to ask you whether you were going to the concert at Father Callaghan's church hall tomorrow night. If so, can I come with you?'

'Sure! Is there a reason?'

Jeanette told her. Peggy gave a whistle. 'Let's hope you're in luck. Bad about Billy, though. Bloody fool!'

Jeanette agreed. She shared the Fry's Cream with Peggy and Elsie, then Peggy left the room and Jeanette got on with her work, looking forward to that evening and the concert tomorrow, as well.

She was pleased to find David waiting for her outside the Cunard Building later that day. 'Happy birthday,' he said, handing her a small parcel. 'I hope you like it.' He brushed his lips against hers.

She removed the wrappings to reveal a square-shaped box. Opening it she found inside a gold heart-shaped locket with a jewel inside on a chain set on a bed of cotton wool. 'Oh, this is lovely,' she said, fingering it. 'I'd ask you to put it on for me now, but perhaps it's best if we wait until we get to the cinema where there's more light.' She managed to stop herself from saying, *You shouldn't have spent so much money on me.* But the fact that he had done so must mean he really was serious about her.

'Good idea,' said David, kissing her again.

She clung to him and returned his kiss. Slowly they drew apart and smiled at each other. 'Thank you so much for my present.' She placed it in her handbag.

'My pleasure,' he said, drawing her hand through his arm.

They began to walk up Water Street, discussing whether to have something to eat before going to the cinema or afterwards. That decision made, she wondered if she should put off telling him about Billy or whether to get it over with. Then she could tell him the news that she had been thinking about for most of the day.

David did not react to the news about Billy as she thought he might. He did not crow over his enemy's downfall but said nothing for a minute or so, then said calmly, 'Nasty. He's going to suffer much more than I did. I remember reading about pilots coming down in flames during the war. Some survived and had to go through the ordeal of having their faces partially rebuilt with plastic surgery.'

'I wanted him punished for what he did to you, as well as for attacking me and stabbing that doorman, but . . .' Jeanette sighed.

They walked on in silence for a few minutes and then she said, 'I do have some other news. Good this time.'

David looked at her questioningly. 'Your brother's changed his mind about me?'

She smiled. 'I think he was in a mood because he'd fallen out with his girlfriend. I'd like the pair of you to be the best of friends. No, my news is about my mother. Apparently the nurse who looked after her after she was rescued could be at the concert tomorrow. I still don't know, though, if she's alive or dead.'

'And if she's alive?'

'I have to see her. I need to know why she deserted me and Dad,' said Jeanette tremulously.

Twenty-Five

'Can you see the person you spoke to about my mother, Father Callaghan?' shouted Jeanette above the din in the church hall the following evening.

The concert had finished and had been received extremely well by a full-capacity audience. She had been surprised to see Tonio Gianelli, Jimmy and Irene, as well as Maggie and Betty amongst the performers. So far she hadn't had a chance to talk to them, although they must be somewhere in the crowd now, enjoying tea and mince pies and bun loaf.

'I can't say I can, Jeanette,' he replied. 'I have been looking out for her. Maybe as it's a foul evening she and her brother changed their mind about coming.'

She could scarcely conceal her disappointment and would have gone home there and then if Peggy had not signalled to her. A few moments later she found herself sitting at a trestle table with the twins, Emma and Jared, Betty and Maggie, as well as Jimmy and Irene. They were chattering ten to the dozen, obviously pleased with their performance. Apparently they all went along to musical evenings at Tonio Gianelli's parents' house, and that was how they had got roped in to perform at the charity concert. They were now talking about their plans for Christmas.

'I'm giving a party in my flat on Boxing Day,' said Betty.

'I thought it was Christmas Day?' said Jeanette.

'No, I changed it so Jimmy and Irene could come. Perhaps you and your David would like to come, Jeanette?'

'Thanks,' said Jeanette, gratified, hoping David would be able to make it.

'How about asking Jeanette's sister to come as well?' suggested Emma quietly. 'I'd like to see Hester again.'

'Why not? The more the merrier,' said Betty, smiling. 'You'll come, too, won't you, Peggy?' She glanced her way.

Peggy hesitated.

Jeanette looked at her. 'Say you'll come. It'll be fun.'

'Yes, do come,' said Pete, gazing across at Peggy. 'I might even get up and have a go at dancing.'

Peggy smiled. 'Now that I'd like to see. Where is your flat, Betty?'

She told them and so it was settled.

When it came to leaving the church hall, Jeanette felt less miserable than she had done on discovering that the nurse was not at the concert. Still, she was disappointed and was not looking forward to telling the family she had no more news about her mother.

As Jeanette neared the house she saw a dark figure emerge from their path. The ring of her heels on the pavement drew the person's attention briefly, and for a moment she caught a glimpse of a woman's face. She seemed to hesitate and then hurried away. Jeanette would have gone after her if the front door had not opened and Ethel called out to her, 'Is that you, Jeanette?'

'Yes, Aunt Ethel, I'm coming.' She went up the path to the lighted doorway. 'Did that woman knock here?' she asked.

Ethel squinted at Jeanette. 'Nobody knocked here, but something was shoved through the letterbox. Probably a Christmas card. Someone saving on the postage.' She peered down at the envelope in her hand. 'I can't make out who it's addressed to.'

'You should have your glasses on,' said Jeanette. 'Give me it here.'

Ethel passed it to her.

Jeanette saw that it was addressed to her and slit open the envelope. She took out a card, but it was a birthday card rather than a Christmas card.

'Come inside and tell me who it's from,' said Ethel.

Jeanette stepped over the threshold and opened the card. A single sheet of paper fell out. She glanced down at the signature and saw that it was 'Laura O'Neill'. Who on earth was Laura O'Neill? Puzzled, she decided to read the letter properly once in the warmth of the kitchen. She did not bother taking off her coat and hanging it up, but went straight in, sat down and began to read.

Dear Jeanette Walker,

You do not know me but I saw your notice in the Liverpool
Echo, *wrapped around a portion of fish and chips, would you
believe? I have information concerning Grace Walker's whereabouts.
I suggest we meet on Christmas Eve at approximately noon at
Bebington station on the Wirral, when all will be revealed. If
you are unable to make this appointment, your mother will be
severely disappointed.*

Yours sincerely,
Laura O'Neill

Jeanette was glad she was sitting down because she felt so odd
that she thought she might pass out and she had never fainted
in her life before. Surely the letter could not be a hoax? Who
was the woman who had delivered it? Could she be Laura
O'Neill who was asking her to go over to the Wirral? It would
have meant her coming all this way on a winter's evening when
she could have posted it. Maybe she had a friend this side of
the Mersey who had performed the task for her.

'It's a birthday card,' said Ethel, rousing Jeanette from her
reverie.

'I know. It was my birthday yesterday.'

'Was it?' Ethel added, 'It's not like me to forget.'

'Huh! All my family forgot.' Jeanette snatched the card from
Ethel's hand and opened it, but disappointingly there was
nothing personal written inside. So why post it through their
door with the letter?

'I'll make us a cup of tea,' said Ethel, getting to her feet.

'Cocoa,' said Jeanette absently.

Ethel glanced at her and reached for the cocoa tin. 'So how
did the concert go?'

Jeanette did not answer.

'I think you're going deaf,' said Ethel. 'Not that I'm really
interested. They're all out. Doesn't matter if I'm here all on
my own.'

'If you were in the old people's home you wouldn't be alone,
so stop complaining.' Jeanette reached for the letter again,
knowing that even if she read it a dozen times, she would not
learn anything more from it. Didn't this Laura O'Neill realize

that she had a job and that Christmas Eve or not, she would be in work on Friday?

'Our George wouldn't put me in an old people's home,' muttered Ethel, lighting the gas under the kettle. 'I saw to it that he was looked after when he was little, despite everything.'

'Stop complaining then and be nice to people,' said Jeanette, picking up the birthday card and reading the first two lines of the verse: *Although we are apart, you are always in my heart.*

'Who's the card from?'

'I don't know, although the letter is from a Laura O'Neill,' said Jeanette.

'Laura O'Neill,' murmured Ethel. 'I'm no good with names.'

'Then why ask?' Jeanette wondered whether she should show the letter to her father, but what if it was a hoax? Some joker who had read the notice in the *Echo* and thought it was funny to have her go chasing across the Mersey in search of her mother. But why the birthday card? Was it to prove that this person knew she'd just had a birthday?

Her mother would know the date of her birth. Had her mother bought the card but for some reason not written in it? Maybe she hadn't had time. She felt a curl of excitement. There was only one way to find out if the letter was on the level, and that was to ask if she could leave work at eleven and make up the hours after Christmas so she could keep the appointment.

But she would tell no one. After her cocoa she would go to bed and if any of her family knocked on her door, when they came in, she would feign sleep.

The following morning, a heavy-eyed Hester said, 'We forgot your birthday, didn't we, Jeanette?'

Jeanette was getting ready for work and wanted to be on her way. 'It doesn't matter. You've had a lot of upset so it's understandable.'

Hester frowned. 'Don't pretend. Of course it matters. I'll get you something before Christmas.'

'OK, thanks. See you.' Jeanette made for the door. 'You look after yourself.'

Hester called her back. 'You haven't said what happened at the concert. Did you see that nurse about your mother?'

'No. Big disappointment. Don't want to talk about it,' said Jeanette.

'OK. How was the Glynis Johns film?'

'Oh!' Jeanette smiled. 'That was fun.'

'Did you notice Dorothy in it?' Hester was remembering Ally suggesting that they go and see *Mad About Men* together and she felt deeply depressed. Her period was due and she had not come on yet. She could have killed Cedric – if he wasn't already dead.

Jeanette coughed. 'You seem to have gone off into a trance. I said, How would I know her? I haven't met her yet. It's time our Sam brought her home to meet the rest of us.'

'Agreed.'

'What about the Christmas tree?' said Jeanette, fixing her with a stare. 'Are you getting it as usual?'

'I haven't given it a thought.'

Jeanette nodded. 'Do you want me to get it? You really don't look well this morning.'

Hester sighed. 'You always used to like choosing it with me.' She tossed some money on the table. 'Take that and see what you can buy on the way home. The shops will be open late tonight and tomorrow.'

Then I'll leave it until tomorrow, thought Jeanette. She had Christmas presents to buy yet and would do that this evening as she was not seeing David.

Jeanette had never felt so nervous as she did that Christmas Eve. She had been told by Elsie that they were always allowed out early that day, but that meant two o'clock, much too late for Jeanette's purpose, so she explained the situation to her boss. Her request was granted and Jeanette wasted no time, heading for James Street railway station as soon as she could. As she sat on the train, she was on pins, praying that she was not on a wild goose chase.

After being underground for a while, she blinked as the train emerged into the daylight. She gazed through the window with interest, thinking that the last time she had crossed the Mersey it had been for a day out in Chester. She had travelled there by bus, passing the model village of Port Sunlight built by Lord Leverhulme, which was situated cheek by jowl to Bebington.

She wondered what Ethel would have had to say if she had told her that she was meeting a woman who knew Grace's whereabouts. Her stomach was churning and she felt slightly sick, thinking about her mother, wondering what they would have to say to each other if they were to meet. She folded her ticket around her finger repeatedly. At last she rose to her feet as the train neared Bebington and began to draw to a halt. Her heart was racing as she climbed down onto the platform and made her way to the ticket barrier, glancing about her as she did so, but there was no one who appeared to be waiting for her on the platform.

It was not until she had shown her return ticket that she noticed a woman in a wheelchair the other side of the barrier staring at her. Her legs were covered by a blanket and her upper body was clad in a tweed jacket. Wrapped around her neck was a brown scarf and on her head she wore a brown pull-on felt hat with a feather in it. She had an attractive, strong-boned face and green eyes, and her lips were painted a bright red. The ground felt as if it rocked beneath Jeanette's feet and it was several moments before everything steadied.

'Jeanette?' said the woman in a voice that quivered.

Jeanette felt a need to cling on to something, but there wasn't anything suitable, so she went down on one knee in front of the wheelchair so that her face was almost on a level with the woman's. 'Yes, I'm Jeanette. But I don't think you're Laura O'Neill.'

'Oh, I am, but that's just one of my names,' she answered.

'I don't understand,' said Jeanette. 'You wouldn't also go by the name of Grace Walker, would you? Your eyes are green and you look so like her photograph that I think you must be my mother.'

'I am your mother.' Grace reached out and touched her daughter's face. 'Beryl said you'd grown so pretty.' Her voice was husky.

'I'm not pretty,' denied Jeanette. 'I prefer attractive or interesting. Pretty makes me think of dolls.'

Grace laughed. 'You always did like to argue. You get that from me, not your father. How is George?'

Jeanette hesitated. 'Hurt. I know you didn't marry for love, but he's missed you since the day you disappeared. He said that you needed a home and someone to take care of you and he needed a mother for Sam and Hester. He explained it was a marriage of convenience, but . . .' Her voice trailed off.

Grace's eyes were suddenly bright with tears. 'George was good to me. I was terribly fond of him.'

'Then why did you stay away?' said Jeanette fiercely. 'Although I don't doubt you're going to say it's because you're in a wheelchair.'

Grace flinched. 'Of course! I didn't want to be a burden, and Ethel would have made herself even more indispensable to your father. I'm a selfish woman, Jeanette, and I couldn't have coped with that. I could only pray that she wouldn't destroy your spirit. I think my prayers were answered.'

'Prayers aren't enough! You should have been there for me,' said Jeanette, her voice shaking. 'It never occurred to me that . . . that—'

'That what, Jeannie? What did you think of when you thought of me?'

'That you were dead, killed in the blitz. But at other times I believed you had walked out on us because Aunt Ethel was forever saying bad things about you. She said that you'd left a note, which she destroyed.'

'I did leave a note once because I nearly left before you were born,' said Grace. 'I fell in love, but I soon realized he was a worthless rogue. When I left the house to visit an elderly friend on her birthday, I fully intended returning home. Then the bomb hit and sadly she was killed, but I survived in this state.'

A woman whom Jeanette had not noticed before bent over Grace. 'Shall we move away from here? We're blocking the entrance and there's a cold wind that could chill you to the bone.'

Grace patted her hand. 'Let's go home then. I'd like Jeannie to see where I've been living for the past thirteen and a half years.' She beamed up at her daughter. 'It's called Little Storeton. And this is Beryl O'Neill who looks after me.'

'O'Neill?' said Jeanette.

'Yes. People believe we're sisters,' said Grace. 'Now it's a bit of a walk but I hope you won't mind that.'

'No, I don't mind a walk,' murmured Jeanette, still trying to come to terms with her mother alive and in a wheelchair.

'I want to hear all about you,' said Grace. 'I know some of what you've been doing over the years, but I could only ever know part of it and I'd like to hear the rest from you.'

'I don't understand,' said Jeanette. 'How is it you know even a little about my life?'

'Beryl is a widow and she has kept an eye on you for me. I knew when you had measles, but there was a period when we lost contact with you because you moved house. Then we found you again. I know that you work in a shipping office and have a boyfriend who is a sailor,' said Grace, her eyes twinkling. 'You and Beryl met once in the snow.'

'That was you!' exclaimed Jeanette, staring at the other woman.

Beryl nodded. 'I almost told you the truth then.'

'You're my only daughter. I was never going to forget about you,' said Grace.

'I never forgot about you either.'

'I realized that when you placed the notice in the *Echo*. Beryl read it out to me, and after the initial shock we puzzled and puzzled over why you should be making enquiries about me after all this time.'

'It was because of the death of a woman. A Lavinia Crawshaw,' said Jeanette.

'Ahhh!' murmured Grace, smiling.

Jeanette was surprised. 'You've heard of her?'

'Of course, she was my mother. Just as I never forgot about you, my mother never forgot about me. She kept a watch on me, too.'

A stunned Jeanette said, 'So the old witch was right! She said you were Lavinia's daughter. Remembers you being born. How strange is it that my father should meet you the way he did?'

'He was a policeman on the beat, so I don't see why you should think it so strange. I was always in trouble when I was a kid. I was a bit of a devil, just like my mother. I knew George was a soft touch.'

'Aunt Ethel thought the worst of you.'

'She had a lot of experience of bad girls and I told your father such fibs. You do know that she was a prison wardress?'

'Yes.' Jeanette grimaced. 'I don't think she's ever forgotten those days in that job. Anyway, when Lavinia Crawshaw's death was announced in the *Echo*, she really went on about my finding you. She was convinced you were still alive.'

'No doubt because she believed there was money in it,' said Grace, looking amused.

'Yes. I was angry with her, but I knew so little about you and then suddenly I was learning something concrete. I didn't like asking Dad too much because it upset him.'

'George was always good to me,' said Grace, her expression softening. 'So kind. He helped me when I was in trouble, whereas some would have let me stew in my own juice.'

'If you cared for him, you should have let us know you were alive at the very least,' said Jeanette. 'He tried to find you.'

Grace sighed. 'That doesn't surprise me. He'd have wanted me to come home and it wouldn't have worked. I was rescued by the most handsome of voluntary firemen. I fell quite in love with him. At the time I was in such a state I couldn't remember who I was and he used to come and visit me. Once my memory returned and I realized I was going to be a cripple for the rest of my life because part of my spine was crushed, I thought it was best to say goodbye to him and let your father and the rest of you believe I was dead. My mother did get in touch with me, though. She tracked me down. Her conscience had bothered her about me ever since she got religion.'

'I suppose you've been able to manage for money because of your mother,' said Jeanette.

Grace nodded. 'She was a rich woman as Ethel knows, but she lived simply and was a bit of a philanthropist. Beryl here is a nurse and was well known to Lavinia. Between them, they took it upon themselves to look after me. Sadly I wasn't able to attend my mother's funeral as I was ill at the time. Her death is a great loss to us,' she murmured, glancing up at Beryl.

'But even in death she's been good to us and provided an income for your mother,' said Beryl. 'We live with my brother in a rented cottage with some land attached. We're pretty self-sufficient because we grow most of our own vegetables and we have fruit trees and keep hens and pigs.'

'And I knit and sew and sell my work,' said Grace, smiling.

'I see,' murmured Jeanette. 'So why is it that you've got in touch with me now if you didn't want to be found?'

'Because you obviously wanted to find me and I had this desire to speak to you and see you close up, instead of from a distance. Besides, the dread of being a burden on your family has long passed. If I'd been less of a coward I would have made contact earlier, but the longer I left it the more difficult it became.'

Jeanette could understand that and did not doubt that her father would, too. She could not wait to tell him that Grace was alive. As for Aunt Ethel, maybe she had got confused about the timing of the note Grace had left?

They came to the village. The cottage was at the end of a row of semi-detached ones constructed of the sandstone of the area, which, according to Beryl's brother, had been quarried for hundreds of years.

He told her so over lunch, adding, 'It's also the same sandstone used to clad the Empire State Building in New York. The quarry has since been filled in with all the rubble and earth dug up when the Mersey tunnel was built.'

'Isn't that fascinating, Jeannie?' said Grace, winking at her. 'Little Storeton might only be a tiny place compared to Liverpool, but it does have its claim to fame. So tell me about your boyfriend and how you met. And how is Hester getting on – and Sam?'

Jeanette was happy to tell her mother all her news and to bring her up to date with some of what was going on in their lives, although she kept quiet about Cedric. Grace appeared particularly interested in Sam's girlfriend making a film of Liverpool women, including Ethel.

'You wouldn't believe the times she locked me in my bedroom,' said Jeanette, rolling her eyes.

'I would, love. I'm sorry. It is possible that she really thought she was doing what was best for you all these years,' said Grace, 'and that's why women like her are a necessity and a danger. Anyway, if you get your own flat you'll be away from her.'

'Yes, but that might not happen for ages.'

Grace smiled. 'Of course, you mightn't be there very long. Your young man, David, do you think you'll marry him?'

'Maybe,' said Jeanette casually. 'It's early days.'

'You must bring him to see me,' said Grace.

'And Dad?'

Grace hesitated. 'If he wishes to see me, then tell him to leave it until the New Year. I'm sure he'll want some time to consider all that I've told you. He might not even want to see me when he knows the truth.'

Jeanette shook her head. 'He'll want to see you. Dad hasn't changed much.'

Shortly after, she decided that it was time she made a move to leave for home. 'It's Christmas Eve and I've been given the job of getting the Christmas tree,' she said.

'Well, choose a good one, Jeannie,' said Grace, reaching out and hugging her. 'And have a very merry Christmas and I'll see you in the New Year.'

Twenty-Six

'That is the perfect-sized Christmas tree for the bay in our parlour,' said Jeanette, breathing in the scent of pine, although she had been told that such trees were really Norwegian spruce.

'It still has its roots,' said the shopkeeper. 'Which means it'll last longer unless you have central heating.'

'Don't be daft,' said Jeanette. 'It would be a heck of a job to put central heating in our old house, even if Dad and Aunt Ethel would agree. They'd consider it unhealthy.'

'It's all that smoke from coal fires that's unhealthy, luv. The sooner the Clean Air Act is passed the better in my opinion,' he said. 'So you've made up your mind? It's this one?' He touched the spur that was used to fasten a silver star or a fairy on top.

Jeanette nodded, and took out her purse.

'D'you want it delivered? It'll cost you extra.'

She gave him a look. 'It's Christmas Eve, you should be glad to be rid of it. Anyway, I'll manage it somehow. I haven't that far to go.'

'Suit yourself.' He took her money and turned to the next customer.

As Jeanette dragged the tree out of the shop, she heard a woman say, 'How much is your mistletoe?'

Mistletoe, she thought, walking along the pavement with the tree following behind like a train on a wedding gown. Should she go back and buy a sprig of mistletoe and fasten it in her hair, just for a joke when she met David later? Perhaps a bit too obvious. Oh, what the hell! She went back and bought a sprig.

As Jeanette dragged the tree round the back of the house, she wondered which members of the family would be in. Would it be easier to tell them all together about having seen her mother, or to get her father alone and tell him first? Or would it be better leaving the telling until after Christmas? New Year was over a week away. Grace's request made it sound as if she was in no rush to see her husband, although she had suggested that he might need time to adjust to the news that she was alive.

'Who's there?' shouted George.

A startled Jeanette panted, 'It's me, Dad! I didn't expect to find you out here.'

'I was putting bread out for the birds,' said George, gazing at his younger daughter in the gathering gloom. 'Is that a tree you've got there?'

'Yes. Hester suggested I picked one.'

'I'm surprised she remembered.'

'She didn't. I did.'

'Not surprising. She's been through a traumatic time and it'll leave its mark on her for a while – if not for the rest of

her life,' said George, frowning as he took a grip on the tree.
'You'll have to be extra kind to her.' He changed the subject.
'We should have got a tree days ago, but I suppose you got it
cheaper and it'll last until Twelfth Night. Come on, I'll help
you inside with it. Glad you've finished work for a couple of
days?'

'That goes without saying, Dad.'

Together, the pair of them heaved the tree into the scullery
and then through the house to the parlour. In the past, after
Christmas dinner, the family had always gathered there to spend
the rest of the day playing games, such as Housey, Housey.
They balanced the tree against the wall near the gas cupboard.

'I'll go and find the tub,' said Jeanette.

'No, luv! It'll be too heavy for you and besides, I can put
my hand on it straightaway,' said George. 'I'll get some soil
from the garden. You make a cup of tea.'

As Jeanette put the kettle on, she decided that whilst they
were alone it was the perfect time to tell him about her mother.
She waited until they had the tree balanced perfectly in the
tub of soil and she had handed him his steaming cup before
saying, 'Dad, I've some news for you.'

He glanced down at her. 'You're not getting engaged to that
David yet, are you?'

'No, it's not that. You know we've only been going out
together for a short time.' She paused. 'It's Mam. I've seen her!'

He blanched and gripped the mantelpiece. 'You're serious?
How can you possibly have seen her?'

'A birthday card was put through the door the other evening
with a note. It didn't say it was from Mam, but a meeting
place was suggested where I would discover her
whereabouts.'

He blinked and then squeezed his eyes together. 'I can't
believe this,' he muttered. 'Why didn't you tell me?'

'Because I didn't know whether it was a hoax and I'd be
let down again,' said Jeanette earnestly, stretching out a hand
and touching him. 'Besides, you've been worried about Hester.
Anyway, I went today and she was there. She's living on the
Wirral in a cottage with a brother and sister. He has a market
garden and she's a nurse.'

'I don't understand! What's she doing there? Why didn't she come home?' He sounded bewildered. 'Is she in love with the brother?'

'I wouldn't have thought so,' said Jeanette. 'She's crippled, Dad. Can't walk. She's in a wheelchair.'

George stared at her and then without a word, he walked out of the parlour. Jeanette hurried after him. 'I know it's a shock, Dad, but I got a shock, too, when I saw her. Part of her spine was crushed when the house she was in got bombed. She'd been to see an old friend. She lost her memory and then when she got it back, she didn't want to be a burden on us.'

A muscle in his throat convulsed. He went over to the sideboard and took a bottle of whisky and a glass from the cupboard and poured himself a generous measure. He gulped it down in one go before going over to his armchair and sitting in front of the fire. Jeanette dragged the pouffe alongside him and placed a hand on his shoulder. 'Are you all right, Dad?'

'How did she manage for money?' he asked hoarsely.

'You're not going to believe this, but Aunt Ethel was right. Mam is Lavinia Crawshaw's daughter and she came looking for her. I suppose you can do that when you're rich and influential.'

He looked up at Jeanette. 'Does Grace want to see me?'

'Yes, but I don't know whether she'll come home. She's built a different life for herself because she didn't want to be a burden.'

He nodded slowly. 'I bet Aunt Ethel is why she stayed away. But Grace and I took vows! For better, for worse, in sickness and in health. I'd have looked after her.'

'How, Dad? You had to earn a living.'

'This is going to take some getting used to.'

Jeanette felt sorry for him because he was obviously deeply hurt and rejected. Strangely, she didn't feel like that at the moment. She wanted to give him a big hug, but already he was pushing himself up out of the chair and pouring himself another whisky.

'It is Aunt Ethel,' he said. 'I'll find her a place somewhere and we'll have a bit of peace without her at last. I'll be retiring soon.' He tossed back the whisky. 'Now tell me what else Grace had to say.'

Jeanette hesitated. 'It's probably best, Dad, if she tells you herself.'

He stared at her and nodded slowly. 'You're right. Write down her address and I'll go and see her tomorrow.'

'Tomorrow's Christmas Day! You can't go. Besides, she doesn't want to see either of us until the New Year.'

He took a deep breath and then reached for the whisky bottle again.

'You're not kidding me?' asked Hester, her expression incredulous as she watched Jeanette decorating the Christmas tree.

'No. Dad's asleep in the armchair. He's downed a couple of big whiskies. If that isn't proof that what I've just told you about my mother is true, I'd like to know what is,' said Jeanette. 'Now, I must get this tree finished because David will be here in about an hour.'

'Where are you going?'

'We're having a meal together and then we thought that later we'd go to church.' Jeanette glanced over her shoulder at Hester and thought she looked as if she had lost weight. 'You could do with feeding up,' she said. 'Dad's going to need something to eat when he wakes up. Make sure you have something proper yourself, too.'

Hester paled. 'The last thing I want is to put weight on.'

'OK, it's up to you. Tell Dad I won't be in until after midnight.'

'I have to go out for a short while,' said Hester. 'There's a few things I have to collect. Does the old witch know?'

'Dad told her and he didn't hold back from blaming her for Mam's decision not to come home.'

'So where is she?'

'God knows! She had a pinched look on her face and stumbled out of the room. She looked dreadful and might have left the house because I heard a door slam. I might have gone after her if I didn't have so much to do.'

Hester nodded, then left the parlour and hurried upstairs. 'First things first,' she muttered, carrying her shopping bag into the bathroom. Her period was late by two days, which was not much but she was always on time. She was going to give her body all the help she could to bring herself on. Her hands shook violently and she struggled to turn on the taps, but managed it at last. She poured in some bath salts. She thought of Ally, wondering if he was back in Liverpool and staying with Wendy and Charley. 'Keep calm, keep calm,' she told herself as she took a bottle of gin from her bag and placed it on the stool beside the bath. 'Don't think of him right now.'

She had heard married women talk of gin and a hot bath doing the trick when they thought themselves pregnant with an unwanted baby, so it was worth a try. She wondered if Betty had done so too, as she removed her clothes and took a towel from the airing cupboard before testing the temperature of the water with her elbow. A bit hot. She ran some more cold and then gingerly immersed herself in the water. She gasped because it still felt scalding. Perhaps some more cold, or would that defeat the object? She needed the water as hot as she could bear it, so she just huddled in the water and reached for the gin. She unscrewed the cap, took a couple of sips and pulled a face. The best medicine always tasted horrible, although lots of people actually loved the taste of gin. What a thing to be doing on Christmas Eve – a time when the Christ child was being welcomed in churches! She drank some more gin and then put the cap back on and cautiously lay down in the water. She felt her belly but didn't feel any pain. It just felt heavy. The only effect the gin seemed to have was to make her head spin slightly. Perhaps she should drink some more.

She was just reaching for the bottle when the bathroom door suddenly opened and Jeanette appeared. Hester froze and her half-sister stared at the bottle of gin. 'I didn't realize you were in here. You should have locked the door.'

'I was in such a state I forgot,' said Hester, feeling slightly hysterical. 'It seems I can't do anything right.'

'What's wrong?' asked Jeanette.

'I'd rather you didn't ask that,' said Hester. 'You can go now.'

'Like hell I will. Do you think you're pregnant?'

Hester sighed. 'Fetch me my housecoat!'

Jeanette ran to get it and was back in moments. By then

Hester had pulled out the plug and was sitting on the side of the bath, rubbing herself dry. Jeanette sat on the bath stool, holding the housecoat. 'I've read about women believing gin and a hot bath is a way of getting rid of an unwanted pregnancy. Did Cedric rape you when you were at the conference?'

Hester sighed even deeper than she had before. 'Yes. A lot of good all my self-defence training did when I needed it. He put handcuffs on me and almost made it impossible for me to breathe, never mind defend myself.' She ground her teeth. 'I shouldn't be talking to you like this. You're only a kid.'

'No, I'm not!' said Jeanette fiercely. 'I'm fed up of people telling me I'm only a kid. I'm eighteen! So are you pregnant?'

'I hope to God I'm not! My period's a couple of days late, but I was so frightened, have been since it happened, so I was having the hot bath and drinking gin in the hope that it would do the trick and bring me on.' A shudder went through her. 'I've already made up my mind to leave home – and Liverpool – one way or the other if I am. Emma would let me rent her cottage, or I'm sure Myra Jones would let me stay with her if the worst came to the worst and I couldn't afford to rent. I had this plan . . .' Her voice trailed off and she swallowed. 'Anyway, I can't stay here any longer. Dad will be really, really upset if I am pregnant. Cedric might be dead, but what if he has left a legacy?'

'You can't leave,' said Jeanette firmly. 'Two days overdue is nothing! I've been ten days before now. You've had a shock to your system. It could just be that which has made you late.'

Hester smiled faintly. 'You really do know how to cheer a girl up.'

'I'm glad to hear you say that. Why don't you get dressed and have something to eat?'

Hester said, 'I have to go shopping. Some of the shops in Breck Road stay open until nine on Christmas Eve to catch the last-minute shoppers and for those workers who have yet to pick up their orders like me.'

Jeanette handed the housecoat to her. 'Promise me you'll come back?'

'Of course I'll come back. I only hope the old witch doesn't get wind of what I was doing. She'll tell Dad and I'd rather he doesn't know unless I have no other choice but to tell him.'

'If the old witch you refer to is me,' said Ethel, poking her head around the door, 'then I heard yer.' She glanced at the gin bottle. 'I'll keep my mouth shut if you put a good word in with your father so he doesn't put me in the old people's home.'

The sisters stared at her and for several moments neither of them spoke. Then Jeanette said, 'It could be out of our hands.'

'You say a word to Dad,' said Hester in a hard voice, 'and I'll see you regret it. For example, between us Jeanette and I could manhandle you into your bedroom right now and lock you in. It might be Christmas Eve but there'll be no mince pies and a glass of sherry for you! Dry bread and water, that's what you'll get.'

'You wouldn't dare,' said Ethel in a quavering voice, backing away from them.

'Just try us,' said Jeanette, a fierce expression on her face as she took a step towards her.

'All right, I believe you!' cried Ethel. 'I'll say nothing.'

They stared at her warily, not quite trusting her to keep her word. 'Promise on the Bible,' said Hester.

'You think that means something to her?' said Jeanette. 'Get her to swear on her dead husband's memory.'

'I don't have to swear on anything. I said I won't tell,' said Ethel, surprising them by darting towards the bath and snatching up the bottle of gin. She scurried out before they could stop her.

'Well, what d'you think of that?' asked Jeanette. 'Maybe she'll drink herself unconscious, just like Dad.'

Before Hester could reply, the door knocker went. 'That'll be your David,' she said. 'You'd best go.'

'OK.' Jeanette hurried out of the bathroom.

Hester grabbed her clothes and went into her bedroom. She rubbed her hair as dry as she could and then took out her best jumper and skirt from the wardrobe and clean underwear and stockings from a drawer. Once dressed, she applied some make-up, brushed her hair which was just dry, put on her shoes, grabbed her best coat, hat, gloves, shopping bag and handbag and left her bedroom.

As she went downstairs, the kitchen door opened and Jeanette came out. 'So you're off shopping?'

'Yes, hopefully I won't be too long and I'll be able to get all I need.' Hester hurried to the front door, opened it swiftly and went out before Jeanette could think of saying, *Come and meet David first.*

There was a nip in the air but no snow to make it feel more Christmassy, although lights shone on Christmas trees in the parlours of houses and her shoes rang out on the frosty pavement, reminding her of bells. She was halfway up the street when she saw a man approaching. He walked like a soldier, shoulders back and with his head held high. Her heart began to thud and she felt a rush of emotion that threatened to overpower her.

'Hester!' His pace quickened.

She stayed where she was because her legs seemed to have turned to water and she feared she might collapse onto the pavement. 'Ally?' she croaked.

He stared into her face and she thought he must have seen something there that caused him to say, 'I know it's Christmas Eve but I couldn't wait to see you.'

'I . . . I was just going shopping.' She paused, frantically searching for something to say that would make him turn about-face. She wasn't ready for this encounter and couldn't think what to say to him.

'Wendy told me Cedric's dead.'

That was the last thing she had expected Ally to say and she could only respond with the words, 'How did she find out? I haven't been to see her. I should have got in touch. It was a real shock.'

'She read it in the *Echo*. I would have thought you'd have known the manner of his death would have hit the headlines,' said Ally.

'I haven't been reading the newspapers. I haven't been well.' She found strength from somewhere to walk past him.

He seized her arm. 'I can't believe that you might have loved him after all.'

She could feel herself trembling. 'I didn't love him. I despised him. I've had a hellish couple of weeks and I just want peace and quiet.' She put up a hand and gripped his arm. 'Now if you'll let me go, I have to collect the turkey and the bacon joint from the butcher's.'

'May I come with you?'

She stared into his face and was aware of such an ache of longing inside her. She wanted him with her, but what if Jeanette was wrong and she was pregnant? She imagined his expression changing and she could not bear it. He would pity her, she felt sure of that. But it wasn't pity she wanted from him, so she walked away without a word.

Hester had not gone far when she became aware that he was following her. She fought against turning and speaking to him, but part of her was glad that he was there. She just could not cope with explanations right now.

When she reached the main road and went into the butcher's, she thought he might change his mind about staying with her and return to Wendy's and Charley's apartment, but he was waiting outside when she emerged from the shop. She looked at him and he smiled. Her cheeks warmed and she gave him a nod before walking past him. The same thing happened when she came out of the other shops, where she bought presents and vegetables.

Eventually he said, 'I want to know why the last fortnight has been so hellish.'

Emotion seized her by the throat and tears pricked her eyes and spilt over. 'I can't talk about it right now. It's too painful.' Her voice was raw.

He reached out and wiped away her tears with the side of his gloved hand before taking her shopping from her. 'Then we don't have to talk about it right now,' he said briskly. 'Come on, I'll walk you home if you've finished.'

She nodded wordlessly.

So they walked silently side by side and she appreciated that he did not try and make conversation. She still felt far too emotional for speech. It was not until they were within sight of the house that he asked, 'What are you doing tomorrow?'

Hester managed to find her voice. 'I'll be helping prepare Christmas dinner for the family.'

'Can I come and see you after dinner?' asked Ally.

She nodded, praying that her life could change for the better overnight.

'Three o'clock okay?' he said.

Again she nodded.

He handed her the shopping and leant forward and brushed his lips against hers. 'Goodnight, Hester. God bless you.'

She watched him walk away until he was out of sight and then went inside the house.

Twenty-Seven

'So what do you think?' asked Sam, standing on the pavement with his arm around Dorothy's shoulders on Christmas Day.

It was almost lunchtime and Sam having left early had returned home only ten minutes ago. He had dragged Jeanette and Hester from the kitchen and now they stood, alongside David and George, staring at the Austin A40 Somerset parked at the kerb.

'I suppose it'll come in useful,' said Hester, her hands tucked inside the deep, wide pocket of her apron.

'Of course it'll come in useful,' said George, clapping a hand on his son's shoulder.

Sam said incredulously. 'Is that all you can say?'

'How old is she?' asked David.

'A couple of years. I couldn't afford a brand-new one.'

'I'm sure you'll get a lot of use out of her,' said Hester. 'Now can I get back to the kitchen or you won't be getting your dinner on time?' She smiled to soften the words before returning to the house. She'd had a splitting headache when she woke that morning to find her period had come. Fortunately there was a packet of STs in her chest of drawers and Aspro in the bathroom cabinet. The song 'Have Yourself a Merry Little Christmas' was playing in her heart.

Jeanette stared after Hester and could have danced up the street. Her half-sister had indicated that she'd received the best Christmas present possible, and that could mean only one thing.

'Well, what have you got to say?' asked Sam, looking at his younger sister.

'I agree with Hester. A car will come in useful.' She smiled.

Sam groaned. 'Women!'

Dorothy chuckled. 'It's what I said. Some girlfriends who had been proposed to might have asked where's my engagement ring, or shouldn't we be saving up to get married? But I accepted that a car will prove useful to both of us.'

'OK, point taken,' said Sam, grinning. 'I just expected a different reaction from my sisters. I know, Dorothy, you're thinking it'll save time when you need to be somewhere fast.'

'Or when she's in a play in another town and you want to visit her,' pointed out Jeanette.

'She's not going to be doing much of that for a while if she's filming here in Liverpool,' said Sam.

'She's got nice lines,' said David, stroking the car bonnet. 'What's the engine like? How fast can she go?'

'You men,' said Jeanette fondly. 'Why does a car have to be a she?'

'It's the same with a ship,' said Dorothy, winking at Jeanette. 'Shall we go inside now? It's cold out here.'

Sam removed his arm from about her shoulders. 'You go in, luv. I want to show Davy and Dad the engine.'

As Jeanette and Dorothy went up the path, they heard George say, 'So how about taking me through the tunnel to Little Storeton? If Christmas Day is about families, then perhaps I should visit my wife.'

Jeanette turned and said, 'Aren't you better waiting, Dad? You don't know what plans Mam has made for today.'

His mouth set stubbornly and for a moment she was reminded of the old witch and thought he was going to insist on going today. Then his expression altered. 'Perhaps you're right. I'll write her a letter and let her know when we're coming.'

'Of course, Jeannie's right,' said Sam. 'Besides, I haven't enough petrol and I can't remember if the tunnel is closed for Christmas.'

'And you a policeman,' teased Dorothy as she paused on the threshold.

'I'm not a traffic cop, luv,' said Sam.

She laughed and went inside the house with Jeanette. 'So where is your Aunt Ethel?' asked Dorothy.

'In her bedroom. I found an empty gin bottle outside her door,' she said. 'The last thing I thought she'd do when threatened with the old folk's home was to take to the drink. Whether she'll come down for dinner, I don't know.'

Dorothy looked thoughtful. 'I know you think she's an old witch, but she's suffered in her time. The wedding she kept secret . . . I've seen her marriage certificate. She found it in a drawer and showed it to me.'

Jeanette raised her eyebrows. 'I wonder what she'll surprise us with next? You're not going to give me a sob story, are you?'

Dorothy rolled her eyes. 'She's a fool to herself. She married her young man when he was dying. He had consumption and there was no hope for him. She risked catching the disease herself to nurse him. He had no one else but did have a bit of money and wanted her to have it.'

Jeanette did not want to believe the story but could not resist asking, 'How did they meet?'

'He was a socialist and was caught up in a riot and arrested. Their eyes met when they passed each other in a corridor in the holding cells beneath the courts in Manchester. She was there with a woman prisoner.'

'Is that how she told it?' asked Jeanette.

Dorothy's eyes twinkled. 'It makes a good story. She was a woman alone who supported herself and her sister until the latter married. After the husband was killed and her sister died, she cared for your father until he was earning himself.'

Jeanette sighed. 'It still doesn't cancel out the way she's treated us.'

Dorothy nodded. 'I agree. I'm just glad it's not my decision to put her in a home. I remember my mother talking about how many people feared destitution and ending up in the workhouse when she was young.'

'You're saying the old people's home is like the workhouse? Surely things have improved since those days?'

'One would hope so,' said Dorothy.

'Anyway, it's Dad's decision not mine,' said Jeanette, relieved. 'But I might put a good word in for her if she behaves herself today. I'd better go and help our Hester.'

An hour later they were all seated around the table ready for Christmas dinner. Almost at the last minute Ethel had appeared like a shadow in the kitchen and placed three bottles on the Welsh dresser: one of sweet sherry, one of port and one of whisky. Then she had sat down before anyone else and kept her head down.

She appeared to have shrunk somehow, thought Jeanette, as she helped Hester dish out the food. After the barest hesitation Hester placed turkey and all the trimmings on Ethel's plate. George had said not a word about the old people's home so far that day. Perhaps Dorothy had told Sam the same tale about Ethel as she had told her and he had told their father. It could be that they were just going to have to accept that the old woman was family and it was not in the spirit of Christmas to cast her out.

It was a merry gathering and they ate their fill, pulled crackers, put on paper hats and groaned over corny jokes. Through it all, Hester's senses were alert for the sound of the door knocker. It banged promptly at three o'clock and she could not contain herself, despite not knowing exactly what she was going to tell Ally about what she'd been through recently.

She removed her apron and paper hat as she reached the front door and flung it open. Her heart seemed to swell as she gazed at the man standing there. He had kept his word and come exactly on time. And not empty-handed.

'For remembrance,' he said, holding out a bunch of yellow mop-headed chrysanthemums.

Her face lit up. 'No one has ever brought me flowers. How lovely of you!' She breathed in their fragrance before lifting her head and staring at him. 'What do you mean – for remembrance?'

'Are you prepared for what I think of as a pleasant shock?'

She gave him a puzzled look. 'What do you mean?'

He smiled. 'How are you feeling today?'

'Much better! Are you coming in? There's a fire in the parlour, we can go in there and you can tell me what this pleasant shock is.'

He followed her into the house and through a door on the left. She placed the flowers on the sideboard and waved him to one of the armchairs by the glowing coal fire. She sat down the other side of the fireplace and stared at him. 'Well?'

'I got talking to Wendy last night. She told me about Mrs Jones who lives in Whalley. I remember her from when I used to go into the village, and once Wendy said you were an evacuee, I remembered you as well. Although I never knew your name and thought when you seemed familiar that it was because we'd met the day of the accident, I realize now that maybe it was also because I saw in you traces of the girl you were when we first met as youngsters.'

She could not tear her eyes from his face. 'Are you saying you're the lad I met on the farm?' she said hoarsely, scarcely able to believe it.

He nodded. 'I know we've grown up and changed a bit since then, but even so, I don't think either of us is that different. The farm belonged to my sister's future father-in-law. It's where she lives now.'

Hester felt as if her heart stopped before increasing its beat. 'It was an incredible, lucky chance us meeting again the way we did,' she said breathlessly.

'Wasn't it just,' he said, reaching out and taking her hand. 'Although I prefer to think it was meant to happen. You will go out with me again?'

'Yes!' She gripped his hand tightly. 'Perhaps we can go and see that film we talked about not so long ago? Our Jeanette said it's fun.'

'That settles it,' said Ally, 'and now there's only one more thing I have to say.'

'Is it about what I said about having a hellish time recently?' asked Hester, a tremor in her voice.

'No. I care about that, of course, but I just wanted to say that I wouldn't bring pressure to bear on you to emigrate. I reckon I can be happy living anywhere with you.'

She blushed. 'I really appreciate you saying that. As for the bad time I've been having, I'll tell you about that another day. Suffice to say that now you're here, I think this is going to be my best Christmas ever.'

He drew her into his arms and she lifted her face to his, and for a while the only sound in the room was the crackling of the fire.

Twenty-Eight

It was the first Sunday of 1955 and Jeanette and George were on the ferry crossing the Mersey. He had said he was more in the mood to go by boat than train and she could understand his feelings. If it had been stormy she would have felt differently, but it was a bright, cold day with only the lightest of breezes, enough to clear the head as they strolled around the deck. Neither of them spoke; she had said all that she wanted to say about her mother, and she sensed her father was naturally feeling a little nervous about the forthcoming reunion with Grace.

Ethel had wanted to accompany them when she learnt that they were going to visit George's wife. Especially when told she had been right in her assumption that Grace was Lavinia's daughter. She had crowed over them and said, 'I told you so.'

George had told her not to push her luck. He had not forgotten she had almost sent Jeanette tumbling down the stairs, and said he had visited the local old people's home so she had better watch her step. The last thing he wanted was Aunt Ethel sticking her oar in when he met Grace.

His aunt had gone pale, especially as Jeanette and Hester had been present at the time. Thinking of Hester, Jeanette smiled. She had liked Ally on sight and was convinced there would be wedding bells for them in the not too distant future. Ally had accompanied Hester to the party at Betty's flat and the pair of them seemed to have plenty to say to Emma and Jared Gregory. Today they had gone to Whalley to visit Myra Jones, and Hester had told Jeanette that Ally had volunteered to help Jared with the renovation of the cottage in his spare time with a view to renting it.

Jeanette had enjoyed the party, despite David being unable to attend as he was working. Peggy had appeared to enjoy it too, and Pete had been true to his word and danced a waltz with her. She had told Jeanette when she had seen her in work the next day that she was not going to think too far ahead where their relationship was concerned.

Jeanette had also liked the flat, despite it being on the top floor, because it had a fantastic view of the Anglican cathedral and the Mersey. As for Betty, she had shown Jeanette some of her paintings and they had talked of visiting the Walker Art Gallery some time before she went to Italy, so they could view her father's painting together. Maggie had told her that she would be leaving the flat once Betty left for Italy to live with her sister. The information had given Jeanette an idea, and once the reunion between her mother and father was over, she was determined to speak to him about leaving home.

'We're nearly there,' said George, rousing Jeanette from her reverie.

They made their way to the side of the ship as it approached Birkenhead and waited with the other passengers. Jeanette noticed that it was Jimmy tying up the boat and wondered how he felt about Betty going to Italy.

'Come on, Jeannie,' said George, 'let's get ashore.'

She linked her arm through her father's and exchanged greetings with Jimmy, wishing him a Happy New Year. Then she and George hurried from the ferry. Soon they were on the bus taking them to their destination.

'You OK, Dad?' she asked as they neared Little Storeton.

'I didn't think I'd be feeling like a lad going on a first date,' he murmured as they stood up.

'Everything will be fine,' she said, despite her own reservations. Her mother seemed to be so settled on the Wirral. Would she want to live with George again? Would she be content leaving her home here and moving back to Liverpool? And what about Ethel?

Before long they arrived at the house where Grace lived with the O'Neills. George's knock was answered almost immediately by Beryl, who smiled when she saw them. 'Do come in. She's been on pins all morning waiting for you to arrive.'

George wiped his feet on the mat that said WELCOME in the small hall, removed his trilby and followed Beryl inside. Jeanette hurried after him, wanting to be there to see how her parents would react when they saw each other. At least her father knew to expect to see his wife in a wheelchair. Even so, after almost fourteen years they had both changed and would need to adapt to those changes if they were to see more of each other.

Grace was sitting over by the window with the light falling on her. The crochet she had been working on slipped from her fingers as they entered the sitting room. The fine lines about her green eyes and mouth creased into a smile. 'How well you look, George! Your hair, so distinguished.'

He cleared his throat noisily and ran his hand over his thick silvering hair. 'I'm getting old, lass. It was dark brown when I last saw you.'

'Being in your fifties isn't old,' she chided. 'You're still a fine figure of a man.'

'And you're just as pretty as the first day I saw you.' He walked across to her.

'I looked a mess that evening you found me.' She reached up a hand to him and he took it, grasping it firmly.

'It seems a long time ago now.'

'Yes. Do sit down, George.' She indicated the chair close by. 'We've a lot of catching up to do.'

'Shall we leave them alone?' said Beryl in a low voice.

Jeanette nodded. She had a strong feeling that today was a new beginning for all of them.